The Falcons of Fire and Ice

Karen Maitland travelled and worked in many parts of the United Kingdom before finally settling in the beautiful medieval city of Lincoln. She is the author of *The White Room*, *Company of Liars*, *The Owl Killers* and *The Gallows Curse*. The latter three titles are available as Penguin paperbacks.

The Falcons of Fire and Ice

KAREN MAITLAND

MICHAEL JOSEPH
an imprint of
PENGUIN BOOKS

MICHAEL JOSEPH

Published by the Penguin Group
Penguin Books Ltd, 80 Strand, London WC2R ORL, England
Penguin Group (USA) Inc., 375 Hudson Street, New York, New York 10014, USA
Penguin Group (Canada), 90 Eglinton Avenue East, Suite 700, Toronto, Ontario, Canada M4P 2Y3
(a division of Pearson Penguin Canada Inc.)
Penguin Ireland, 25 St Stephen's Green, Dublin 2, Ireland (a division of Penguin Books Ltd)
Penguin Group (Australia), 250 Camberwell Road,
Camberwell, Victoria 3124, Australia (a division of Pearson Australia Group Pty Ltd)
Penguin Books India Pvt Ltd, 11 Community Centre,
Panchsheel Park, New Delhi – 110 017, India
Penguin Group (NZ), 67 Apollo Drive, Rosedale, Auckland 0632, New Zealand
(a division of Pearson New Zealand Ltd)
Penguin Books (South Africa) (Pty) Ltd, Block D, Rosebank Office Park,
181 Jan Smuts Avenue, Parktown North, Gauteng 2193, South Africa

Penguin Books Ltd, Registered Offices: 80 Strand, London WC2R ORL, England

www.penguin.com

First published 2012
002

Copyright © Karen Maitland, 2012

The moral right of the author has been asserted

Set in 13.5/15.5 pt Garamond MT Std
Typeset by Jouve (UK), Milton Keynes
Printed in Great Britain by Clays Ltd, St Ives plc

A CIP catalogue record for this book is available from the British Library

HARDBACK ISBN: 978–0–718–15996–2
OM PAPERBACK ISBN: 978–0–718–15637–4

www.greenpenguin.co.uk

MIX
Paper from
responsible sources
FSC
www.fsc.org
FSC™ C018179

Penguin Books is committed to a sustainable
future for our business, our readers and our planet.
This book is made from Forest Stewardship
Council™ certified paper.

ALWAYS LEARNING   **PEARSON**

Time and chance happen to all men. For man knows not his time. As the fishes that are taken in an evil net, and as the birds that are caught in the snare, so are the sons of man snared in an evil time, when it falls suddenly upon them.

Ecclesiastecus 9:11–12

I am the enemy you killed, my friend.

'Strange Meeting', Wilfred Owen (1893–1918)

First World War poet

Tantum religio potuit suadere malorum.
So potent a persuasion to evil was religion.

De Rerum Natura, Titus Lucretius Carus

(c. 95–55 BC) Roman poet

Cast of Characters

Iceland – 1514

Elísabet – pregnant woman
Jóhann – her husband

Portugal – 1539

Manuel da Costa – glassblower
Jorge – physician
Benito – Spanish Marrano

Portugal – 1564

Isabela – daughter of the Royal Falconer
Ana – Isabela's mother
King Sebastian – sovereign of Portugal, a boy of ten years old
Cardinal Henry – the king's great-uncle and Regent
Dona Ofelia – wife of royal courtier
Jorge – physician in 1539 and now elderly neighbour of Isabela
Ricardo – adventurer
Dona Lúcia – rich widow
Carlos – Dona Lúcia's nephew
Silvia – Ricardo's lover
Filipe – potboy at the local tavern

Iceland – 1564

Eydis – oracle and shaman
Valdis – twin sister of Eydis
Fannar – local farmer
Ari – hired farmhand
Unnur – Fannar's wife, and mother to daughters
    Margrét and **Lilja**
Heidrun – friend of Eydis
Pastor Fridrik – Lutheran clergyman
Jónas – stallion owner and father to little daughter **frída**
Pétur – breeder of horses

On Board the Ship

Dona Flávia – wife of a merchant
Marcos – physician
Vítor – map-maker and collector of curios
Fausto – diamond hunter
Hinrik – ship's boy from Iceland

Prologue
Anno Domini 1514 – Iceland

'I killed them, Elísabet, I killed them!'

Elísabet heard the sobs tearing at her husband's throat. She knew Jóhann was desperate for her to comfort him, begging her to assure him that no evil would come from the terrible thing he'd done, but she couldn't speak. She couldn't even bring herself to turn and look at him. She stared at her own hand grasping the iron ladle. She watched her reed-thin fingers stir the dried stockfish in the steaming pot, as if her hand was a strange animal she didn't recognize.

'I had to do it, Elísabet . . . I had no choice.'

Her back snapped upright. 'I begged you not to go. Did you listen? No, as usual you . . .'

But even as she turned to confront him, her eyes glittering with fear and rage, her words died away in a horrified gasp. Jóhann was standing close behind her in the tiny cottage, bathed in the mustard light of the fish-oil lamp. But if she hadn't heard his voice, Elísabet would never have recognized the creature staring down at her as her husband.

His face was a mask of blood. It ran down his cheeks, and pooled in the creases of his skin, staining his pale beard crimson. Blood oozed too from numerous deep gashes on his arms and hands. Even his hair was soaked and matted with gore. If it hadn't been for his clothes, which she had woven and stitched with her own hand, Elísabet would have sworn he was the ghost of some ancient Viking who'd perished in battle.

Jóhann's legs buckled beneath him and he sank down on the wooden platform that served as both bed and chairs in the tiny room. That was enough to jerk Elísabet into action. Although her belly was swollen with child, she moved with a swiftness that she had not managed for weeks, hurrying to dip a handful of raw wool into the water pail and return with it, dripping, to her husband's side. Gently she began to wipe the scarlet stains from his face, but even as she washed the blood away more ran from the wounds to cover the blanched skin. Jóhann, wincing, caught her wrist and, pulling the hank of wet wool from her fingers, pressed it to his forehead. He closed his eyes and, for a moment, Elísabet thought he was going to pass out, but he didn't fall.

'Did you . . .' She swallowed hard. 'Did you get the foreigner what he wanted?'

Jóhann reached beneath his shirt, flinching as the coarse woollen cloth rasped over the cuts on his hand. He pulled out a leather draw-string purse and let it fall on to the bed. The purse looked well stuffed, but that told Elísabet little about the value of the coins inside.

'He has the chicks, both of them,' Jóhann said wearily. 'They're alive . . . and strong enough to survive the sea voyage back to Portugal.'

'But to kill the white falcons . . . the last white falcons on this mountain . . . Don't you understand what you've done? Anyone who kills that bird is cursed until the day they die. You promised me, Jóhann, you promised that no harm would come to the adult falcons . . . You took an oath on the life of our unborn child.'

Elísabet touched her rounded belly where only the night before her husband had laid his own warm hand, as he'd sworn to her he would not hurt the birds.

'The foreigner will pay good money for the chicks,' he had told her. 'The falcons will have more young next year and I'll see to it that nothing disturbs them, even if I have to guard their nest day and night. But I must do this. I have to pay back the money I borrowed for the cattle, and with the baby coming, this is the only way we can survive. What else would you have me do?'

He meant the *dead* cattle, which had all perished the same summer he'd bought them when the cloud of gas from the volcano had poisoned the grass. Four years of misery and hunger for man and falcons alike, when the grass had withered and the ptarmigan, the prey of the white falcons, did not venture into the high valley. Before the poison cloud swept over them, a dozen white falcons had circled in the skies above the river of blue ice. But they had starved to death or flown away to the north, and the single pair that still soared over the frozen river had not laid eggs for three years.

'Don't you see, it's a good omen,' Jóhann had told her. 'The falcons have bred once more, that means they know the ptarmigan are returning and the grass is sweet again. With the money I'll get for the chicks we'll be able to buy more cattle. The foreigners will give a heavy purse for the white falcons they sell to the royal houses of Europe.' He laughed. 'They say that kings will pay more for a single white falcon than for a whole palace.'

Elísabet stared down at her husband's bloodied head. Last night Jóhann had been so sure that their luck was changing. Now look at him – was this the change of fortune he'd promised her?

'But you swore to me, Jóhann, on our child's life . . . Why . . . why have you done this to us? What possessed you to call down such evil on us . . . on your own family?'

Jóhann opened his eyes, but he didn't look at his wife. He gazed fixedly into the flames of the cooking fire as a despairing man stares down at the sea before he drowns himself. Finally, and in a voice that barely rose above a whisper, he answered her.

'We waited until the adults had gone hunting. I've never climbed so high up the cliff face before. It was a long, slow climb. Then, just as I was within a man's length of the nest,

3

the adult falcons returned. They began diving at me, slashing me with their talons, screaming at me till I was so deafened I couldn't think. My arms were stinging from the gashes and my fingers were so slippery with my blood that a dozen times I nearly fell from the rock face. I realized I'd plunge to my death if I tried to carry on, so I climbed back down.

'The foreigner was yelling at me. I didn't know what he was saying, but I didn't need words to understand he was furious. The Icelander who had brought him to me told me that if I didn't go back up and get the chicks, they would tell our Danish masters that they'd caught me trying to raid the nest. He said the Danes would hang me on the spot.'

Jóhann looked up at his wife, his tired blue eyes pleading for understanding. 'I didn't want to do it, Elísabet, but . . . if I was to have any chance of capturing the chicks and getting back down safely, I had to drive the adults off. I thought if I shot an arrow at one of them, the other would fly away. I aimed for the male, which was flying low. I only meant to clip his wing feathers, but he crashed down on to the rocks. The female circled higher and higher, till I could no longer see her. I was certain she'd taken fright and had gone.

'I started to climb back up to the nest, but just as I reached it she dived at me again. I was slashing at her with my knife, trying to keep a grip with my other hand on the rock. As if she knew I'd killed her mate, she fastened her claws on my shoulder, stabbing at my head with her beak. I was in agony and terrified she would blind me. I lashed out wildly with my knife. I didn't mean to kill her, just to make her let go. Then I felt her collapse against me. But even though she was dead, her talons gripped my shoulder as fiercely as ever.

'When I carried her chicks down from the nest her claws were still locked deep into my flesh. Her dead body was swinging from my shoulder. Even when I reached the bottom, her talons were still impaled in me. They had to cut them out of me, before they could tear her body off me . . .

4

But I can still feel her talons gripping me. She won't let go of me. She'll never let go of me.'

He was sobbing, and Elísabet knew she should go to him and put her arms around him, but she couldn't. She could see the white bird beating its wings against her husband's face. She could hear its cry of fury. The whole room was suddenly full of flailing wings and the screams of *murder, murder!*

Elísabet fought her way out of the tiny cottage and ran as fast as her swollen belly would allow, but too soon she was forced to stop and gasp for breath. It was summer, but the great river of blue ice that lay below the cottage never melted, never moved. And now the chill, damp air rose up as if every breath she took sucked the cold towards her, turning her lungs to ice. She stared up at the clear blue sky above, but it was empty. Not a single bird flew, not a single cry was heard, as if every creature in the world had died with those falcons, the last falcons in the valley.

A boom echoed round the mountains, louder than a thunder clap. Startled, she stared down at the ice. A huge crack had opened in the frozen river, leaving a hollow in the ice like the inside of a giant white egg. Even as she gazed at it, Elísabet saw a great black shadow running down the valley, staining the sparkling blue-white ice until it was as dark as the bog pools. Terrified, she glanced up. It was only a cloud passing over the sun . . . only a cloud creeping out from behind the mountain . . . only a cloud where there had been none before.

Elísabet gasped as the child in her belly kicked. Tiny fists punched into her, thrashing furiously as if her child was trying to fight its way out. She could sense its fear, feel the small heart fluttering and racing like the heartbeat of a snared bird. But even as she listened to the tiny frantic pounding, she realized there was not just one heart beating in her belly, but two. Two little heads butted her. Two pairs of minute arms thrashed about inside her in their terror. She sank to the ground, pressing her hands to her belly, gently rubbing their little limbs through her skin, trying to comfort them as if she could grasp those frightened, angry little fists and calm them.

'They know,' a voice said behind her.

Elísabet twisted herself around as best she could. A young woman was standing in the shadow of a rocky outcrop. She was taller even than Jóhann and she held her back as straight as a birch tree.

'An oath sworn on the life of an unborn child cannot be broken without a terrible price being paid. You should not have let him swear on the infants in your womb. If an oath was to be made, it should have been on your own heads, not on innocent lives. Your daughters are marked now. The spirits of the falcons have entered your belly. But I will do all I can to protect them if you entrust them to me.'

Elísabet stared aghast into the eyes of the stranger, eyes that were as grey and dark as a winter's storm. She saw something else too in that handsome face, a tiny ridge beneath the nose where a groove should have been.

'Get away from me,' she screamed, desperately trying to scramble to her feet. 'I know who your people are. You're evil, wicked, every last one of your tribe. You're child killers. Everyone knows what happens to the children you steal from decent people like us. I won't let you near my babies. I won't let you take them, do you hear? Get away from us!'

Her eyes wide in terror, Elísabet backed away, desperately making the sign of the cross over herself and her belly as if this would drive the stranger off.

But the woman regarded her impassively as she might have watched a screeching gull riding the wind. After a long moment, she reached beneath her shawl and unlooped a long knotted cord of white and red wool from about her waist. She drew the cord three times through her right hand, before holding it out to Elísabet.

'This will help ease the birth and undo some of the harm

6

that has been done. Loosen one knot each time the pains come upon you.'

Elísabet backed away, holding her hands behind her as if she feared the cord might fly into them unbidden. 'I don't want it! I won't have it in my house. I'd never take anything you or your filthy brood have touched.'

The stranger's placid expression did not change, but she tossed the cord on the ground between them. The scarlet and white cord lay among the rusty grass stalks, limp, inert. Then the stranger lifted her hand and without warning the cord reared up in front of Elísabet and slithered towards her. But even as she cried out, it burst into flame and vanished into smoke.

The woman lifted her head and her eyes were as sharp and hard as the black rocks on the mountains of fire. 'Remember this – in the days that are coming it is not my people you should fear. You have cursed your own babies and day by day, as they grow, so will your dread of them, until you and all your people will become more terrified of your daughters than of any other creatures on this earth. When that day comes, we will be waiting!'

Chapter One
Anno Domini 1539

The queen of Spain once had a dream, that a white falcon flew out of the mountains towards her and in its talons it held the flaming ball of the sun and icy sphere of the moon. The queen opened her hand and the falcon dropped the sun and the moon into her outstretched palm and she grasped them.

The falcon perched upon her arm and spread its wings. And, as it stretched them, the white feathers grew longer and wider until they enveloped the queen like a royal mantle.

Then the queen dreamt that a traitor had entered her presence and at once the white falcon rose and flew to him. It alighted on the man's shoulders and the talons of the falcon were so strong and sharp they severed the man's arms from his body. Streams of blood poured out from his body and the queen knelt and drank the blood of the traitor.

Lisbon, Portugal

***Enter** – a term meaning to give a falcon the first sight of the prey which the falconer wants it to hunt and kill.*

On a bleak winter's morning in Lisbon, in front of a howling mob, Manuel da Costa was burned alive. Only he died that day, a lone, pathetic figure on the pyre. He was a poor man, an insignificant man, a man that few would have troubled to mourn. But hundreds of men and women who even then were huddling behind closed doors would have chilling cause to remember Manuel's death. And all through the bitter, blood-soaked years to come they would whisper into the darkness how on that winter's day and in that very hour the devils of hell were made flesh and dwelled on earth.

If young Manuel had only kept his head down, averted his eyes, held his tongue, if he had just kept walking, he might have stayed alive. And if he had survived, who knows, maybe the thousands of others who came after him might have lived too. But Manuel had no warning of the nightmare that was about to ensnare him. How could he?

So, just as he did every day, one February morning, shortly after dawn, he closed the door of the tiny room he rented and hurried through the narrow, twisting streets of Lisbon. Even a passing stranger would have spotted Manuel's occupation at once, for though he was only in his twenties his chest was already as round as a barrel from years of blowing glass and his olive hands scarred with a hundred healed burns.

With his head hunched down against the wetted wind, Manuel would never have noticed the small crowd gathered at the far end of the square in front of the church had it not been for a small boy who ran headlong into him. With a curse worthy of a sailor the brat dodged around him and scampered across the square. Only then did Manuel lift his head to see what was attracting the lad. The crowd was swelling fast, with men, women and children hurrying towards it in twos and threes. As they joined the gathering, they simply stood and gazed at the church as if it was the most astounding thing they had ever seen.

Manuel hesitated, torn between curiosity and his fear of being late for work. Curiosity won. He hurried across the square and joined the back of the crowd. An old woman, dressed in widow's black, was trying to elbow her way to the front. Manuel knew her. She occupied one of the tiny squalid rooms two houses down from his own lodgings. He wasn't surprised to see her here. If there was any trouble or misfortune anywhere in the neighbourhood she was always the first on the scene. He sidled closer to her.

'What's everyone looking so thunderstruck for?' he whispered, then, just to bait her, he added with a grin, 'You'd think the Virgin Mary had farted in the middle of Mass.'

The old crone turned and glared furiously at him, crossing herself rapidly.

'How dare you speak so of the Blessed Virgin? If your poor mother was alive today it would kill her to hear such wicked words on your lips.'

She hobbled around to the other side of the crowd, darting poisonous glances at him. Manuel grinned broadly at the outraged expression on her face. That would give the old witch something to complain about.

A man standing on the other side of Manuel pointed through the heads of the crowd to a notice pinned to the door of the church.

'What's it say?' he demanded.

Manuel shrugged. He'd never learned to read much more

than his own name, but even if he had been a scholar, at that distance it would have been impossible to make out the words.

The question was taken up by others who were unable to get close to the door. They began insisting that those at the front should either move aside or tell them what had been nailed up there. So, in scandalized tones, the ripple of the words spread back through the crowd, passing from mouth to mouth until it reached Manuel's ears.

The Messiah has not yet come. Jesus is not the Messiah.

Manuel was as shocked as any in that crowd. It was one thing to make jokes, but what was nailed on that door was nothing short of blasphemy. Even as the words spread through the crowd, an angry buzzing began. Strangers and neighbours alike were demanding to know who could have committed such an outrage.

Manuel felt a cold shiver of unease. It never took much to inflame a crowd in Lisbon. If a few hotheads started whipping up the anger of the mob, they would turn violent in minutes. And he knew only too well whom the crowd would turn on first. Somehow, the Old Christians of Lisbon could always tell if you were a Jewish convert. They could scent the presence of a New Christian and would attack with the savagery of a pack of wild dogs.

He broke away and hurried off in the direction of the glassblowers' works. As he scuttled through the streets he passed two more churches and saw to his disquiet the same heresy nailed to their doors and other angry mobs beginning to gather around them.

By noon everyone in the city knew that the blasphemous proclamation had been pinned not only to every church door in Lisbon, but also on the very door of the great Cathedral itself, and King João had offered a reward of 10,000 silver crusados to anyone who could discover the author of this evil.

That night when Manuel returned to his lodgings, he found the house packed to the rafters with frightened men and women. Men and women like himself who were *Cristianos Nuevos*, New Christians, or, as the Old Christians mockingly called them, *Marranos*, meaning pigs. They were Jews fled from Spain, or their descendants, who had been forced to convert to Christianity, and now practised the Catholic faith. But to the Old Christians they were filthy foreigners come here to take their jobs, their homes and their women, and no matter how much the New Christians swore they were now good Catholics, they still remained what they had always been in the eyes of the Old Christians – Christ killers.

Manuel squashed himself into the darkened doorway of one of the rooms. Jorge, the physician, was holding forth amid a crowd of men all murmuring nearly as loudly as the crowd outside the churches.

Jorge held up his hands for silence, raising his voice to make himself heard.

'There is no cause for fear. The Pope issued a bull declaring all New Christians free and cancelling all the charges brought against us. He's forbidden the Inquisition to act against those of us who were forcibly converted or against the children of converts.'

'But for three years only.' Benito's white beard trembled as he rasped for breath. 'Those three years are now ended. I have lived through it all before in Spain, trust me, you cannot rely on the promises of kings or popes. It will happen here, as it did there. Our people will be rounded up and murdered one by one till not so much as a newborn infant remains alive.'

He swept his clawed hand around the room. 'Are you all so blind? Don't you see they will blame us for these notices on the churches; who else will they blame? Who else do they ever blame? Every Catholic in Portugal will soon be screaming for our blood. The king will have all the backing he needs to unleash the dogs of the Inquisition. It is no secret he hates us. He is looking for any excuse to purge Portugal of us.

Who knows, maybe King João himself nailed the notices to the churches deliberately to turn his people against us.'

At that, several of the men leapt to their feet, shouting at the old man to be quiet. Weren't they in enough danger already without him adding the charge of slandering the king to their troubles? They glanced anxiously over at the shutters. They were fastened tightly, but all the same, you never knew who was listening outside on the street.

'Enough, enough.' Jorge waved the men back to their seats. 'Benito has a point. There are some who will try to blame us. So it is up to us to make certain we are not blamed. Now listen,' he said, lowering his voice to a whisper, 'tonight . . .'

But Manuel did not wait to hear what they would do tonight. He'd grown up in this community and he knew that the old men would still be arguing about what they would do 'tonight' come daybreak. All he wanted to do was sleep. Dawn would come only too quickly and, with luck, by then the people of Lisbon would have found some new scandal to divert them.

But the following morning found another notice pinned to the Cathedral door. This time the crowd that rapidly gathered around it read the proclamation:

I, as the author, declare that I am neither Spanish nor Portuguese, but I am an Englishman, and even if 20,000 gold escudos were offered, my name will never be discovered.

The crowd read it, but they did not believe a single word of it.

Two nights later, Manuel woke with a start as the light from a lantern shone full into his face. Even as his mind registered the fact that this was the middle of the night, a wave of cold fear washed over him. As his eyes struggled to adjust to the light, he was dimly aware of four hooded figures looming over him. He could hear their breathing like the hissing of snakes.

Manuel tried to scramble out of bed, but his legs became entangled in the bedclothes and he tripped, sprawling at the feet of one of the black-robed figures. The man stared down at him as if he was a beggar whining for alms. His face was concealed by a pointed black hood, and in the lamp-light his eyes glittered through the slits, the eyes of a cobra rising to strike.

'Manuel da Costa, by order of the Grand Inquisitor you are to accompany us for questioning.'

Sheer terror washed through Manuel, almost emptying his bowels. 'No, no, please, you have the wrong man. It's a mistake. Why would you want to question me? I know nothing . . . I swear, by all the Holy Saints, by . . . I . . . I am a good Catholic. I go to church regularly every week. I never miss Mass. Never miss confession, you ask anyone.'

'A good Catholic does not blaspheme the Holy Virgin.' The hooded man raised a warning hand as Manuel opened his mouth to protest. 'We have a dozen witnesses who will swear they heard you mocking the Virgin even as you denied with your own hand that her Son was the true Messiah.'

They dragged Manuel down the stairs – they had to, for his legs had buckled and he couldn't manage to stand, much less walk. From behind the many doors they passed along the street there came only the sound of silence as heavy as a stone coffin lid. All lights were extinguished. All shutters closed. All doors barred.

Only the old widow, her eye pressed to a crack in the wood, watched and chuckled. Ten thousand crusados they'd promised her. It was a fortune, more than enough to move away from this street of pigs into a respectable district and live in comfort for the rest of her life. They had explained that she would only get her reward if the accused confessed his guilt, but she didn't have the slightest twinge of concern about that.

And Manuel did confess, of course . . . after his muscles and tendons had been ripped from his bones on the rack; after every joint in his limbs had been slowly dislocated by the ropes biting into his thighs, shins, wrists and ankles. Day and night without sleep, they whispered, shouted and cajoled, until they had even him believing that he must have nailed those notices to the church doors.

But, as his inquisitors said, his admission of guilt was not enough, not nearly enough to demonstrate his repentance, for how could one man alone have nailed those notices to the churches all over Lisbon in one night without being seen? Manuel must have had accomplices, unless the Devil himself aided him. He had only to name those men and his suffering would be over, his pain ended. They would let him rest.

Give us a name, any name, that is all we want – JUST ONE NAME.

He could have named his friends, his acquaintances, even his enemies, especially his enemies, most did. He could have uttered any name at all that surfaced in his pain-crazed mind, uttered it without even knowing if he was dreaming or speaking it aloud. But although Manuel prayed with every fibre of his being for an end to his torment, his inquisitors could not make him name another soul. Now, that kind of defiance takes a rare courage.

In the end, they carried him to the square. There, in front of a blood-crazed mob, they sliced through his wrists, separating skin and flesh, muscle and bone, severing the hands with which those foul words had been written. In truth he scarcely recognized the pain of the knife, for what was left of his limbs was already half-dead from the rack. He had thought himself in so much anguish that he could feel no greater torment, but when they tied him to the stake, and he felt the burning flames licking around his body, he knew that he could. The Inquisition had, as always, left the most exquisite agony to the last.

Chapter Two
Anno Domini 1564

According to Norse legend, at the birth of the world an ash tree was created, Yggdrasil, the tree of life, of time and of the universe. On the topmost branch sits an eagle, and perched between the eyes of the eagle is Vedfolnir the falcon, whose piercing gaze sees up into the heavens and down to the earth, and below the earth into the dark caverns of the underworld.

All the good and evil this falcon sees he reports to Odin, the father of gods and men. For the falcon and the winds are one, and the winds blow across every blade of grass on the earth and every wave that foams on the sea. There is no escaping the wind.

Lisbon, Portugal
Isabela

Stoop – *the rapid descent of a falcon from a height on to its quarry.*

'You must not avert your gaze, Isabela. Whatever you see, whatever you hear, don't let your face betray you. You must look as if you approve of everything that is done.'

My father had given me the same instructions at least a dozen times, and every time he said it, it made me more nervous, certain that I would not be able to control my expression. For the only thing he and my mother could agree upon was that I always wore my feelings on my face.

Though dawn was only just breaking over the rooftops of Lisbon, my hands were already sticky with sweat. The bread and olives I had eaten sat in a hard lump in my stomach. I'd felt too nauseous to face breakfast, but my father had stood over me, forcing me to eat for fear I might later draw attention to myself by fainting. It wasn't lack of food that was likely to make me faint, but being laced into the rib-crushing corset and farthingale petticoat, with its many whale-bone hoops. Together with heavy, voluminous skirts, the whole contraption swayed so alarmingly whenever I moved, I was sure I was going to tip over. Simply crossing the room was like trying to take half a dozen over-excited puppies for a walk.

Back home in Sintra, I never wore such things, but my father was determined that today at least I must look like a lady. My mother had snorted at the very idea, and for once I was forced to agree with her. Nothing could have induced me to dress up in this cage had I not seen the desperate anxiety in my father's eyes. Whatever was troubling him – and it had been for weeks – it was far more serious than me not disgracing him by dressing, as my mother so kindly put it, like a dung collector's brat.

Father peered into the mirror, adjusting the scarlet cap on his head, so that the three white falcon feathers were plainly visible from the front, his badge of office as the Royal Falconer. He turned and studied me, his head on one side, frowning in concentration as if I were one of his hawks and he was deciding whether or not I should be flown.

Conscious of his critical gaze, I smoothed my new skirts. Father had selected the colour of my gown himself. It was emerald green, much to my mother's disgust. She always complained that my skin was too dark for a well-bred Portuguese lady and the green, she said, only emphasized it. But for once my father overruled her. Green was the colour of the Holy Order of the Inquisition and we had to be seen to show our loyalty.

Father shook his head. 'Where do the years go? It seems only yesterday, you were a wild-haired little chick. I blinked and here you are now, sixteen years old, a woman already. How did I miss that?'

'If I'd had feathers you'd have noticed,' I teased.

He smiled, but it didn't soften the lines of anxiety permanently etched around his eyes. He was only in his forties, but lately he had begun to look like an old man. He reached out, grasping my shoulders gently.

'You are truly a beautiful young woman, and yet to me you are still only a child, *my* child. I hate myself for making you do this. But we must all act our parts in this play today, even the young king, him most of all.'

I knew little King Sebastian well, for he spent as much

time as he could at the summer palace in Sintra with my father and the falcons. He was only ten years old, yet he had more riches than any boy in the world could dream of possessing. But the only thing he seemed to care about was his falcons. He loved those birds even more than my father did. If ever their sovereign was missing, the servants always knew where to find him. There he'd be with the falcons, but most especially with the pair of royal gyrfalcons, those exquisite white falcons with their great dark, liquid eyes. Sometimes the way Sebastian looked at them reminded me of that rapt expression of adoration on my mother's face whenever she knelt before the altar of the Holy Virgin.

He'd spend hours with my father exercising the birds and, unlike the other nobles who were only interested in hunting with them, he was eager to learn every aspect of their care. He and my father had high hopes that the pair of gyrfalcons would breed next season. They'd been excitedly planning how the chicks might be hatched beneath a bantam hen and then hacked to teach them to return, a method my father had not often had cause to try, since most falcons and hawks, except the royal gyrfalcon, could be so easily replaced by trapping wild adult birds in migration.

Motherless and fatherless, all the lonely little boy's affection was poured into those white falcons, and I believe also into my father whom he treated like a wise grandparent. I confess to feeling a pang of jealousy sometimes when I saw the two of them together. Little Sebastian so absorbed in helping my father to mend a broken feather. My father smiling down at him in the way I could imagine he might have smiled at his own son had he been blessed with one. My father would have denied it vehemently, but I knew I could never make amends for not being a boy.

'But Father, surely little Sebastian won't be there today? He's only a child.'

My father grimaced. 'His great-uncle, the Regent, insists

he witness the *auto-da-fé*. He says Sebastian must learn to recognize and hate the enemies of the Church and of Portugal. I only hope for the boy's sake he will be able to do what is required of him. It is something no human being should have to see, let alone a child. And you . . .' He stroked my hair sadly. 'Isabela, please believe me, if I could have brought your mother instead of you, I would have done so, but we both know . . .' He trailed off miserably.

I tried to smile. 'I know. Mother is too . . .' It was my turn to grope for the word. 'Sensitive,' I finished lamely.

There was a whole bible of words you could use to describe my mother – beautiful, volatile, caustic, bitter – but *sensitive* certainly wasn't one of them. What my father meant, what we both meant, was that she couldn't be trusted not to open her mouth. Whatever thought slithered through her mind seemed to wiggle its way out between her lips without any attempt at censor. And most of her thoughts were vicious ones. Not that I blamed her, not really. Her husband, me and her whole life had been a constant disappointment to her. We'd all let her down, as she was forever reminding us in her sighs, her clenched-teeth humming and the crashing of pots and pans.

When she had married a man newly taken into royal service, she had expected a life of luxury at Court, of dancing and entertainment, of pearl-encrusted gowns and jewelled necklaces. Everyone said she was certain to be chosen as one of the ladies-in-waiting to the queen herself, for my mother had been strikingly handsome in her youth. But instead she was dealt a life scarcely better than a peasant's, exiled to Sintra and married to a man who, she said, cared nothing for his family or for bettering himself, but only for his lousy stinking birds.

My father, faced with one of my mother's furious tirades, would always gently reply that he was simply more content to spend his years peacefully among his falcons instead of having to tiptoe his way through the spiteful intrigue and rivalry of the Royal Court. And I didn't blame him, though, of course, I never dared say so in front of my mother.

Father took both my hands in his. 'Isabela, listen to me carefully. You must not look at any individual in the procession for too long or it will appear to others as if you are taking an interest in them. These things will be noticed. Try to let your gaze wander indifferently over the penitents as if they were a flock of sheep being driven to market. If among the penitents you should see anyone you know, a neighbour, a friend even . . . don't let your eyes meet theirs. No one must see the slightest flicker of recognition in you, not for any of them.'

I gaped at him. 'But we don't know anyone who is a heretic.'

I could just imagine my mother's outrage at the very suggestion. We were Old Christians from good Catholic stock and proud of it, as she never ceased to remind me.

Father gnawed at his lip. 'No one knows who will be brought out of the dungeons until the procession begins. But what I do know is that they will have planted spies everywhere amongst the crowd. They will be watching everyone who comes to witness the spectacle, looking for any sign of sympathy or pity, and if they see it they will report it to the Inquisition. The *auto-da-fé* takes many hours, but no matter how tired and hungry you become, you must not relax your guard for an instant.'

'Do try to keep up, child. We must hurry if we want the best seats.'

Senhora Dona Ofelia peered anxiously behind her to ensure I was still with her. But much as I would have liked to lose her, it would have been impossible, for that vast billowing scarlet gown was surely visible even to ships far out at sea. Dona Ofelia was the wife of a Court official and my father had persuaded her to act as my chaperone, for he was required to attend upon the young king's pleasure.

I stared glumly at her massive backside as she deftly squeezed her hoops between the benches on the raised platform. I was still struggling to force my skirts to walk in a straight line in the street without knocking over small children or dragging stray dogs and startled pigeons in their wake.

Dona Ofelia sat down, then immediately stood up again, moving along the bench before sitting and at once bouncing up again, trying half a dozen positions until she had assured herself she had secured the best possible view not only of the square, but of the royal dais to the side of us. Opposite us a great altar had been erected, on which stood huge fat yellow candles and what I guessed must be a cross, though it was covered with a heavy black cloth.

The benches around us were filling up fast with families of Court officials, town dignitaries and wealthy merchants. The ordinary populace of Lisbon was gathering along the other two sides of the square and lining the streets beyond. The air throbbed with chattering and laughter, and with the bellows of the street vendors offering wine or cooling sherbet drinks; and for those who were hungry there were oranges, olives, cheese, almonds, custard pastries, roasted sardines and hot spiced bread fresh from the ovens. Friars and priests were trying to drive them away, for the *auto-da-fé* was supposed to be witnessed while fasting, but the standing crowd had come determined to enjoy themselves and no disapproving priest was going to stop them.

Dona Ofelia snapped her fingers, attracting the attention of one of the vendors who was renting out well-stuffed cushions. She rejected the one he proffered and insisted on pinching and poking almost a dozen until she found two that she considered worthy of our posteriors.

'Some of these cushions have more lumps than a cobbled

yard,' she said. 'You don't want to get one that's been sat on by a great fat sow like her, ruins them,' she added, nudging me and gesturing to a woman two benches down from us, who looked as thin as a whippet compared to Dona Ofelia.

Finally settling herself with a sigh of contentment, she drew out a long fan and flapped it vigorously, though the morning sun had barely risen above the great buildings.

The banners of the Holy Office of the Inquisition fluttered from the roofs and balconies around the square. On each flag was painted a bright green cross flanked by an olive branch and a sword, to reassure everyone that the Inquisition dealt equally in forgiveness and justice, mercy and punishment.

I peered around, trying to see my father, and glimpsed him standing among the throng of courtiers behind the royal dais. His head was bowed slightly as he listened to the chatter of the man beside him. He wouldn't say much, he never did. Mother said he was a fool for not pushing himself forward. She complained that he made no attempt to ingratiate himself and win friends who could help him rise.

Dona Ofelia nudged me and gestured towards the royal dais itself. A line of soldiers stood guard in front of it, their breastplates polished until their own nostril hair was reflected in them. At the slightest movement of their chests, dazzling bursts of sunlight bounced off the metal and darted about the square like dragonflies.

'There's King Sebastian himself.' Dona Ofelia levered herself up for a better look. 'See how regally he holds his little head. Bless him. Poor little mite, he's the whole weight of the kingdom on his tiny shoulders. But he's going to be a heartbreaker, that one. When he was born, the astrologers said that every noblewoman in the world would throw themselves in his path. Not that you need the stars to tell you that – who wouldn't want to be his queen?'

I craned around the head of the man in front. A small blond child sat on a great gilded throne that would have dwarfed even a fully grown man. His tiny feet, clad in red leather boots, rested on an embroidered footstool. I had never seen him in his royal robes before or looking so clean. It was hard to believe it was the same little boy who would emerge from the mews covered in bird muck and blood after feeding the falcons with scraps of raw meat.

But there was no look of rapt attention on the young king's face today. He was fidgeting and leaning over the arms of his throne, peering down at the soldiers below him as if he'd much prefer to be standing guard with a sword in his hand than sitting on a throne. Two priests dressed in severe black cassocks stood just behind him. One of them bent down to whisper something to the king and the boy jerked upright, evidently obeying an order to sit still. It was the first time I had seen these two men among the young king's retinue and they certainly did not seem to behave with the deference most of his other courtiers showed towards Sebastian.

'Those two priests,' I whispered to Dona Ofelia, 'who are they?'

'The king's new tutors. Jesuits, very devout men. They fight against the heresy of the evil Protestants. I hear they keep a strict hand on the young king, as they should.' She pursed her red lips and nodded approvingly. 'Boys, even kings, must be taught to –'

But what boys must be taught I never learned, for Dona Ofelia was interrupted by a fanfare of trumpets, and she struggled to her feet, pulling me up with her. Everyone rose, except the boy-king, as another figure mounted the royal dais. He was a tall, gaunt-faced man dressed in the scarlet robes of a cardinal. He turned to face the crowd lining the square, repeatedly making the sign of the cross in blessing over them, as his imperious gaze swept over the throng. As the raised hand moved in their direction, the people bowed their heads, hastily crossing themselves as if his blessing was more like a curse to be warded off. Only when the robed figure took his seat on the empty throne next to the boy did those of us lucky enough to have benches sink back down on to them again.

'Ah,' Dona Ofelia sighed with satisfaction. 'That's who we were waiting for. Now the procession will begin, you'll see. That's Cardinal Henry of Évora, the King's great-uncle. He used to be the Grand Inquisitor.' Dona Ofelia suddenly raised her voice so that her words must have been audible at least three rows in front and behind us. 'We're fortunate to have such a godly man as Cardinal Henry for Regent.' Then, in case there should be any doubt where her loyalties lay, she declaimed, 'There is none more dedicated to purging Portugal of evil than the Regent.'

A cry of *Viva la fé, Long live the faith*, rose from the crowd as the first glimpses of the procession were visible, approaching the square.

'What kind of monks are those?' I whispered, as a phalanx of hooded men in black bowed low to the royal thrones. They each carried a wooden rod.

'Monks!' Dona Ofelia echoed indignantly. She looked at me through narrowed eyes as if she wasn't sure if I was mocking the procession or was just extremely ignorant. She evidently decided on the latter. 'They're not monks, child. They're the Guild of Charcoal Burners. They provide the wood for the fires, so the cardinals have given them the honour of leading the procession. Has your father not described the procession to you?'

I was spared the necessity for a reply, as Dona Ofelia was distracted by the entrance into the square of a man bearing the red and gold standard of the Inquisitor-General. The Inquisitor-General himself strutted behind his flag bearer, flanked by two lines of his own soldiers and followed by a long procession of priests and monks from many different orders, all anxious to prove their support for the Inquisition.

Some of them staggered under the weight of the crosses, icons and reliquaries they carried reverently in their hands. The remainder shouldered biers on which rested life-sized statues of saints. A bejewelled statue of the Holy Virgin followed them, smiling distantly at the crowd below her as if she wished herself anywhere but here. Sunlight flashed from the gold and silver crosses and from the many precious stones that encrusted the reliquaries and the robes of the wooden saints. Many of the crowd sank to their knees, stretching out their hands in supplication, and wailing out their prayers as the holy objects were whisked past them.

But they rose just as quickly to their feet as the Dominican friars entered, and the pious prayers of the crowd turned to hisses and shouts of rage, for the friars carried ten life-sized wooden figures into the square. These were not hung with jewels or crowned with halos. The monks stood them in a neat straight row before the altar, like children lining up toy soldiers. Each crudely carved wooden figure had what looked like words inscribed on its chest. I leaned forward trying to read the letters, until I realized Dona Ofelia was watching me.

'You recognize one of the names, child?'

I snapped upright. 'No, I was ... I just ... the statues, they're not saints, are they?'

Dona Ofelia closed her eyes and crossed herself. 'Those are the likenesses of the wicked men and women who escaped before the Inquisition could bring them to mercy,' she whispered in awed tones, as though running away to avoid arrest was too heinous a crime even to be spoken aloud.

I could see her lips moving, but whatever she was saying now was drowned out by the renewed hissing and shouted obscenities of the crowd as several more friars appeared bearing small coffin-shaped boxes.

Dona Ofelia thrust her face so close to me I could smell

what she'd eaten for breakfast – spicy *morcela* blood-sausage, judging by the stink of her breath. 'Those coffins contain the bones of the wicked heretics who died in the Inquisition's dungeons,' she bellowed down my ear, 'and those who've been found guilty of heresy after their death. Their bodies have been dug up, so they can be punished. They needn't think that dying will let them escape,' she added with grim satisfaction.

As the tiny coffins were borne past, people began spitting and throwing clods of excrement and rotten vegetables at them. But they seemed to be exceedingly bad marksmen, for most of the missiles hit the friars instead of the coffins, much to the amusement of many young lads in the crowd, who whooped with delight and slapped one another on the back. The friars glared furiously, but could do nothing.

A sullen silence now descended as forty or fifty men and women limped and shuffled into the square, each one flanked on either side by two black-hooded *familiares*, the lay agents of the Inquisition, who in some cases were virtually carrying the prisoner between them, for these emaciated figures could hardly stand, never mind walk. I felt my heart begin to race. This was the moment my father had warned me about. I dug my fingers into the palms of my hands and fought to keep my expression blank.

The prisoners were all dressed in the *sanbenito*, the uniform of the heretic. It was a broad yellow tabard reaching below their knees on which was painted the cross of St Andrew, with single, double or half cross-pieces according to the severity of their crime. On their heads they wore a tall hat, like a bishop's mitre, painted with flames and grinning devils. Nooses of thick rope hung from their necks and in their hands they carried unlit candles. Some of these cowering creatures were aged, their hair grey, their faces the colour of a blade of grass that has been kept too long from the light. Others were as young as the boy-king himself, their cheeks sunken and wizened like tiny goblins who dwelled deep in the earth.

I told myself that I mustn't look at the faces, but I couldn't help it. They stood in a miserable huddle, some gazing around them at the other prisoners or at the crowd, desperately searching for a glimpse of their family members who had been arrested with them. I watched their eyes dart to the little coffins. I knew they were heretics and I should be glad they'd been caught. But I just felt so sorry for them, and then I felt guilty for feeling sorry.

The hissing in the crowd began again, like a fire racing across a field of grain. The final little group was dragged in. A dozen or so men and women, they too wore the yellow *sanbenito,* but their tabards as well as their hats were painted with leaping flames and devils. All of them had leather gags tied tightly over their mouths.

Dona Ofelia was on her feet, shouting along with the crowd – *Heretics, blasphemers, Jewish pigs, sons of the Devil!*

She turned to me, her eyes glittering with excitement. 'They're the ones who are to be burned. There'll be no escape for them. They'll burn in this world as their souls will burn in hell.'

I glanced over at my father. He was staring anxiously at me. Our eyes met and he gave the briefest jerk of his head. I knew he wanted me to stand and join in the jeering. But I wouldn't. The crowd opposite were howling and throwing every piece of dung and filth they could lay hands on at these broken, terrified wretches. And for the first time in my life, I felt my mother's anger at Father's timidity – *Behave like everyone else, don't draw attention to yourself.* Why should I? The Inquisition couldn't arrest you if you hadn't committed a crime, and certainly not for refusing to behave like a savage ape.

The crowd were trying to surge forward now and vent their fury on the prisoners. The guards fought to hold them back. Then suddenly a young boy in the first group of penitents seemed to recognize one of the condemned. Before his two *familiares* could stop him, he had dropped his unlit candle and stumbled towards the group, his arms held out. 'Mother! Mother!'

For an instant a woman lifted her head and her arms jerked forward as if she was reaching out to him, then they dropped back by her side, and she turned away. The *familiares* grabbed the child and led him back to his own group. I thought he would cry, but he didn't. He didn't even look at the woman again. He hung between the two men like a frayed rag, as if the last spark of life in him had suddenly been snuffed out.

The crowd fell silent once more as the Inquisitor-General donned his bishop's mitre and climbed up to the altar. He was a thin, lean man with a long, straight nose, made longer and sharper by the upward tilt of his chin.

In nomine Patris, et Filii, et Spiritus Sancti, Amen.

When the High Mass was ended the Inquisitor-General took up his staff of office and, descending the altar steps, solemnly strode across the square towards the diminutive figure of the king, closely followed by a young altar boy staggering under the weight of a huge leather-bound and jewel-encrusted copy of the Holy Gospels.

As the Inquisitor-General approached, little Sebastian edged so far back into his throne I half-expected him to crawl out of the back of it. The Inquisitor-General took the massive book and held it out towards the king. At the urging of the two Jesuits behind the throne, the boy placed his right hand on the book and in a shrill, quavering voice, promised to 'support the faith and the Inquisition and do all in my power to extirpate heresy'. He stumbled over this last phrase and it took three attempts to get it right. Sebastian glanced fearfully up at his great-uncle, Cardinal Henry, but he received only a stern frown by way of reassurance.

Dona Ofelia produced a finely embroidered handkerchief and dabbed her eyes. 'Ah, bless him, the little lamb. Such a pure, innocent child, he has no notion what wickedness there is in this world.'

One by one those penitents to be spared death were dragged forward to have the name of their sin proclaimed to the crowd. As each crime was announced, Dona Ofelia, fervently clutching at the silver and ebony rosary that hung about her neck, gave an exaggerated gasp of horror as though she was about to swoon at the wickedness of it all. Some of the penitents had confessed to being Lutherans, witches or adulterers, or had broken the law by neglecting to display an image of the Virgin Mary on the walls of their houses. But Dona Ofelia reserved her greatest shrieks of outrage for those who were accused of Judaizing – relapsing back into the Jewish faith.

'I knew it,' she said, as each was dragged forward. 'You can tell he's a Jew just by looking at him.'

If Mother had been with us, her horror would have been even greater than Dona Ofelia's, for according to my mother and our parish priest, Judaizing was the most unforgivable crime you could ever commit against Christ. Father Tomàs reminded us of the list of thirty-seven signs of Judaizing almost every Sunday at Mass. He said that if you saw a friend or neighbour showing any one of these signs it was your duty as a faithful Christian to report it at once. Did your neighbour wear a clean shirt on a Saturday? Was he seen giving fruit to a friend in September near the time of the festival the Jews called the Feast of the Tabernacles? Was there no smell of pork fat in the smoke from his cooking fire? Had the fishmonger remembered that they had never bought eels from him? Did you see a mother wash her infant too soon after it had been christened? Even a person cutting their fingernails on a Friday might be a sign that they were practising their Jewish faith in secret.

Father Tomàs assured us that the accused would never learn who had reported them, so no one need fear retaliation from the accused's family or have cause to worry about being cursed by these heretics. On the contrary, whoever denounced their masters or their servants, their neighbours or even their own parents, would be blessed by the Church and God for their piety and devotion in helping to rid Portugal of this evil. My mother would nod emphatically in agreement each time Father Tomàs reminded us of this. For our family could trace our Catholic lineage back almost to St Peter himself, even counting abbesses and bishops among our forebears, so she was constantly vigilant for any suspicious signs among our neighbours, proud and eager to play her part in purifying Portugal.

It was late in the afternoon now, my mouth was dry and my stomach was growling with hunger. Sitting in the full glare of the merciless sun, the penitents must have been crazed with thirst, but they were herded to kneel before the great altar to repeat after the Inquisitor-General phrase by painful phrase the lengthy public abjuration of their sin.

The sentence for most was to be seated upon a donkey, the women bare-breasted, and flogged with two hundred lashes through the town. *The shame*, they called it. Children were taken from their parents to be re-educated in the Catholic faith. Then, after the shame, most of the penitents would be taken to the secular prison, there to remain for the rest of their lives. Those lucky few who, after their ride of shame, were set at liberty would have to appear in public in the *sanbenito* for the rest of their lives, so that all decent Christians would know what they were and shun them.

'What a pity your mother could not attend today,' Dona Ofelia said suddenly.

She vigorously fanned her deep puckered cleavage, down which rivulets of sweat ran from the great mounds of her breasts like melting snow from mountain peaks.

'She's ill,' I told her. It was the excuse Father and I had agreed upon.

'But witnessing the *auto-da-fé* is a pious act. Why, I have known people brought here on their deathbed to witness the procession who have leapt up and walked home on their two feet, cured by God for their faith.'

'She has a contagion.'

Dona Ofelia looked at me suspiciously as if I was one of her maids she had caught out in a lie. 'Do convey my sympathies to her. She must suffer a good deal from poor health. I seem to recall your father saying she was unwell on the last occasion too. But perhaps she does not understand how important it is to witness the *auto-da-fé*, for you seem to know so little of what occurs. Has your father not shared with his family the mercy of the Inquisition? Perhaps he does not altogether approve?'

'Of course he does,' I protested hotly. 'My father doesn't talk much, but there is no one who is more loyal to the Inquisition than he is, and my mother is constantly —'

She reached across and patted my hand. 'Don't get upset, child. I'm sure you're right. It is just that there has been some talk. You know how gossip spreads through the Court, not that I ever listen to it myself, naturally.'

'What have they been saying?' I demanded, furious that anyone should question the loyalty of my parents. We came from one of the oldest Catholic families in Portugal, probably a great deal older than hers. How dare she?

Dona Ofelia's eyes flashed. She was not accustomed to being addressed in such a tone. I knew it was dangerous to offend a woman with her husband's influence.

I tried to swallow my temper. 'Forgive me, Dona Ofelia, I was worried that people were saying things that were untrue.'

'I'm sure I must have misheard and they were talking of someone else. It is nothing for you to worry about, child. Forget I even mentioned it.'

She smiled soothingly, but I knew I had ruined any chance

I had of finding out more. She turned her head firmly in the direction of the altar as if she was riveted by the stumbling words of the penitents. But I couldn't forget. She knew they had been talking about my father, but what could a man as quiet and self-effacing as he ever have done to provoke gossip? I glanced uneasily over at him, but his gaze too was fixed on the Inquisitor-General.

The public abjuration had at last drawn to a close and thick shadows stretched out their dark fingers towards the centre of the square where the penitents knelt. Over the rooftops, the sky blazed gold and purple and blood-red as the fierce sun sank from view. The notes of the choir rose into the evening air. The castrati's high-pitched voices rang out like angel song over the square and stilled the restless crowd, sending shivers of awe up my spine. Even a few of the penitents raised their haggard faces as if they thought the light of heaven was descending upon the town.

A priest stepped forward to light the candles in the penitents' hands as a token that they had been brought back to the light of Christ. The penitents gazed in wonder at the tiny, fragile flames which sprang up in their hands. The Inquisitor-General raised his arms, his deep voice booming out in exaltation and triumph through the unearthly soaring of the castrati's song as he pronounced the Absolution.

Then, with a conjuror's flourish, the Inquisitor-General swept away the black cloth, which all this while had covered the altar, to reveal the rugged green cross of the Holy Order of the Inquisition, the sign of God's mercy, love and forgiveness. The Church had triumphed over heresy and God once more would turn the smile of His countenance upon Portugal. The crowd roared and cheered and stamped their feet as if a vision of Christ himself had appeared over the altar.

Dona Ofelia hugged me, beaming through her tears. 'I swear even a stone would be moved by that dear man's mercy.

Isn't he magnificent?' she said, reaching out a trembling hand towards the Inquisitor-General as if she longed to caress his face. Then she suddenly blushed like a love-sick girl.

But the day was not yet over. There was still the little group of condemned prisoners to deal with. The king, the Regent, the Inquisitor-General and all the monks and priests processed out of the square and eventually, when the royal procession was far enough ahead, the rest of us were permitted by the soldiers to follow them in solemn procession to the huge square of Terreiro do Paço, in front of the royal palace. Dona Ofelia clung tightly to my hand lest she should lose me in the crush.

A second dais had been erected for the king and his great-uncle, but in front of it was no altar. Instead, on the far side of the square, furthest away from the palace walls, was a huge platform made from dried faggots of wood with a dozen or more posts rising up out of them.

It was dark now. Only the blazing torches on the palace walls illuminated the scene, sending snakes of red and orange flame writhing up into the indigo sky. Midges swarmed around the flames in great misty clouds and over our heads bats, drunk on moth blood, lurched in and out of the pools of light.

A twisting rope of candle flames wound down the street towards us. The candles were held in the hands of monks and the castrati who were singing a *Miserere*. The voices of these beautiful beardless men rose and wheeled like the flight of a merlin climbing higher into the heavens, until the very stars themselves seemed to vibrate with notes.

The crowd, restless and hungry after the interminable day, were prowling around like caged animals, and when they saw the condemned enter the square, they surged forward in a great wave, howling and shrieking in anger and disgust. It was all the soldiers could do to beat them back and stop them tearing the heretics limb from limb before they could even reach the pyre.

The condemned were hauled up one by one on top of the faggots of wood and dragged to a post, where they were chained facing the screaming mob. One of the black-hooded *familiares* held up a flaming torch beside each man and woman so that those binding them could see clearly enough to fasten the locks. The Judaizers were still gagged for fear that they might cry out that they were innocent, or worse still, shout some desperate prayer to their Hebrew God.

Next to them on the pyre, the friars positioned the effigies of those who had fled rather than face capture. The wooden statues would help to burn the relatives and friends they had left behind. It was an irony not lost on the crowd, who repeated the joke loudly to one another.

Finally the boxes of bones were placed into the hands of some of the penitents spared the flames, who were driven forward to the edge of the pyre. Most carried the boxes without giving any sign that they knew what they held, either numb to any emotion now or so relieved to have escaped death they would gladly have kissed the feet of their jailers.

But one young girl began to sob so hard the sound rose even above the chattering people. Tears streamed down her face, and she clutched the box in her stick-thin arms so fiercely that the friars had to strike her with canes several times before she would set it down on top of the unlit pyre. Even then it seemed she could not pull her hands away from the box, as if her fingers were frozen to it. She clutched at it until she was dragged away.

'That'll be the bones of her lover or one of her family in that box,' Dona Ofelia said with glee. 'Now she'll watch them burned to ashes so there can be no hope of resurrection for them, which is what all heretics deserve, don't you agree, child?'

I smiled and nodded as vigorously as I could. Trying to look as if I couldn't wait to see them blazing.

When all was prepared the crowd fell silent. A hush of

expectation fell across the darkened square. Slowly and solemnly the Inquisitor-General stalked across the square towards his sovereign, his footsteps suddenly echoing hollowly in the darkness. The torches flickered, lengthening his shadow and sending it slithering towards the gaping crowd. As it crept close to them people stepped back, as if the mere touch of his black ghost would send the chill of death through their bones.

He bowed before King Sebastian, handing him a scroll of parchment on which were written the names of the prisoners, now released by the Inquisition into the hands of the king. For the Church could not execute anyone. The ultimate sentence of justice must be carried out by the State. The boy-king gingerly took the parchment in his hands, holding it as if he thought it would burst into flames.

A Moor with a chest as broad as an ox took up his place behind a condemned woman chained to the first post on the pyre. His features, like those of the *familiaries*, were concealed beneath a black hood. He was stripped to the waist and the thick corded muscles of his ebony arms gleamed with a sheen of sweat in the torchlight.

The prisoner cringed away as far as her chains would allow. She was a small, hollow-cheeked woman with long grey hair that hung in tattered shreds from beneath her hat. One of the *familiaries* loosened her leather gag. As soon as the gag was removed, she began to sob and scream. She was crying so hard that her words could hardly be distinguished, only the odd phrase torn from her parched throat filtered through her tears – *repent . . . abjure . . . abjure . . . I abjure.*

It was enough. Before I even realized what he was doing, the Moor had placed an iron chain around her fragile neck. Fear contorted the woman's face as he pulled the chain tight in his great fists. She struggled desperately for breath as the chain bit deeper and deeper into her throat, then finally her head lolled sideways and her body sagged limply from the wooden post, a look of abject terror frozen for ever in her bulging eyes.

The crowd screamed and howled, half-excited by the death, but at the same time frustrated that in repenting she had cheated them of the spectacle of her writhing in the flames. The executioner removed the iron chain and moved to stand behind the next prisoner. And so they worked down the line of the condemned. As one by one their gags were removed, a few shouted their repentance so there could be no mistake they wanted the mercy of the garrotte. But through fear or pain or raging thirst, most could do no more than whisper their confessions to the friars, who declaimed them theatrically to the square. As the garrotte crept agonizingly slowly down the line towards them, the waiting prisoners trembled and tried desperately to pull themselves out of their chains. One lad pissed himself in fear, and the crowd jeered and whooped with delight.

When they came to the sixth man, they once more untied the leather gag. He was old, his hair white, his cheeks caved in as if all his teeth had gone, eyes sunk so deep into their sockets they looked like two black holes in his skull. The soldier lifted the blazing torch higher over his head, ready for the executioner to do his work. Up to then I hadn't seen the old man's face clearly because of the gag. But as the light fell full upon him, I realized with a jolt there was something familiar about the way he held his head, something about the mouth . . . the eyes . . . but why? Why did I think I'd seen him before? Then horror shuddered through my frame as I finally realized who the old man was.

'Senhor Jorge! No, not him!' The words were out of my mouth before I could stop them.

Dona Ofelia turned a startled face to me. 'Did you say something, child?'

I tried to smile, even though I was trembling so much I was certain I was going to vomit.

'I thought . . . I . . . I saw a friend in the crowd.'

She smiled. 'I expect you did, dear, half of Lisbon is here. But you said, "No, not him."'

'Did I?'

Mercifully, before I was forced to think of an explanation, Dona Ofelia's attention was captured once again by what was happening on the pyre. Unlike the other prisoners, Senhor Jorge had said nothing when his gag was removed. The *familiaries* and friars jostled around him, urging him even now to recant and be spared the agony of the flames. But as if he'd heard me cry out, he ignored them and, turning his head, stared directly at the spot where I stood. He opened his mouth and in a hoarse, cracked voice, proclaimed, 'You Christians are all idolaters; you bow down before idols and worship a man instead of God . . . *Shema Yisrael* . . .'

It was all he could get out before they forced the gag back into his mouth. With a single bellow of fury, the enraged mob rushed towards the pyre, determined to tear him apart with their bare hands, and the soldiers had to beat them back. Several people fell to the ground, bleeding and senseless, before the soldiers could regain control of the crowd.

When they were satisfied that the gag was tied so tightly around his mouth again that not a single word could escape, the friars and the executioner moved on down the line. But Senhor Jorge stood quite still with his chin lifted, his eyes staring up at the starry sky above, as if he was back in his own flower-filled courtyard in Sintra. And just for a moment I was sitting there with him again, crouching on a stool at his feet, a wide-eyed little five-year-old, listening entranced to his stories, stories his Spanish grandmother had once told him when he was a small boy long, long ago. Jorge would sip his wine and lean back in his battered old chair, peacefully contemplating the heavens.

'That is Lilith's star, Isabela. You watch, over the next few nights she will grow dim and then bright again, like a great eye winking in the sky. Lilith . . . now, did I ever tell you of her? She was the most beautiful creature who ever lived and she used to boast that she could make any man in the world fall so hopelessly in love with her that he'd give all he owned for one night in her arms. But the angels said there is one man on earth who is too wise ever to fall in love with you, and that is the great King Solomon.

'Lilith was determined to prove them wrong. So she disguised herself as the queen of Sheba and went to visit the wise old king. And he did find himself falling in love with her, just as she said he would, but he decided to test that she really was who she claimed to be. So he built for himself a floor of glass, sat down on the other side of it, and sent for Lilith to come to him. When she drew near, she saw the glass shining in the sun and thought it was a pool of water, so she raised her skirts to wade through it and then King Solomon saw to his horror that instead of human legs she had the hairy legs of a goat. And he knew then that she was no mortal woman at all, but a wicked demon sent to tempt him.'

Seeing my mouth open wide with amazement, Jorge popped a sugared almond into it and laughed.

Gentle, wise old Jorge, how could he be here in this vile place, chained on that pyre? All his life he had been a physician and had done nothing but help and heal both neighbour and stranger alike. What had he done to make the Inquisitors think he was a Judaizer? Who could have reported him? Which of our neighbours would have done that? I wanted to scream out they had arrested an innocent man. But he wasn't. Those words he shouted out before they gagged him again meant he wasn't innocent at all. He was a heretic. But even though I knew that, I still couldn't bear to see him punished. I tried to look somewhere else as my father had warned me to do, but I couldn't tear my eyes from him. I felt as long as I kept looking at him, I could keep him alive. I could will him to live.

By the time the Moor reached the end of the line of prisoners, three of them remained alive – Jorge, a woman and a young lad. All had refused to confess their guilt and renounce the faith of Abraham. The friars were still standing beside them, urging them to repent in the hope that their courage would fail them and in their terror of the flames they would finally throw themselves on the mercy of the Church and its swift garrotte. The Church wanted no martyrs for another faith.

All heads now turned to the royal dais. The two Jesuits standing behind the king's throne prodded little Sebastian to rise. The crowd drew in their breath as he descended the steps. They watched the slow progress of their tiny king as he marched alone across the dark square, his cape trailing after him in the breeze. The gold coronet about his brow turned to blood-red in the light of the torches.

When Sebastian drew level with the Inquisitor-General, the commander of the soldiers stepped forward and with a low bow handed him a blazing torch almost as long as the boy was high. The officer respectfully pointed to the place on the edge of the pyre where Sebastian must light the pyre. The sticks at that spot glistened in the dancing flames. They had been coated with tar so that they would catch fire at once. The Inquisitor-General stood to one side, his head bowed. It was up to the king, not the Church, to light the fire that would burn the living and dead to ashes.

The child held the burning torch awkwardly, recoiling from the heat of it. He stared wide-eyed at the flames, holding the torch as far away from himself as he could, as if he feared that the flames would set light to his hair. But he was not tall enough to balance the heavy weight at arm's length. He advanced a couple of steps, then he lifted his head and looked up at the figures above him on the pyre. His gaze seemed to rest upon the young lad, who stared directly into the little king's face. The leather gag masked his mouth, but his eyes were as large and liquid as those of a fawn.

For a moment the boy-king and the young prisoner just stared at each other. Then the officer, perhaps fearing that Sebastian had forgotten where he was to light the pyre, bent down to whisper to him. Sebastian whipped round, his chin jerking up defiantly, his brow creased in anger. Then he turned and hurled the torch as far away from the pyre as his strength would allow. It crashed on to the flagstones and continued to burn there, as Sebastian stalked back to the dais.

The crowd gasped. For a moment no one moved. Finally the officer retrieved the torch and looked helplessly at the Inquisitor-General, plainly uncertain what to do next. The Inquisitor's face was a portrait of undisguised rage. For a moment he looked as if he was going to wrench the torch out of the officer's hands and light the pyre himself. You could see he was itching to burn these heretics, but that was the one thing he did not have the power to do.

The crowd started up a rhythmic mocking chant – *Burn them! Burn them!* – stamping their feet and clapping their hands. The king's great-uncle rose from his throne and almost leapt from the royal dais. His red robes flying out behind him, he strode rapidly across the square. He seized the torch with one hand, whilst with the other he struck such a blow with his leather-gloved fist that he lifted the officer off his feet and sent him sprawling on the ground a yard or more away. The Regent lifted the torch high above his head, then thrust it into the tarred sticks, as viciously as if he was thrusting a dagger into a man's body. The wood caught at once, and flames clawed up into the black sky. The crowd roared and cheered.

The fire surrounded the box of bones that the young girl had placed on the pyre. For several minutes the box sat in the centre of the blaze, unscathed, like a phoenix in its nest, then it burst into flames and was consumed.

It seemed a lifetime before the flames reached the back of the pyre, where the living prisoners were tied. They writhed in the scorching heat, watching the flames creep closer to them, waiting for the orange tongues to dart out towards the hems of their robes and lick up around their bodies.

I had never in my life prayed for someone's death, but I did so now. I prayed that Jorge and the woman and the young man would be suffocated by the smoke before the flames touched them. Was it blasphemy to pray that heretics should be spared pain? I never knew if my prayers were answered, for by then the flames at the front were too high, the smoke too dense for me to see when they died. If they could have screamed through the leather gags, no one would have heard them for the cheering and insane bellows of laughter from the crowd.

I pretended it was smoke that made the tears run down my face, but I don't think Dona Ofelia believed me.

Belém, Portugal
Ricardo

Lure – a piece of padded wood, to which meat and feathers have been bound, which is swung on a line to attract the hawk to the falconer.

'Senhor Ricardo da Moniz, at your service,' I announced.

I swept off my green feathered cap and bowed low, kissing Dona Lúcia's plump jewelled hand. Pio, my diminutive pet monkey, standing on my shoulder, doffed his miniature cap and bowed in imitation of me. Dona Lúcia simpered at us both.

Sweet Jesu, that ruby in her ring was the size of a pigeon's egg! I could hardly bear to tear my lips away from it. All right, so maybe it was not quite that large, but where's the harm in embellishing a little? The point is that it was as plain as a nipple on a whore that Dona Lúcia was elderly, wealthy and best of all a widow, with no one to lavish her money on except herself and her overstuffed lapdog.

'Won't you sit with me, Senhor Ricardo?' she cooed, patting the silk cushion next to her on her seat under the arbour.

Ricardo – it has a debonair ring to it, don't you think? I'm quite proud of that one. The name came to me on the spur of the moment in the fish market when I first encountered Dona Lúcia's adorable little maid, with breasts like a couple of soft ripe peaches and such a fetching little dimple in her right cheek. *Senhor Ricardo*, she repeated when I told her, and the syllables purred delightfully in her slim white throat.

47

Anyway, it's a damn sight better than *Cruz*, which my benighted parents thrust upon me. What on earth possessed them to name their youngest son after the Holy Cross? If they hoped that it would turn me into a priest, they were sadly mistaken. Now, if they had christened me with an elegant saint's name like *Teodósio* or *Valerio*, who knows, I might have tried to live up to that, but not Cruz. It's the kind of name that's bound to bring out the Devil in you from the very first time your mother sets you on your infant feet and says, 'Now, be a good boy, Cruz.' I ask you – wouldn't that make you determined to rebel?

At Dona Lúcia's invitation I settled myself on the long bench beside her under the canopy of ancient twisted vines in the small courtyard. It was the most delightful spot; enclosed by the high walls of her house, the floor of the courtyard was tiled with an intricate Moorish design of twisted blue and yellow flowers. The scents of jasmine, orange and lemon hung in the air, and from a small fountain in the centre jets of water tinkled into a marble pool, making the air feel cool and refreshingly moist after the scorching heat and dust of the narrow streets beyond.

Dona Lúcia's black slave boy brought us glasses of hot mint tea. I produced a tiny cup for Pio, my little monkey. He crouched between us on the bench, sipping like a gentleman and graciously accepting fragments of almond cake from Dona Lúcia's own fingers, much to the insane jealousy of her own yapping lapdog. Pio ignored it. Even a monkey could see the dog was so plump it could do little except sit there panting. It so much resembled a frying sausage I had an urge to prick its rump, sure that if I did so, it would burst wide open.

There is nothing like an animal to attract the ladies of any age. I used to have a little lapdog myself, but I realized women only really have affection for their own dog which, however revolting it is, they believe far outshines any other dog in intelligence, affection and cuteness. The monkey proved far more effective. I had dressed him in a miniature version of my own clothes, a cream doublet with gold trim and padded breeches slashed with scarlet. Together we looked quite striking.

Once the slave had withdrawn to the far side of the courtyard and Dona Lúcia's interest in feeding Pio was beginning to wane, I worked the conversation round to the reason for my visit. I told her I needed funds to equip a ship to sail to Goa, and I launched into a glowing description of all the riches she might garner for herself if she were to invest a modest amount in such a venture, which, I assured her, could not possibly fail.

'Unless you have seen this wondrous isle with your own eyes as I have, Dona Lúcia, you would never believe the half of its treasures. It is with good reason that it is called Golden Goa. All the riches of the world are traded there – costly spices, precious stones from Burma, jewels from the crowns of princes, the finest silks, delicate plates from China, the very best glass from Venice, horses from Arabia, elephants from India. All of it just waiting to be loaded on to ships and brought back to Portugal to be sold here for four, five, even ten times what was paid for them. That is, of course, anything you did not want to keep for yourself.'

'Do you really think I should keep an elephant?' Dona Lúcia asked.

She gazed round the courtyard as if contemplating whether such a beast might be installed in here to frolic in the fountain and nibble at the clipped balls of orange trees in their tall, elegant urns. I tried not to let my exasperation show on my face. Why do women have to latch on to your most inconsequential remarks and ignore the important things?

'I was merely explaining the variety of goods that are traded on this isle, Dona Lúcia. Naturally I would not be bringing back elephants. I would purchase rare spices, fine silks, delicate ornaments from China and beautiful jewels.

The kinds of things that any wealthy Portuguese man would want to adorn his home and his charming wife.'

Her large bug eyes grew misty with tears. She looked down at the numerous rings glittering on her wrinkled fingers. 'My late husband, God rest his sweet soul, often brought me jewels. He was such a fine man, Senhor Ricardo.' She glanced up at me from under her heavy lids outlined with black kohl. 'He looked just as handsome as you when we were first courting. But then, I was considered a great beauty in my time.'

'*Was*, Dona Lúcia? No, no, you must never say *was*. You *are* a beauty. Why, there isn't a jewel in all the royal palaces in India that wouldn't be eclipsed by the diamonds that sparkle in your eyes.'

She frowned. For a moment I thought I had gone too far and she thought I was mocking her. But then she favoured me with the kind of coquettish glance that must once have had men throwing themselves in front of charging bulls for her.

'Do you really think so, Senhor Ricardo?'

We talked on about the venture, the length of the voyage, the equipping of such an expedition. I told her about the sturdy ship I had found, the *Santa Dorothea* – such a pious and blessed name – and described with fulsome praise the vast experience of her captain. Then finally I drew the conversation to its purpose – the considerable sum of money I would need to embark on such a voyage. Money that I assured her she could not invest in any venture more secure or profitable.

'Why, on the last occasion I returned from Goa I made six times what I had put into the expedition and my only regret is that I was unable to invest more at that time, but now . . .'

Dona Lúcia frowned until the two strips of black mouse skin that she had stuck on over her own shaved eyebrows bumped noses in the middle of her forehead.

'But what I don't understand, Senhor Ricardo, is if you made such a good profit on your last expedition, why could you not use that money to fund another voyage?'

I hung my head in shame. 'I regret it is almost all gone. My friends said I was a fool, but alas, it is too late.'

I glanced fleetingly up at Dona Lúcia and saw her bridle.

'Your friends would appear to have more sense than you do. A young man who wantonly squanders his fortune is certainly a fool. I wager that women, drinking and gambling were your ruin. That's usually how a man and his money are parted.'

I let her scold. The more harshly she judged me now, the more guilty she would feel later. And when a man or woman feels guilty they always assuage their conscience by giving far more money than they would otherwise do.

'What, no fine words, Senhor Ricardo?' she said. 'You were eloquent enough just now. Are you ashamed to admit the truth?'

'I confess that I am, Dona Lúcia. You see before you an abject wretch who has failed his duty as a son. For the truth of it is, my poor dear father became sick. I took him to all the best physicians and bought whatever treatments they prescribed in a desperate attempt to save his life – rare herbs, pearls crushed in wine, tonics and purges. One physician recommended pure cold air, so I paid porters to carry my father into the mountains. Then another physician said the mountain air was harmful, instead we should bathe him in sea water, so I rented the best rooms I could find at the sea, but it was all to no avail. He sadly died. He was relying on me and I failed to find the cure for him in time.'

I bowed my head to hide my tears and it was several moments before I was able to continue.

'My sweet, gentle mother was heartbroken and terrified for the future, for I had five unwed sisters all needing dowries so that they might catch respectable husbands. I could not let the poor woman fret over such a burden. So all the money I had left from paying for my father's treatments I gave to my mother to provide for her and my little sisters.

I am a fool, as my friends so rightly say, for I left myself almost penniless, but what else could I do?'

I sighed heavily, and Pio, who has been well trained, reached out his tiny paw and stroked my cheek, laying his little head on my shoulder in a most affecting manner.

Dona Lúcia sighed almost as deeply as I had and, taking her cue from Pio, stroked my hand. 'That such a thing should happen is tragic, tragic! But you mustn't blame yourself. You did everything you could. You have been a jewel of a son to your parents and your sisters. A saint! No mother on earth could ask for better.'

I almost wished my mother had been there to hear me called a saint. Then she would realize that there are some people in this world who do appreciate my talents. But it was just as well she wasn't for she might have disputed a few of the trivial details of my story. It was entirely true that I was half an orphan. You didn't think I'd lie about something like that, did you? But my mother would tell you it was shame over my wicked and dissolute behaviour that killed the old man. Rather an unfair accusation, if you ask me. But then she had thought me a sad disappointment ever since I said my first word, which apparently was a word no mother would ever want to hear her son utter. She could be a harsh woman at times.

Dona Lúcia, on the other hand, was a charming if blessedly gullible creature, who was perfectly content that I was whatever a mother could wish for in a son. And that kind of touching faith is bound to bring out the best in any fellow. I swear by the time I left that perfumed courtyard she was almost on the verge of adopting me as her own kin.

I was to return in five days' time when she would have my money . . . *her* money . . . ready for me to collect. She had originally proposed two weeks to gather the finances, but I had persuaded her that the ship needed to sail within the week in order to catch the trade winds. A few days, I told her, could make all the difference between a journey lasting mere weeks and a voyage of many months, as I knew from my own experience, having seen ships becalmed for days on end.

I explained to her that men grew so sick from lack of food and water as their supplies dwindled that by the time they found the wind again, the crew were too weak to man the sails. I told her how I'd seen innocent young boys plunge to their deaths from the rigging, too faint to hold on, and men, driven mad by thirst, leaping into the waves thinking the water was a meadow and they could see their own wives and children running across it. She dabbed her eyes most touchingly at that.

Finally, after we agreed that the money had to be found as quickly as possible if she didn't want their deaths on her conscience, I left her house, clutching a basket of grapes and peaches 'for dear little Pio'.

Tomorrow I would pay a call on a friend of mine, a clerk, and get a document drawn up. Dona Lúcia would expect a written contract before she parted with a single crusado. My friend could produce the most impressive documents ornamented with great flourishes and couched in such obscure legal phrases that the Devil himself would sign away his own soul and not realize he was doing so. This clerk would draw up whatever I required for nothing. He owed me. He'd managed to pocket some nice little sums from his employer over the years, but he'd become greedy and careless, and was perilously close to getting himself arrested. I'd helped him point the finger of blame at another employee who even now was languishing in prison, but my friend knew that one word from me and he could find himself in that dungeon instead.

'Just think, Pio,' I said, as we feasted on the fruit in the stifling heat of my lodgings, 'in five days' time that bastard of an innkeeper will be bowing and scraping and begging us to accept the best wine his poxy tavern can offer. But I've a good mind never to set foot in there again. He can whistle for his money. Throwing me out as if I was a beggar instead of a gentleman. By rights he should be paying me to drink that muck he serves just to get rid of it. And I should sue him for giving me a bellyache every time I sup it.'

Pio snatched another grape from my plate, and leapt up on top of the battered old cupboard to eat it, spitting the seeds at me. I popped a grape into my own mouth and, as if he thought I was stealing his food, Pio screamed at me in indignant fury, before finally turning his back on me and refusing to look at me at all.

When he was in this mood, he was nearly as bad as Silvia. The sulky little witch was always flouncing and throwing tantrums. I didn't have enough fingers on my hands to count the number of times she'd threatened to leave me. Now she had finally done it, but I knew she wouldn't stay away for long, not once she got a whiff of the money.

'How long do you reckon it'll be before that whore comes crawling to me? Want to place a wager, Pio? A month, you say. I'll bet you a whole barrel of figs it'll be a week at most, you'll see. Then she'll be twisting her pretty little arms round my neck and begging me to take her back.'

I lay back on the narrow stained straw pallet and stared up at the sagging beams above the bed. God, but I missed her. Silvia drove me mad when she was here with her whining and nagging, but when she was gone I was crazy with longing for her. I tried not to think about whose bed she was lying in now. And she would be lying with someone; she was not the kind of woman to spend even a single night alone. With that wild mane of raven hair, lithe brown limbs and full soft lips, not even a Jesuit could have remained true to his vows in her company.

Even when we lived together I could only be sure that Silvia was faithful to me when she was actually in the room with me. Not even then sometimes, for she often had that melting look in her wide indigo eyes that told you she was

thinking of someone else. I frequently became insanely jealous. But when I shouted at her or implored her to give the
other men up, she only laughed at me. Jealousy made no
sense to her, for she was easily bored and would wander from
lover to lover like a fly aimlessly buzzing around a butcher's
stall. She couldn't ever understand that a man wants to believe
he is a woman's only lover.

What had made her stalk out this time, I couldn't remember. We'd had a fight. But that was nothing new. Silvia loved
to whip up a storm, to rage and scream and hurl her shoes at
my head, and once even a full chamber pot. But if our fights
were wild, our lovemaking afterwards was wilder still. All
that fury in her exploded into passion and she rode me like a
marauding Tatar until we both collapsed into sleep from
sheer exhaustion.

But there'd been no intoxicating gallop this time, that
much I do remember through the brandy fumes fogging my
head. When I'd finally awoken the next morning, with a
tongue as furred as a donkey's arse, she was gone. I was sure
she'd return that night but she didn't, and no one at the inn
had seen her since.

'But it's only been four days, Pio. As soon as she hears I've
got money to buy her dresses and jewels, she'll slither back in
here. Just you wait and see, Pio. All the soldiers in the king's
army couldn't keep her away.'

A bright green lizard scuttled across a patch of rotting
wood above my head. Sweet Jesu, but it was hot. The sweat
was trickling down my face and stinging my eyes. The stench
of putrid fish guts, tar and dried seaweed wafted in through
the broken shutters, but there was scarcely a whisper of
breeze to cool the tiny room. I slapped at a bedbug crawling
into my armpit and tried to settle myself more comfortably
between the lumps in the straw mattress.

Below my window, I could hear the rustling and squealing
of the rats fighting among the rubbish, too insolent even to

bother to wait for the cover of darkness. But for the first time in weeks I didn't resent any of these daily torments. Only five more days and then I'd be out of here for good, with money jangling in my pocket and a belly full of rich food. Life was a tree laden with sweet ripe peaches for those who knew how to pick them, and I was about to pluck one of the juiciest.

Iceland
Eydis

Mews — *the building where hawks are kept, especially while they moult, or mew.*

My sister died today. I felt the life go out of her as I cradled her tightly to me. I had always thought the spirit took wing from the body like a beetle flying upwards to the light. First would come the shiver of death in the slow opening of the wings, testing, balancing, and then a sudden upward thrust and the soul would be gone.

But it was not like that at all. It was water dripping slowly out of a cracked beaker. It was an icicle melting drop by drop. There was no moment of death, only a slow haemorrhaging of life, the heartbeat growing softer, a drum fading into the distance as the drummer walks away.

Valdis didn't speak, but I knew what she was thinking, I always knew. She was thinking of the mountain and of the river of blue ice that creeps from it so imperceptibly you cannot see it move, although you know it does. She and I used to watch it for hours when we were small children in the hope of seeing it change, but we never did. At night, tucked up together in the little bed we shared, we'd hold hands and listen to the ice-river singing to us under the bright cold stars. But some nights it did not soothe us with its lullabies. It crackled and cracked so loudly the boom of it would echo around us as if the mountains themselves were crashing into the valley. Then we clung to each other, afraid.

57

That's what Valdis was thinking of when she died, the nights of the blue ice. We always promised ourselves we would see that river again one day. One day we would leave this cave and climb up again to the light. We would run across the grassy plains, and slide across the frozen lake, and scramble over the sharp black rocks to reach the mountain where we were born. One day, we said . . . one day. We promised each other.

Our mother brought us to this cave when we were both seven years old. That is the age at which the gift of second sight awakens in a child. I remember thinking how vast it was. First the descent through the slit in the rock, narrow as a woman's crack, hidden from any mortal view unless you knew it was there. Then we climbed down and down over ledges and boulders into the darkness below and all the time the sound of rushing water grew louder, and the heat more intense.

Finally we stood on the wide flat floor of the cave, bigger even than our cottage above the river of ice. The rocks were warm against our bare feet. At the far end of the cave a deep, clear pool of hot water bubbled up from an underground river far below. It streamed out into a second cave where narrow tunnels crushed and squeezed the water until somewhere far off, or so we were told, it finally thundered out of the rock and into the light.

Valdis and I were terrified of that pool of steaming water when first our mother brought us here. We feared that some great beast lay at the bottom of it, a dragon or monster, which would rise out of it while we slept and devour us. We tried to take it in turns to sleep, but in the end we both slept. The cave was too warm, the sound of the water too intoxicating to resist sleep for long. But now I am alone with that pool. Now there is no one to keep watch over me, sleeping or waking.

For fifty years there has always been the two us. We were twins, constant companions, day and night, sleeping and waking. Not even lovers could know the closeness we felt. I used to look at people who were alone and wonder what it must be like to have only your thoughts for company, hear only your own heartbeat in the night, feel only your own breath in the darkness. My sister was as close to me as my soul is to my body, and I can't conceive of life without her.

I knew we would die one day, every mortal dies, but I had thought we would die together. It didn't seem possible that one of us could go on living when the other was gone. In truth I can't even be certain that I do live. I feel numb inside as if my thoughts are frozen, my tears petrified as ice, and yet my body can still feel the heat of the water gushing through this cave. My eyes can still see the flames of the pitch torch burning on the rock wall and the glowing ruby embers of my little cooking fire. My ears can still hear the wind whistling over the slit in the rock high above, far out of my sight, playing the hole like a child plays the pipes. How can these things be when Valdis is dead?

When she first brought us to this cave, our mother gave us little pallets stuffed with eiderdown to rest on, baskets of dried fish and whale meat, smoked mutton and sweet dried berries. She gave us lamps filled with fish oil and torches dipped in pitch. We had water aplenty in our underground lake.

The blacksmith who bolted the chains deep into the rock wall was kind to us. He took great care to ensure that when he fastened the chains to the iron hoops about our waists they were long enough to let us walk to the water, even to allow us to bathe if we wished, but we were too afraid to enter that pool. He returned several times over those first few years to fit us with new hoops as we grew to womanhood, but we were never to see our mother again, not after that day she brought us here. And that was the last time we ever saw the sun or the moon.

Others came, of course, bringing food and oil for our lamps, gifts of clothes or spring flowers. Everyone who comes brings an offering to us. They lay them out for our inspection and then they ask us their questions.

'My red mare is missing, where should I look for her?'

'My daughter has two suitors, which should she take as a husband?'

'My husband has not returned from the sea, has he drowned or has he left me?'

'Shall I buy my neighbour's farmstead, will it prosper?'

'My son has been murdered, who is his killer?'

They want curses to punish their mothers-in-law, spells to defeat their rivals, blessings to protect their infants and cures for their ailing cows. We hear all life as it passes through here in their quarrels and triumphs, their griefs and their joys, but we do not see life, except in our visions. We do not live it.

They are afraid of us, afraid of what we might do if the iron rings are removed from our bodies. They know it is only those rings that keep our spirits in this cave. If that iron ever broke, we could transform ourselves into falcons. We could fly into the blinding sunlight, or soar among the frosted stars, and like our mother who brought us to the cave, they are terrified of what we might do then.

But in here we are tamed, their captives, and they need us, now more than ever, for a long shadow of evil creeps across the land. The Lutherans have destroyed the abbeys and monasteries, driven out the Catholic priests and executed the bishops. They raid homesteads and cottages, searching for the images of saints and the charms and amulets of the wizards and wise women that have protected the Icelanders since the old gods ruled this land. All the old certainties, the faith, the hope that people clung to down through the centuries, have been torn away from them. They are frightened. They are lost. They are defenceless. They need us. And I need Valdis.

One day, my sister, one day we shall return to the blue ice. I will find a way back to the light. I will take you back. I swear to you on your corpse, I will not fail you.

Chapter Three

Tamerlane wanted to possess the power of his great enemy Khan Tokhtamysh. He knew that if he could steal the eggs from the khan's prize gyrfalcons he could weaken the mighty khan and gain his strength. So Tamerlane bribed one of the khan's guards to smuggle out the falcons' eggs and give them to him.

When the eggs hatched, Tamerlane reared the birds with his own hand. As the falcons grew, so Tamerlane became stronger, and the khan weakened. And thus it was that when next they met in battle the great Khan Tokhtamysh was defeated and fled.

Sintra, Portugal
Isabela

Bow-net – *a baited trap to catch a falcon, which springs
around the bird when a peg is dislodged.*

'It was his own fault,' my mother said savagely. 'The old man
should have confessed when he had the chance. Then they'd
have given him the mercy of the garrotte before they burned
him.'

She scraped five sardines smoking and blackened from
the griddle on to my father's pewter plate, and set it down
with such a heavy thump in front of him on the table that the
candle flame trembled. I shivered, pulling my shawl tighter
around me. The sun had not yet risen, and the tiny room was
icy, as if the heat from the charcoal stove was being pushed
back by the chill of the room.

'What was the point of holding out? All that needless
pain. It was his own fault he suffered. You tell me, what was
the point of it?' It was the only question she had asked since
Father had told her about our neighbour Jorge, and she just
kept repeating it, as if the answer held the key to all the mys-
teries of the world.

'You can't simply confess,' my father told her. 'They won't
believe you have repented, unless you give them the names
of others.'

'Not when he was already sentenced to death. Once he'd
been handed over to the king, they couldn't do anything. He
could have recanted on the pyre. Then it would have been

over in a trice. But no, he wouldn't do it, would he, the stubborn old fool.'

I shuddered. We had returned from Lisbon only yesterday evening, a full three days after the burning, but I could still smell the stench of that bonfire.

Mother banged another plate down in front of me, causing the three salt-crusted sardines on it to leap as if in a bid for freedom.

'Jorge was a good man, a brave man,' Father said quietly. 'To endure the flames rather than betray anyone else, that takes the courage of a saint.'

Mother snorted her contempt. 'A saint! Is that what you think? He was a heretic, a Christ killer. It was the Devil in him who stopped him confessing his sin, that's what it was. To even think of comparing a man as evil as him with a saint who died for the true faith is . . . is . . . is obscene!'

'He was our neighbour. Don't you remember how kind he was to little Isabela when she was a child? She loved him like a grandfather.'

'And how many times did I warn you not to let her go round there? Filling her head with his silly stories and goodness knows what else. I warned you not to let her go mixing with Marranos, and now I've been proved right. They pretend to be good Catholics, but all the time they are practising their devilish rites in secret and plotting to murder us all in our own beds.' Mother rounded on me. 'You stay away from the lot of them, do you hear? Isn't it bad enough your father can't provide a decent dowry for you? How do you think you are ever going to get a good, respectable husband, if anyone finds out you are mixing with these converts? And now you have seen for yourself how dangerous it is to make friends of these pigs.'

'But, Mother, Jorge was a good man, a great physician. You used to take me to him yourself when I was sick, and don't you remember that time when you —'

'Enough, Isabela.' Father shook his head, warning me not to continue.

'Who reported him, that's what I want to know!' I burst out angrily. 'Who would even think of doing so, betraying a harmless old man?'

'Harmless!' Mother snapped. 'He was a heretic, and you heard what Father Tomàs said in Mass. Anyone who does not fight against heresy is himself guilty of betraying our Blessed Lord. It's our duty to God and the king to report these people. Our duty, do you hear?'

'But who –'

'Please, Isabela.' Father's tired eyes begged me to let the matter drop. 'Jorge is dead. All the words in the world cannot change that. Let us speak of something else.'

I glared at him, torn between wanting to punish my mother for her contempt of that poor old man and not wanting to hurt my father. But in the end I said nothing and vented my anger by stabbing furiously at the belly of the little charred fish. There was much which was never spoken of in our household for fear of upsetting my mother. It was the eleventh commandment in our family.

Mother crossed to the small shrine in the corner of the room and picked up the statues of the Virgin Mary and St Vincent of Saragossa clutching the gridiron on which he was martyred. She moved the statues reverently to one side, then gathered up an assortment of rosaries, dried flowers and candles. Shoving aside my father's half-eaten breakfast, she laid them on the table in front of him. My father grabbed his plate just in time to prevent the faded and crumbling wreath falling into his griddled sardines, and retreated to a bench in the corner to continue eating.

The shrine was my mother's pride and joy. She dressed it according to the feasts and festivals as diligently as if it was an altar in the great Cathedral in Lisbon. My earliest memories were of her holding me up in her arms in front of that shrine, gripping my chubby fingers painfully tight as she helped me light a candle to the Holy Virgin.

'My mother came from one of the oldest Catholic families in Portugal,' she would say. 'You must always remember that and see that you light a candle every day, just as she did and her grandmother before her.'

I didn't really understand then what Catholic was, but I could tell from the tone of my mother's voice, and the way she lifted her chin when she said it, that this was something to boast about.

Mother would show me the black wooden rosary with the silver cross left to her by my great-great-aunt who was an abbess of a convent. And if I had been a good girl, she would unwrap a little square of silk and let me hold the tiny tin wheel, the emblem of St Catherine, once worn by one of my father's ancestors in the Crusades when he fought under the Holy Cross. If she couldn't be proud of her husband or her life now, she could at least take pride in her heritage.

Mother flapped her goose-wing brush vigorously over the shrine, sending a cloud of dust into the air.

'Ana, my dear, must you start to clean so early?' my father protested gently. 'It's not even light yet. Sit, rest, eat your breakfast.'

My mother turned on him, her hands on her scrawny hips, her dull-brown eyes for once flashing with life. I cringed for my father, knowing that even after twenty-two years of marriage, he had once again walked blindly into the hole she had dug for him.

'Rest!' she snapped. 'When do I have time to rest? I suppose you have remembered that the girl who washes for me is sick again. Well, she says she is sick, but is it just a coincidence that her lover's ship has put into harbour? She'll be in bed all right, but mark my words, it won't be her own bed, that's for sure. If we had a black slave, like every other respectable family, I wouldn't be wearing my fingers to the bone, waiting for some little slut to decide whether or not she can be bothered to work. The spice merchant's wife says their slave paid for herself in half a year with the wages they saved by not having to employ a maid, and the slave they have costs practically nothing to keep for she eats less than a hound, and needs no meat. But no, you'd rather see your own wife work herself into an early grave than buy a slave.'

Father raked his fingers wearily through his hair. 'Ana, please, no more. If this girl is not reliable then look for another, but I've told you I will not buy a slave. We've discussed . . .' He shrugged, but did not finish the sentence, as if after all these years of trying to reason with her, he had simply exhausted his store of words.

He had never told me why he would not give in to my mother over this. It would have made his life so much easier. He said, whenever she pressed him, that we could not afford it, but I had to admit that my mother was right, poorer families than ours had at least one slave, for they were cheaper by far than hiring a man or maid by the hour. But my father's reason for refusing remained unspoken, like so much else in our lives.

He pushed his half-eaten meal away and began to fasten his shoes.

'And what about her?' my mother demanded, as she replaced the objects on the shrine. 'I hope you're not planning to take her with you today?'

I mouthed a silent 'please' at him, begging him not to leave me behind, for I knew mother would be in a foul temper all day.

Father grimaced and shook his head.

I pressed my hands together in supplication. 'Please, please,' I mouthed silently again.

'I . . . I have a falcon with broken feathers in its tail. I will need an extra pair of hands to hold the bird while I glue in new feathers.'

'There are plenty of boys at the mews who can do that. Isabela should be here learning how to be a wife and mother, not playing about with those birds. Unless you intend to marry her off to some stinking stable hand.'

My father shrugged to show me he'd tried his best. 'Perhaps your mother is right. She needs you more than I do today with the girl being sick, and –'

The bell of the courtyard door jangled and at the same time someone hammered on the stout wood. All three of us froze. We stared at one another. No neighbour or pedlar would knock so early or so insistently.

The bell clanged again, ringing over and over. From the thundering at the door, it sounded as if someone was beating on it with metal rather than with their fist.

'It could be someone in trouble,' my father said as he crossed the courtyard. But I don't think even he believed that. For the long minutes it seemed to take him to cross the few flags of the courtyard, I felt as if I could see through the solid wood, see the hooded, black-robed *familiaries* of the Inquisition standing outside our little house. Had Dona Ofelia reported me for showing sympathy for a heretic? Had they come to question me?

Father's hands were trembling as he fumbled to turn the key in the lock. Mother moved to my side and put her arm around my shoulders, drawing me close to her, breathing in short little gasps. Side by side we watched through the open door of the kitchen, as the lock of the courtyard door yielded, but even before my father had pulled it open, someone was flinging it wide from the other side.

A tall man in the king's livery pushed his way into the courtyard, followed by two soldiers. I realized I had been holding my breath and it almost exploded out of me in relief. It was not the Inquisition. Father was wanted at the royal palace; that was all. Perhaps the young king wanted to go hunting or –

'You are under arrest, Falconer, by order of the king.'

My mother gave a little shriek and started forward, but my father motioned her back. He drew himself up as straight as he could, though he was no match for the height of the officer.

'Arrest? On . . . on what charge? May I ask what crime I have committed?'

'The charge is murder.'

My mother moaned, swaying so violently that I rushed to her side, fearing she was going to collapse. Even my father seemed too stunned to answer.

'Murder, but who am I supposed to have murdered? When? Until yesterday I was waiting on the king in Lisbon and since then I have been nowhere alone, nowhere except to tend the king's falcons.'

'So you admit it,' the officer said. 'You admit that you were alone with the king's birds.'

'Yes, of course. Why shouldn't I be? I am the Royal Falconer. The birds are my responsibility. I went to see that they had been well tended in my absence the moment I arrived back in Sintra.'

'And had they been?' The officer's expression remained impassive.

'Yes, the boys had been diligent in their duties. Perhaps not cleaning the dung from the wall behind the perches as well as I would have liked, but I will see to it that they do so this morning. I assure you that —'

'So there was nothing amiss with the birds last night?' the officer persisted.

The two soldiers were leaning against the wall, yawning and picking their teeth, evidently paying little attention to the exchange.

'The birds were fit and well,' my father said, his face showing his bewilderment. 'One of the peregrines has damaged his wedge a little, but I will soon mend —'

'And you personally locked the mews when you left?'

My father nodded. 'I left one of my lads to sleep with the birds, as I always do, in case they should become disturbed during the night.'

'Then it seems we have come to arrest the right man,' the officer said. 'This morning one of your other lads found the body of a gyrfalcon lifeless and cold.'

My father groaned, pressing his hand to his mouth, shaking his head sadly. I knew he was devastated. He loved every one of his birds as if they were his own children, but particularly the gyrfalcons, the royal falcon, rarest and most beautiful of all the hawks of the lure. But I still didn't understand. The officer had spoken of murder and arrest, but what did the death of a bird have to do with that?

'It happens,' Father said with a sigh. 'The gyrfalcon is a powerful bird, but also the most delicate. They can die without warning. Which one was it, do you know? Did the boy say?'

'Oh, he told us, all right, Falconer, and I've seen it with my own eyes. It wasn't just one bird. It was both of the gyrfalcons. The royal birds are dead. The most valuable birds in the mews are now so much carrion. Now, how do you account for that, Falconer? They both decided to fall off their perches at the same time, did they? So how did you kill them, Falconer?'

My father gasped in horror. 'But I didn't! I would no more hurt those birds than I would murder my own child. They're my life. Something must have happened, a sudden illness . . . perhaps something frightened them . . . The lad who slept with them, he must surely tell you how this misfortune came about. Have you questioned him? What did he say?'

'Oh yes, we questioned him all right, though we had to find him and untie him first. You see, he'd been bound, gagged and hidden behind some sacks of sand. He doesn't remember being trussed up. What he does remember is settling down to eat his supper after you left. The usual fare except for an unexpected treat, a custard pastry had been left on his platter, the kind they sell in the market places of Lisbon. Naturally the lad being hungry, as they always are at that age, gobbled it up. Next thing he knows he felt dizzy and unaccountably sleepy. He collapsed and doesn't recall a thing until he came round the next morning to find himself bound up ... I noticed you keep a great many jars of herbs and flasks of potions in the mews.'

'Every falconer does,' my father said distractedly. 'If a bird gets sick or it's not thriving it must be treated at once. But have you discovered who drugged the boy?'

'It must have been someone with great knowledge of herbs – someone who knew exactly what would keep a lad asleep for several hours so that he couldn't raise the alarm and also which herb would poison a bird so swiftly that it would die in those same hours, isn't that so, Falconer?'

Before my father could reply, the officer grabbed my father's shoulder and spun him around, pressing his face into the rough stone wall of the courtyard. One of the two lounging soldiers finally sprang into action and bound my father's wrists tightly behind him.

The officer pushed my father towards the open door. 'You know what they used to do to a falconer who carelessly lost a valuable bird, don't you? They sliced the weight of the bird out of the falconer's own chest. If that was the punishment for letting a bird escape, what do you imagine they will do to a falconer who has deliberately murdered the king's favourite birds? How much do you think a pair of gyrfalcons weighs, Falconer? I reckon there's not going to be a lot of flesh left on your chest once they've finished, in fact I don't reckon you're going to have enough meat on your chest to equal the weight of those birds. So maybe they'll just have to take the rest from your charming wife, or your pretty little daughter.'

Belém, Portugal
Ricardo

Make in – *to approach a falcon after it has made a kill.*

'Álvaro, Álvaro, wake up, you lazy dog!'

A clatter of stones hit the broken shutter of my window and pattered on to the wooden floorboards. Pio chattered angrily and retreated to the top of the cupboard. I groaned and turned over, trying to force my eyelids open, but shutting them against the cruelly bright morning sunlight.

'Álvaro! I know you're up there!'

Another hail of stones, one bouncing hard off my back, finally made me sit up. Even so, it took me a few moments to realize that the idiot throwing stones was actually addressing me. I'd become accustomed to thinking of myself as Ricardo these last few days, so that I'd almost forgotten that up to then I had been *Álvaro*, at least to those who shared the miserable squalor of this quarter of Belém.

'Álvaro!'

'I heard you! I'm coming!' I bellowed. 'And stop chucking stones, you fuckwit! You'll have my eye out.'

I struggled out of bed and crossed over to the window. The acid from last night's cheap wine rose up, burning in my throat, and I coughed violently as I bent forward to see who was disturbing me at this unholy hour. How anyone can face being up before noon is a mystery I have never fathomed. What is the point of mornings, you tell me that? The taverns aren't open, the whores haven't unlocked their doors, and cock pits are empty, so what is there to get up for?

I blinked down into the street below. It was crowded with jostling people trying to edge around one another with barrels and baskets. Women balanced trays of fruit or pitchers of water on their heads, men held live chickens fluttering under their arms, and donkeys swayed under the weight of laden panniers or huge mounds of hay. In the midst of all this bustle, a solitary man was standing resolutely under my window gazing upwards. He was being shoved forward and backwards as those on the move barged into him, cursing him roundly for blocking the path, but he was ignoring all of them.

He was a scrawny-looking fellow, with fleshy ears that stuck out between the locks of his straight hair, like the handles on a flagon. I dimly recognized him as one of the potboys from the inn. What was his name – Felix . . . Filipe . . . ?

He beckoned with a frantic flapping of his hand as if he was trying to bat at a wasp. But I had no intention of going down there until I knew what he wanted. Had the lousy innkeeper sent him to collect the money I owed? Did I owe this Filipe some money as well? I couldn't remember, but it wouldn't be the first time I laid a wager after one too many glasses and not recalled the incident. If I was honest, I'd have to confess I've been told of many things I've done when I'm drunk that I don't have the slightest recollection of, but then the world is full of liars. And, as I always say, if a man can't remember laying a bet, then he was in no condition to make one. If you are going to trick a drunken man into making a wager, you can't expect him to honour it when he's sober.

I peered cautiously out of the window again. 'What do you want?' I yelled down.

'It's your woman . . . Silvia. You have to come.'

My heart began to thump against my ribs. 'Silvia, but . . . Wait for me. I'll have to dress. I'll be as quick as I can.'

I knew it! I knew Silvia would be begging me to take her back, and it couldn't be for the money, because she didn't know I was about to acquire such a sum. She was coming back because she loved me, adored me in fact, and she'd found she couldn't live without me, any more than I could live without her. She'd lay down conditions, of course; she had her pride. She'd make me promise I'd never do it again, whatever it was she thought me guilty of, and I would swear to it on my mother's grave. But we'd both know she wouldn't have sent this lad to fetch me if she hadn't already made up her mind to return.

I gathered up the soiled clothes from the floor where I'd scattered them as I'd lurched to bed. Although I dressed as rapidly as possible, without paying any attention to the way I looked, it still seemed as if the simple task was taking hours to accomplish. My hands were trembling so much that I fumbled uselessly with every button and lace. I even managed to put my breeches on backwards and then had to fight to take them off again.

As soon as I crossed to the door, Pio leapt from the cupboard on to my shoulder, expecting to accompany me as usual, but I gently swung him on to the bed.

'No, Pio, not today. You stay here.'

Silvia did not much care for Pio. He had the habit of springing on her back without warning and pulling her hair. It particularly amused him to do so when her hands were full and she couldn't defend herself. Once, when I was nearly choking with laughter watching her struggle, I made the mistake of telling her that he only did it because she squealed, and if she ignored him, he would tire of it. I think that was the time she threw my dinner at me, and the names she called that innocent little monkey couldn't be repeated even in a dockside tavern.

So on balance it seemed diplomatic to keep Pio out of the way until after Silvia had agreed to return. But Pio wasn't used to being left behind. He made another rush at me, squeaking with anxiety, but I quickly closed the door in his face before he could slip through and heard his screams of rage behind me as I clattered down the stairs.

Filipe was squatting against a wall, waiting for me. He rose swiftly as I approached, and with another agitated flapping of his hand strode off down the narrow street, weaving in and out of the crowd with such agility that, several times, I lost sight of him altogether. At the end of the street, I turned in the direction of the inn, assuming that was where Silvia would be waiting, but I felt a hand on my sleeve, tugging me in the opposite direction.

'This way, she's down by the harbour,' Filipe said.

I obediently trotted after him. So she'd found a bed some-where along the waterfront. But just whose bed had she found? She wouldn't have spent this past week alone, I knew that. I felt the sharp spike of jealousy plunge into my bowels. Who was he? Some sweaty hulk from the docks, all muscle and no brain? One of those oily musicians who play in the inns and wink at girls, or a foreign sailor with gold in his pocket? Was that why she wanted to see me again, because her lover's ship had sailed?

I realized I was clenching my fists and I was probably mut-tering furiously to myself, because a middle-aged woman with a pannier of fish on her back squashed herself hard against the wall to avoid me, her hands raised across her face as if she thought I was going to attack her. I smiled and bowed, but she scuttled away, throwing terrified glances over her shoulder.

I tried to calm myself. There was no point in asking Silvia where she had been or who she had been with, that would only start another fight. For both our sakes, it was safer to ignore it. I must kiss her, cajole her and woo her again. That's what she wanted, to be the centre of attention, to be made to feel the most desirable woman on earth, and she was too.

Sweet Jesu, my groin was throbbing just at the thought of her. It had been a week since I'd held her, and my body ached for her more than any drunkard craves his wine. I could picture her now, naked save for that amulet in the form of the eye of God which nestled unblinking between her sweat-beaded breasts. She was straddling me, her back arched, her eyes closed and her lips parted in a cry, my hands pushing up over her slim waist, towards those soft round breasts.

I was so consumed by the image that I would have walked straight past the shack, had Filipe not grabbed my arm again.

'She's in there.'

He indicated a rough wooden hut, thrown together from old ship's timbers black with tar, and from driftwood bleached to ash-grey by the salt sea. The doorway was covered by a piece of frayed sacking and outside several nets lay drying over barrels. The stones around the hut were stained with rusty splashes of dried fish blood, and littered with empty mussel shells. It was a typical fisherman's hut, the kind of shelter he would use to mend his nets and clean his catch. The place stank of fish guts, salt weed and cat pee. It wouldn't be hard to persuade Silvia to abandon such a rat hole. However handsome her fisher-boy, her ardour would cool as rapidly as sea wind if she was forced to spend time in this hovel.

But Silvia would never admit that. She'd be in there now artfully posed, draped seductively over a bench, waiting for me. She'd try to look as if she hadn't been waiting at all, but I'd just happened to come in whilst she was resting. She'd feign complete indifference until she considered she had punished me enough with her coldness. But she knew only too well it was that very aloofness and disdain that drew me to her like a dumb fish to a juicy worm, no matter how many times it gets hooked. Even though I knew every twist and turn of the game she was playing, I was powerless to resist it. I took a deep breath and pulled aside the sacking curtain.

But what I saw was not Silvia reclining on a bench. Light shining in from the broken board in the wall revealed two men sitting on upturned barrels, fishermen judging by the stench and filth on their breeches. In one glance I took in the grappling iron lying within a hand's reach of one of them, and the sharp knife tucked in the belt of the other. Not that either of them would have needed weapons to attack a man, not with their great fists.

As rapidly as I had stepped in I backed out again, crashing straight into Filipe, who squealed as I trod heavily on his toe. But I was in no mood to apologize to him. The little rat had set me up. I'd get even with him later, but right now the only thing on my mind was to get as far away from that hut as fast as I could. I turned to run, but Filipe yelled after me, 'Wait! They need to tell you about Silvia. Come back!'

I turned. The men had made no move to follow me. I hesitated, then cautiously edged my way back towards the hut, torn between curiosity and a healthy desire to stay out of danger. I am not a man who enjoys pain and besides, I needed my face to remain intact to earn a living, not to mention all my other appendages, of which I had grown rather fond.

'What,' I asked Filipe, 'do those two cod-buggerers know about Silvia that you couldn't have told me back at my lodgings?'

The tips of Filipe's jug-ears turned scarlet and he squirmed like a schoolboy told to drop his breeches.

Comprehension dawned. 'Ah, I see it. They want money for their information, that's it, isn't it? Well, you can tell them from me I haven't got the price of my next meal, and even if I came into a fortune I wouldn't give as much as a bag of goat's droppings for information about that bitch. I don't care where she is or what trouble she's got herself into.'

Filipe cringed and darted an embarrassed glance towards the hut. It suddenly occurred to me that Silvia might be hiding somewhere near, waiting until the fishermen had been paid. I raised my voice so she could hear.

'If she wants money, tell her to sell herself on the streets, she's had enough practice. And when she's sick of doing that, she knows where to find me, but she'd better hurry because if my bed gets any colder, I'll be moving Bárbara in to warm it.'

I stole the name from the wind, for the truth was I didn't actually know any Bárbaras, apart from an elderly aunt with a hairy black moustache, and I certainly didn't intend inviting her into my bed. But I could have met someone since Silvia had left me and there was no harm in letting her believe I had.

Filipe was flapping at me like an agitated duck. 'No, no, don't say such things. Silvia is . . . I didn't know how to tell you. That's why I brought you here. I thought you should see for yourself. If it is her, I mean. I think it is . . . I'm sure it is.'

He ran back to the shack and held the sacking curtain up, pointing to something lying on the floor inside. A cold hand seemed to have thrust itself inside my chest as I realized what he was trying to say. But it couldn't be true. I would have known. I would have felt it.

Slowly, on legs that felt as heavy and dead as ship's timbers, I edged towards the door. The two fishermen hadn't moved from their barrels.

The older of the two removed the long strip of dried fish he was chewing, and waved it at the curtain. 'Drop it. Don't want everyone seeing our business.'

Filipe nudged me inside and, following hard on my heels, dropped the sacking back in place.

Between the two fishermen a long bundle was stretched out on the floorboards, wrapped in a piece of old sail cloth. I hadn't even noticed it when I'd first entered, in my shock at finding the fishermen inside.

'Caught her in the nets this morning. Knew there was a

floating corpse even before our nets snagged her, could see the gulls following something.'

The younger of the two men leaned down and peeled back a flap of the sail. I tried to stifle a cry as I reeled backwards into Filipe, the bile jumping into my throat. The body had evidently been in the sea for some time. I could only see its head and shoulders, but it appeared to be naked. The eyes were open but milk-white, the face grotesquely swollen and bloated. The skin was peeling away. Something had been nibbling at the lips and nose and they were half-eaten away, revealing sharp white teeth. Salt crusted the matted black hair, turning it grey even as I stared at it.

Gagging, I clapped my hands to my mouth, trying to stop myself vomiting. The two fishermen glanced at each other with undisguised contempt for my weak stomach. I stared up at the broken roof boards of the hut, and when I could finally trust myself to speak without retching, I shook my head.

'That's not Silvia. It looks nothing like her.'

Filipe laid a hand on my shoulder. 'I know she's swollen up in the water, but look at that amulet round her neck. It's the eye of God. Silvia always wore –'

I did not look. 'Thousands of women wear that amulet,' I snapped.

'But most wear a crucifix too, and that eye is much larger than –'

'It isn't her, I tell you. Some woman jilted by her lover probably. Hundreds of women a year drown themselves over men or unwanted brats or just from plain melancholy. Women are like that; they always have to make the dramatic gesture.'

''Cept this one didn't drown herself,' the old fisherman said quietly. 'Not unless a corpse can rise and walk down to the sea. I reckon she was dead long before she ended up in the water. Look at those black marks about her neck. Plain as anything she's been strangled, she has, had the life throttled out of her, then her body dumped in the sea.'

I couldn't bring myself to look again at the body. I knew I'd be sick if I did. All three men were watching me intently. I could read the question written in their faces. But surely they couldn't think that I would . . .

'Don't look at me like that. I didn't hurt Silvia. I swear I never laid a finger on her. She's alive. She's found some other fool to take her in, but she'll be back as soon as she becomes bored with him, you'll see.'

Filipe shook his head sadly as if I was some dim-witted child. 'Look at her, Álvaro, really look at her. It is Silvia. I'm . . . I'm not saying that you –'

'No, no,' I screamed at them. 'That creature is not my Silvia. Don't you think I'd recognize my own lover? It's not her, I tell you. It's some old witch, a monster. You don't know Silvia like I do, a woman like that with so much life in her, so much passion, can't just die. I'd know if she was dead. I'd know it!'

I turned and tried to push through the sacking, and only succeeded in tangling myself in it. In the end I ripped it from the doorway and strode out.

As soon as I got outside I did vomit. Two women walking along the waterfront crossed themselves and rapidly retreated back the way they'd come, as though they feared to pass me in case I had the plague. I was shaking violently, but I forced myself upright and staggered back towards my lodgings, trying to obliterate that grotesque face from my head, but the image was seared on to my eyeballs.

It couldn't be her. Why on earth would they even imagine it was? There were hundreds of dark-haired women in Belém, and who was to say she even came from this town? Why, she could have been thrown into the sea miles up the coast and drifted here, or even fallen from a ship. It wasn't her. My Silvia was not dead.

It suddenly occurred to me that I hadn't asked the fishermen what they were going to do with the body. Would they quietly dump it back in the water? They often did with corpses, safest way. No one wanted the trouble of reporting it, never mind losing a day's work answering all those questions. And no man wanted his family threatened or worse if the murderer got to hear that he had reported a body. But if too many people already knew about the corpse, the fishermen would have no choice but to hand it over to the authorities.

Would Filipe swear on oath it was Silvia? If he did, I'd be the first person they would come looking for, and unless I could produce Silvia alive, there was no way I could prove my innocence. I had to leave my lodgings and leave now, today, before they came looking for me. It occurred to me then that Filipe had shown me the body to give me the opportunity to flee. If he was hoping for a reward for reporting the crime, then it would doubtless salve his conscience to give the man he was condemning to death a fighting chance to escape.

And I did have a chance, a damn good one. Dona Lúcia had promised to give me the money tomorrow. All I had to do was stay free for a night and a morning, then I could leave this town for good with a small fortune, enough to take me so far away from Belém they'd never find me.

I ran back to my lodgings and threw some clothes into a leather bag. Not all of them, of course. If Filipe did lead the authorities here, it must look as if I might return at any moment, and with luck they'd stay here to lie in wait for me.

Pio leapt for my shoulder, and I kissed him and stroked his tiny head, but I knew I couldn't take him with me. You can't sit in the dark corner of an inn or pass down a street with a monkey on your shoulder, without some child remembering.

I opened the shutter and placed him next to the window.

'Go on, Pio, take yourself off.'

But he only turned his sad brown eyes on me and sat there squeaking plaintively. He was still sitting there, watching me, as I closed the door.

With the closing of the door, Álvaro vanished. Tomorrow Ricardo would charm the money from Dona Lúcia and then a third man, a stranger, would leave Belém for good. What he'd be called I didn't yet know, but I had all night to work on that. As for Silvia, my poor little Silvia . . . no, no I couldn't think about that now. I must keep my wits about me. All I had to do was stick to my plan; it was simple enough.

But the trouble with even the best-thought-out plans is that other people make them too.

Iceland

Eydis

Tiercel — *the male hawk, from the Latin 'tertius' meaning 'a third', for the male is a third smaller than the female.*

I sensed the two men coming. Now I hear them scrambling down the rocks. There is another with them, someone both living and dead. I sense life and yet the life is not in this world.

I pull the veils over my sister's face and my own. When people come to consult us we always keep ourselves veiled. They prefer it that way, not seeing our faces, as if they know their secrets will also be kept concealed. They are frightened of our naked gaze. We might see too far inside them. We might curse them with our stares. Our veils are their shields against us.

There is only one woman who has never feared us, Heidrun, an old, old friend. She told us she had watched over us whilst we were still in our mother's womb, though my mother had never spoken of it to us. The first time I recall seeing Heidrun was the night that Valdis and I became seven years old. We'd been sleeping in the bed we shared and had woken in the dark to find Heidrun sitting in the room.

We had not been afraid. It seemed to us that we already knew her and had been expecting her to come. She had put her finger to her lips and held her hands out to us, pulling us from our bed and leading us out of the cottage right past where our parents lay sleeping. It never occurred to us to protest or ask her where we were going. We followed her as trustingly as if she were our own mother.

The year was drawing towards the end of summer, and though it must have been the middle of the night the sun hovered only just below the horizon, washing the sky behind the mountains with a shimmering pearly glow. It was neither dark nor light, but that strange owl light where rocks and people have no shadow and no substance, just an outline so thin and grey you think they might dissolve like smoke.

Heidrun strode over the short, springy turf and we scurried along behind her. I don't know how long we walked, but we were neither cold nor tired, though we were climbing all the time. She led us between two towering rocks, black and sharp, that looked to us like crouching men, and we finally emerged in a valley which we had never entered before.

A turf-covered longhouse rose out of the valley floor. It would have been invisible had it not been for the lights blazing out from the open doorway. Heidrun reached the doorway and stood aside, smiling and motioning us to enter. Clinging tightly to each other, we edged inside. The longhouse was full of people, young and old, adults and children. A great fire blazed in the centre, musicians were playing, and the table was spread for a feast.

All eyes turned to us, and there was welcome written on every face. It seemed that they were all there to celebrate our birthday. A priest with a grave face but gentle voice gave his solemn blessing over the food and over us, for we had in that very hour become seven years old. Then we were whisked up to sit in a great chair that held the two of us side by side, and food was pressed into our hands – cakes sweetened with honey, fish so fresh and tender they must have been pulled from the lake no more than an hour before, and pungent pieces of shark that had been long buried in the earth till the flavour was as rich and strong as molten lava.

As we all ate, the musicians sang and soon the dancing

began. People joined hands and danced in a circle around our chair of honour, their heels thumping on the earth floor. The wooden pillars of the hall vibrated to the pulse of that drum, which was covered with white bear skin and beaten with a long yellow bone. The rhythm of the dancers and drum was intoxicating, hot and heavy. The eyes of the dancers glazed over and their heads flopped forward or back, and still the drummer beat on and on, like the hammering of a mighty dragon's heart.

The black ravens of the Lutherans had forbidden the circle dance, but it was still danced in those hidden valleys, even sometimes on the mountain tops to welcome the sun as our ancestors had done since the days when old gods ruled. Valdis and I had never seen the dance before, only heard it whispered about among the hired men and women who came to work on the farmstead. Our parents never talked of such dangerous things for they lived in constant fear of the Lutheran ravens.

The pulse of that drum must have soothed us, for stuffed with food and drunk with the music, we fell asleep in that great carved chair. Heidrun and others carried us back to our home, and slid us back into our bed as quietly as we had been taken from it. Our parents never knew we had gone. They would never have permitted us to go to such a place. But when we woke on that morning of our seventh birthday, our mother saw what she had long dreaded to see in our eyes, and that was the day she brought us to this cave.

The men are anxious, afraid. I wait for them, crouching in the shadows against the wall of the cave. It will be the first time anyone has come to our cave since Valdis died. The stench of her rotting corpse grows a little stronger each day. In the heat of the cave it can hardly do otherwise. They say if you live with a smell night and day you cease to notice it. It is true that for a brief time it floats away from you, circling like an anxiety that you try not to dwell upon, but like your fear, it is always there, ready to force itself upon you again when you least expect it. But there are stronger stenches in the cave, so everyone tells me, the smell of bad eggs from the hot-water pool and a lifetime of our excrement accumulating in a dark corner. Maybe those smells will be strong enough to mask the odour of decay.

I do not want them to know she is dead, not yet. They will feel orphaned. Only one voice to guide them, can that ever be as certain as two? They trust two voices; the unity comforts them, assures them that our predictions will come to pass. And they will ask themselves what the death of one of the oracle sisters portends. They will believe it is a bad omen for them and for the land. And that much is true.

I need time to grieve before I can strengthen myself to help them deal with her passing. Her death means so much more to me than just an omen, a sign from the spirits. For that is all we are to them, that is all we have ever been since we were brought here – a sign, an oracle, a twin voice that speaks the same word.

The first of the men, a young, agile lad, lowers himself down through the slit and seems almost to be bounding down the rocks until he is nearly at the base. Still I cannot see him for the passage that leads to the entrance is hidden from the cave by a rocky outcrop. I hear him call up and a rope slithers and thumps down towards him. They are lowering a bundle down into the cave, but it is not dried meat or wood. I know the sounds of those. A second, heavier man climbs down with careful deliberation, as a man moves when his joints are stiffening with age.

The two of them come into view around the rock. Between them they carry a bier, fashioned from birch poles, covered with sheep skins hastily lashed together with leather thongs. The man who lies on it does not stir, not even when they lay the bier down in front of me.

The older of the two men I know. Fannar, he is called. He has a small farmstead in the next valley. He has visited me a few times over the years, wanting remedies for barren ewes, a sick child, even a feud with his wife's brother. The younger man I have not seen before. Most likely he is one of the hired hands who travel the country offering to work for any farmer or fisherman that will take them on for a few weeks or months. The clothes of both men are beaded with tiny drops of water. It must be raining up there in the world. It has been so long since I have felt the cool patter of raindrops on my face. I miss it.

Fannar briefly nods to me by way of a greeting. He nods also to Valdis.

'She is sleeping,' I explain.

The boy jerks back when he first catches sight of me, then he recovers himself. Fannar must have warned him about my appearance, but still I know it comes as a shock even when they have been warned. I am not offended. I have seen that expression on the faces of others ever since I was in my cradle. The boy will get used to it in time. Now he is politely looking away as if he does not want to be caught staring. Which is worse, I wonder, when they stare or when they refuse to look? But either way, I know they mean no disrespect.

Fannar jerks his chin towards the bier. 'He's hurt bad. Can you help him, Eydis?'

I shuffle closer. The long chain fastened to my waist rasps and clangs over the rock as I drag it behind me. The man's face is swollen with bruises. His eyes are blackened and puffy, his nose clearly broken and perhaps his jaw too for it hangs open at an odd angle. His hair is matted with dark fluid. Blood has pooled in the creases either side of his nose and dried on the black stubble of his skin. Beneath it, his complexion is as blanched as a man's trapped in ice.

'Who is he?' I ask.

Fannar grimaces. 'A foreigner, we reckon. He's the look of one of those men come up from Spain or Portugal to fish for cod in these waters. Though he's a good way inland for a fisherman. What cause would he have to come here? Cod don't graze on the mountains. Most of the foreigners venture no further than the villages along the coast or the Westmann Islands, especially now that the black devils are swarming everywhere.'

He spits on to the floor of the cave as if the very mention of the Protestant clergy brings a foul taste to his mouth.

Fannar continues. 'Anyhow, the boy here says some Lutheran lads ran into him along the track, gave him a right hammering. I reckon they were Danes, bound to be. Arrogant young goats. Come here and think they can lord it over us whose families have farmed these lands since Thor and Odin ruled the heavens.'

Fannar, like most crofters, has always resented Danish rule of Iceland, but out here in the interior it never really affected their lives until the Danish king forced Lutheranism upon them. It is the Danes who have driven out or slaughtered the Catholic priests, monks and nuns; closing the abbeys; destroying the altars, books and holy objects, and forbidding the Catholic Mass or any rites of the old Church. That was when the resentment of Danish rule really began to boil in their veins. Now any Dane who is foolish enough to travel alone on dark nights in these parts will be fortunate indeed to see the dawn.

I turn to the lad, who is staring with fascination at the water bubbling up in the hot pool. He is short but stocky, built like an Icelandic horse for stamina and distance. He still has the soft, fair cheeks of a girl, but a beard of sorts is trying to colonize his chin and looks set to be the same red-gold hue as his thick, shaggy tangle of hair.

'You saw him attacked, boy? Why did they beat him?'

He glances back at me, his chin raised so as not to look

at the bloody pulp of a man which lies on the ground between us.

'They were walking towards him on the road. They started joking about him even before they came close, how he looked like a foreigner, with his dark skin and all. Then they saw the crucifix about his neck. They circled him and told him to take the crucifix off, throw it into the dirt and piss on it, but he wouldn't. They tried to take it from him, but he fought back. He was strong, far stronger than any man I've seen. He fought like Thor himself. But there were seven or eight of them and they all had long, stout staves. He was unarmed. They told him they were going to teach him a lesson in the true faith. They were battering him from all sides. I saw what they did, but I . . . I was afraid to try and stop them.' He flushes and bows his head, shamed by his cowardice.

Fannar slaps the lad's shoulder. 'Don't blame yourself, son. If you'd tried to interfere, you'd be lying there bleeding alongside him. They'd have killed the pair of you. You did the best thing you could, lad, in running to fetch me. Eydis and Valdis'll take good care of him.'

'I wish we could. But he needs help beyond our skill, Fannar. It's a physician, a bone setter, he wants.'

'Can't risk fetching a physician,' Fannar says. 'They left him for dead. If they know he still lives, he'll be arrested for practising the old faith, and any that try to help him will be made to suffer too. Try what you can, Eydis. I don't know if any power on earth can raise him to his senses again, but you're the only hope the poor soul's got. I'll pray to the Holy Virgin for him. And I'll pray too that those Danish bastards rot in hell for what they've done,' he adds with a scowl.

I send them both away with instructions to bring me the herbs I will need and some dried mutton so that I can make him a broth if he wakes, for I judge that it will be a while before he can chew, if he ever can again.

Now that the men are gone I move close to him, preparing

to strip him so that I can examine him properly. I reach out a hand towards him, and hear a clicking and rasping of wings. A mass of black beetles emerges from the dark recess of the cave and takes flight above me. Although many beetles live in the crevices of the rocks, I have never seen them flying together before. They circle over the body, round and round, faster and faster, like a whirlpool of black water. I try to flap them away, but they will not be deterred. They keep spinning round the man, as if they are trying to bind him in ropes of smoke.

I become aware of another sound, like the frightened scream of some tiny dying creature. One of the beetles alights on my shoulder. I try to shake it off, but the scream rises higher and higher, until my eyes water from the pain of it.

'Let him die, Eydis. Do not touch him. Let him die. He must die.'

The voice is so faint, so high-pitched, that I can scarcely make out the words. But I recognize that voice. I would have sworn it was my own, yet it is so far off I know it is not coming from my head.

I turn to try to catch the beetle in my hand, but the man suddenly screams as if he is being torn in two. His body convulses in agony. Beneath his closed eyelids, I can see his eyes flicking back and forth as if he is trapped in a terrible nightmare. I have to help him. I cannot simply leave a man to die. I might not be able to save him, but at least I can make his last hours comfortable.

I cross to the underground pool, pulling my chain behind me, and scoop out a bowl of hot water. Then, returning to the injured man, I moisten a rag intending to wipe his bloody lips. The black beetles stop circling. They fly up and swarm about my face, their sharp wings scratching and beating against my skin. I raise one arm to fend them off, while with the other I lay the wet rag to his face.

The instant I touch him with my fingers, the beetles scatter, scuttling back beneath their rocks, vanishing as if they are fleeing from a predator. I stretch out my hand again to wipe the bloodied face when, out of the corner of my eye, I see something moving. A huge shadow is oozing over the wall behind the body of the man, spreading like a dark stain until the whole side of the cave is engulfed by it. I cannot move. The shadow bursts from the rock and roars across the cave, snuffing out the burning torches as if the flames have been doused with water. The cave is plunged into darkness and silence.

A tiny shrill voice echoes around me. 'Sister, my sister, what have you done? You have betrayed me, Eydis. You have damned me!'

Chapter Four

When the French King Philip II was laying siege to Acre, his prize gyrfalcon broke its leash and flew up to perch on the city walls. He sent an envoy requesting the bird's return, which, not surprisingly, was refused. The bird was delivered to the Saracen leader, Saladin, who was camped with his army outside the city.

Philip was so anxious for the bird's return that he dispatched a procession to Saladin accompanied by trumpeters, heralds and envoys offering 1,000 gold crowns for the safe return of the gyrfalcon. Saladin, however, regarded the capture of this white bird as a most auspicious omen for his troops and flatly refused to return it even for that sum.

Sintra, Portugal
Isabela

Falcon – *the female of any species of hawk, as opposed to the tiercel or male. It is also used to refer to the category of long-winged hawks in general.*

The knock came again at dawn, four days after my father's arrest, but this time it was for me. They'd only sent one soldier, for I was only a girl, what resistance could I offer? They hadn't reckoned on my mother, who clung to me with the tenacity of an octopus. As soon as he had prised one hand off me, she clamped on somewhere else. In the end the soldier had to hold her off with the point of his sword.

'Don't be so eager to join your daughter, Senhora. Your turn will come all too soon and I promise you, then you will wish it hadn't.'

He did not bind my wrists but instead gripped my upper arm and led me up the hill through the narrow twisting streets towards the king's summer palace.

I was trying desperately to fight down my fear, though every muscle in my body was aching to tear myself from his grip and flee. The only way I could keep from crying in terror was to force myself to think about the place I was in now and not what was awaiting me. I told myself to remember the town as it looked on that morning, for I might never see it again.

The ridge of Sintra was swaddled in a soft white mist that intensified the silence of the early morning. The rocky plain below was hidden by the fog, so that it felt as if Sintra had drifted off high in the sky among the clouds, like a child's kite that has broken its string. The air was soft and moist, laden with the scent of resin from the pine groves and the perfume of the camellias whose pink blossoms lay so thick upon the path that it felt as if a carpet lay beneath your feet. From the walls of the houses and gardens, lush dark green ferns and soft fat cushions of moss dripped with moisture. How could I leave this? How was it possible that pain and death should be hiding amongst such intensity of life?

We were already at the palace. I tried to turn and take one last look behind me, but I stumbled and would have fallen on the steps had the soldier not hauled me painfully up by my arm. We passed under the arch of the arcade, as dark as the mouth of some great cave, where water dripped into a great basin, echoing like the tolling of a single bell. Then out into the courtyard behind. The red tiled roofs of the cluster of buildings were all but hidden by the mist, but I'd seen them often enough to know they were there, as were the two great white conical chimneys that carried the smoke and steam from the roaring kitchen fires high into the air, so that it should not blow into the windows of the royal chambers. The clatter of plates and irons in the kitchens and stables mingled with the soft tinkling of the many fountains that studded the patios in front of the chambers, but these sounds drifted towards me like ghosts without substance.

Servants loomed out of the mist, vanishing again as they hurried off about their tasks. A few glanced at me, but those that did quickly averted their eyes. I thought I saw one of the boys from the mews, but as soon as he saw me he fled around the corner of a building as if he thought I had the evil eye. The soldier suddenly pulled me into the shelter of a building and held me there as two of his comrades marched past, as if he didn't want to be seen by them. Then he dragged me forward again.

In the far corner of the palace grounds stood a square white tower. The soldier ducked under the low doorway and led the way up a narrow, winding staircase, until we reached a thick, stout door. He pushed me through it and slammed the door behind me.

I stood too terrified to move, trying to make sense of what little I could see in the dim interior. There were no windows, save for some thin slits in the wall far too high for anyone to reach and too narrow for anything but a songbird to escape that way. The thin blades of light scarcely did more than illuminate the beams high above me.

Ever since my father's arrest I had been conjuring in my mind the horrors that might lie behind a door like this, but as my eyes grew accustomed to the darkness I saw with relief that the room contained nothing but a long wooden table with two high-backed chairs placed at either end. It seemed too commonplace to be real. Yet, as I stood there, I felt the coldness of the stone walls eating into my flesh and I began to understand that it is not always necessary to inflict pain to induce fear.

The door opened again and the soldier leaned in. 'I've relieved the guard, but he won't be gone for long, so you must hurry.'

The bewilderment I felt must have been written on my face, for he stepped further into the room. 'Your father asked me to bring you here. He wants to see you. They'll be taking him to Lisbon any day now; he may not get another chance. Come on, hurry.'

'I thought you'd been sent to arrest me.'

He grinned. 'Your father didn't want your mother to know he sent for you. It's you he wants to see, not her. Only way I could think of to get you here without her following. Worked, didn't it? Bet you thought you were going to find yourself in chains.' He chuckled gleefully as if he'd just pulled off some great practical joke.

I tried to smile, since he obviously expected me to admire his ingenuity, but my face was frozen. My legs were still trembling as I followed him back down the stairs. When we reached the level of the courtyard, the soldier unlocked another door with a great iron key and, darting anxious glances out through the archway, he motioned me inside.

'Watch your step when you get to the bottom, those stones are slippery. Always wet down there.'

Behind the door the steps continued down beneath the tower, until I found myself standing in a long passage lit by burning torches in brackets on the rough stone walls. The walls were black with mould, and an overpowering stench of excrement, urine and rotting straw burned my nostrils. The soldier led me past several low doorways in which were set iron grilles. I couldn't help stealing a quick glance through one of them, but the interior was too dark to see what lay inside, though something or someone did, for I could hear the straw rustling and a kind of whimpering moan – whether it was animal or human was impossible to tell.

At the furthest end of the passage the soldier stopped and, selecting another key from the great ring of them in his hand, wiggled it into the lock. The lock was evidently rusty for he needed both hands to turn it. He jerked his head, motioning me in, before he pulled the door shut again and turned the key once more. I could barely stand upright in the tiny cell, which was no longer or broader than it was high. The only light seeping through the small iron grille came from the burning torches a way up the passage, and at first I could see little except the dim smudge of the walls.

'Isabela, my dear child! He brought you. I was afraid he would not.'

The voice came from the floor, but it was in darkness. I crouched down to avoid blocking the light from the door, and as my eyes adjusted I saw my father sitting on a heap of straw with his back to the rough stone wall.

I held out my arms, expecting him to rise and hug me, but as he moved his arms I heard the clanking of heavy chains and realized he could no more embrace me than he could stand, for his wrists were fettered to an iron ring about his neck, which was bolted to the wall.

I put my arms about him as best I could and kissed him. His face was wet, but whether from my tears or his, I didn't know.

'Have they hurt you, Father?'

'No, no, Isabela, the king has been merciful and for now I am under his protection, but I don't know for how long.'

'I should have brought you some food and clothes. But I didn't know that I would see you. I thought . . .' I trailed off. To say that my only thought had been fear of what was going to happen to me made me feel suddenly ashamed.

'They would have taken them from you in any case,' he said with such a weary resignation in his voice that it sounded as if he had aged twenty years. 'Listen, Isabela, I gave the guard my ring to bring you here, but I don't know how much time that will buy us and there is much I have to tell you. Much I should have told you before, but I hoped you would never need to know. Look outside in the passage, is the guard there?'

I peered through the grate, but the passageway seemed deserted.

'Come close then, in case others in the cells are listening.'

I crept nearer and sat beside him on the filthy straw, my head pressed to his.

He lowered his voice to a whisper. 'In case we are interrupted, I must first tell you this. You must take your mother and leave Sintra tonight. She will not want to go, but you must force her. I've hidden a little money and some small items of value under a loose flag beneath the linen cupboard. I've been saving a little when I could, in case it should ever come to this. It is not a fortune, but it will help. Don't let her try to pack her possessions, just set out with whatever you can carry in a pack. Tell the neighbours you are going to spend a few days in Lisbon, but don't go there. Make for Porto to the north. So many go there to trade, the arrival of two strangers will pass unnoticed. Many artisans work there. It will be easier to find respectable work. The money won't last for long, Isabela, and I fear that you may have to seek work to support yourself and your mother. She can't . . .'

We both knew that though my mother laboured harder than any field hand in her own home, the shame and humiliation of having to take orders from a master or mistress would kill her.

'I am so sorry that I have failed you, Isabela. I thought always to provide for you and your mother.' I could hear the shame in his voice. 'But promise me you will leave Sintra today.'

'We can't just abandon you here, Father,' I protested.

'My child, don't you think my pain would be a thousand times worse if I knew you and your mother were suffering in prison as well? I can bear whatever they do to me, but it would kill me if I knew they were hurting you or your mother and I was powerless to stop them. If you want to help me, leave tonight so that at least I don't have to fear your arrest too.'

'But why should they arrest us? Father, listen to me, you mustn't lose hope.' I gripped his shirt. It was as wet as the walls of his cell. 'They will find you innocent, I know they will. How could they not? Sebastian knows you'd no more kill the falcons than you would harm your own family.'

My father closed his cold fingers gently over mine. 'This is about something far more serious than the birds, Isabela. The gyrfalcons were killed deliberately, so that I would be blamed. I am sure of that.'

'But I don't understand, Father. Who would hate you enough to do that?'

I couldn't imagine that my mild, unassuming father had ever made an enemy in his life, and certainly not one who would plot to see him dead.

'The Inquisition,' my father said bluntly.

'But –'

'Please, child, just listen. There isn't much time. There is something I should have told you long ago, but your mother would not allow us even to speak of it, and I was too much of a coward to challenge her. It seemed easier just to keep the peace. Isabela . . . I know your mother has always told you that we are Old Christians. I think she has really come to believe it herself, but it is not the truth.'

'I don't understand.' He had told me not to interrupt, but I couldn't help it.

He bowed his head as if he was ashamed. 'I convinced myself that it would be safer if you didn't know. You were always such an inquisitive child. Even if your mother had refused to tell you anything, you might have asked questions of old Jorge or me, and knowledge of the old ways is dangerous. But the truth is our grandparents, mine and your mother's, were once Jews. Our parents were born Jews, though they were so young when they were converted they remember little of it. But it is easy for the Inquisition to find out these things, when it is determined to uncover the truth.'

I couldn't take in what I was hearing. Ever since I could remember, my mother had told me that we were Old Christians. She was so proud of it. And my own father had sat in the room when she had boasted of it, never once contradicting her. It made no sense. I'd seen the rosary which had belonged to my great-great-aunt, the abbess. I had held it, just as I had held the emblem of St Catherine that my father's forebear had worn in the Crusades. How could they own such things if they were Jews? All my life, my mother had taught me that the Jews were the enemies of the Holy Church, and

Marranos were worse for they were demons hiding among the good Christians. But now, if my mother and father were . . . if *we* were . . . But my father was still talking in a low urgent whisper.

'Isabela, you saw at the *auto-da-fé* how the young king refused to light the bonfire? That very morning, those courtiers who stood with him had been whispering about how the king was showing sympathy for heretics. It's no secret at Court that the Regent, Cardinal Henry, is determined to cleanse Portugal of heretics. But Henry's influence over Sebastian will last only until the boy is old enough to take the reins himself. Kings have tried to limit the power of the Inquisition before, but Henry is determined that, once he is no longer Regent, the Inquisition's power should rival, if not surpass, that of the sovereign. He was Grand Inquisitor before he was Regent and may well take up that post again once the young king is of age. He wants to ensure that nothing stands in his way then, certainly not a king who is sympathetic to the Marranos.'

None of this made sense to me. I was still struggling to grasp the idea that I was not who I had always been told I was. My parents were not who I had always believed them to be. It felt as if I had awakened to find that the familiar solid floor of my house had suddenly turned to a bottomless lake. Words had suddenly reversed their meaning. *They* were Marranos, *them* our enemies, now suddenly Marranos meant *us, me*. Then who were the enemies now?

I wanted to scream at my father, demand to know why he had lied to me all these years, yet even as the rage boiled up in me, he shifted himself in the filthy straw, trying to ease his cramped limbs. I heard the clank of heavy chains and the gasp of pain as the sharp iron collar bit into his neck, and I understood with sickening clarity why he had kept the truth from me.

I touched his hand. It was as cold as a gravestone in winter. I tried to speak softly.

'But, Father, I don't understand what the Regent has to do with the gyrfalcons. I thought they'd arrested you because of the birds, not because . . .'

I was still too shocked to say the word, as if uttering it aloud would make it true.

'Cardinal Henry knows how much young Sebastian loved those birds, and anyone in the king's service will have told him how many hours the boy has spent with me, how close we have become. Henry was bound to want to find out all he could about a man who could potentially have so much influence over the child. In my heart I knew the danger, but I refused to admit it to myself. I should have discouraged Sebastian from coming so often to the mews, but I didn't have the heart to turn the boy away. The poor little lad was so lonely and the falcons were his only refuge from his uncle and those Jesuit tutors who never give him a single kind word. And the truth was, I loved the boy's company. He was the son I never . . .'

He trailed off, and squeezed my hand apologetically.

'I don't know if Henry gave the orders himself or if it was the Jesuits, but I'm sure one of them came up with the plan to kill the gyrfalcons and to make it appear that I had done it. They wanted to poison the young king's mind by letting him think a Marrano had betrayed him and murdered the creatures he held most dear. Nothing could possibly hurt the boy more or make him feel more betrayed than if he believed the man he trusted the most had slaughtered his falcons knowing how much the birds meant to him. It would be easy then to persuade the boy that all Marranos were treacherous and wicked. He would not falter again when it came to lighting the next bonfire, he would be begging to do it.'

'But, Father, Sebastian worships you and he knows how

much you loved those birds. He's watched you tend them a thousand times. He could never believe that you would harm them. Can't you ask to see him, explain?'

'I have seen him,' my father said, with such despair in his voice that I found my eyes stinging with tears. 'But the young king was not alone. I could see Sebastian didn't want to believe the tale. But I had never confessed to him I was a New Christian, why should I? It was never something he asked or even thought to imagine. But clearly others had already persuaded him that I had deliberately concealed the truth from him and so there was already a seed of doubt in his mind. If I had hidden that much from him, what other lies had I told him?

'And even if he believed me, he is just a child. How can he stand up to adults around him? How can he argue with them, especially his uncle and his tutors? He's terrified of them. Little Sebastian did the best he could. He tried to say he didn't believe I was guilty, and when one of his advisors told him he must sign the papers for my execution, he stoutly refused . . . that is, at first.'

'No, Father, no!' I clapped my hands over my mouth and moaned.

With a great effort he lifted his hand and pressed my cheek. The heavy chain clanked.

'Please don't cry, child . . . I need you to be strong . . . you must or you will not survive this. My time is not come yet. When Sebastian refused to sign, one of the Jesuits proposed a test. He said that if I was innocent and a good Catholic, God would prove it to be so by bringing the birds back to life. Sebastian is a bright lad. He said that the birds had already been buried for more than three days, and not even Jesus had been that long buried. The Jesuits were furious. One of them looked as if he would strike the boy, king or not.

'But Dona Ofelia's husband quickly stepped in to smooth

things over. He suggested that Sebastian simply demand that I should replace the dead ones by producing a new pair of gyrfalcons. He said it as a joke and everyone laughed, for they knew that to be impossible. Where would a falconer find that kind of money, never mind be able to lay his hands on a pair of white falcons? But the young king didn't laugh. He seemed to grasp at the idea as if it was a way out of his problem. He waved his hand for silence and then formally announced that I had a year and a day to produce a new pair of white falcons. If I did, he would pardon me.'

At my father's words, my heart felt as if it would explode with relief.

'Blessed Virgin, thank you!' I breathed. 'You see, all is well, Father. We'll find the money. You said you had hidden a little, and I have some necklaces I can sell. And Mother has rings and clasps. There will be other things. At least he has given us plenty of time to raise the sum we need, but I promise we will do it as soon as we can, so that we can get you out of here. We can borrow –'

'No, Isabela. That's not why I sent for you. You must take the money, every valuable thing you have, and leave tonight. The king has bought me . . . us a little time, and I am grateful for that. But the Jesuits would never let a mere child get the better of them, even if he is the king. It's not in their power to make a king change a proclamation, but they did force him to add another condition. If I fail to produce the new birds, they will have me executed, but not just me alone . . . you and your mother will die too, and the execution they have planned is not . . . *merciful.* And I believe it will not end there. They will try to track down other members of our family too. My sister and her children . . . no member of our family will be safe. All of us will pay a terrible price for this crime. So you see, you and your mother must get away tonight. I'm sure that they are planning to arrest you both in the next day or two and hold you until the time has elapsed, in case you escape them. You must not be found. You must get word to your aunt also, but only once you are safe.'

I felt as if my blood had turned to ice. It was well that I was already sitting on the ground, for I was sure my legs would have collapsed under me. The vision filled my head of those prisoners tied to the stake, the flames leaping up around them in the darkness, the mob screaming for their blood. But this time when I saw that scene it was me staring out at them through the heat and smoke, straining in vain against my chains as flames crept towards me.

I forced myself to speak, but my voice was shaking, though I tried to sound confident. 'But it won't happen, because we won't fail, Father. We will get the money somehow.'

'It's no use hoping for miracles, child. Even if you could raise the fortune it would cost to buy the birds, where would you buy them? The gyrfalcon is a royal bird. The king possessed the only pair in Portugal. If it was a lanner falcon or an eagle, you could easily buy another. There are many traders bringing them in every year. But the gyrfalcon comes only from the frozen lands of the North. And the kind of gyrfalcons which are the largest and whitest, like the ones Sebastian owned, are only found in Iceland. That land is ruled by the Lutherans. They'll never permit their royal birds to go to a Catholic king, particularly not in a country where the Inquisition holds sway, for the Inquisition murders the Protestants as fervently as they do the Marranos. No child, you must promise me that you will –'

My father stiffened as we heard footsteps hurrying down the passage towards us. The key grated in the lock and the door creaked open.

The flickering orange torchlight from the passage was obscured by the massive bulk of the soldier who had brought me.

'Hurry, the guard's finished his breakfast. I saw him from

the window. He's gone to the latrines for a shit, but he'll be back any minute.'

He grabbed my wrist and yanked me to my feet, tugging me back out through the door. I didn't even have time to say goodbye to my father, never mind hug and kiss him.

As the soldier pulled me along the slippery passage towards the stairs, I heard only a single word follow me. *Promise!*

I did not go home. I couldn't. I didn't even want to look at my mother, much less be forced to talk to her. The cold, damp stench of the dungeon still clung to me and I couldn't bear the thought of being inside any building, even my own house. I needed to be outside in the fierce, hot sunshine, breathing in pure, sweet air. I climbed high into the pine forest, wading through the ice-cold streams and scrambling past the great moss-covered boulders. The thick, sinuous roots of the trees had grown around and over the great stones. And even where the trees had fallen in a storm, or stood dead and blackened, the roots would not relinquish their stranglehold on the boulders, as if they had become rock themselves.

I was so intent on getting as far as I could from that stinking dungeon that I didn't even pause if my skirts became entangled on branches. I simply strode on, letting them tear as I pulled them after me. The sound of ripping fabric was almost a relief, I needed to rip and break, to hurt and smash.

I was so frightened for my father and so bewildered by what he'd told me. Last night I prayed to the Blessed Virgin for him, certain of who he was and who I was, and in a single hour all that had been swept away. I was one of the despised, a Marrano, a Jew, and yet I could no more enter their world than I could return to the world of my childhood, for that door had been slammed shut and sealed for ever.

But I knew I had to return home eventually. Where else could I go? The sun was already low in the sky when I entered the kitchen. My mother was sitting at the table, her head resting in her hands. I had never come into the house before without seeing her bustling about, engaged in her ceaseless war against dust and dirt. Now her neat hair was dishevelled and her eyes red with weeping. She raised her head and stared at me as if I was a corpse risen from a grave. Then, with a little cry, she threw herself at me, hugging me so tightly I thought my ribs would crack.

'What happened? What did they ask you? Did they hurt you?'

I felt the wetness of her tears on my cheek and heard her breath coming in heaving sobs. And for a moment I felt a twinge of guilt, as I realized that all this time she had thought that I'd been arrested and was chained up in some prison somewhere or worse.

'Have they released your father too? Is he with you?' she asked eagerly, peering over my shoulder as if she thought he was going to walk through the door behind me.

I felt a coldness come over me, a sudden hatred of this woman. My mouth was so dry I couldn't answer her. I pushed her away and crossed to the big clay water jar in the corner, dipped in a beaker and drank it in a single draught, refilling it several times before my thirst was slaked. I sank down on the bench where only a few days before my father had retreated to eat his breakfast of sardines, while she had told us why poor old Jorge deserved to die. I couldn't bring myself to look at her.

I told her all that my father had said, with a brutal harshness, sparing her nothing, not even the fact that my father had paid for *me* and not her to be brought to him. I knew I was hurting her, but for the first time in my life I didn't care. I refused to play the game of pacifying her any more.

She stood pale-faced, her hand gripping the crucifix around her neck so tightly I could see the whiteness of her knuckles. I wanted to tear it away from her throat, just as

I was ripping away the whole necklace of lies she had so proudly worn throughout her life.

'All those foul things you said about poor Jorge and the other heretics, yet all the time you were saying them, you knew that we were exactly the same as them.'

'We are not,' my mother spat. 'We're not like them. They're filthy Jews and always will be. There are no Jews in my family, nor in your father's. We've always been Catholics. Always! Your father doesn't know what he's saying. Goodness knows what they've done to him in that place. It's enough to turn anyone's wits. They're making him confess, but it's not true. It's all lies. We are Catholics, do you hear? Good, decent Catholics.'

A horrifying thought struck me. 'Were you the one who reported Jorge?'

She flushed a dull scarlet and I knew it was true.

'Why?' I screamed at her. 'Why would you do that? Don't you see that it was as unjust as what they've done to my father?'

'I am a good Catholic. I did it to prove I am a good Catholic. Your father wouldn't do it, so I had to. Father Tomàs had been asking questions, asking if we knew Jorge, how long we had known him, how often we went to see him. I knew that meant they suspected him. Someone had to protect our family. You have to prove you are loyal. You see what happens if you don't. You see what they've done to your father, because he refused to denounce Jorge.'

I felt the anger drain out of me. I saw now what my father had long understood, that arguing with her was hopeless. Even after all I'd told her she still wouldn't accept why her husband had been arrested. I don't believe that even the Grand Inquisitor himself could have made her admit the truth. She had lived the lie for so long, that like the tree roots and the rocks, she and the fantasy she clung to could not be separated.

'We have to leave tonight,' I said dully. 'We must start packing.'

'Leave here? But we can't just go. This is my home. What about all my things, my furniture, my pots and linen? It will take weeks to pack. Besides, they're bound to release your father soon, when they realize it's all been a mistake.'

'Mother! Haven't you listened to a word I've said? They are not going to release him. They are going to kill him, kill us all, unless I can give them a pair of gyrfalcons in exchange for our lives.'

'And just how do you propose to do that? You think we have the money to buy such birds?'

'I will have to take them from the wild.'

My mother snorted. Contempt for my father's occupation had become such a habit with her that even now she could not keep the expression of distaste from her face.

'I know you and your father think I am stupid, that I don't know anything about his precious birds. You both like it that way, don't you? That private little world you share with him, laughing at me behind my back, cutting me out of your conversations. But you can't be married to a man like your father for twenty-two years without learning something, and I know that gyrfalcons only breed in the Northern lands. They're not passage birds. They don't migrate through these parts. So you can't set traps for them or take the chicks from the nest, because there are no wild gyrfalcons in Portugal.'

'Then I will have to go to where I can capture them,' I yelled.

It was only when I heard the words burst from my lips that I suddenly realized that was exactly what I had to do. There was no other way.

'Don't talk nonsense,' my mother began. 'Even if you were the son your precious father always wanted, it would be impossible, but you're only . . .'

I didn't wait to listen to the end of her speech. I was not a son. I was not my mother's daughter. I was not an Old Christian. In truth, I didn't know what I was any more. The image flashed into my head of the young Marrano girl, weeping and clasping the little box of bones to her chest as they forced her to put it on the pyre and watch it burn. The only thing I knew for certain at that moment was that I would not become that girl. I would not stand there and watch the flames creep across the faggots of wood towards my father, as I had watched them slither towards Jorge.

I seized the edge of the linen cupboard, heaved with all my strength and felt it grate across the floor as I inched it away from the wall. *Under a loose flag*, my father had said.

'What are you doing?' my mother demanded.

'The only thing I can do – I am going to the Northern lands to steal a pair of gyrfalcons.'

Belém, Portugal
Ricardo

Passage hawk – *a hawk captured during migration.*

'Move aside, you useless pail of piss. You think I've got all day?'

A man hefting a huge bale on his bare shoulder pushed past me, almost pitching me into the stinking water of the harbour. I turned to remonstrate with the fellow and then saw that the oaf was a good foot taller than me and as broad as an elephant's backside. I concluded it wasn't worth giving the man a lesson in manners; he wouldn't have understood a word.

It was impossible to walk in a straight line along the water-front. If you weren't sidestepping mooring ropes and gangways, you were being shoved aside by lumbering herds of sweating, reeking peasants all rushing to and fro carrying boxes, kegs and bundles of produce. Moorish slaves ran along the street with long planks of wood balanced on their heads. Girls wove in and out with baskets of silver fish, and men with accents as thick as their breath threw sacks to one another across the gap between ship and shore with the ease of a dolphin tossing a fish.

I forced myself to slow my pace to that of a hobbled mule, but only succeeded in being buffeted from one side to the other like a football in a scrum of boys. But it wouldn't do to arrive at Dona Lúcia's house too early. She might think I was overeager for the money, and worse still, that I had nothing better to do than wait on her. I was supposed to be organizing the supplying of a ship. I would have a thousand tasks to do, better to arrive a little late. Not late enough to cause offence, but just enough to convince her I was a busy man.

I paused to gaze out across the harbour at the Torre de Belém, the fortified tower that lay just offshore. The waves lapped all around her base and the white stones of her battlements sparkled in the sunshine. Silvia always used to stop just here when we were out for a stroll, especially at night when the tower was lit up by a hundred lamps that shone down on the black water. She dreamt of being entertained in one of the Governor's private rooms, which she had convinced herself were decked out like a palace. She thought it was the most romantic place in Belém. Was that where the bitch was now? Had she finally succeeded in snaring an officer or even the Governor himself and installed herself as their whore?

As I turned away, I saw two soldiers approaching. My heart began to race. Were they looking for me? I crouched down near a fish seller and feigned interest in a basket of mussels, trying to keep my face averted until they had passed by. The rheumy-eyed old man who sat on a low stool beside his basket grew quite animated at the prospect of making a sale and prised one of the shells open, thrusting the contents halfway up my nose to prove they were fresh. When, out of the corner of my eye, I saw the soldiers strolling away from me, I pushed the old man's trembling hand away and strode on, his whines following me.

Then I suddenly saw her, Silvia, walking ahead of me along the waterfront, a scarlet bandanna wound through her mane of glossy black hair. She was swaying with that easy stride of hers that made her hips swing as if she was beginning a dance. I called to her, but she couldn't hear me. I hurried after her, shoving my way through the crowd, ignoring the curses and insults as I elbowed people aside.

'Silvia! Silvia!'

Her head turned slightly, but she walked on.

I barged into one old lady with such force that she staggered and would have fallen had the press of the crowd not been so great, but a cascade of bright oranges tumbled from her pannier and bounced on to the street. She screamed curses at me as she struggled to retrieve them from under the feet of the crowd, but I didn't stop to help her. I pushed on through.

Silvia had vanished. I gazed frantically round and finally spotted the scarlet bandanna disappearing round the corner of a side street. Mercifully this street, though narrow, was less crowded and I sped after her, dodging round piles of pots and dishes that the shopkeepers had stacked out in the street. I had almost caught up with her.

I seized her arm. 'Silvia, my angel, I've been –'

She gave a squawk of indignation and pulled her arm out of my grip, turning to face me. I felt as if someone had thrown a bucket of icy water over me. It wasn't Silvia.

Muttering incoherent apologies, I backed away straight into a teetering stack of jars that wobbled alarmingly. Trying to right myself and steady the jars at the same time, I heard the girl's mocking laughter behind me, but I did not turn around.

I walked a few paces around the corner and sank down on my haunches under the shade of an almond tree. I'd been so sure it was her, but even as I touched her I'd known it wasn't. Where the hell was she? Surely someone must have seen her. Was she still in Belém?

I hadn't dared go to her usual haunts the previous night in case Filipe or the fishermen had reported the body and named me as her killer. I'd spent the night a short way out of the town, huddled behind a small shrine, with precious little sleep. Most of the night was spent cursing that witch Silvia. It was she who'd dropped me into this pile of dung. As

I tossed and turned on the stony ground, without even the solace of a flagon of wine to comfort me or soothe my grumbling belly, I bitterly imagined how Silvia was spending the night. She'd be laughing and drinking in a tavern, tearing great strips of hot roasted chicken off the bone with her sharp white teeth and rolling into a warm soft bed with her newest lover. I can tell you that long before the morning sun had finally stirred its fat arse and bothered to clamber over the horizon, I was actually wishing Silvia really was lying dead on the floor of that stinking fisherman's hut.

But, although every instinct told me I should keep walking away from Belém, whatever the danger I was forced to return. One hungry night was enough to remind me that I could not afford to be on the road without a good sum of money in my pocket. Some men may survive sleeping rough and scrounging a crust or two where they can, but a man of my sensitivities needs good food in his belly, fine wine in his cup and a thick mattress beneath his bones. I could not bear to delay any longer. The sooner I had that money, the sooner I could get away from here.

The church bells were just sounding noon when I stood before Dona Lúcia's gate, slapping the dust from my clothes and tugging on the bell rope.

'No monkey today, Senhor?' the black slave said as he opened the door. He looked mildly disappointed.

'Pio is sick,' I told him.

'I am sorry,' he said. 'But a rich man like you can afford to buy many monkeys. You will get another.'

If only that were true. Nevertheless I felt a bubble of pleasure rising up my spine, knowing that by the time he showed me out again I would indeed be as rich as he imagined me to be.

As I followed the slave through cool, dark reception rooms into the bright sunlight of the courtyard, I glimpsed Dona Lúcia's enchanting little maid peering out from one of the doorways. She shook her head at me, making agitated flapping motions with her hand. I blew her a kiss and walked on. If she was hoping I would take her out on her next day off, she would be gravely disappointed. These girls are always dreaming of catching some wealthy, fond old man or a handsome young fellow who would set them up in a pretty little house where they could play at being mistress instead of maid. But adorable though the maid was, I was too cunning a fish to bite at that particular fly. She had served her purpose.

We did not turn, as I had expected, into the courtyard. Instead, the slave led me into a small room which was so crowded with chests, bowls, plates and huge clay jars that it put me in mind of a merchant's shop. The shutters on the windows were fastened and the only light came from a star-shaped oil lamp attached to a chain that hung from the beam above the centre of a long wooden table. Five tiny flames burned at the end of each arm of the lamp.

Dona Lúcia was seated at the far end of the table, which was lined on either side by many high-backed chairs draped with white cloths, so that in the dim light it looked as if she had invited a host of ghosts to dinner. I bowed low and kissed her plump hand.

'Dona Lúcia, how delightful to see you again. I swear you look even younger and more radiant than when I last saw you.'

'Always the flatterer, Senhor Ricardo. But you should save your pretty words for your young sweetheart.'

I pressed my hand to my heart. 'Alas, Dona Lúcia, now that I have had the pleasure of your company, any foolish young girl would seem insipid by comparison.'

The slave drew out a chair at the end of the table opposite the old widow and whisked the cloth from it. With a bow, he indicated that I should sit. Something under the table began growling and yapping alternately and I felt a wet nose snuffling around my ankles. I tried to resist the urge to boot it away.

'Now stop that, my darling,' Dona Lúcia cooed. 'Leave the poor man alone.'

The revolting little dog waddled out from under the table and flopped down on the cool tiles. Dona Lúcia may not have grown any younger, but I swear that little beast of hers had grown fatter since my last visit.

'Now tell me, Senhor Ricardo, how are your plans progressing for your voyage? This ship, what was its name?'

'*Santa Dorothea*. Yes, she is ready to sail as soon as she can be provisioned and the sailors hired. The captain has a list of the crew he wants, the most experienced navigator, master, quartermaster and carpenter, as well as the toughest seamen. They have all been offered work on other ships, for they're known to be the best, but the captain has persuaded them to wait until this evening before signing with another ship, on the promise of a generous advance on their wages if they make their mark upon our papers. But if I cannot pay them tonight . . .' I spread my hands, leaving the rest of the sentence hanging.

I heard a dry cough behind me and the swish of a curtain being pulled aside. As I turned, a man stepped out from a doorway that, thanks to the infernally dim light of the room, I hadn't even noticed. I half-rose from my chair, but he pushed me back down, his fingers digging into my shoulder as if to make it quite clear he was willing to exert more force should it be required. He settled himself on a chair next to mine. From the excellent cut of his clothes, the rich gold trim on his doublet and the silver-inlaid ebony sword sheath that dangled from his belt, I didn't need introductions to tell me that this was no servant.

'I understand from my aunt that I have the pleasure of addressing Senhor Ricardo da Moniz.'

But he did not look as if it was a pleasure, quite the opposite in fact. The tone of his voice was so cold it would have frozen a dragon's breath. My stomach was churning and not just because I was ravenously hungry. Dona Lúcia hadn't mentioned any nephew. The last thing I needed was some heir with an eye to his aunt's fortune asking awkward questions. I could convince the old lady of anything, but this fellow didn't look like a man who would be easily conned.

I took a deep breath. Hold your nerve, I admonished myself. Perhaps she's told him what a good investment she has found and he wants a share of it. Play this right and you might yet prise both these oysters open and take two pearls instead of one.

I met his gaze and tried to smile confidently. 'At your service, Senhor . . . ?'

He continued to stare hard at me, but did not supply a name.

'It's a pleasure to meet the nephew of such a charming lady. How truly fortunate you are indeed to have such a wise and noble woman as your aunt.'

I beamed at Dona Lúcia, but she seemed not to be listening and was engrossed in feeding a titbit to her revolting dog, which had lumbered back to her chair. My stomach growled. It was all I could do to stop myself wrenching the piece of cake from the dog's jaws and devouring it myself.

'Dona Lúcia has no doubt told you of the marvellous venture which she and I are to embark on?'

'My aunt has told me of your conversation.'

'Then,' I said with a brightness I certainly did not feel, 'I take it that she has invited you here to read and witness the contract between us. A very prudent precaution, if I may say so, Dona Lúcia. One cannot be too careful these days; there are so many rogues who try to take advantage of a woman alone. I am delighted that you have someone to safeguard your interests.'

I pulled a folded parchment from the inside of my jacket. My friend the clerk had done an excellent job, and the lettering with all its embellishments looked impressive enough to have been a royal proclamation. I loosened the ribbons that secured it and handed it to the man. He unfolded it, his eyes running rapidly down the page. A smile curled the corners of his mouth, but it was not a pleasant one.

'Well drawn, well drawn indeed. You must give me the name of the man who wrote this for you. I would be most interested in seeing more of his work.' He tossed the contract on to the table and leaned back in his chair, the tips of his fingers pressed together.

'Since my aunt told me of your visit, I have been making a few inquiries of my own into this venture of yours. I thought at first this ship might be – how shall I put it? – as *fanciful* as this contract of yours. But I found that there is a *Santa Dorothea* in harbour and she is indeed bound for the isle of Goa, where, as you told my aunt, her captain is intending to buy many rich and rare treasures to sell in the markets of Lisbon.'

My stomach, which had been knotting itself tighter and tighter, suddenly relaxed.

Dona Lúcia smiled happily at the end of the table. 'You see, Carlos, I told you this young man was to be trusted. I always say you can trust a man who loves animals. They always know, don't you, my poppet?' She held out another morsel of cake to the drooling dog. 'Please forgive my nephew, Senhor Ricardo. He always thinks that someone is going to take advantage of his foolish old aunt.'

I bowed my head graciously. I could afford to be magnanimous now that the deal was almost sealed.

'You're fortunate to have such a devoted nephew whose only desire, I'm sure, is to protect you from the wickedness in this world, as I always endeavour to protect my own dear mother.'

My own dear mother would doubtless have said that it was the world that needed protection from me, but then she never had the faith in me that a mother should.

'If your nephew is now assured that all is in order, perhaps he would care to witness our signatures, unless, of course, Senhor Carlos would like to join us in this little venture?'

I turned to him hopefully. 'The rewards, as I'm sure your aunt has explained, are beyond anything a man might hope to gain by investing here. Chinese silks and dishes, for example, can be bought for a mere trifle in Goa, but sell them in Lisbon and you may name your price.'

'I have no doubt at all about that, Senhor Ricardo. And doubtless the *Santa Dorothea* will come back loaded with such goods, and make a fortune for her backers, just as you say.'

He picked up the contract. I felt that same glorious shiver of excitement rise up through my body that I always did when I knew a fighting cock I had backed was about to be declared the winner.

'There is only one small problem, Senhor Ricardo. It seems that the *Santa Dorothea* is already crewed and provisioned, but not, it seems, by you, rather by a group of merchants represented by one Henry Vasco. In fact, the captain has never heard of you, Senhor Ricardo. Now, how do you account for that?'

He shifted his weight in the chair, leaning forward, his hand inching towards the hilt of his sword.

'What's this?' Dona Lúcia said sharply, ignoring the whining dog.

I tried to keep a relaxed smile on my face. 'Of course he hasn't heard of me. As you say, Vasco is representing me and my fellow merchants. That way there can be no possibility of Dona Lúcia's name being involved. As I assured your aunt at the beginning, I guarantee discretion. It would be vulgar to link a noblewoman's name with base commerce.'

Carlos's eyes narrowed. 'You have just told my aunt that you needed the money today to secure the services of the experienced crew. Yet I have been told they are already signed up and are aboard.'

'Because I swore to them that I would have their money tonight. They trust me as a gentleman.'

'Is that so? A gentleman?' A cold smile slid across Carlos's mouth. 'Well, as luck would have it this Henry Vasco is coming to Belém this very day to deliver some cargo to be shipped to Goa. Why don't you and I pay him a visit? I'm sure he will be delighted to see an old acquaintance such as yourself.'

I rose with as much dignity and control as I could. 'That will be delightful, Senhor Carlos, shall we say seven this evening? Now, dear lady, I must beg you to excuse me. I have some urgent matters to attend to.' I bowed. 'Till this evening, Senhor Carlos.'

I began to back towards the door, but Carlos was already on his feet with his drawn sword in his hand, the tip of the blade pointed exactly at my heart as if he could see it thumping in my chest.

'I'm afraid your business will have to wait, Senhor Ricardo. I have a mind to pay my respects to this friend of yours immediately.'

He took a step closer. I backed away and collided with a heavy wooden chest.

'Come now, Senhor,' I said. 'Sure . . . surely you would not be so ill-mannered as to draw a blade in the presence of a lady? If you are so eager for me to come now, you have just to say the word and I will be only too delighted to accompany you. There's no need to use force, I assure you.'

All the time I was speaking my hands were groping behind me over the chest, trying to find something I could use to defend myself. My fingers closed on a cold, heavy object. With one swift movement I hurled it at Carlos.

The statue of the saint hit him on the nose and he staggered backwards. Dona Lúcia screamed and the dog started barking, but I didn't stay to watch. I turned on my heels and ran through the archway into the passage beyond, making for what I hoped was the door to the street. But I must have turned the wrong way, for I found myself facing a staircase that led upwards. I started to retrace my steps, then I heard Carlos bellowing above the yapping of the dog.

'Guard the doors, damn you, don't let him escape.'

Footsteps were hurrying in my direction. There was only one way to go. I scrambled up the stairs and just managed to flatten myself into an alcove at the top as servants rushed through the hallway below. My heart was thumping so loudly I was sure it was echoing off the walls.

'Search the house! I want him found!' Carlos bellowed. I could tell his temper had definitely not been improved by that bang to the nose.

Something warm and soft touched my hand. I jumped, barely suppressing a squeal. Dona Lúcia's maid pressed her fingers to my lips. She peered cautiously over the rail of the stairs. I didn't need to look. I could hear crashes and shouts as the slaves and servants searched every conceivable hiding place below, and the excited barks of that nasty little dog as it waddled round behind them.

The maid tugged urgently on my arm and pulled me across the passageway into a room, locking the door behind us. I found myself standing in a sumptuous bedchamber. The floor was tiled in a delicate mosaic of jewel-bright flowers, fish and frolicking dolphins. Images of saints and innumerable depictions of the Virgin Mary smiled serenely down at me from all the walls. A silk rug lay to one side of an enormous bed, which was piled high with cushions and draped in light gauze hangings, whilst on a carved black table a silver mirror was drowning beneath an ocean of delicate glass phials, gilded bottles, ivory combs and silver brushes.

'The mistress's bedchamber,' the maid whispered, though I could see that plainly enough for myself. 'Hers and that dog's.' She picked up one of the silver-backed hairbrushes. 'That's his, the spoilt little brute. She brushes him with this, but she won't even give me so much as a wooden comb for my hair.'

'I can't hide in here,' I said, aghast. 'If I'm found in her bedchamber, that nephew of hers is going to run me through on the spot.'

She gave a little giggle. 'I think he's planning to do that anyway.'

'I'm glad you find it amusing,' I snapped. 'But it's my life hanging by a fingernail. How am I going to get out of here?'

Instead of answering, she moved closer and, standing on tiptoe, she slid her hand around my neck and pulled me down towards her, kissing me full and passionately. I put my arms around her, feeling the warmth of her hot little body against my legs. There was a familiar stirring in my groin and she nuzzled in to me. For a few blissful moments, I entirely forgot that I was being pursued and could think of nothing else except the delightful little creature in my arms. Well, to be more truthful I wasn't actually capable of thinking at all, I had just given myself up to the thrill surging through me.

But my cock went as limp as a drowned kitten as soon as I heard the furious shouts outside the door of the chamber.

'Quickly,' the maid said, pulling me across the room. She thrust me out on to a narrow stone balcony. 'You'll have to climb. Go on,' she urged.

I stared down into the courtyard below. 'I can't go down there.'

Several of the servants were peering hopefully behind the pots of the miniature orange and lemon trees as if I might somehow be concealed behind them.

'Not down, stupid, up. You'll have to get up on the roof. If you stand on the balustrade then you'll be able to heave yourself up. Once you're up there you can cross to one of the roofs of the other houses and climb down to the street.'

'I'll break my neck.'

The girl shrugged. 'If he catches you, he'll probably cut your head off anyway.'

'There must be some other –'

I broke off as someone rattled the door of the bedchamber. Now here was an interesting choice – death by falling from a roof or death at the hands of an apoplectic, sword-wielding maniac. Which, I wondered, was the more attractive proposition?

I clambered on top of the balustrade, praying that none of the servants below would look up. I tried to swing myself up on to the roof above, but was fearful of bringing the tiles clattering down.

'Wait, you'll never do it like that,' the maid whispered. She grasped the balustrade to steady herself. 'Stand on my shoulder.'

I wasn't at all sure she could bear my weight, but there wasn't time to debate the matter. I placed one foot on her little shoulder and pushed hard. She gave a gasp, but managed to keep standing until I had pulled myself up on to the roof.

The girl instantly vanished back into the chamber, closing the shutters to the balcony behind her. For a few minutes I just lay there, too terrified to move in case I rolled off the steep slope of the roof. The tiles were painfully hot from baking under the fierce sun, but even the pain of that couldn't induce me to stir until I heard a thunderous hammering at the door of the chamber.

'Are you in there, Ricardo? You'll have to come out sometime. You're trapped. There's no way you can escape. Now, open this door and give yourself up, and I won't kill you, but if you don't, I'll break the door down and cut you into dog meat.'

The strange thing about fear is how readily you overcome it when threatened by something even more terrifying. If I had been too frightened to move up to that point, I suddenly found myself positively eager to crawl across a roof even a cat would refuse to venture upon. Trying hard to resist the temptation to look down, I inched my way along the tiles until I came to the side of the building and with a monumental effort dragged myself over the ridge tiles and round the corner. At this point, a low palisade ran along the side of the roof and I gratefully crawled behind it and lay there, panting and shaking. On this side, the roof overlooked one of the narrow streets. The palisade was too low to shield me completely, if someone should chance to look up as they sauntered along, but it was the only cover I had and at least it would stop me slipping off.

I don't how long I lay there with the sun scorching my back and the hot tiles blistering my hands, sweat pouring down my face and my throat so dry I would have gladly drunk a barrel of horse piss, before I finally heard Carlos and some of the servants heading off down the streets away from the house. They had evidently realized I was not inside and had decided to search the streets for me. Carlos was bound to report the incident. In fact, he'd probably already sent a servant to summon help. It wouldn't be long before the place was crawling with soldiers.

Trying not to raise my head too high, I examined the building next door. It had a balcony on the upper storey with a high wall around it. The doors to the room that opened out on to the balcony were tightly fastened, and the catches were rusty. It looked as if they had not been opened for some time, for leaves and other wind-blown debris had accumulated behind the wall. If I could get down there I could safely hide on the balcony in the shade and wait until dark. Anything would be better than being grilled alive on this roof.

There was nothing for it but to move quickly and pray no one would look up. I grabbed the palisade and dragged myself over the tiles until I reached the point where I was directly above the balcony of the neighbouring house. Then, praying to every saint I could name and to all those I couldn't, I jumped down.

For once the saints must have taken pity on me for I landed on the wall of the balcony, teetered precariously between life and death, then managed to fall the right way and tumbled down inside. There I lay bruised and winded, not daring to move in case someone inside the house had heard me. But no one came running or flung open the shutters, so I eased myself into a sitting position in the blessed shade and breathed a great sigh of relief.

I'd made it! I'd escaped! All I had to do now was wait until dark, then climb down into the street below, leaving that arrogant, pompous jackanapes Carlos chasing himself up his own tight little arsehole. I grinned to myself at the thought that even now he was pounding around the sweltering streets working himself into a raging sweat, while all the time I was lying cool and relaxed just above his head.

The exhaustion of the chase and the sleepless night before it had taken its toll and I must finally have drifted off into a doze, because I was jerked awake by a clamour of voices below in the street.

'We may as well call off the search here and start to cast our nets wider, Senhor Carlos. The villain will be long gone from this area by now.'

'No!' Carlos roared. 'I stationed men on the end of every street leading out of this quarter and I tell you he's still in this warren somewhere. I want that scoundrel found.'

I shrank down beneath the wall as low as I could get.

I could hear them banging on doors, questioning people up and down the street, but all denied seeing anything, though they promised to report it at once if they did. Carlos's voice was growing more distant as they moved further up the street. I released my breath. My mind was racing, trying to work out an escape route which would avoid the lookouts Carlos had posted. If I could slip through a house and emerge on a different street, then . . .

There was a chattering just above me. For a moment I thought it must be birds quarrelling on the roof, but then something black and white scampered along the top of the balcony wall. I twisted round. My little monkey, Pio, was standing on the wall just above my head, squeaking in ecstasy at having found me.

'Where the hell did you come from?' I whispered.

His chattering grew more noisy and excited.

'Be quiet, Pio! Shush!' I implored him.

He was standing up on his hind legs on top of the wall, waving his arms about.

'Pio, come here. Good boy, that's right, come to your master.'

I lunged at him and he bounded away along the wall, uttering high-pitched screeches of rage at my attempts to grab him.

'Go, get away! Go! Go!' I flapped at him frantically.

Picking up twigs that lay scattered on the balcony, I hurled them at the enraged little demon, trying to make him flee to the roof top, but he refused to budge. His screams intensified. I made another grab for him, but he neatly evaded my hand, and as I turned to try again, the doors on the balcony crashed open and I found myself staring up into the coldly triumphant face of Carlos.

'I thought the creature would find you. They say masters become like their pets, so I should have guessed you'd be clambering over roofs like a monkey.'

I scrambled to my feet and swung my leg over the wall.

'You can certainly jump if you want to, Senhor Ricardo,' he said with an icy smile. 'But I really wouldn't recommend it. If you look down you'll see the soldiers are waiting directly below with their pikes and swords. So your landing won't exactly be comfortable.'

He gestured towards the door leading back into the house. 'Please be so good as to step this way. I'm afraid, Senhor Ricardo, or whatever your real name is, your days of charming naive old ladies out of their money are about to come to an end . . . a very painful end.'

Iceland

Eydis

Jesses – *short leather thongs permanently attached to the legs of a hawk to allow the bird to be held securely by the falconer or fastened to a perch.*

'I've brought you the herbs you asked for.' The lad squats opposite me on the warm rock floor.

He is the same young man who helped the crofter, Fannar, bring the injured man to me.

'Does he live?' he asks.

'He is not dead.'

The body of the man lies between us, like a loaf of bread placed between a guest and his host on a table. Something given, something taken, something shared, which forms an unbreakable bond between strangers. But though he is the pledge between us, neither of us looks at the man.

'Fannar is not coming?'

The lad frowns. 'The priest has come to hear confessions and to administer the sacraments of Mass. He's in Fannar's hall even now. Fannar sent me to his neighbours to tell them to come, for who knows when Father Jon will be able to return . . . or even if he will ever return. Fannar said to tell them they must come quickly for the priest must be away before first light. It's too dangerous for him to remain on the farmstead more than a few hours. Fannar will guide him out of the valley before dawn.'

The lad nervously fingers the ties on his leather jerkin. 'I did offer to guide the priest myself. I'm not a coward!' he adds vehemently, his eyes flashing from under his heavy fringe of red-gold hair.

It is plain that he still feels shame over his failure to defend the foreigner from the Danes.

He scowls down at his grimy fingernails. 'But Fannar wouldn't let me do it. He said he knew the land better, could show the priest a pass over the mountains that's hidden from view. I think he only wanted to protect me, though, in case the priest is caught. But I don't need protecting! I know ravens are everywhere watching us, but I'm not afraid.' He thrusts his chin out as if defying the Lutherans to come and take him.

Fannar is wise not to entrust the task to him. The boy is desperate for a chance to show he is no coward and might deliberately take risks to prove himself, which will put not only him but the priest too in danger, for the ravens are indeed watching everyone. Although every man, woman and child is officially a Lutheran now by order of the Danish king, still many like Fannar practise the old Catholic faith in secret. And the black-clad Lutherans have eyes everywhere, trying to catch those hidden priests still celebrating the forbidden Mass, as well as the ordinary men and women who shield them.

Fannar is taking a huge risk by inviting others to come to confession. How is he to know for certain which of his friends or neighbours is not simply pretending to be Lutheran as he is, but has in his heart really converted to the Protestant faith and might betray him? Even those who have no love for the Lutherans might be persuaded to spy for them, if they are offered enough gold.

'Fannar must trust you, Ari.'

The lad looks startled. 'Did Fannar tell you my name?'

'Fannar trusts you,' I repeat, 'and yet you did not tell him the truth about this man.'

Ari's cheeks flush, but he mutinously thrusts out his lower lip. 'I told him what I saw.'

'That some Danes beat him.'

'It was the truth.' He scowls as if challenging me to dispute it.

'But you let Fannar believe you didn't know the man, that he was a stranger to you. And Fannar is a good soul. No matter if it was a friend or stranger, human or beast, if Fannar saw any living creature hurt or hungry he would try to help, even if it meant sharing his last loaf of bread or cutting his only blanket in two. You, I think, are much like him, and if that man had been a stranger, you would have helped him just as Fannar would. But there is something more here. Something I think you will not admit even to yourself.'

I pause to watch him. Although I am veiled, still he refuses to look at me, but stares sullenly at the pool of hot water bubbling up through the rocks. He is not going to admit anything without a deal of persuasion.

'If this man really was a stranger to you, Ari, you would have looked at his face with curiosity that first day you brought him here, but you didn't. I thought then that you were sickened by the sight of blood, but that wasn't what was upsetting you, was it? Then again tonight when you came in, any other man's gaze would have been drawn at once to him as soon as they entered, to see if his wounds were healing and if his eyes had opened, but yours was not. You know this man and you are afraid of him. Why?'

Ari scrambles to his feet. 'I have to go. Fannar will have need of me to keep watch.'

'Ari, tell me. We need to know. There is danger, grave danger, hovering around this man, that we can sense, but we cannot yet see the shape of it.'

The boy hesitates. He stares into the clear waters of the pool, the flames of the burning torch rippling over his face so that he dissolves and re-forms in a hundred different masks.

'I should have left him to die on the track, I know I should. But I couldn't just walk away. What if I'd been mistaken? Do you think it's better to let an innocent man die rather than risk saving a man who should not live? I didn't know what to do, Eydis, and I still don't.'

'Tell us the truth, Ari. We have to understand what we are dealing with. You must help us. If you don't, you could be putting everyone in danger.'

But he stubbornly shakes his head. 'No, I must be sure first. When he wakes then I will know.'

'And what will you do then, Ari?'

He covers his head with his arms as if trying to shield himself from a great boulder that is about to crash down on him. Then he turns and scrambles over the rocks towards the entrance of the cave. I hear the shower of small stones rattling behind him as he hastily climbs back up and out through the slit.

The cave seals itself again in silence, save for the gentle bubbling and gurgling of the pool. I look down at the man. At his temple a tiny pulse flickers beneath the skin like the wingbeat of a moth. That is the only sign of life in him. Since they brought him here, he has not moved nor opened his eyes, but beneath her veil my dead sister, Valdis, turns her head towards me and laughs, a dreadful mocking laugh, and the walls of the cave tremble.

Chapter Five

A fable relates how once a falcon refused to return to his master's fist. A cockerel, watching this, thought, I am just as fine a bird as any falcon, yet I am forced to scratch for scraps in the dust at my master's feet. Why should I not ride upon his fist and be fed choice meats from his fingers?

So the cockerel flew up on to his master's fist. His master was delighted and praised the bird for its cleverness. Then he killed it, and held up its body as a lure for the falcon, which at once returned to his fist and devoured the cockerel's flesh.

Torre de Belém
Ricardo

*Man – to accustom the hawk to being handled by the falconer
and to make the bird accept the equipment used to control it,
such as hoods, jesses, etc.*

The guttering orange flames of the torches high on the walls
of the dungeon glinted on the black water as another icy
wave surged in and splashed across my legs. I shivered violently. My bare chest was wet with the salt spray. I could no
longer feel my feet as I stood knee-deep in water, and my
arms were numb from hanging in the chains. But at least I no
longer felt the terrible panic of the first night, when the
guards had chained me here promising that, with the coming
of the high tide, the dungeon would flood. They roared with
laughter as they climbed up the stairs of the tower, leaving
me to wait in agonized terror for the first wave to come rolling in through the openings and race across the stone slabs.
Just how high would the tide reach?

I had stood there in the darkness with my hands gripped
painfully either side of my head by the fetters that bolted me
to one of the great pillars, feeling the water creeping higher
and higher up my legs with each breaking wave. How long
before the tide was at its highest? How many hours had
passed? And the cold! Oh, sweet Jesu, that bitter, biting cold.
I had no idea how agonizing cold could be. It was as if my
bones were being slowly crushed in the vice of it.

Then, when something solid bumped against my groin, it

suddenly occurred to me that eels, octopuses and worse, much worse, also made their home in the sea. If the water could flow in, what was to prevent them swimming in with it? Was that an eel even now gnawing at my numb flesh, or a crab tearing strips of my skin off with its claws? Was that just a ripple I could see in the torchlight, or some huge fish carried in on the tide, a stinging jellyfish, a shark? What was swimming around me in that dark, swirling water, its mouth open, its teeth dagger-sharp?

But I was not drowned or devoured that night, nor had I been in the fourteen tides that followed, for I count my days in tides now. But what would happen when there was a storm? And sooner or later there would be one. I'd seen the waterfront at Belém flooded more than once when high winds lashed the sea. I knew just how much higher those waves could rise. And tall as I was, they would only need to rise a few more feet to cover my head.

But even when the tide was low and the water had drained away, I couldn't get warm. The heat of the sun didn't penetrate the dungeon of the tower, though I could glimpse it sparkling on the blue water through the openings in the walls as if it was put there to taunt and torment me. A priest told me that once a year the damned in hell are permitted to glimpse the beauty of the heaven they can never enter, to comfort them in their suffering. When I saw the reflection of the sun on the sea, I knew that if those in hell are shown heaven it's not an act of mercy, but just another torture inflicted on them.

The sea wind funnelled through the arches of the dungeon, flaying my wet flesh. The skin on my feet and legs, especially the tender parts around my cock, was cracking open and peeling, leaving raw wounds and sores which stung viciously with each new flood of salt water, and itched madly as the salt on my skin dried at low tide. With my hands chained either side of my head, I couldn't even relieve the torment by scratching my crotch. Merciful heaven, to think it was summer now! How much worse would it become if I was still chained up here in winter?

They had rowed me out to the tower within hours of Carlos seizing me. Dona Lúcia's nephew was a wealthy man, and the rich can buy vengeance which is denied to the poor. Had I robbed some poor market woman of every miserable thing she had ever owned, I would have merely ended up in the town jail, not comfortable perhaps, but not torture. Try to borrow a few escudos from a woman who's so rich she wouldn't even notice the loss, and they chain you up in here. There's no justice in this world.

And to think that just a few short weeks ago Silvia and I had stood, arms round each other, her head resting on my shoulder, gazing out from the shore at the tower, its windows glowing with soft yellow light. Silvia had thought it so romantic with its little turrets and graceful arches. Believe me, the romance dies pretty quickly when you see it from this angle.

A guard clattered down the stone steps, swinging a pail in one hand and half a loaf in the other. He stopped somewhere behind me and addressed another prisoner hidden from my view.

'How are we today, Senhor? In a better humour, I trust.'

The only response was an incoherent mumbling, punctuated by sudden shrieks of demented laughter.

I knew there was someone else chained up behind one of the other great pillars that supported the vaulted ceiling. I'd never seen him, but I could hear him talking to himself, though if I shouted a question at him he'd immediately fall silent. Each time the tide started to roll in, he'd begin whimpering and crying, and as it rose he'd start howling above the wind like a starving dog. How long had he been here? Had he been mad when they brought him here or had he gradually lost his wits chained up in this place, month after month?

How long were they going to keep me here? Until I was as crazed as he was?

I had given up asking the guards what was to happen to me. They simply laughed, sometimes drawing their fingers across their throats, or else twisting their heads sideways and making their tongues loll out in the grotesque mockery of a hanged man. But they never answered me.

The footsteps moved towards me again and the guard rounded the pillar, a grin on his lopsided face. I stared at the quarter of the loaf remaining in his hands. I was sure he'd given that other prisoner the bigger share. He stuffed the bread into my chained hand and watched me lean my head towards my fingers until the bread was close enough to my mouth to eat. I devoured it as rapidly as I could. If I took too long, the guard would become bored and wander away without giving me anything to drink. But I had learned from painful experience to hold the chunk of bread tightly, for if my numb fingers dropped it, the guard wouldn't pick it up and return it to me again. He'd simply walk away, leaving it on the floor where I couldn't reach it. And the sight of the bread, so near yet so unattainable, would only make my stomach ache more with hunger.

The guard dipped a ladle in a stinking bucket of water and held it to my lips, tilting it only slightly. I sucked as fiercely as a baby at the nipple, before the water could dribble down my chin. To my surprise he dipped the ladle a second time and then a third. I'd never been given more than one before. For a moment I wondered if he'd pissed in it or poisoned it, but frankly I was so thirsty not even that would have stopped me drinking it.

'Thank you,' I said, when he picked up the pail ready to depart.

The guard snorted. 'Not me you want to thank, it's your visitors. Said they wanted you in a fit state to talk, they did.'

'Talk? You mean they want to question me?' My stomach contracted so fast I nearly vomited what I had just drunk.

'They didn't come here for the good of their health. In fact, one of them's looking decidedly peaky. I'd always heard of people turning green, but I never believed it until I'd seen him. I don't reckon he enjoyed that crossing much. He's up in the Governor's room now, taking a little port for his stomach, and if I were in your shoes I'd be praying it improves his temper, otherwise I don't give much for your chances.'

'Who . . . who is it? Senhor Carlos?'

The guard chuckled. 'These are no senhors,' he said, as he walked away.

'Wait, please! At least tell me who –'

'You'll find out soon enough,' the guard called back, as he ambled towards the stairs. 'Don't be so impatient. Not as if you've got anything else to do today, except hang around.' Laughing at his own feeble joke, he vanished from view.

As if he too shared the joke, the unseen prisoner also began to laugh, a high-pitched, insane giggle that ended in a sob.

I don't know how long I waited. There was no way to measure time except by the relentless tides. My ears were straining for the sound of footfalls on the steps and my thoughts were spinning in a maelstrom. What did he mean, *these were no senhors*? Were my visitors women? Had Dona Lúcia taken pity on me? Did she feel guilty that her own nephew was responsible for my unjust incarceration and had come to negotiate for my release? Perhaps that adorable little maid of hers had persuaded Dona Lúcia that I was innocent of any crime, which indeed I was, since I hadn't actually taken any money from her. There was no denying the kiss that girl had pressed on me had all the taste and passion of love, and she had tried to help me to escape. She would be distraught that I had been taken.

I was so preoccupied with thinking of the maid coming to release me that it wasn't until they had rounded the pillar that I saw them, two black-robed men, their cassocks held in place by a long girdle tied about the waist. They moved round either side of the pillar and came together in front of me like a giant claw closing. They seemed to be gliding an inch above the ground for their sandals made no sound at all on the wet paving stones.

It took me a moment or two to realize who they were. I'd never before been within spitting distance of one of their kind. But when I recognized their habits, a douche of icy panic shot through my bowels. *Jesuit priests!* What the hell were they doing here? There was only one reason I could think a priest would visit a prisoner – to hear his confession and give him the last rites before he was executed. I stared wildly from one to the other, but neither spoke.

Faced with their icy silence, my brain seemed to freeze. I couldn't think of a single coherent story with which to defend myself. Instead I began to babble wildly like some callow farm boy caught stealing a chicken.

'Please, you have to understand I've done nothing wrong. It was just a business arrangement, that's all . . . I didn't take the money . . . You can't hang me without a trial . . . Don't listen to Senhor Carlos, he completely misunderstood the situation. He . . . he wasn't there at the beginning, you see. I had no intention of borrowing any money from the old lady, quite the reverse. In fact I'm the one who was the victim here. I was completely deceived by Henry Vasco and the captain of that ship. It's them who should be here, not me . . . I . . . the truth is . . .'

My voice faltered and died away. Both men's faces were expressionless. They did not so much as nod their heads to show they were listening. Both stared at me with unblinking eyes as if they were searching my soul and despised what they saw. The only sounds to be heard were the waves lapping against the outside of the tower and the wind whining between the pillars. Even the mad prisoner had fallen silent.

The older of the two men gave a dry little cough. He was a well-fleshed man with a bulbous nose and small, sunken eyes which even in the shadow of the dungeon seemed to be permanently squinting against a non-existent glare. His companion, in contrast, was a shorter, leaner man, with sharp features, but whose black eyes burned with a dark fire that I had only ever seen in men who are consumed with lust for a woman. Sweet Jesu, surely he didn't mean to ... I mean, you did hear of prisoners who were raped by their jailers, but not by a man in holy orders surely?

The older priest coughed again. 'I am sure you realize by now that you are in serious trouble, Senhor Cruz. Oh, yes, we know your name, in fact we know all the names you call yourself. But let us not trouble ourselves with a list of those. Why don't we stick to the name that will appear on your death warrant, just to simplify matters?'

'Death ... but I told you I am innocent. I didn't take a single crusado from Dona Lúcia.'

'But you tried to. A thief who is apprehended in the midst of his crime is no less guilty than one caught afterwards.'

'A servant who puts poison into his master's wine is still executed whether his master drinks it or not,' the younger man added.

'But I was tricked, I –'

The older priest held up his hands. 'Don't waste words lying to me. It's not the first time you have committed such a fraud. True, the ship was a little more ambitious than some of your other schemes. Remember the olive grove you sold that you did not actually own? The girl you promised to marry and then abandoned after you had talked her into giving you her jewellery to buy medicines for your dying mother? And then there were boxes of rare nutmegs you procured for the noble lady which turned out to contain, what was it – apricot stones? Need I go on?'

'That wasn't me. You are mistaking me for someone else, I swear.'

'We could, of course, bring these people as witnesses to your trial,' the priest said in a bored tone, as if he was discussing the price of hay instead of my life.

'They wouldn't testify, because they know it wasn't me,' I retorted, trying to sound far more confident of that than I felt.

'I grant you many of them wouldn't want to admit in public they had been taken as fools. But let me assure you that the girl's father as well as Senhor Carlos are so hungry to see you hanged they'd don the executioner's hood themselves, if we allowed them to.'

He paused. His gaze wandered to somewhere behind me. I turned my head and was sure I glimpsed the sleeve of a black cassock sticking out from behind the pillar to which I was chained. There was a third priest in the dungeon. Why didn't he step out where I could see him? Was he going to garrotte me from behind? I was horribly conscious that my hands were chained fast. There was nothing I could do to defend myself, not even cover my face.

The older priest was speaking again. 'But it would be a pity to let a man with your skills go to the gallows when he could perform a great service for his country and for the Holy Church. Our Blessed Lord does not like us to waste the talents he has given us.'

The younger priest gave a half-smile. 'Indeed.' He nodded respectfully to his companion, before turning to me. 'The Holy Church wishes you to carry out a task for her. If you succeed, on your return you will be set up in a well-appointed house many miles from Belém and your accusers. Furthermore, you will be granted an income more than sufficient for all your needs, such that you will never again have to put yourself to the trouble of finding, shall we say . . . a less honest means of earning a living.'

I gaped at him. I couldn't take in what he was saying. Just minutes ago they were talking about death warrants and gallows, now they were suddenly offering me houses and money. Had my wits finally fled and I'd become as mad as the unseen prisoner? Perhaps I was imagining all this and the priests were just hallucinations. I jerked my hand and felt the iron shackle cut into my wrist – the pain was certainly real enough.

'Are you saying I'll be released . . . with no charge? Will there . . . will there be a penance?' I asked anxiously.

I had witnessed the ghastly humiliation of those the Church forced to do public penance for their crime and always thought I'd rather die than suffer that. Although now that it had come to just such a choice, I realized I would do anything to stay alive, even endure public shame.

'We feel that the task you will undertake will involve sufficient hardship so as to render any further penance unnecessary. You might say that what the Church requires of you is in the nature of a pilgrimage.'

'You mean to Compostela or the Holy Land?'

The abject fear that had gripped me was beginning to ease a little. Pilgrimages could be quite jolly affairs, or so I'd been told. True, the journey could be a little rough at times, but if one had plenty of money there was always good food, desirable women and juicy entertainment to be had in the inns along the way.

'I fear the pilgrimage you are about to embark on is to somewhere a little colder and damper than the Holy Land.' The young priest glanced round the dungeon at the water marks on the pillars and the puddles of sea water on the floor. 'But after this place such a journey should be no hardship. We want you to go to Iceland . . . you have heard of Iceland?'

'Somewhere in the North, isn't it? Nothing there but cod

and sheep, so I heard. Why would I go on pilgrimage there? Are there even any shrines in Iceland?'

'It's not the destination that makes the pilgrimage, Cruz, it is the journey,' the older priest said. 'A pilgrimage is a journey you undertake to purify the soul, but in this case it is a journey you will make to purify the Holy Church, and Portugal, even the young king himself.'

The older priest glanced behind me again, as if he was seeking confirmation from someone standing just out of my sight in the shadow of the pillar. Whatever answer he got seemed to be a signal to continue, for he nodded briefly and returned his gaze to me.

'A young girl has arrived in Belém. She has been making inquiries about ships bound for Iceland. We believe she means to go there to capture a pair of gyrfalcons which she intends to present to King Sebastian. It is vital for the future of Portugal that she does not succeed. You will sail with her and use your considerable skill at charming women to befriend her. We want you to ensure she does *not* return with the white falcons.'

I don't know quite what task I'd been expecting them to charge me with – delivering a package to someone, or even stealing a holy relic for them from a shrine – but stopping a girl capturing a couple of birds was definitely not what I expected to hear.

'I can't imagine why a gift of a few birds should affect the future of Portugal,' I said. 'Why don't you just tell her the king doesn't like birds and suggest she stitch him a nice shirt instead?' I tried to grin, but my lips were too cracked and sore.

The two priests regarded me with an icy contempt. It was a look that reminded me that my life still dangled precariously in their hands.

I added hastily, 'What I mean is, Father, if . . . if you don't want the girl to go and find these birds, why don't you arrest her or simply forbid her to leave?'

'She must be seen to go to Iceland, and she must be seen to fail in her quest. If she is arrested or if she should fall mortally sick before she has a chance to sail, there is a danger that His Majesty, being at an impressionable age, might express a certain sympathy towards her and her family. This he must not do. You must see that she is well away from these shores before any . . . *accident* befalls her. What happens after that we will leave to your discretion.'

What did they mean – *accident*? Were they suggesting I trip her up and break her leg? In my bewilderment I had almost forgotten that my arms were chained. I tried to gesticulate, gasping as the iron cut into my already raw and bruised flesh.

'Look, why don't I simply seduce her and then talk her out of the whole venture? It won't be easy if she is stubborn, but you may rest assured that I know how to handle any woman and win her round. There's really no need for either of us to set foot on board any ship. What with the cold and the rotten food – I wouldn't be able to function at my best. I don't travel well. It's impossible to seduce a woman if you are constantly vomiting with seasickness. I assure you I work much better on dry land.'

The younger of the two priests swallowed hard as if the mere mention of the word *seasickness* was enough to make him want to retch.

The older priest's lip twitched in a faint smile. 'Come now, Cruz, an experienced seaman such as you surely does not fear such a journey? You have weathered storms at sea before many times, have you not, when you voyaged all the way to the island of Goa, as you so vividly described to Dona Lúcia? You don't mean to tell me that was a lie.'

'You know it was.'

'Lies have a way of becoming truth, as you are about to discover, Cruz.'

He waved his hand about the dungeon. 'Of course, you could always choose to stay here. I promise you, as winter approaches it will become just as wet and cold in this tower as on board a ship, more so in fact, for at least at sea you will have fires to warm you and blankets to sleep beneath. And all the while you hang here in your chains, drenched and frozen, night and day, you will be dreading that really bad storm. Do you see that?' He pointed to a stain on the pillar opposite, high above my head. 'I believe that is the height waves surged to last winter in a gale.'

My throat, which was dry before, was now so tight that I feared I was going to choke.

'But this girl, you said an *accident*. What did you mean? You're surely not suggesting a *fatal* accident?'

The elder priest raised his eyebrows as if I was a particularly dull-witted pupil who had, at last, with much prompting, managed to stumble upon the correct answer.

'But . . . but you're priests, you can't ask me to kill someone.'

It was the younger priest's turn to smile, but there was no humour in it. 'Have you at last found a conscience?'

'I may have parted some fools and their money, but only rich ones who could well afford to lose the trifle I took. I've never killed anyone, much less a woman. I admit I don't attend Mass as often as my mother would like, but the last time I was there I was sure that the priest mentioned something about murder being a mortal sin, or was I dreaming through that sermon too?'

'If you were to kill a Christian man or woman, it would indeed be a mortal sin,' the young man agreed. 'But this girl is no Christian. She is a Marrano, a Jew, a heretic. And Christ rejoices over the death of a heretic. Whoever cleanses Portugal of such an evil abomination is blessed in the sight of God and the Holy Church.'

'Then let the Holy Church do it,' I retorted. 'Hand her over to the Inquisition. I won't commit murder for anyone. I'd rather spend the rest of my life in jail than kill a girl who's never done me any harm. It may be hard for you to believe, but I do have some principles and I draw the line at murder, especially the murder of a woman.'

I hoped I sounded a lot braver than I felt, but just at that moment I was so outraged by what they were proposing, I couldn't even think about the consequences.

The elder of the two Jesuits looked inquiringly at whoever was standing in the shadows behind me. Then, with a slight nod, he strode back across to the stone steps with only the whisper of his robe to betray his movement. The younger priest did not move, but continued to watch me in silence, like a hound pointing at the quarry awaiting the arrival of the huntsman.

A few minutes later I heard the sound of two pairs of footsteps lumbering down the stairs and crossing the stone floor towards me. My stomach tightened. These were no priests. Had he sent for the guards to beat me into doing what they wanted, or worse?

But when the guards came into sight they were carrying a long wrapped bundle between them which they dropped with a dull, heavy thud on to the stone floor. The older Jesuit returned behind them and, with a wave of his hand, dismissed the guards, waiting until they had retreated back up the stairs before continuing.

'Cruz, understand that I am not a gullible old woman or a foolish young one. I cannot be seduced by your pretty tongue. I have been very well trained in rooting out lies. I can look into any man's eyes and read the truth there. But in your case, I don't have to. The proof is here. Yet another crime to add to your ever-lengthening list – the crime of murder.'

I stared at him. 'I haven't . . . I'll admit to the other things, but of murder I am innocent. I swear by all the saints in heaven. I have never killed anyone.'

The Jesuit's voice became even more measured; I could feel he was taking pleasure in this. This was a man who prided himself on using words, not violence, to eviscerate his victims.

'How easily one forgets one's sins. Though I am surprised you have forgotten this particular sin so rapidly, Cruz. After all, it was committed less than a month ago. Silvia, I think you called her. Your method was not very subtle, I admit. There are many men who possess a far greater skill in making a murder look like a natural death such that not even the most suspicious person would think to question it. But then at sea or in that benighted country to the North, who needs subtlety? What is required is certainty, and I am certain, Cruz, you are the man we need.'

'No, no, you've got it all wrong. I didn't kill Silvia. That idiot Filipe saw a drowned corpse and mistakenly thought it was her, but I'm telling you it wasn't Silvia, because she isn't dead. She's still alive. I never saw that woman before in my life and I certainly didn't kill her, any more than I killed Silvia.'

'But how can you swear you don't know this woman, Cruz? I haven't shown her to you yet.'

He gestured towards the younger Jesuit who, clamping a hand over his mouth and nose, knelt down and gingerly began to unpeel the cloth that covered the body.

'No, no,' I screamed. 'Don't unwrap it, I beg you. I've seen it once before. I can't stand it . . . I tell you it isn't Silvia. I swear I have no idea who she is.'

'Come now, Cruz,' the older priest murmured. 'It is only fair and just that we should show you of what you stand accused. In fact, I think we should leave her with you for as long as you manage to stay alive here, so that you may grieve properly and say prayers for her soul. I would hate to part two such devoted lovers. I think I will ask the guards to chain her corpse to the pillar facing you. You wouldn't want her to be swept away by the tide, would you? As the weeks pass and you watch her rot before your eyes, you can be comforted by the thought that soon you will look just as she does. And when the waves finally close over your head, you and your beautiful lover will once again be reunited in the cold embrace of death.'

The younger priest paused in his unwrapping. His eyes were closed and he was swaying and heaving, as if unable to make up his mind whether he was going to faint or vomit. In the end he scrambled madly to his feet and raced across the floor to the archways where he could lean out over the sea, gulping in the fresh air.

The older Jesuit remained unmoved. 'We will leave you alone now to gaze upon the face of your lover, but we will return before the next high tide to ask for your decision. Perhaps by then you will have realized just how much you might enjoy the benefits of a healthy sea voyage.'

He ripped the cloth from the corpse lying at my feet. I screwed my eyes shut, but as I stood there helpless, chained to the pillar, nothing, but nothing, could shield me from the stench of the rotting, maggot-filled corpse rolling up towards me.

Chapter Six

Henry II of England cast his falcon at a heron. The heron seemed to be on the point of escaping the falcon, when Henry swore aloud, 'By God's gorge, that heron shall not escape, even if God Himself wills it.'

No sooner were these words uttered than the heron rounded upon the falcon and, as if by a miracle, struck the falcon's head with its beak, killing the bird instantly. Thereupon the heron cast the dead falcon at the feet of his master King Henry, to prove to all those who witnessed it that God's will must always prevail even above that of a king, though it turns the natural order upside down, and causes the prey to become the hunter.

Belém

Isabela

Eyas – *a young hawk taken from its nest in the wild before it can fly and reared in captivity.*

'You'll all sleep here,' the ship's master said gruffly. We were standing in a low compartment beneath the forecastle in the bow of the ship. Two narrow openings in the wooden walls on either side showed tiny glimpses of water and of the quayside. The sun blazed down through the hatch above our heads, illuminating a space that contained little except for a line of small wooden chests and bulkheads hung with wooden and metal tools and coils of rope as thick as my arm. I glanced up at the square of blue sky above us and wondered how dark it would be in here if the hatch was shut. I swallowed the lump that rose up in my throat as I thought of my father sitting there in the damp, stinking darkness of that dungeon, unable to stand or even lie down. How long could a man live like that before sickness took hold of his body, or despair seized his mind?

The master continued, 'There's a chest apiece to stow your belongings in, and see that your bedding is rolled and hung on the sides at first light. Seamen need to get to their tackle and they don't want to be falling over your blankets, especially not in rough seas.'

A plump, middle-aged woman squawked in a mixture of alarm and disgust as she surveyed the bare boards, on which white lines marked out the sleeping space allotted for each passenger. 'But where are my husband and I to sleep? My husband is a wealthy and distinguished silk merchant, you know.'

'I told you,' the master said wearily. 'All passengers sleep here.' He glanced at me and then back to her, for we were the only women in the party of eight passengers. 'Some ladies like to hang a blanket in the corner to screen themselves when they're dressing.'

'A blanket!' the woman echoed, her voice shrill with disbelief. 'When we were on the pilgrimage last year the better class of passenger all had private cabins with locks on the doors and beds suspended on chains from the ceiling. The cabins were hardly bigger than my linen press at home, and the beds were far too hard and small, but they were at least proper beds. And I put up with all that discomfort and inconvenience without a single word of complaint, isn't that so, husband? For one expects to suffer on a pilgrimage. But this . . . this dog kennel isn't even fit for slaves to sleep in.'

'This, Senhora, is a cargo ship, not a pleasure trip,' the master said tersely. 'But my men would be glad to swap places with you if you don't fancy sleeping here. Perhaps you'd rather bed down with them in the hold among the grain and spices.'

'Now see here,' the small, stout merchant said, indignantly puffing out his chest. 'I won't have you talking that way to my wife.'

'Then you'd best disembark now while you still have a chance, for as master on this ship I talk to passengers and crew alike any way I please. All that matters to me is getting this ship safe to Iceland and back again and I'll not let any passenger endanger that.'

'Iceland?' the merchant said sharply. 'What business has a cargo ship to do with Iceland? You cannot trade there. They'll not permit traffic with any Portuguese merchants, not even with the English now. I'm reliably informed that any halfway decent harbours on that island that are able to accommodate a ship have been leased by the German merchants, mostly from Hamburg, and what remain are in Danish hands. I can assure you I have investigated the matter very thoroughly, for if trade were possible, I myself would be taking my business to that island.'

The master gave a twisted smile, displaying a mouthful of crooked, yellow teeth. 'And who says we're going to land any goods? There's no law against landing people, and if a few barrels should happen to fall over the side whilst we're helping the passengers off . . .' He winked. 'My lads are sharp enough at sea, but put them anywhere near land and they're as clumsy as ducks on ice.'

The merchant's wife positively trembled with outrage, her double chin wobbling like a chicken's wattle. 'The agent gave us to understand this was a lawful voyage. My husband is a respectable merchant. He has a reputation to uphold and I will not have his name linked to any nefarious dealings. I have no intention of sailing aboard a . . . a . . . *pirate* ship.'

'Pirates seize goods, Senhora, they don't land them, as you'll soon find out if we have the misfortune to encounter any. Besides, you're bound for England, what do you care where we go after that?' The master glared around at the rest of us.

'Now mark me well. You'll get two hot meals a day. When you hear the trumpet sound, make haste to the table and eat. When it sounds again, finished or not, you've to rise and make way for the captain and his officers. So you'd best eat quick, for the captain doesn't like to be kept waiting. If you want more food or drink, you'll have to use your own provisions, so I suggest you stock up well at any inhabited port we call at, for it is getting late in the season now, and we will more than likely run into the first of the autumn gales as we sail. And if we're forced to spend more weeks at sea than we reckoned on, then be sure of one thing, the captain will not allow his men's rations of food or water to be shared with passengers, for if the sailors become too weak to work, then we'll all perish.'

At these words the matron swayed alarmingly as if she was about to swoon, and some of the other passengers looked equally frightened. I also felt an icy shiver. It was not fear of running out of food but of time that frightened me. I could not afford to be delayed at sea, for with every day that passed the shadow of my father's death crept closer.

With final instructions not to distract the sailors when they were working, not to touch any rope, chain, pulley or windlass, in fact not to do anything at all except eat, sleep and stay out of the seamen's way, the master grunted that we'd best get what luggage we had brought with us safely stored aboard, for we would be sailing with the next tide.

As soon as he had climbed the steps and disappeared back up through the hatch to the deck, the merchant's wife immediately claimed a strip in the far back corner, which she deemed to be the most sheltered from draughts, and ordered her husband to stow the towering stack of her bundles and boxes into what seemed by comparison to be a pathetically inadequate ship's chest.

One of the male passengers bent towards me and whispered, 'She won't find that spot so cosy when all of the passengers are vomiting and gasping for air. Take my advice and sleep near one of the anchor holes. It'll be cold, but the air will be fresher.'

I was about to do as he suggested when the merchant's wife seized me by the arm. 'No, no, my dear, you must sleep next to me.' She lowered her voice. 'Sailors are little better than savages. The sight of a woman after weeks at sea drives them mad with lust. We must place ourselves as far as possible from the hatchway in case one of them should try to creep down in the night. I tell you, I'll not be able to shut my eyes all night for fear that they might try to molest me.

I begged my husband to allow me to bring my tiring maid, but he refused to pay her passage. Says it will be cheaper to hire new servants when we arrive. But how he expects me to manage without servants on the voyage, I'm sure I don't know.' She glared balefully at her husband who was anxiously examining some cargo tallies, oblivious to his wife's distress.

The young man who had spoken to me before squeezed past me again. 'Careful you don't find yourself pressed into service as her slave.' He smiled at me and his hand brushed mine so lightly that I could not be sure if he intended it or not.

A trumpet sounded, and the matron looked up eagerly. 'Food? Make haste, husband.'

She waded through the chaos of bundles and bedding towards the steps that led up through the hatch, elbowing the other passengers aside in her haste to be first to set her foot upon them. But when we followed her up the creaking steps, we found that the trumpet blast had not been sounded to summon us to a meal.

All the sailors were assembled on the deck and a priest stood up on the poop deck in the stern, the highest deck on the ship, a young altar boy at his side dangling a censer of burning incense from its chain in one hand and clutching a silver bowl with hyssop in the other. The sailors one by one removed their caps, and the priest began his blessing of the ship. He was mumbling away in Latin, his voice drowned by the clamour of the voices on the quayside. The boy swung the censer vigorously back and forth, but the incense smoke blew away before it could reach our nostrils. The priest dipped the hyssop twigs in the silver bowl and flung the drops of holy water over the ship, but they too were snatched by the salt breeze before they could touch the timbers.

The altar boy began to sing the hymn to the Virgin Mary in a clear sharp treble, *Salve Regina, Hail Queen of Heaven.* The ship's boys joined in and the men's deep voices plodded after them. Each of the weatherbeaten faces relaxed for a few moments into expressions of certainty and devotion.

I felt suddenly afraid. All my life I had known what I believed. Known that the Holy Virgin and her saints were watching over me, as my mother had always told me they were. I had looked up at that shrine in the corner of the kitchen and seen them smiling serenely down at me. When the thunder echoed round the valley so deafeningly that I was sure the great boulders in the mountains were rolling down to crush me, I would run to the shrine and pray with all the fervency of a nun, in the knowledge that the Virgin would protect me.

But whenever I was naughty as a child, I had guiltily avoided the unblinking stares of the statues, knowing that they had seen me steal a fingerful of honeycomb from the jar or watched me as I tried to hide the plate I had broken. I was always convinced they would tell my mother what I'd done. Yet even then, I had known beyond any doubt that when I lay down to sleep in my little cot, if I did not wake I would be carried by the angels up to heaven.

Now, for the first time in my life, I did not know where I would go when I died. If there was a storm and the ship foundered, would any saint bear me up in the waves, knowing what I was, who I was? Would the Virgin Mary Misericordia open wide her cloak and shelter me beneath it? The Holy Church and my own mother had declared the Marranos heretics, and Mary did not spread her cloak to comfort those who were to burn in hell. I was alone, cast out from all the protection that once had surrounded me. My own God had rejected me as a heretic. Yet if there was a God of the Marranos, I did not know him or where to find him.

The agent who had accepted my money and negotiated my passage had asked no questions of me save one – 'Are you an Old Christian?' I assured him I was. The lie came as easily to my lips as it had to my mother's. Indeed, like her,

I had for a moment found myself still believing it was true, until I remembered. He had insisted on hearing me recite the Creed and the *Ave* in Latin. But though I had known the words all my life, I suddenly began to stumble over them, as if my tongue was swelling up as I tried to say them. The agent seemed satisfied, however, and had held up his hand halfway through to stop me.

'That'll do for me,' he said. He winked. 'I have to check. They don't want those Marranos escaping, but I say, what if they do? Good riddance to them, we don't want their sort here. In fact I reckon we should get together the oldest and leakiest hulks we can find, pack the lot of them on to them and send them all off to the New World. And if the ships founder before they get there, who's to care, that's what I say. But no one listens to ordinary folk like us, do they?'

My blood instantly turned to iced water. I had been so afraid I would not be able to find a ship that it simply hadn't occurred to me that I might be arrested for trying to leave the country. Of course, I knew that the Marranos weren't permitted to leave Portugal. I had grown up knowing that, but then I had also grown up knowing that I wasn't a Marrano, so the decree had no meaning for me. As an Old Christian I was free to come and go as I pleased. But now suddenly I realized that I was one of those forbidden to leave.

The agent must have seen my stricken expression, for he reached across his table and grasped my hand unpleasantly tightly, his mouth twisted into a leer. 'Now, don't you be fretting, my darling. There's no danger of your ship sinking. Smartest and most seaworthy ship on the seas she is. You'll be sailing in luxury. Course, if you'd have gone to anyone else, it would have cost you three times as much, but I'm a friend of the captain, so he gives me special rates.'

Along the quayside a small group of black slaves shuffled past from one of the ships newly put into port. They were naked save for filthy loincloths, their feet weighed down by iron shackles, their necks chained together. A few stared wildly around, their bloodshot eyes darting from side to side in fear at the strange sights and sounds that assailed them on every side. But most gazed sightless at the ground, moving listlessly as if they were already dead. I winced as I remembered the heavy fetters biting into my father's limbs and neck. My guts felt as if they had been twisted into a knot so tight it would never be loosed.

I retreated to our sleeping chamber the moment the blessing was over and peered out of the anchor hole, holding my breath each time a soldier approached the gangplank. Once, when two soldiers paused to chat to the seaman on watch, I thought I would be sick with fear. Eventually they strolled away, but still I remained terrified that any moment they might discover who I was and drag me from the ship. When finally I watched sailors casting off the mooring ropes and I heard the gangplank rasping up over the side, I breathed easily for the first time in days.

We sailed on the evening tide and ate our supper – mutton and a pudding of bruised wheat – by the light of the swaying lanterns. The merchant's wife, who announced that she was to be addressed as 'Dona Flávia', complained that the mutton was tough, the pudding not sweetened enough, the wine watered, and the boat rolling so much she'd never be able to eat a bite, but such shortcomings did not prevent her from devouring every dish with such haste that I was sure she would be ill.

The other passengers seemed anxious to obtain as many fragments of information about one another as could be snatched between mouthfuls of food. I listened, but I didn't attempt to join in. Up to the time of my father's arrest, I had rarely spoken to anyone who was not a friend or neighbour of my parents. We seldom had visitors at home, and even if my father and I chanced to encounter servants and courtiers at the summer palace on our way to the mews, I was expected to do little more than curtsy, smile and listen without interrupting the conversation of my elders.

But with Dona Flávia presiding over the table, I didn't need to talk. She immediately informed us that she and her husband were travelling only as far as England, if, she added with disdain, 'this wretched hulk manages to get us that far'. There her husband was to do business with only the finest shops to which he planned to sell a large quantity of silks and other rare fabrics. She, meanwhile, would decide if there was anything at all worth buying for her daughter's trousseau, though she very much doubted that England would have anything half as fine as could be purchased in Lisbon. She proceeded to launch full-sail into a detailed description of her daughter's forthcoming lavish wedding, while her husband sat morosely tearing his bread to pieces and muttering to anyone who'd listen that he hoped the English shopkeepers were feeling generous since he'd have to sell three full warehouses of silk to pay for what his wife had planned.

Finally, he interrupted her and addressed himself to the elderly gentleman sitting next to a lumpish, baby-faced boy who, though he looked no more than twelve, was already twice the size of his tiny wizened father in girth, as if the boy had been feeding on his father like some great leech and had sucked all the juices from the old man. The lad, it seemed, was the youngest of the man's many children. The father was taking his son to France where he was to be enrolled as a student in Paris and would, his father anxiously assured us, become a scholar.

The lad didn't look very scholarly and, judging by his scowl, he didn't seem to want to be. But it appeared his father was in despair to know what to do with his son. He wasn't suited to the life of a craftsman, for several apprenticeships had been obtained for him and none had lasted more than a few weeks. So it was either the life of a scholar or the lad would be obliged to take holy orders and become a priest or monk. At which pronouncement the boy's scowl deepened, and he savagely kicked the bench on which he was seated.

Attention now turned to the three other men at the table. All three looked to be of a similar age, in their late twenties, but that didn't seem to make them friends, for they eyed one another warily, like strange dogs circling as if to test one another's willingness for a fight.

The one sitting next to me was a gaunt-looking man, with eyes as blue as the deep of the sea. His head was wrapped in a turban of black velvet cloth trimmed with a silver thread. It so completely enveloped his pate that I suspected underneath it he might be bald. He leaned across the rough wooden table to help himself to more of the mutton and the over-long sleeves of his doublet trailed in the juices on his plate.

Dona Flávia gestured imperiously at the cook, who was bending over the two great pots bubbling in the cookbox, half-hidden in a great cloud of smoke and steam.

'Where is the man who serves the food?' Dona Flávia asked in a voice that must have carried from stern to bow. 'He should be waiting on us. This poor gentleman's clothes are quite ruined.'

The cook gave no sign that he heard her.

'I fear we have to fend for ourselves, Dona Flávia,' the man said, dabbing ineffectually at his sleeve with a handker-chief. 'Like you I am, of course, used to a manservant, but I dare say we shall learn to make shift for ourselves.' He gave up trying to clean his sleeve and attacked the mutton again with almost as much gusto as Dona Flávia.

'It's not good enough, not good enough at all,' Dona Flávia grumbled, then, raising her voice so that any of the seamen could hear her, she said, 'Husband, I insist you com-plain to the agent who booked our passage, the moment we return. Tell him we did not expect to be treated like common peasants on this voyage. I'm sure you agree, Senhor . . . ?'

'Marcos,' the man helpfully supplied through a mouthful of food.

'And are you also a merchant, like my husband, Senhor Marcos?'

'Alas, no. I am but a humble physician.'

Dona Flávia beamed and clapped her hands with delight. 'How fortuitous! Did you hear that, husband? This gentleman is a renowned physician! I am a martyr to a sick stomach, as my husband will tell you. And to know I shall have you to call upon is a great weight off my mind.'

Marcos looked thoroughly alarmed. 'I am merely travelling to Iceland in search of new remedies that might be concocted from undiscovered herbs and lichens. I hadn't intended to treat . . . there must be a ship's surgeon on board. He will have much more experience than I in dealing with maladies at sea.'

But Dona Flávia waved a dismissive hand. 'I don't doubt he is perfectly able to provide crude remedies for these rough sailors, but a lady of my sensibilities needs the gentle touch of a learned man who understands complex cases such as my own. My husband will gladly pay any fee you command. We always buy the best of everything.'

The merchant winced. Then he patted his wife's arm. 'Now then, my dear, let's not tempt providence by speaking of illness. I'm sure you will remain perfectly well on this voyage, so there will be no need to trouble Senhor Marcos.'

And, as if desperate to divert his wife's attention from her illness, he said almost without drawing breath, 'I have heard, Senhor Marcos, that there are ancient bodies preserved in the mud in Iceland. They tell me all the skin and flesh remain intact, though every bone has mysteriously vanished from the corpse, but not a cut is to be seen on the skin. And such corpses when rendered down provide much more powerful medicine for every kind of ailment than even the dried mummies brought from Egypt. Although I understand they are so rarely found that even a king's ransom would not buy a whole corpse.'

Marcos offered that kind of faint, polite smile which people make when they have no idea of what is being discussed and fear to reply in case their remarks appear foolish. I wondered if he was actually listening, or was still cowering in fear from Dona Flávia's attention.

The merchant waited politely, but seeing Marcos was not inclined to add anything, he turned to the man sitting to Marcos's right. 'And you, Senhor, what is your profession?'

The man he addressed was the one who had so kindly advised me to sleep near an anchor hole. Now he smiled pleasantly, as if he had been waiting to be asked this question.

'Please call me Vítor, and I am by profession a maker of maps and a collector of curios.'

Dona Flávia's head swivelled round to face him, her pursuit of the physician quite forgotten.

'How thrilling! Do tell us, what curios are you searching for on this voyage?' she asked, apparently dismissing maps as quite unimportant.

Vítor paused to consider the matter for a moment. His gaze travelled towards me. For a long moment he seemed to be studying me, his eyes veiled by long, dark lashes that would be the envy of many a girl. He wore such an intense, hungry expression that I found myself blushing. Then, just as swiftly, he looked away and smiled again at the merchant's wife.

'There are two curiosities I long to possess, Dona Flávia – a sea monk and a sea bishop – both are to be found in the icy Northern waters. These creatures are described most admirably by Guilielmus Rondeletius in his book *Libri de Piscibus*

Marinis. The sea monk is a fish the size of a man with a human head like that of a tonsured monk, long scaly robes and two fins which resemble human arms. But its superior is the sea bishop, which has two legs, two hands and the head of a bishop complete with mitre and a covering upon its back resembling a cloak.'

The merchant's wife stared at him with a spoonful of pudding suspended halfway to her mouth. 'And have any such creatures been found?'

'Indeed they have, Dona Flávia. For Rondeletius has made fine drawings of them from his observations. And furthermore, a sea bishop was captured and taken as a gift to the king of Poland, though it did not remain in the palace for long, despite being shown every honour and courtesy due to a personage of the rank of bishop. The creature made it plain by signs that it disapproved of the impiety of the Court and wished to be returned to its life of contemplation beneath the waves, and so it was.'

Dona Flávia glanced out at the foaming black water, as if she expected to see the sea bishop floating towards us, praying.

'Are such creatures . . . dangerous?' the elderly man asked nervously, and even his son stopped kicking the bench.

Vítor looked uncomfortable, as if he suddenly regretted mentioning the fish at all. 'It's thought they are mostly harmless. They don't attack ships or eat those who fall into the sea, but they are inclined to a little – how can I put it? – mischief. I believe the sea monk has on occasion whipped up a violent storm, when it is displeased.'

Dona Flávia clutched at her chest. 'Then I absolutely forbid you to capture one, Senhor Vítor. Tell him, husband. Tell him he must not attempt such a thing. We have no wish to anger this monster.'

'My dear, have you forgotten, we are disembarking in England, and Senhor Vítor has explained these fishes are found in the cold seas to the North. We shall be safe on land long before the ship reaches the dwelling places of these creatures.'

But his wife seemed far from reassured and glared furiously at poor Vítor as if he was the cursed Jonah and should at once be thrown overboard to save the ship.

'And what of you, Senhor?' Dona Flávia said, pointedly turning her back on Vítor and addressing the last man at the table. 'I hope you are not intending to drown us all by recklessly antagonizing ferocious sea monsters.'

He pressed his hand to his heart and, half-rising from the bench, made a gracious bow, beaming first at Dona Flávia and then at me. 'Senhor Fausto, at your service, ladies.'

The man had a pinched, drawn look as if he had recently suffered an illness, but that only served to emphasize the fineness of his features.

'I assure you, gentle ladies, you need have no fear. I will not attempt to arouse the wrath of any dragons or monsters. Mine is a far more civilized quest and one of which I'm sure you will approve, for I am bound for Iceland to seek diamonds and gold to adorn the necks of lovely women like you.'

The merchant frowned. 'I didn't know such things were to be found there.'

'Ah, there speaks a man with knowledge of the world's wealth,' Fausto said. 'It is true that none have so far been discovered there, but few men have looked, for the natives of that isle care only for their sheep. But in a land where mountains spew forth fire and rivers run hot from the heart of the earth, who knows what treasures may be found? And if I find none, why then, I'll take the next ship on to the vast lands of Canada and try my luck there.'

The merchant snorted. 'Then you are a fool, Senhor. Have you not heard, some Frenchman by the name of Cartier went on an expedition to Canada and returned to France claiming he brought back a fortune? Seven barrels of silver he reckoned to have, eleven barrels of gold and a whole basket filled to overflowing with uncut diamonds and other precious gems. None of it was what he thought it was, and the only use there was for those stones was to fill in potholes in the road. He'd have got a better price if he'd fetched back eleven barrels of dog dung – at least he could have sold that to the tanners, isn't that right?' He nudged Vítor sitting next to him and laughed heartily.

But Fausto's smile did not waver, though his eyes were cold and hard as jade. He was not a man who could laugh at a joke made at his own expense.

'This Cartier clearly knows nothing about the diamond trade and is unable to distinguish a diamond in the rough from a common pebble. I, on the other hand, have learned my trade from the best.'

He leaned forward across the table. 'When I was travelling in India, I came across a merchant who had the biggest and most perfect diamonds for sale. I asked him where they came from, and for a long time he refused to tell me. Then one day this merchant was attacked by a band of thieves, who tried to strangle and rob him. I saw the attack and galloped in to assist him, fighting furiously until I had helped him beat them off.

'In his profound gratitude he offered to give me any diamond of my choice from his stock. But I asked instead to be taken to the source of these diamonds. At first he refused, but since he owed a debt of honour to me, he finally agreed to take me to the place, on condition that I allowed myself to be conveyed there and back blindfolded and hooded, so that I could not disclose the route to anyone.

'I allowed myself to be hooded and was led through the mountains on a mule. It was a terrifying journey since I could feel the steepness of the mountainside as the beast struggled up. I could hear the stones dislodged by the mules' feet crashing down hundreds of feet below, so I knew the track must be wild and dangerous, but I could do nothing except trust the man in front to lead me safely. Then finally the merchant called for us to stop and my blindfold to be removed. We were standing on the edge of a huge ravine, so deep that great trees below looked like tiny blades of grass, and clouds hung below the cliff edge. The merchant explained that once a mighty river had run through the ravine, carrying with it such a quantity of diamonds that now they lay on the dry bottom in great heaps.'

Dona Flávia's jaw had dropped open and she had even forgotten to eat. 'Even the peasants who live there must be as rich as emperors. Imagine such wealth,' she breathed in awe. 'It must be paradise.'

'Ah, but there is always a serpent in paradise, dear lady. The sides of this ravine are sheer rock, much of it overhanging such that no man may gain a foothold, and it is so deep that it would be impossible for anyone to be lowered down by a rope. Many have tried in vain to breach the defences of that ravine, as their skeletons bear witness.'

'Then forgive me, Senhor Fausto,' the old man said, 'but I thought you said this merchant took his diamonds from this place. How is such a thing possible, unless you are telling us the man could fly? Now, that would be a fine tale, Senhor.'

Everyone laughed at this, but Fausto simply smiled. 'In a manner of speaking, you are correct, Senhor, the merchant did use wings, but not his own. He commanded his servants to take from the panniers pieces of raw meat, sticky with blood, and throw them down into the ravine. Then he whistled. Almost at once, four or five eagles appeared and flew down into the ravine to snatch up the gory feast. The birds were trained to carry the meat up to the cliff top where the servants would take it from them. And there, sticking to the meat, were the diamonds. When the men had gathered sufficient diamonds they rewarded the eagles with their supper.

'I saw this done with my own eyes and I was determined that I would return alone and try the same trick myself, but as I said, I had been blindfolded and when I did return I could not find my way back to that ravine again. I searched for many weeks, till I was half-dead from exhaustion, but in those mountains I could have searched for a hundred years and not found it. But I assure you, Senhor, unlike this Frenchman, Cartier, I will know the real diamonds when I find them.'

'The merchant had trained these wild eagles himself? But how did he man them?' The words were out of my mouth before I could stop them.

'The people of India are much skilled in the art of falconry. But your words tell me you know something of falconry yourself. Are you interested in the art, Meniña? Which hawk do you favour?'

I could have slapped myself for my stupidity. How could I have given myself away so carelessly and the voyage only just begun?

'I'm afraid I know nothing about hawks,' I said hastily. 'I was just fascinated by your story. I've never heard of such a wondrous thing before.'

'I agree, my dear,' the merchant said. 'I too have never heard such an *incredible* tale. But you must be careful not to believe everything travellers tell you. Young girls inexperienced in the ways of the world may easily be dazzled by fine words.'

Fausto glared furiously at him and half-rose as if he meant to be revenged for such an insult, but however he intended to retaliate, he was forestalled by Dona Flávia who suddenly seemed to remember that she knew nothing about me.

'And what brings you aboard this ship, my dear? You are very young to be travelling alone. Have you no parents or kin? Is there no chaperone with you? Was Senhor Fausto correct to address you as Meniña? Are you unmarried?'

'Yes . . . no, I mean, I am married.' If my face was as red as it felt, I was sure I was lighting up half the ship like the flames in the cookbox.

'And your husband is allowing you to make a long sea journey alone?' Dona Flávia looked scandalized. 'Whatever –'

But at that moment the trumpet sounded again and two bare-footed boys came scampering across the deck as if they had been waiting for the signal. They began to gather up the wooden bowls and plates with such haste that some of the passengers were left holding their spoons suspended in mid-air as the bowls they were eating from were whisked off the table.

The cook, having ignored us up to now, strode up to the table, wiping his greasy hands down the front of his breeches. 'Come along, let's be having you. Lads have to lay up the table for the captain. Shift your arses. The lads are scrawny but they're not ghosts, they can't work through you.'

'This is an outrage,' Dona Flávia spluttered, attempting to wrest her bowl back from the hands of one lad who was equally determined to keep hold of it. 'We haven't finished eating yet.'

'Then you'll know to eat faster next time, won't you?' said the cook with complete indifference. 'There'll be plenty of time for you to gab on this voyage. Nothing else for you to do, is there? So what you want to remember is mealtimes is for eating and the rest of the time for talking. You'll soon get the hang of it.'

One of the young lads sniggered, and the cook cuffed him across the back of his head, causing him to lose his grip on the dish he was attempting to wrest from Dona Flávia. The dish jerked upwards and the remains of the wheat pudding, her third helping, landed with a wet plop on her neck. For a moment no one seemed able to do anything except stare as the mess slowly began to ooze down into her ample cleavage.

Then Dona Flávia gave an ear-piercing shriek. The boy fled and the cook reached out his hand as if he was going to attempt to grab the mess before it disappeared down inside her gown. This only seemed to alarm the poor woman more, and clutching her dress to her as if she feared he was going to rip it off, she fled, howling, to the passengers' quarters as fast as her bulk would allow, pursued by gales of laughter from those seamen who had witnessed her misfortune.

The cook wiped his perspiring face with his sleeve. 'Senhor, your wife . . .' He seemed to be struggling to control his face. 'Rest assured I will thrash that boy till his back's as black as a tar barrel. Not that it will do the slightest good. Captain bought young Hinrik there from his father in Iceland when he was seven, that was nigh on five years ago, but you'd think he only came aboard yesterday, he's that clumsy. No amount of beating him seems to knock any sense into the lad. Reckon his father didn't sell him 'cause he needed the money, but just to get shot of the useless blockhead.'

'I would not have the lad beaten,' the merchant said. 'On this occasion he was not entirely to blame. But I believe it would be wise to allow my dear wife a little privacy just now . . . so that she can change her gown, you understand.'

He glanced anxiously towards the passengers' quarters. He evidently wanted to avoid returning there for as long as possible. I didn't blame him and I certainly had no intention of going back there either, at least until Dona Flávia was safely asleep.

Fausto and Marcos were engrossed in discovering which seaman had the best wine for sale on board, and the merchant and Vítor had wandered over to join a small group of sailors who were sitting on coils of rope eating their meals and listening to a young lad singing about the women left behind in every port.

I found a dark corner in the stern of the boat and stood there, watching the lights of the ship's lanterns trailing across the black water. The flames separated into a thousand tiny reflections as if a shoal of bright yellow fish was following the ship. The waves foamed white in the darkness and the wind, though still warm, tugged at my clothes. Closer inshore tiny fishing boats dipped up and down on the waves, and occasionally the outline of a man would appear, stripped to the waist and silhouetted against the boat's lanterns, as he pulled in his nets. Yellow and red lights dotted the distant shoreline, like jewels on a black velvet gown. And above them, a great arc of white stars hung in the sky. For a moment, staring up at them, I could feel blessedly alone.

But a raucous gale of laughter from the sailors quickly reminded me I was very far from alone. I was trapped with a score of others, any one of whom might discover who I really was and inform the captain he had a heretic on board. I had seen the way those seamen blessed their ship. Sailing with a heretic on board would, in their eyes, be worse than if someone had hidden a curse-doll on the ship. I had to think of a plausible story to protect myself. Dona Flávia would not be diverted for long and, as the cook had reminded me, we would be many weeks aboard this ship, and what else would there be to do but talk? I couldn't hide from her for ever.

The ship juddered as a large wave rammed it and the huge square sails snapped as a sudden gust of wind filled them, making it leap forward like a startled horse. I shivered in the wind. Then I felt something heavy envelop me. Vítor was standing behind me. He had swung his short cloak from his shoulders and wrapped it about mine.

'I hope you have some warmer clothes for when we get further north, else you'll freeze.'

In truth I hadn't even considered that. I had brought a few clothes from my closet at home which I wore through the chilly days of winter on the hilltop of Sintra. Would it be colder than that? Would I be able to buy warm clothes there? I gnawed at my lip, thinking of how much I had paid for the voyage, and I had yet to find a ship to bring me home. I dared not spend too much on other things.

Vítor put his head on one side. 'Trying to avoid Dona Flávia?'

'No, of course not,' I said too quickly, then, seeing the exaggerated rise of his eyebrows, I smiled. 'Are you avoiding her too? Afraid she might lecture you again about the folly of provoking sea monsters?'

He laughed. His breath was sweet, but not from wine. 'I shouldn't have mentioned that. Though I don't think Senhora Flávia has anything to fear from sea monsters, it is they who would take fright at the sight of her.'

'Are you really intending to capture such beasts?'

'Capture, perhaps not. If I brought such a fish aboard this ship, bishop or not, the cook would soon have it broiling on his fire.'

'Then why are you travelling to Iceland?'

His smile vanished abruptly. 'Must a man have only one reason for going on a journey? I might ask you the same, Senhora, or is it really Meniña?'

'I am married,' I snapped with the kind of indignation that flares up when a lie is questioned. 'My husband's in Iceland. He promised he would send for me when he was settled and now he is.' I was glad that it was too dark for him to see my face.

'A Portuguese settled in Iceland. That is unusual – a Catholic in a Protestant land.'

'He's a Dane. I . . . met him when he came here to trade. We fell in love.'

'So you are married to a Protestant. Is that why you travel alone? Have your family disowned you?'

I nodded. That much at least did not feel like a lie. My mother and I had parted on the worst of terms. She was going to stay with her sister, and I knew they would take her in. But when I told her where I was going, my mother had torn open the bodice of her dress telling me to cut out her heart and eat it in front of her. Why not, she said, that was what I was already doing to her – ripping out her heart. For an only child, a daughter no less, to abandon her mother at a time like this, was a crime more wicked than murder.

As I stood there on the rolling deck, her face swam before me again, white and pinched, her eyes wet with tears, but not softened by them, her voice as harsh as a seagull's screaming at me that we were not Marranos. How could I even suggest such a thing? It was all a lie, a wicked lie, and how could I be so cruel as to taunt her with this, hadn't she already suffered enough by losing her husband? She spoke as if he had already been taken by the angel of death, as if she was now a grieving widow. Maybe that is what she would tell her sister – that her husband was dead. And she would say it as if it was the truth, for in her head, like so much else in her life, she had already convinced herself it was.

I was so preoccupied with my mother's words that I didn't realize that Vítor was still talking.

'. . . when we reach Iceland. But in the meantime, Isabela, allow me to offer myself as your protector, if only from the dragon, Dona Flávia.'

I didn't register what he had said at first, the name was slipped in so smoothly among the words.

'It is Isabela, isn't it?' he asked softly. 'A beautiful name for a beautiful woman and one you can be sure I will remember.'

Iceland

Eydis

Pelt – *the dead body of the hawk's prey or quarry.*

I keep the man alive because I have to do it. Like Ari, I ask myself a thousand times a day if I should let him die and I know beyond any doubt that I should. But I also realize now that he will not simply cease to live, for in truth I am doing little to keep him alive. I have bound his wounds and covered them in herb poultices so that they do not fester. Five times a day I wash his mouth with water and put honey beneath his tongue. But these ministrations are not enough to help him recover. He is injured in ways I can never heal. Any other man would have died within hours of being brought to the cave, but he lives. Not waking, not stirring, but still he lives.

Jónas carries little Frída into the cave in a sack tipped over his shoulder, with only her head visible and not much of that, for her face is wrapped tightly around with a shawl. Frída is nearly seven years old and lives up to the name that we revealed to her mother, for she is both *beautiful* and *fair*. Her mother gave birth to her in this cave and Valdis and I brought the child into the world and bit through the cord to loose her from the womb.

'Is the child sick, Jónas?'

He does not answer, but lays her tenderly on the floor. She begins writhing like a maggot, trying to free herself from the sack, and her eyes are blazing with fury.

Jónas glances over at the man lying motionless in the corner.

'He still lives then,' he says without curiosity. 'I heard what happened.' He spits to show his disgust. 'He was a fool to come inland. A shark-sucker does not leave the shark, why should a sailor leave the shore?'

'Why have you bound your daughter?' I ask, not wanting to talk about the man.

Jónas grunts and turns his attention back to his thrashing daughter. 'She tried to throw herself into a boiling mud pool.'

'But she's a sensible child, old enough to know that the pools are so hot they would kill her instantly.'

'She knows. We've taught her since she could crawl that it is dangerous even to walk on the ground around the boiling mud pools in case the crust of the earth gives way. But she ran at the pool and tried to jump in. Her playmates caught her and dragged her away, but she fought them and kept trying to reach the scalding mud again. In the end three of them had to sit on her to hold her down while one of them came running for me.'

It is not unknown for men and women to throw themselves into these pools of boiling mud, when a great melancholy comes upon them. I have heard of women killing themselves in this way in grief over a lost lover or a dead child, but for one so young to be in such despair . . . Whatever could have brought about this change in her?

'Loosen the shawl. Let me speak to her.'

Jónas fumbles with the knot and pulls the shawl from her face.

The moment her face is uncovered, Frída screams that it hurts and then she utters such obscenities that I never thought to hear fall from a child's lips. Her father makes to cover her mouth again, but I stop him.

'Where does it hurt, Frída? Tell me where you feel the pain.'

But she stares at me, her eyes wild. 'The whales are singing on the land. The birds are flying in the water. And flowers, I saw flowers in the snow.'

She thrashes her head violently from side to side, her pale hair flailing about her face. It is only now that I notice the thick black line down the side of her face, but the mark is not swollen. I have seen enough bruises on the man in recent days to know that this mark was not caused by a blow or a fall.

Jónas hastily ties the thick shawl about his daughter's head and face again, plainly worried that she will dash her brains out on the rocks. 'You see how she is? Her mother and I can do nothing to bring her to her senses.'

'That mark on her face. How did she come by it?'

'In the same hour that she lost her wits,' Jónas says sadly. 'Her mother thought it was soot and tried to wash it off, but it will not budge.'

'You said that she was playing when the madness came upon her. Did her friends tell you what happened?'

Jónas frowns. 'They did, but what they say makes no sense. They were scattered about the pasture, throwing a ball one to another, when one of the children said she heard a hissing in the air. She looked up to see a cloud, a small black cloud, approaching them. It was so low and coming towards them with such speed that at first she thought it must be a big black bird of some kind. It seemed to her that this cloud brushed past Frída's face and at once my daughter fell to the ground, screaming and holding her head. As they clustered round her trying to find out what ailed her, she leapt up and ran towards the mud pools, screaming and babbling so wildly, they had to run after her to grab her.'

'Your neighbour has done this. A Sending has been conjured to harm the child.' The voice which suddenly booms out in the cave might have been my own and yet I did not speak. There is a harshness to it which I do not recognize.

Jónas turns to look at my veiled sister. 'My neighbour?' he asks, as if he expects her to answer him, and I cannot understand why, until I remember he does not know she is dead.

'Is there anyone who has a grudge against you?' the voice says.

I stare at the body of the man lying in the corner of the cave, even though I know it is my sister's voice I can hear. But he remains motionless, his eyes closed, his lips cracked and still.

'Pétur, it has to be that bastard Pétur,' Jónas says vehemently. 'I sold him a stallion to cover his mares, but he said the beast died. Claimed it was sick when I sold it to him. He's come to my farm several times demanding the return of the money, but I wouldn't give it to him. It's been more than three months since I sold him the stallion. If the horse had been sick when I sold it to him it would have died long before this, but he wouldn't listen to reason. Now he's taken his revenge on my poor innocent daughter. What can I do to help her?' Jónas is still addressing my sister as if he expects her to answer him.

'If you do exactly what I say, the child's wits shall return,' she says.

My hands are trembling. I slowly turn my head towards Valdis's body, not wanting to look but knowing I must. There beneath the flimsy cloth of her veil, I can see her lips moving.

'Go to the graveyard,' she says, 'and open a grave of one newly buried. Take from it the coin that is placed on the man's tongue. Carry the coin to Pétur's farm and there hide it in the bed of the stream at the place where his mares come to drink. But make sure you do this during the daylight hours. At night, the ghost of the corpse will follow his coin to the farm to take back what has been stolen from him, but ghosts cannot enter running water, so he will not be able to retrieve the coin. In his frustration, he will take his vengeance out on the nearest living creatures, Pétur's mares, and kill them. Then the child's wits shall be restored.'

Jónas shudders. 'The wretch deserves to lose his mares and more besides after what he's done to my beautiful daughter, but I would sooner kill his horses with my own hand than rob the dead.'

'Dark magic harmed your child, only vengeance from the spirit world can undo the curse. It must be done as I have told you,' Valdis tells him.

I am so horrified at hearing the voice come from my dead sister's lips that I have barely taken in what is being said, but the words finally penetrate through the veil of fear and revulsion in my head. I know what she is telling him to do is wrong, terribly wrong.

'No! No, that is not what ails the child.'

Jónas turns to me, puzzled, as well he might be, for my sister and I have always before uttered the same thought.

'The cloud was not a Sending. There was no malice in it, no life in it, no spirit.'

'Just look at the child,' Valdis jeers. 'How can you say there is no malice in this?'

'The child is sick, but I sense that no human hand lies behind this. The cloud came from the mountain, not from your neighbour Pétur. Frída will –'

But Jónas interrupts me. 'Your sister Valdis is right, whoever heard of a cloud moving so fast and why did it make straight for my daughter? Her friend said it was as if an arrow had been fired at her.'

He scoops the child up and slings her again over his shoulder, his face grim with resolve.

'What Valdis says about the Sending is the only explanation that makes sense. I'll do as she says. I'll take a dead man's coin to Pétur's farm. Even if I have to dig up a hundred corpses before I find such a coin, I will do it to cure my child. What father wouldn't be prepared to risk the wrath of a thousand ghosts if it was the only way to save his daughter?'

'No, please listen, Jónas,' I beg, but he strides away, determined not to hear me.

As soon as I hear him scrambling out of the crack in the rock above, I steel myself, then slowly pull the veil from my sister's face. Beneath the cloth, her skin is yellowed like old parchment, the features wizened and sunken as if every drop of moisture has been sucked from her body by the heat of the cave. Her lips have shrunk back from her teeth. Her arms swing limp, the fingernails blackened, the skin cold as the grave.

But though I closed her eyes tenderly when she died, now suddenly they are wide open and looking straight at me. But it is not my sister's soft blue eyes that stare up at me. I have known and loved her eyes all my life. I could not mistake them now. The blue is gone, the whites of the eyes have vanished, only two huge black pupils remain like great gaping holes. I am staring into twin open graves. I gasp in horror and the eyelids slowly blink.

Chapter Seven

A French nobleman was suspicious that his wife had a lover. So he locked her up in a high tower, with only a narrow window at the top and walls no man could scale. Then he set his sister to keep watch on the tower whenever he was absent from it. But when the nobleman left the tower each day to go hunting, the woman's lover transformed himself into a goshawk and flew in through the narrow window. There he turned into a man again and made love to the woman, before flying away. And so they continued for many months, blissfully happy in each other's arms.

But the woman's sister-in-law noticed the goshawk flying in and out of the tower. One day she followed the bird, and when he alighted on the ground, she watched him resume his human form. She told her brother, who fitted sharp spikes to the window, then pretended to go hunting. The lover, believing it was safe to visit the woman, transformed himself into the hawk and flew in through the window, and impaled himself on the spikes. The wounds were fatal and he died in his lover's arms. But his beloved was already pregnant with his son and that infant grew up to become a great hero of France.

Coast of France
Ricardo

Ruff – *when the falcon strikes its prey without seizing it.*

'The men will row you ashore now,' the ship's master said. 'Take your water kegs. There's a stream and my quartermaster says the water is sweet. You can fill them before we return.'

'Why are we disembarking here?' the merchant demanded. 'The bay's deserted. There's no town. Not even a house to be seen for miles. We must continue to a well-appointed harbour where –'

'Where we can sleep in a decent bed on land and eat a meal that's fit for civilized people,' his wife finished for him. 'Why should we set one toe on this desolate beach? How do we know you won't just sail off and leave us there to starve? I've heard about such things – passengers being abandoned on some remote island to die, or sold to marauding pirates.'

'You'd have to pay pirates to take that harridan,' I muttered to one of the sailors waiting to help us to climb down into the shore boat.

He grinned, showing a mouthful of stubby, blackened teeth. 'They wouldn't take her if you gave them all the gold in the New World. A night with her and they'd be begging the judges to hang them.'

'Senhora,' the master said, in the tone of one who was barely restraining himself from throwing her overboard, 'the ship will not abandon you because she will not be sailing tonight. Have you not seen?' He gestured towards the towering clouds rising up over the distant headland. 'There's a storm coming. We know this coastline well. The nearest inhabited port is miles away, and with this wind against us, we haven't a hope of reaching it before the storm breaks. If we attempt to sail any further we'll be sailing straight into the storm and we'll be caught out at sea when the full force of it hits us. This bay at least offers us some protection, though we'll still take a beating.'

'And you expect a fragile, delicate woman like my wife to spend the night on the beach in a storm?' the merchant said, his expression as black as the gathering clouds.

The sailors sniggered. Dona Flávia was about as delicate as a whale.

The master spat copiously into the waves below. 'She can stay aboard, if she's a mind to, as can any of you, but I warn you now, you'd best make sure that you are lashed down as tight as the boxes and barrels, for once the ship starts being pounded, you'll be thrown around so much you're liable to get your brains dashed out on the bulkheads. And I hope you've a strong stomach, for if you've felt seasick before now, I can assure you that you'll all be praying to drown once this ship starts plunging up and down.'

Dona Flávia shrieked and clutched frantically at Isabela's arm as if it was a holy relic. 'But if the storm is going to be so terrible, we'll all be swept away by the sea if we spend the night on the beach. We'll all drown!'

The master closed his eyes as if he was praying. 'Then I suggest, Senhora, you *don't* spend the night on the beach. The boatswain tells me there is a stone cottage among the trees beyond the beach. It's not inhabited, but it will shelter you for tonight. Now, unless you want to ride out the storm on the ship, get into that shore boat before the wind grows any stronger else you'll all end up at the bottom of the bay.'

I don't know who invented the rope ladder, but whoever it was should have been made to dangle from it over a pit of vipers while men swung it violently to and fro, because that's exactly what it felt as if I was being forced to do, as I clambered down from the ship's towering side into the pathetically small shore boat below. The boat was not only bucking up and down, but also crashing into the side of the ship and then rolling away, leaving a great yawning gap of churning water just at the precise moment when you were trying to step into it.

I finally managed to hurl myself into the little craft, but not without banging my shin hard on the gunwale. I hunched in the boat, massaging my leg, as the wind dashed icy water into my face, and long before the next passenger had climbed down I was already soaked to the skin. I closed my eyes against the stinging salt, and the bloated, rotting face of that drowned woman rose up in front of me. Once again I was back in the tower of Belém, feeling the cold waves creeping up my legs. I opened my eyes rapidly.

Most of the passengers had climbed down into the boat now except the girl Isabela, and the merchant and his wife. Isabela already had her little foot on the ladder. I stood up, ready to help catch her as she descended. I hadn't planned it, but it came to me as suddenly as the image of the drowned woman, that I could cause that accident now. One little push as she stepped down on to the gunwale of the boat and she would slip over the side, between the boat and the ship. With luck, she'd hit her head as the two vessels clashed together, and would sink like a lead coffin. The scene played out perfectly in my head as if it was already happening.

The girl stood on the bottom rung, both arms clinging to the ladder, gazing fearfully down as the boat was dragged back from the ship. As the sailors hauled on the ropes, trying to pull the boat closer to the ladder again, she raised her foot in readiness. I reached up to clasp her waist, but at that moment a wave lifted the boat, and I overbalanced. I found myself slipping over the side. I flailed desperately, but could find nothing to grab on to. Then I felt a strong hand seize the back of my doublet and haul me into the boat again, where I sat trembling with shock.

'Do you want to get yourself killed, Senhor?' the boatswain shouted. 'Sit down and leave it to us. You nearly pulled the girl into the sea along with you.'

He put his brawny arm about Isabela's waist and lifted her bodily into the boat, seating her firmly on the plank in front of me.

She took a few gulps of air to steady herself, then smiled trustingly at me. 'Thank you for trying to help me, Senhor. It was very kind, but you shouldn't take such risks for me.'

I tried to return the smile, hoping that she would not notice how my hands shook. But Isabela was already distracted by Dona Flávia's shrieking descent. Her husband had insisted that a rope be fastened under his wife's armpits, in case she should slip, though it would need the anchor windlass to winch her up again if she did.

Dona Flávia thrashed wildly around with her foot trying to find the next rung. She looked like a cow attempting to dance. Isabela's face was a picture of concern, though she was biting her lip as if she was trying to suppress her laughter, while the sailors and other passengers made no effort to conceal their grins.

Isabela was a pretty little thing. Her skin was a rich sweet caramel, lighter than my Silvia's nut-brown body, but at least it wasn't as pale as those insipid skins of the noblemen's daughters who are constantly shielded from the sun and who are so colourless they remind me of fat white grubs dug up from the earth.

Isabela's eyes were a greenish-blue and couldn't seem to make up their mind which shade to be. Her hair, though dark and curly, was not the great silky mane that Silvia possessed, but the kind that tends to frizz up at the first sign of dampness. Her breasts weren't Silvia's either. I grant you that

I hadn't had the opportunity to examine them in any detail, but they swelled over the top of her gown perkily enough, though they were as small as half lemons in comparison to Silvia's luscious ripe fruits. In short, she was not wildly beautiful or voluptuous, but she possessed the kind of sudden radiant smile that would entice any man to her side.

And had things been different I would probably have amused myself by seducing her. I might have found my task easier to accomplish if I had. But the moment I set eyes on Isabela I discovered that knowing you are going to murder a girl cools any lust you might feel as rapidly as water thrown over an amorous dog. The thought of killing a woman might excite some men, but not me, not if I was going to have to murder her in cold blood. It's different, of course, if you don't know that a woman will one day die at your hands, then you can enjoy her to the full. But if there was one thing I was certain of on this voyage it was that Isabela had to die and I was the one who would have to ensure that she did.

I'm sure I don't need to tell you what answer I gave to the two Jesuits when they returned to the tower of Belém. It wasn't the promise of the wealth they offered me. Naturally, if it had been a simple matter of theft or deception, I wouldn't have hesitated to take their money, except, of course, to try to bargain my fee up. But murder, that's an entirely different matter.

But it was the sight of that corpse which persuaded me to agree, knowing that after weeks of torment, one day the tide would rise and keep rising until it was over my head and then I would become that foul abomination lying on the paving slabs. You think I was a coward? Well, you just imagine descending into a crypt, gagging on the foul stench of maggots and decay, then lifting a coffin lid and seeing your own rotting face in that coffin staring sightlessly up at you. Picture that if you can, then tell me honestly, if you'd been offered a way out of that accursed tower, would you have chosen instead to hang there in chains, unable to move as the cold waves broke over you, and wait day after day for that fatal tide? Would you have chosen to stay and watch that body rot before your eyes? Would you?

The Jesuits had seen to it that I was bathed and given such clothes, bedding and money that I would need for the voyage. They had ensured not only that Isabela found a suitable ship, but also that I obtained a passage on the same one. The agent had been bribed with a generous purse not to demand papers or inquire too closely into the identity of his clients. The priests had done all they could to make things easy for me, as they said. What happened after that was in my hands. But the question was – how to do it? And I had no more ideas about that now than I'd had when I first boarded the ship.

Isabela must have felt me studying her for she suddenly turned and bestowed another of her smiles in my direction. 'Poor Dona Flávia. I do believe she will kiss the ground when we reach England.'

And so would I. At least with her and her husband gone from the ship, I might be able to get Isabela alone. Every time I had tried, particularly after dark, Dona Flávia descended like a huge blubbery angel determined to defend the girl's honour. She seemed to regard safeguarding Isabela's virtue as her personal mission, though of course she made use of the girl as if she was her own daughter, sending her to fetch things from the sleeping quarters or massage oil of lavender into her temples when she declared herself unable to sleep.

But even if I could get the girl away from Dona Flávia I couldn't just walk up behind her and pitch her overboard. There were always too many eyes on watch and though I had made a friend of one of the sailors by buying wine from him, paying double what the dog piss was worth, I was pretty sure even he would raise the alarm if I tried to throw someone into the sea. It had to be made to look like an accident.

Even when pig-boy and his father, and Dona Flávia and her husband had all left the ship, there would still be two other passengers who were travelling on to Iceland and those two men seemed equally determined to make friends with Isabela. Hardly surprising since she was the only girl aboard. But it was going to be hard to prise their attentions away from her.

The boat rocked alarmingly as Dona Flávia finally plopped down into it, gasping and wailing that she would never, *never* set foot on that rope ladder again. When her husband mildly pointed out that she would have to climb up it again tomorrow as there was no other way back on board the ship, she declared she would rather stay on the shore and live in the stone cottage for the rest of her life. The sailors smirked at one another and cast off.

By the time we reached the shore, though, no one was smiling or even had the energy to talk. With our rolls of bedding slung over our shoulders and little water kegs tucked under our arms, we staggered over the sand behind the boatswain, who carried a stout barrel hoisted on one shoulder, which I devoutly prayed was full of wine.

My clothes were sodden and the roll of blankets felt no drier. So much water had washed into the boat that my shoes had filled up and my numb toes were splashing about in their own private pools. The wind buffeted us so fiercely that it was hard for any of us to walk in a straight line. The blown sand savagely stung our skin and we were reduced to peering through our fingers to stop ourselves being blinded.

We floundered over a steep dune, our feet sinking in the loose sand, and saw, stretched out in front of us, an area of dry scrub and gorse which seemed to be growing right out of the sand. Behind that a dense forest rose up all around, obscuring any view of what lay beyond. The towering trees were already swaying and bending in the strengthening wind.

'There you are.' The boatswain nodded to a low stone

building half-hidden among the bushes. 'Nice little nest for the night.'

Dona Flávia gave a squawk that put me in mind of an affronted hen. 'The captain cannot mean us to sleep in there. Have you brought us to the right place, my man? There must be a house somewhere, this is just a byre.'

She peered earnestly around the scrubland as if there might be a commodious mansion or castle in the vicinity which we had somehow failed to notice.

'This is it,' the boatswain said, with the cheerfulness of one who thinks watching other men being tortured is the height of entertainment. 'Course, if you don't fancy spending the night here, you can always come back with me and climb that rope ladder again.'

He flung open what was left of the wooden door and dumped the barrel inside before emerging. 'Stream cuts through the dunes over there. So you'll not want for water. If the storm passes, captain'll want to set sail first light, that's if there's no repairs to make. If it hasn't blown over we'll maybe be stuck here for a day or two, more even, so you'd best ration the food in case. But don't go wandering off too far. When the captain's ready to sail he'll have the trumpet sounded and the shore boat'll come back to take you off the beach. So make sure you stay within sound of the ship. He's not a patient man, isn't the captain. And he'll not waste precious sailing time searching for any man or woman that doesn't come back to the beach when the trumpet's blown.'

Suddenly, this wild, empty corner of the world didn't seem so bad. Maybe I wouldn't need to kill the girl, after all. All I had to do was to ensure she didn't get back on that ship. If she was left behind it would be up to her whether she survived or not. There was bound to be a town or village somewhere beyond the forest. If it took her two or three days to walk there, so much the better, there'd be no chance of her catching up with the ship or finding another. When

I returned without her, I could tell the priests she was dead and there'd be nothing to prove she wasn't. She'd never show up in Portugal again, not if she had any sense. Who in their right mind would walk back into the wolf's lair, after they'd escaped? But if she perished from starvation here, then it wouldn't be my fault. I'd have given her the chance to live. My conscience would be clear.

Coast of France
Isabela

*Wake – when a falconer sits up all night with a newly trapped
falcon in order to tame her by keeping her awake.*

We all crowded into the tiny one-roomed cottage, if indeed
that was what this place had once been. But it must have
been many years since anyone had called it home. Only the
rotting remains of a table crouching in the corner and a
faded red crucifix painted crudely above the door showed
that humans had ever inhabited this place. The floor was
covered in sand that had blown into small drifts against the
far wall. The timber tiles on the roof were cracked, and the
shutter had long since fallen from the only window. But its
thick stone walls still provided some shelter, or at least a flock
of goats had evidently thought so, for the floor was littered
with their droppings and strands of their hair were caught on
the stones of the wall.

For a few minutes no one in the party seemed to know
what to do. We just stood there, clutching our bundles, staring around as if we expected an innkeeper to come bustling
in and show us to our rooms.

Vítor set his bundle down against the wall. He glanced at
me, then looked round at the other passengers.

'We should quickly gather as much dry kindling and firewood as we can, enough to last for several days, and stack it
in here before the storm breaks. We must separate and hunt

for whatever we can find, especially thick branches of dried wood which will burn the longest.'

'I hope, Senhor Vítor, you are not expecting me to go out gathering wood. I'm not a peasant,' Dona Flávia said indignantly.

'Naturally I did not mean you, Dona Flávia. I thought you might stay here and perhaps collect up the goat dung to clear the floor. The pellets seem dry and will burn –'

'Me! Gather goat dung!' Dona Flávia's indignant shriek must surely have been heard back aboard the ship. 'I've never heard anything so preposterous in my life, but what can you expect from a man who thinks it sport to see us all devoured by ferocious sea monsters?'

'I assure you sea monks don't devour –' Vítor began, but was cut short by Marcos.

'Dona Flávia, as a physician I would strongly advise that after your terrible ordeal getting here, you should not exert yourself at all, but simply rest as best you can in here.'

Dona Flávia beamed at him. 'What a blessing it is to have someone who understands my frail constitution. Senhor Marcos, I insist you stay with me in case I should become faint. Besides, suppose pirates or Frenchmen should burst in upon me when I am alone. I've heard about the French, Senhor. Their men have an insatiable appetite for women.'

But I don't think it was fear of Frenchmen or pirates that caused the look of panic to flash across the poor physician's face.

'I'm sure the boy will stay here and keep you company, Dona Flávia,' he said hastily. 'He's a strapping lad, he'll look after you. And he could also make himself useful clearing the floor of dung and heaping it ready to burn.'

'Certainly he will,' the boy's father answered for him, glancing anxiously at his glowering lump of a son as if he had grave doubts whether the boy was equal to even this simple task.

Fausto picked two of the water kegs and, sidling up to me, murmured, 'Dona Isabela, will you accompany me to fetch the water while the others search for wood?'

But though he spoke low, Vítor must have been watching him, for he rounded on him savagely.

'Have you no sense? Isabela will hurt herself if she tries to carry full water kegs. Do you really expect someone of her slender size to heave great weights about?'

'I'm quite capable of –' I tried to protest, but neither man was listening.

'Isabela can help me to gather wood,' Vítor said.

'And you think that easier work, do you? Hauling logs about,' Fausto retorted.

'I have no intention of permitting her to carry logs, you imbecile, just twigs and bracken for kindling.'

Furious, I turned on my heel and stalked out of the cottage. What gave them the right to debate what I was and wasn't able to do as though I was a child? I was more than equal to the task of carrying a bundle of wood or a small keg of water, which scarcely weighed any heavier than a pail. What did they think I'd been doing all my life? Sitting around being waited on by servants? I was in such a temper as I strode towards the forest that I found myself deep among the trees before I even considered where I was going.

Though the trunks broke the strength of the wind, it howled through the branches above, making them bend and creak, and sending twigs flying off like stones from a catapult. If this kept up there would be plenty of wood to burn come morning. One thing was for certain, I was determined now I was not going to collect kindling twigs. I'd return with good stout branches even if I had to walk all night to find them. But the sky was already bubbling black with clouds and beneath the canopy of trees it was darker still. Every tree and herb, leaf and twig was turned to grey in the fading light. Any fallen wood that had lain all summer and was dry enough for burning had merged into one colour with the forest floor of dry leaves, and it was impossible to distinguish it at any distance.

As always when foraging, I convinced myself that if I took just a few more steps I would find what I was searching for, and so I just kept walking, another few yards, then another. Then suddenly as I pushed my way between two bushes I found myself in a small clearing. The ground was uneven, moulded into a series of long humps and hollows, as if waves had formed in the earth. Perhaps these were ancient fallen tree trunks which had over the years been covered by the leaf mould.

In the dim light I saw what I took to be several branches sticking at odd angles out of the ground. They weren't exactly logs, but they were definitely thicker than kindling. I picked my way towards them between the humps, but as I came closer I saw these were not branches at all, or rather they had been, but someone had lashed them together to make three crosses, still standing at drunken angles. There had once been more of them, for there were fragments of others scattered about and half-buried under the leaves.

It was only when I saw them for what they were that I realized just where they had been placed. The humps were not decaying tree trunks at all, they were graves. Six long ones and two shorter graves beside them, perhaps even a third, though it was so tiny it was hard to be sure. Were these smaller ones the resting places of children? What were they doing out here so far from any church or charnel house? Perhaps they were the graves of the people who once lived in the deserted cottage. But what terrible disaster had overtaken them? And who buried them and made such hasty crosses for their resting places?

From sheer curiosity I knelt down and peered at one of the crosses to see if there was any name or date inscribed there. But there was nothing. These people had been buried without names. Then I saw something pale half-buried in the leaf mould. It stood out starkly in the sickly light of the coming storm. Without even thinking about what I did, I began to brush away the dried leaves and scooped it into the palm of my hand before I registered what it was. I peered at it, then froze. It was not the sight of the iron ring lying in my palm that shocked me, but what was inside the ring. It was a white finger bone, still with scraps of parchment-like skin clinging to it.

Behind me, even over the moaning of the wind, I heard a long-drawn-out shriek of rage and at the same time the snapping of twigs as if something was running fast towards me. I scrambled to my feet and whirled round. Something was moving behind the bushes, something was hiding there. Still clutching the bone, I ran. I didn't know where I was going except that it wasn't back towards the cottage, because whatever it was that was pursuing me was coming towards me from that direction, as if it was driving me from any place of refuge. I pelted through the trees, stumbling over roots, tearing my skirts on bushes and my hair on branches.

The wind was roaring overhead and my own progress was so noisy that I couldn't hear how close the creature was at my heels. At any moment I expected to feel sharp claws fastened on to my back, teeth sinking into my legs. My blood was pounding in my ears and my breath rasping in my throat. I turned as I ran, trying to get a glimpse of what it was that was hunting me. Then, with a sickening jolt, my foot stepped into nothing. The ground fell away and I was tumbling down and down.

Coast of France
Ricardo

Sharp set – a hungry hawk. A bird should be kept sharp set before it is taken out to hunt.

I could hear Isabela crashing through the forest even above the wind. Damn it, every creature in there must have been able to mark her progress as she blundered into branches and tore through bushes. You wouldn't think such a dainty little thing could lumber about so clumsily, but she was plainly as terrified as I. That shriek was chilling enough to turn your guts to ice. Unlike her, though, I couldn't run. I cowered down behind the bush where I was hiding and tried desperately to work out where the hell the cry had come from. I peered into the gloom, trying to get a glimpse of the beast that had uttered such a cry, but the branches and bushes were being whipped back and forth so fiercely by the winds that even if a bear had been rampaging through the forest, I wouldn't have been able to distinguish it from a tree in that gloom.

The noise of Isabela's flight had almost faded into the distance now. The evening was growing darker by the minute and I was desperate to get back to the cottage before I lost my way entirely. Spending the night lying in goats' shit with the great she-whale and pig-boy was beginning to feel strangely enticing compared to a night out here alone in the storm. But I dared not move until I knew what it was that had made that noise.

Then I heard a long-drawn-out scream. I'd heard enough

screams like that in my time to be quite certain it was a woman's cry, a woman in pain, a woman terrified. It was far away, but I knew it was Isabela. Whatever that beast was, it must have caught up with her and seized her in its jaws. I almost started in the direction of the sound, thinking I should do something to help her. But I quickly pulled myself together. If she was hurt, dead even, wasn't that exactly what I wanted? Besides, who knew what had attacked her? Judging by that unearthly shriek, it was a monster no man alone could hope to tackle.

But the girl had conveniently drawn it away from me, and now was the time to run for it while it was safely occupied devouring its kill. Then a chilling thought occurred to me. If there was one monster out there, might it not also have a mate, even a pack? Although it made my flesh crawl to think of it, it also pushed me into action. I had to move and move now. I certainly didn't intend spending the night alone in a forest full of slavering beasts. With luck, if there were more of them, they'd be drawn to the corpse by the smell of blood.

I rose cautiously and peered about me, trying to work out which way I'd come. The trouble was, I'd been so intent on following the girl that I hadn't taken much notice of landmarks, and one tree was beginning to look dismally like another in the dark, not that they didn't in daylight. I've always loathed the countryside, and this evening's events had certainly done nothing to endear it to me.

I edged out from behind the bush and started off at an ungainly trot back in what I hoped was the direction of the stone byre. The wind swirled among the branches, plunging down through any small gap in the trees, sucking up fallen twigs and dried leaves in stinging spirals. Then the rain began to fall, big fat drops plopping down through the branches. I hurried as fast as I dared, peering around me all the time in case that beast, having tired of the girl, had doubled back and was now stalking me. But after I almost pitched headlong several times over tree roots and crashed painfully into branches, I realized that I was in grave danger of breaking a leg or knocking myself unconscious. And if I did, I'd be at the mercy of any passing predator who fancied an easy meal. So I forced myself to concentrate on getting clear of the trees as quickly as possible.

The rain was pouring down now. Between the darkness and the rain driving into my eyes I could only see my own hand, white as a maggot, moving in front of me as if it had become detached from my body and was its own creature. The leaves were now so wet under foot that several times my feet slipped from under me and I had to grab at branches to steady myself, but finally I burst out from the trees into the scrub. I staggered backwards as the full roar of the wind and the crashing of the waves on the shore exploded in my ears.

I could see no sign of the cottage and began to fear that I had emerged from the forest on to a different shore altogether. I clawed my way up the nearest dune on my hands and knees, for there was no way I could stand upright against the immense force of the wind. At the top, lying on my belly, I peered out into the bay. Even in the darkness and blinding rain I could see the great white foaming tops of the black waves as they reared up, racing towards the shore. But I could make out nothing else. I scrubbed the water out of my eyes with my sodden sleeve. Then finally, to my great relief, I glimpsed them, tiny pinpoints of yellow light rising up over the water, and sinking down again to be hidden from view by the great black roll of the sea. I watched them rise two or three times more, just to assure myself it was the ship's lanterns I could see. At least now I knew I was on the right beach, unless of course there was some other ship riding out the storm.

By the time I eventually found the cottage and burst in through the remains of the wooden door, my limbs and face were so wet and numb with cold that even the draughty interior of the cottage felt like a hot summer's afternoon in Portugal.

I was greeted with howls of protest as the wind rushed in with me, swirling the sand on the floor into a dust storm and almost extinguishing the flames of the small fire. The merchant hurried over and fought to close the door, stuffing the dislodged cloth back into the gaps in the wood.

'Have you found them?' Dona Flávia demanded, the moment she had finished an exaggerated bout of coughing.

I stood speechless, dripping on to the floor. Rain was running into the cottage in half a dozen places through the cracked tiles on the roof and forming small puddles on the sand. The party were all huddled round a small fire in the far corner of the room where the roof tiles seemed to be least damaged, warming their hands. A small pot was bubbling on the edge of the fire, the steam smelling distinctly of salt pork and ship's biscuit.

'Well? Did you see them?' Dona Flávia demanded, taking not the slightest notice that I was half-drowned and near dead with cold.

'Who?' My teeth were beginning to chatter. I shuffled to the fire and rudely pushed between pig-boy and his father, crouching down to hug the pitiful heat from the flames.

'That poor child, Isabela, and Vítor, of course,' Dona Flávia said, waving her hand around the little circle as if even a blind man could see they were not there. I would have been more startled if I had seen Isabela sitting by the fire, but I was too sodden and numb to register who else was present apart from the great she-whale herself, of course. No one could fail to spot her.

'Are they missing? And in this terrible storm? What happened?' I tried to sound suitably appalled, and fancied I made a convincing job of it. But although the absence of Isabela was no surprise, I can't say I was exactly distressed that Vítor was missing too. Come to think of it, it was poetic justice – a map-maker getting himself lost. I almost giggled, but fortunately my face muscles were too stiff with cold to permit a grin.

Pig-boy's father shook his head gravely. 'When Senhor Vítor brought the wood for the fire and discovered Dona Isabela had not returned, he feared she'd met with some accident or could not find her way back, so he went to search for her.' He glanced towards the door which was rattling violently in the wind. 'A hopeless task, and I fear that, noble though the gesture was, on a night such as this it may cost the poor fellow his life.'

The merchant grimaced. 'I should have gone with him, perhaps the two of us –'

'A fine thing that would be, running off in the middle of the night to search for a girl we barely know and leaving your own wife unprotected and at the mercy of the storm. Goodness knows what may be lurking out in those woods.' Dona Flávia shuddered, as did I when I remembered that shriek.

As if to make quite sure that her husband would not even think of trailing out after Isabela, Dona Flávia sent pig-boy to fetch some wooden bowls that had been packed into the provisions barrel the sailor had brought ashore and began to ladle out portions from the steaming cooking pot. Hers, of course, was the largest measure, though on this occasion not even the pig-boy seemed anxious for a greater share.

Ship's biscuit had been simmered in water until it formed a lumpy porridge that was so thick and gluey it had to be vigorously shaken from the spoon in order to persuade it to relinquish its hold. I was trying hard to convince myself that the black pieces in the greyish mess were burnt biscuit and not boiled weevils. The merest hint of any kind of flavour was provided by a few strips of salt pork which had mostly found their way into Dona Flávia's and her husband's portions. We all gazed at it in dismay, for *hot* was the most charitable thing you could say about the mess that lay suppurating in our bowls.

'How much wine did the sailor leave us?' I asked, hoping for something pleasant that would wash down the glutinous lump stuck in my throat.

The merchant shook his head glumly. 'He left no wine, just biscuit and pork. May the Blessed Virgin, in her mercy, still this storm before morning. I can't stand many more meals of this.'

'If you don't like it, you certainly don't have to eat it, husband.'

Dona Flávia seized the half-finished bowl from him and began scraping the contents back into the cooking pot.

'I'd like to see anyone do better with mouldy biscuit and pork that's too tough even for shoe leather, but I'm sure I won't bother again. Perhaps you think that girl Isabela can whip up a meal more suited to your tastes. Well, perhaps she should have tried instead of running round the forest in the middle of the night like some common harlot. And her a married woman, or so she claims.'

'My dear,' her husband said, consternation written across his brow, 'I'm sure that poor child isn't still out there by choice. No one —'

'You men always fall for that helpless act. But take it from me, she's not as innocent as she looks. I've seen her sneaking off to have whispered conversations with that Vítor, who thinks it's so amusing to torment me with his tales of monsters. He was very keen to go after her tonight. It wouldn't surprise me if they had arranged a tryst before we even landed.'

'On a night like this?' the merchant said incredulously, and as if to give credence to his words, the wind ripped another wooden tile from the roof with a resounding crack. A stream of freezing rain poured in through the hole, forcing pig-boy's father to struggle to his feet and pull his blankets away from the puddle before they were completely soaked.

Nothing much was said after that. Dona Flávia had plainly decided to punish her husband, and indeed all the men in the room, by refusing to speak, which was a blessed relief to the rest of us, though not to the merchant, who kept glancing nervously towards his wife as if she was a loaded cannon that might fire at him without warning.

We tried to dry our bedding around the fire, only succeeding in making it steam a little. But we rolled ourselves in the blankets as best we could and bedded down for the night. Pig-boy's father, who was still anxious that two of our party were lost in the storm, said that we should hang one of the lanterns outside to guide our missing couple back, but I managed to persuade him that the wind would smash it even before he had closed the door and he reluctantly conceded that the gesture would be futile.

Exhausted though I was, I found it impossible to sleep. I was not accustomed to nodding off without a good measure of wine in my belly, save for those nightmare days chained up in the tower of Belém, and, believe me, I had not been doing much sleeping there. But even if I'd drunk half a keg of wine, the roar of the wind and the drumming of the rain and the constant splashing of the water into the puddles on the floor would still have kept me awake. Trying to sleep on the ship was bad enough with the creaking timber and crashing waves, but the rolling, once you got used to it, was somehow soothing, and I found I was missing it.

Besides, I couldn't stop thinking of Isabela. When I had followed her out into the forest I hadn't much of a plan. My original idea, when we landed on the shore, had been to accompany her as she collected wood or water, and in doing so coax her away from the others and then dump her like a sack of unwanted puppies, far enough from the beach so that she couldn't find her way back. Naturally I realized that if I was able to find my own way back to the cottage, so would she, and probably quicker than me too, since she no doubt had more experience with that purgatory they call the countryside. So I knew I'd have to stop her returning somehow, tie her up perhaps. She'd get herself free eventually, but by then the ship would have sailed.

But I hadn't reckoned on her stalking out of the cottage alone, spitting like a cat whose tail's been trodden on. It was all the fault of that gormless, slug-brained ninny Vítor. Did he have no idea how to handle women? Tell any female that she can't do something and that is precisely what she will insist on doing. He'd nearly ruined everything. In that mood she certainly wasn't going to let anyone walk with her.

I had followed her as soon as I could, but it was sheer luck that I stumbled across her standing in the middle of that clearing. I had already taken the precaution of picking up a good stout branch that I'd found. If she saw me with it she would not be suspicious, she would assume I was collecting wood. I'd hidden behind a bush, waiting for her to move back into the trees. I crouched there ready, with the wood grasped tightly in both hands. I didn't intend to kill her, just knock her out. But when she knelt down in that clearing and bowed her head, she looked like a prisoner meekly awaiting the executioner's axe. It was as if she was inviting me to do it, begging me even. I stood up and had almost taken my first step into the clearing, when we both heard that unearthly shriek.

Now I felt strangely miserable. I liked the girl, even if she was a heretic. God knows I was no saint myself. I honestly hadn't meant for her to die. I'd hoped it wouldn't need to come to that. But I knew she had to be dead now, or would be by morning. Even if that animal, whatever it was, had merely wounded her, lying out there in this rain and biting wind she would surely perish in a few hours. But at least I could console myself with the fact that she hadn't died at my hand.

But would the Jesuits believe she was dead? Would they expect some proof – bloodstained clothing, a severed hand? Nothing would induce me to go back into the forest and look for her corpse. Besides, they hadn't asked for proof. An accident, they said, well away from Portuguese soil. Just ensure she doesn't return. Well, they'd got their *accident* all right.

And I would have my pardon, not to mention a house and money, enough money to make Silvia crawl out from whatever sweaty bed she was holed up in. Silvia wasn't dead, she couldn't be. If only I could remember something, anything. If I could just picture her in my head walking out of that door alive. Her throat, I could see her slender throat, the fragile pulse beneath her jaw. Had I put my hands about that long, slender neck? Had I squeezed until that tiny throb was stilled?

I groaned as I felt an urgent stirring in my groin. I turned over, pressing myself into the hard cold floor, and tried to kick the image of Silvia's lithe, naked body out of my head. I would find her. I would leave the ship at the very next port and buy passage on the first boat sailing back to Portugal. I could be home within the month and holding her in my arms.

I must have drifted off into sleep eventually, for I woke sweating from a dream in which Dona Flávia was ladling out soup into bowls, and when I dipped a spoon into mine and raised it, I saw the decaying, bloated head of the woman's corpse balanced on my spoon gazing up at me, the rotting lips parting, begging to be kissed.

I sat up, stifling a cry. A pale light was filtering through the holes in the roof, but apart from the occasional drip where water still dribbled through, the puddles beneath the holes lay still. It had stopped raining and the wind had died down too. The storm had blown over.

We were manfully attempting to swallow the remains of the biscuit and pork porridge, which, though it scarcely seemed possible, had grown even more foul having festered in the pot overnight, when we heard the distant sound of the trumpet signalling that they were launching the shore boat from the ship. Dona Flávia hurried to the door and wrenched it open.

'Hurry, husband, we must be on the shore before they think we have all perished and sail without us.'

She waddled out of the door with such eagerness that I wondered if she had entirely forgotten that she was going to have to scale that rope ladder again. Her husband collected his wife's water keg as well as his own, together with their blankets and several other items Dona Flávia had abandoned in her haste to get to the shore, and the rest of us gathered up our own possessions and extinguished the fire.

Outside pig-boy's father stared anxiously at the forest. 'What of Senhor Vítor and Dona Isabela? Should we not wait for them?'

'We can't wait,' I told him. 'You heard the ship's master; the boat will sail without anyone who doesn't return at the signal.'

'Then we should search for them. They may not have heard the trumpet and if they are lying hurt, unable to move . . .'

Last night I had convinced myself she was dead, but that certainty had ebbed away with the passing of the storm. If Isabela was still alive and she heard the trumpet, then she might have got her bearings from the sound and be even now making her way towards us. I couldn't risk that.

I took his arm and pulled him around away from the forest. 'Senhor, that forest is vast. Even if they still live, they could be anywhere. We could search for days and not find them and the ship will not wait.'

'But . . . we cannot just abandon a young girl,' he protested, twisting his neck around to stare once more into the trees.

The merchant staggered past us, donkey-laden with his own possessions and those of his wife.

Pig-boy tugged at his father's sleeve, whining like a five-year-old. 'Come on, Pa. She's only a dumb girl. I'm hungry and I'm not eating any more of that stinking cowpat we had for breakfast.'

His father looked mortified and began a stumbling apology to the merchant for his son's rudeness.

But the merchant grinned sheepishly. 'Believe me, I've no more appetite for my wife's cooking than the boy has, but I beg of you, don't tell her I said so.'

Heaving his many burdens more firmly over his shoulders, he staggered up the sand dune and the rest of us followed.

The shore boat was already bobbing in the shallows of the bay by the time we reached the water's edge. The sea was sparkling in the sunshine, the tiny waves pouncing playfully on the sand, like harmless kittens. To see the ocean now you might easily be convinced the raging storm of barely a few hours ago had been nothing more than a fevered dream. Once we had all waded out and clambered into the boat, Dona Flávia being carried by two burly sailors who grunted with the effort, the boatswain counted us.

'Where's the girl? There's a man missing too. Miserable-looking fellow, never buys any wine, what's his name?'

'Senhor Vítor,' Dona Flávia supplied. 'And as to where they are, we haven't laid eyes on them since last evening. We think they went into the forest. Doubtless Senhor Vítor went hunting for more of his monsters. He'll probably return with a savage-toothed manticore or basilisk and insist they are perfectly harmless pets.'

'Went off with the girl, did he?' The boatswain winked at the other sailors. 'In that case I don't reckon it was monsters he had on his mind.' He jerked his head at the young lad, Hinrik. 'You, boy, get up to that stone cottage and collect the provisions barrel and while you're up there give a good holler into the forest. Listen to hear if they shout back, but don't linger too long and don't go wandering into those trees. Master'll keel haul me if I lose one of his crew, even one as useless and bone-idle as you.'

We watched Hinrik trudge up the beach and disappear from sight. He seemed to be gone an age. I felt the tension knotting my stomach tighter. What if he had heard something in the forest and had gone to investigate? I could stand the suspense no longer. I stood up and tried to pick my way over the plank seats towards the boatswain.

'Where do you think you're going?' the boatswain yelled. 'Sit still, can't you, you'll have us all in the water!'

I flopped awkwardly down on to one of the seats. 'Listen, my good man, the lady is becoming chilled and we are all hungry. I think you should take us back to the ship at once.'

'Oh you do, do you? Well, if you think I'm going to row you lot all the way across the bay with one man short at the oars, and then row all the way back for my lad, you're an even greater blockhead than you look.'

'How dare you speak so to a paying passenger,' Dona Flávia snapped. 'He was only thinking of my comfort and he is quite correct. It's outrageous that we should be kept waiting like this. If your boy –'

The merchant interrupted his wife. 'Look, the young man is returning, my dear.'

All eyes turned to Hinrik who was weaving down the beach towards us, staggering under the weight of the provisions barrel awkwardly hoisted on his shoulder. I let out a huge sigh of relief. He was alone.

Despite the fact that the ship and boat were not rocking anywhere near as violently, Dona Flávia's progress up the rope ladder was no less ungainly than it had been coming down. In fact it was worse, since she now had to heave her bulk upwards. Men heaved on the rope from the top and the boatswain, much to her indignation, grabbed her great hams and pushed from below, and finally she was hauled on to the deck. To make matters worse, she had insisted on going first, so the rest of us were obliged to wait below on the bobbing boat, until we could follow her up that swaying ladder.

The other passengers all made at once for their quarters in search of their own supplies of food and wine. But I was too anxious to think of eating. I stood on deck watching the distant shore. Hinrik had said he'd called and whistled several times, but there was no answer. That was it then. Isabela and Vítor had vanished. The ship's master was barking orders. Men feverishly cranked the windlass to haul up the great anchor, while high above me, the gromets, as they called the apprentice seamen, were already swarming over the rigging.

I willed the seamen to hurry. Just a few more minutes and we would be sailing out of the bay and all my problems would be marooned for ever on this shore. That old familiar thrill shuddered through my belly, as it did whenever I was certain I was going to win on the throw of the dice. It was all over and I hadn't had to do a thing.

Naturally, that would not be the story I would tell the Jesuits. I wasn't going to give them any excuse not to pay me what they had promised. I would confess to her murder. Confessing a sin you haven't committed is no crime. There were saints who confessed to sins of pride and lust, greed and faithlessness every day. How could they be saints and have committed those sins? It was merely excessive humility on their part. Yes, I'd confess sorrowfully to her murder. They'd ask me how I'd done it, of course. And I would tell them that I –

My breath turned to stone in my throat. There was someone hurrying down towards the beach. Vítor, was it Vítor? He was clutching what looked like his bedroll in his arms. Suppose Isabela was following behind him? He might have run on ahead to alert the ship. I turned sharply away. Maybe no one else would see him. The sailors were all intent on their tasks. The anchor was clear of the water. They were just securing it. I searched for the ship's master. He was standing on the forecastle, his hand shielding his eyes from the sun as he squinted up into the rigging. *Give the order to set sail*, I willed him. What was he waiting for? Everything was ready. *Go! Go!*

As if he heard me, the order came: 'Set the mainsail.'

But the words were barely out of his mouth when that ship's brat, Hinrik, scampered up the steps like a monkey and tugged on his arm, gesticulating wildly towards the shore where Vítor stood. I haven't ever in my life felt a greater urge to strangle a lad than I did at that moment.

I turned once more and looked again at the man standing on the shore. As he waded out into the shallows, I realized that the bundle in his arms was not blankets but something far more substantial. A woman? Was it Isabela? If it was, she was not moving.

Iceland

Eydis

Haggard – *a wild falcon which is more than a year old when it is captured and has passed through its first moult, or mew, and therefore has its mature plumage or livery.*

I wake suddenly to find Heidrun looking down at the man. I did not hear her enter the cave. I never do. She is just as I remember her though it must be five years or more since I've seen her, tall and slender, her back as straight as a razor cut. Her hair is as grey as the cloud over the mountains and her eyes, I know, are the colour of the winter's sky, though she does not turn to greet me.

'He should not have lived, Eydis. You knew that. You sensed that.'

'But I do live,' the dark voice growls from Valdis's lips.

'I did not know his spirit would enter my sister, Heidrun. Tell me how I can force him to release Valdis. You know these things.'

The dark voice laughs. 'It's no good pleading with her, Eydis. She is as powerless to force me out as you are, my sweet sister. Tell me, woman. You walk through the world. You know all that passes. I charge you to tell me the truth of it. Did the farmer Jónas do what I told him?'

Heidrun turns and for the first time looks at Valdis and me. Over all these years she has hardly changed since the first time I saw her when she took us to the circle dance on the night of our seventh birthday, the night of our awakening.

She has an angular but handsome face, though where most people have a groove above their upper lip, she has a ridge. But now her pale eyes are cold with a fury I have never seen in them before.

'Pétur's mares were seized with fright and they all galloped madly off, running further than any horse would ever do had it merely been affrighted by a human whipping it or a noise startling it. Pétur and his sons tracked them on foot for two days, but by the time they found them it was too late. They'd run over the edge of a cliff and smashed themselves on the rocks at the bottom. When Pétur's sons climbed down they found some of the mares still lived, but their bones were so badly broken they could do nothing to help them except cut their throats to put them out of their pain.'

'And Jónas's daughter?' I ask her.

'Frída recovered, as you knew she would. If Jónas had listened to you, she would have come to her senses without the need for any healing herb or charm save that of time. You read her malady well. The cloud came from the mountain, not Pétur.'

'And does Pétur know who slaughtered his mares?' I ask.

'He will,' Heidrun says with an icy certainty. 'His thoughts are creeping towards that knowledge even now. When he returned from tracking the horses, Pétur was in such a rage, he made all in his household swear on the Holy Book to say what they knew of the matter. His serving girl tearfully confessed that she had slipped out to meet her lover and thought she saw in the distance a man crouching near the stream where the mares come to drink. She couldn't be sure and, besides, didn't want to alert her master for fear he would demand to know why she was wandering abroad when she should have been about her work on the farm. Pétur's sons searched the place where she said she had seen a man and found the death coin glinting in the stream. It will not take long for Pétur to discover who placed the coin there, and when he does, he will take revenge on Jónas and all his kin.'

This is exactly the outcome I had dreaded. If Pétur took revenge, then Jónas and his family would retaliate. Such blood feuds have been known to last for generations and involve even distant relatives and hired help from both farmsteads.

'I tried to stop Jónas,' I tell her. 'But he would not listen.'

Heidrun's expression is grim. 'You had the power to stop him, but you didn't. For as long as you and Valdis spoke with one voice, you needed no more than words to control the people. Even a gentle shower of rain if it continues long enough will persuade a man to cover his head, so you let your words fall softly on them and they hurried off in the direction you sent them. You had grown used to that and thought nothing more was needed. So you've let the power you were born with shrivel up like an unused limb. But now you must fight to make your words heard.'

My sister's black eyes stare up at Heidrun. Her peeling lips part as the voice speaks through them.

'Eydis can't fight me. I tell the people what they want to hear, and so they will do it. Prince or pauper, priest or pagan, a man will always listen to the words that echo the desires of his own soul, and he will act on them.'

'Who is it that speaks through my sister's mouth, Heidrun?' I ask her, trying desperately to ignore the mocking voice. 'You above all must know.'

'He was not born on this isle. Every man, woman and child whose birth blood has fed this land is known to me by name, but not those who come from over the water. The boy, Ari, knows where he comes from, I think, but he will not speak of it. He is afraid.'

'And so he should be,' the dark voice says with pride.

Heidrun ignores him. 'But though I don't know his name, I know what he is. He is a draugr, a nightstalker.'

A cackle of mocking laughter pours from my dead sister's lips and echoes from the walls of the cave as if the man has a hundred brothers hovering behind him in the shadows.

A deathly fear grips me. I sensed from the moment they brought him to me that his life was not of this world. But I refused to trust my own gift. As long as I could convince myself he was only a man, I could go on believing that if only I could make his body live, then his spirit would leave my sister and possess its earthly home once more, but now I know it will take far more than that to force him out of her.

'Heidrun, tell me what to do. Tell me how to save Valdis.'

She walks across to the pool of bubbling water and for a long time says nothing as she gazes into its clear depths. The palms of her long hands move over each other as if she is grinding something between them.

I wait in silence. Valdis's head swivels round in the direction of the pool. The draugr is waiting too.

At last Heidrun turns back to face us. 'You know already the man's body must be kept alive, if his soul is to leave your sister, for only when his body and spirit are reunited can the wrong which has been done to this man be undone and he can be freed. But his body can't live long without his spirit inside it. Soon it will be past the point where the spirit can re-enter it. You must heal the physical wounds, and you can. You possess that knowledge and skill, if you will use it.'

Once again she makes the grinding motion with her palms. 'But, Eydis, you must know that only those who are themselves dead can force his spirit to return to the body, only they can control him for he comes from the realm of the dead. You must summon a door-doom, a door-doom of the dead who walk. They shall pass sentence upon him. Only their judgment can rule him. I cannot help you bring their spirits here. I don't have the power over them, but you do.'

'But I do not. You above all people know that I do not!' I seize my chain and strike it furiously against the iron hoop about my waist. The clang echoes from the walls of the cave. 'Have you forgotten, Heidrun, I am bound by iron? They did this to us so that we would have no power.'

'No power to send your spirit out into the world. But there is much you can do in this cave.' She points with a long, sharp finger towards my sister. 'Remember, a band is fastened about her waist too. As long as she is bound by iron, so too is the spirit that infects her. You and he are matched in your limitations and your strength. Only your fear of him can make you weaker.'

'But she does fear me,' the dark voice growls. 'Even bound by iron I am three times stronger than her. I can sense her every feeling. I know her most fleeting thought. I know her more intimately than any lover and can be that too – her lover, her master, her destroyer. I have not even begun to show her what I can do.' Valdis's head twists around to gaze first at Heidrun and then at me with those great cavernous black eyes.

But Heidrun ignores the voice as if it had not spoken. She walks away across the cave floor as noiselessly as she entered. Is that all she is going to tell me, all the help she will offer me? Does she not understand that I am trapped alone with this creature? I need her. I desperately want to beg her to return, but I cannot, for then the draugr will know how much I fear him.

Heidrun pauses beside the rocky outcrop which screens the passage to the entrance. 'If he escapes this cave he will bring terror and death to every hovel and farmstead across the land. Where he crosses a threshold by night not a man, woman or child in that dwelling will be found alive come dawn. Where he walks along a path, no human soul who crosses that track will live long enough to reach home. You must send him back to his body, while you are both bound by the iron. That is your only hope and it is the only hope for the hundreds of innocent men, women and children who will lose their lives if you fail. If he is freed from the iron, neither you nor anyone will be able to stop him destroying every living thing in his path.

'But there isn't much time, Eydis. The mountains are stirring again. The rivers of fire will run. Remember the black cloud that struck Jónas's child? You spoke the truth about that cloud. You know what it means. The mountain has spoken, and soon the pool in this cave will answer it. When it does, you will know time is running out – for all of us.'

Chapter Eight

In the later half of the thirteenth century a Mongol emperor was so passionate about hunting with falcons and gyrfalcons, that he ordered the sides of a valley near the palace to be sown with a huge variety of grains to help breed more wild partridge and quail for the hunt. Near his palace in Chandu he enclosed a park with rich grazing and many streams in which he kept deer and goats which were bred purely to feed the two hundred falcons kept there during their moult. He also kept eagles for hunting wolves.

Every year in March the emperor went to Manchuria for the great hunt, taking ten thousand falcons and an equal number of soldiers to guard the hunting birds. The emperor rode out in a pavilion covered with cloth of gold and lined with lion skins, which was borne by four elephants. Inside he kept his twelve favourite gyrfalcons and twelve favourite officers to amuse them. When those on horseback reported the sighting of game he would open his curtains and cast off the falcons.

When they finally reached the plains, a camp was set up for the falconers, nobles and the emperor's wives, who also had their own falcons, and for a month they would disport themselves with hunting.

Each falcon bore on its leg a tiny silver tablet giving its owner's mark, and a man known as the 'guardian of the lost' would set up his tent on a rise with a banner flying above it so that in the vast camp he could easily be seen. Any owner seeking a lost bird would go to him, and any man finding a lost falcon would take it to the guardian, so that the one might be reunited with the other.

Off the Coast of Iceland
Isabela

Frist-frast – *a pigeon's wing used to stroke birds of prey.*
Stroking with the bare or gloved hands removes the natural
oils from the falcon's feathers and her feathers
become soaked if it rains.

I am lying in a shallow pit. A searing pain, worse than I have ever known in my life, is burning through my chest. I can't move. I'm too terrified even to try. I want to gasp for air, but I have to make my breathing as shallow as I can. I must make the men think I am dead. If they do they will go away. My baby is crying. But I can't go to him. I can't reach him to comfort him. They tore him out of my arms and I was powerless to stop them.

My baby's cries cease and I know they have silenced him. None of my children are crying now. Perhaps they too are simply holding their breath until the men have gone away. They can't be dead. Please don't let them be dead! Even these murderers would not slaughter innocent children. I lie staring up into the darkness, listening to the wind wailing among the trees, waiting, biting back the pain.

The men have not gone. I can hear their breathing above me, hard and rough. I lie rigid, trying to stop myself doubling up as the pain surges back through me. Something heavy falls into my lap. I will myself not to move. Great clods of earth are raining down on my feet, my legs, my chest, my arms, my face. They are burying me in a grave, but I am still alive. I try to scream. But no sound comes. I push and push, trying to force the air from my lungs, but I cannot make a sound. I fight with every splinter of strength I have left.

My own scream woke me, and for a few minutes I lay trembling on my pallet, until the sound of the waves crashing against the timbers and the rolling of the floor convinced me I was safe in our quarters under the forecastle of the ship. Nightmares had haunted my sleep ever since we'd left France. I couldn't seem to shake them off and I had no idea what they meant. Were they a bad omen?

I shivered in the biting cold and huddled deeper under the blankets. Since the departure of Dona Flávia and her husband in England, I had taken myself into the far corner of the passengers' quarters, the spot once occupied by Dona Flávia, to try to find some shelter from the icy wind that flooded through the anchor holes. As we drew further north from the isles they call the Shetlands, the seas had grown stormier and the wind so bitter that I could no longer bear to be upon the deck. The boards were constantly slippery with rain, and the ship tossed so much that I was afraid of falling and hurting myself again.

The bruises I had received in France had all but vanished and my knee was healing well, but the slightest awkward movement sent a sharp pain flashing up my leg which often made me cry out before I could stop myself. One of the sailors, a kindly man, had fashioned me a crutch so that I could take the weight from my leg. But I was praying desperately for my knee to heal by the time we reached Iceland. How was I going to capture the birds if I couldn't even walk far enough to find them?

Marcos, Vítor and Fausto had each come to me in turn, murmuring that they would gladly carry me to wherever I wanted to go on the ship, but I refused to allow them to carry me anywhere. All three of them made me uneasy.

I almost longed for the return of Dona Flávia to shield me from their attentions, though her manner had grown colder to me after that night on the beach. Perhaps it was the way that Marcos the physician was constantly fussing round me, and not attending to her own imagined illnesses, but several times I heard her pass some remark loud enough for me to hear about wanton young girls and sluts, as if she thought me one of them. She never asked me what had happened in the forest. No one did, as if to do so would mean having to explain why they abandoned us on that shore.

I was relieved they didn't ask. For I didn't understand the events of that night myself, much less feel able to give an account of it to others. I could still hear that shriek in my head and I often woke in panic, thinking myself back in among those graves, until I realized where I was, and knew that the moan I could hear was only the wind in the rigging.

When I had fled that clearing, the shriek seemed to pursue me, as if something was rushing towards me in the wind, tearing after me like a kestrel stooping down on a mouse. Perhaps it was a hunting animal I'd heard, a vixen, even an owl, though none I know could have made that sound. Maybe it was just the wind shrieking in the branches. I'd once heard the wind whistling through a mountain cave and sounding almost human. But could I really have been that foolish as to flee from nothing more sinister than the wind?

But as I ran I'd been more concerned with looking back over my shoulder than with where I was going, until with a sickening jolt I found myself stepping into thin air. There was nothing I could do to stop myself falling. I landed at the bottom of a great steep-sided gulley. Dried leaves had formed a thick layer over the soil. But there were rocks sticking out of the leaf mould and it was against these that I hit my shoulder and in the same instant felt a searing pain as my knee twisted under me when I crumpled to the ground.

Stunned by the fall, I curled myself up into a ball and lay

there whimpering, clasping my knee and fighting for my breath. For a few moments the pain in my leg was so all-consuming that I couldn't think of anything else. If whatever it was I had heard in the forest was still shrieking somewhere, shock and agony blocked it out of my head. Then, as the full white-hot intensity of the pain began to subside a little, I heard a rustling of dead leaves and the sound of something slithering towards me. Some creature was scrambling down the slope into the pit. Still cradling my knee, I whipped my head around and saw the dark figure of a man standing behind me. In his hand was a thick branch. The figure raised the lump of wood high above my head, ready to strike down hard. I think I must have screamed. I covered my head with my arms, cowering away. I braced myself for the blow, but it did not fall.

After a few moments I glanced up, though I was afraid to lower my arms. The stick was still raised above me, frozen in the air, as if the man was debating whether or not to bludgeon me. Instinctively I hauled myself backwards by my arms, dragging my injured knee through the carpet of leaves, knowing even as I did so that retreat was useless. He only had to take a few quick steps to catch up with me and strike. But he didn't move. Finally he seemed to come to a decision. He slowly lowered the branch and pushed back his hood, though it was still too dark to recognize him.

'Isabela, are you hurt?'

He advanced a few paces and I shrank back, for he was still gripping the branch firmly in his hand.

'It's me, Vítor. I came to look for you. When you didn't return to the cottage, I was concerned. I thought you might be lost or hurt.'

'How . . . how did you find me?'

He made no answer but instead fell to his knees and, laying down the branch, reached for my injured leg. The gesture startled me and I jerked my leg away from him, a movement which sent waves of pain flashing up my body.

'Your knee, have you cut it? Let me see.'

Reluctantly I held my leg still, but the moment his fingers felt it, though the touch was light, I gasped with pain and pushed his hand away.

'I think you may have dislocated it,' Vítor said. 'But I don't have the skill to straighten it. You need a bone-setter. We'll have to get you back to the cottage.'

For the first time I became aware of my surroundings. The gulley I had fallen into was narrow but long, shaped like the hull of a ship. The sides were steep and though in the darkness I could scarcely make out the top, I could see from the protruding tangle of roots above me that even if I could stand up, the top of the gulley would be a good two or three feet above my head.

Vítor rose and took another pace towards me. I cringed and grabbed the branch he had discarded, prepared to defend myself as best I could, but he stepped over me and felt his way along the gulley.

'The sides are much less steep at this end and not so high,' he called back. 'This is our best way out.'

I heard his shoes scuffing through the leaves as he returned. Then without warning he slipped his arm around my back and I felt the fingers of his other hand sliding under my legs.

'Don't touch me!' I swung the branch at him.

He leapt back and held up his hands as if to show me he meant no harm. 'Forgive me, Isabela, I was only trying to lift you up. I'll have to carry you. You can't walk.'

I stared up at him. Just minutes before he had been standing over me with a branch preparing to smash my skull open. Now he was offering to carry me?

'Get away from me. I can walk and I will!' I dug the end of the branch into the ground and tried to lever myself up. He proffered his hand which I ignored. But though I leaned heavily on the branch I couldn't manage to raise myself more than a few inches before I sank back down on to the leaves again. He offered his hand once more and this time I was forced to take it. I managed to drag myself to the end of the gulley, using the branch and his arm to steady me. But though the wall of the gulley was indeed less steep there, the top was still level with the top of my head and there was no way that I was going to be able to scramble over it.

As we stared at the bank the rain began to fall. Hard, heavy drops falling fast and furiously. Desperately I reached up to pull myself out, but found myself holding only a handful of slippery wet leaves. I groped through the leaf mould, trying to feel for a tree root that I could use to haul myself up, but I could grasp nothing solid except chunks of earth which came away in my hand. The rain was blinding me and I was on the verge of tears from pain and desperation.

Vítor grasped my wrist as I scrabbled frantically through the sodden leaves.

'It's no use trying in this rain. We may as well stay here until it's light. Then I can find a way to heave you out. At least it's sheltered from the wind down here.'

He swung me up in his arms and by this time I was too weak to resist. Every step he took jolted my knee and sent stabs of pain shooting through me so violently they exploded in white lights in my eyes. I allowed him to carry me back to the higher end of the hollow. There he set me down gently against the side of the gulley, removing his own cloak and wrapping it round me, though it was already soaked through. He scraped piles of wet leaves over my lap and legs to keep out the cold, before settling down to sit beside me. The rain beat down upon us. I knew I should offer to wrap the cloak around the two of us, but I couldn't bear for him to touch me for I was in too much pain, and besides, I still didn't trust him.

'It was foolish to wander so far from the cottage and the beach,' he said.

It was too dark to see the expression on his face, but I

could hear the accusation in his voice. He blamed me for us both being out here. How dare he?

'No one asked you to follow me. I could have found my way back. I wasn't lost until that shriek startled me.'

'Shriek? What shriek?'

'You must have heard it. Anyway, you didn't answer the question I asked you before. How did you find me?'

'I heard something crashing through the bushes and I followed the sound.'

'Rather foolish thing to do, wasn't it? It might have been a wild boar.'

He snorted. 'I can tell the difference between two legs running and four.'

I was still firmly grasping the branch. I lifted it a few inches. 'And exactly what did you intend to use this for?'

The answer came swiftly. 'Firewood. What else would I want to do with an old branch?'

It was obvious when he said it. He'd told everyone in the cottage he was going to find wood. Why should I doubt for a moment that's what he'd been doing? And yet I still couldn't throw off that image of him standing over me.

'But when you climbed down in the gulley, you had the branch raised as if . . .'

I didn't finish the sentence. I didn't want to say what I feared aloud, as if the words, once uttered, would make it true.

'As if I was defending myself?' he finished. 'Of course I was. It was dark. I could see something moving at the bottom of the gulley. And couldn't be sure it was you. It might've been some wild beast.'

But I didn't believe him. He had held that branch raised above my head long after he must have realized that it was me. Besides, only an idiot would climb down into a pit if they really thought there might be a savage animal trapped in it, and I had a feeling Vítor was no fool.

We spoke little more that night. He seemed to be lost in thought and I was consumed with pain. I huddled into the sodden cloak and as I pulled it tighter around me, my fingers brushed something hard on my chest, caught in the wool of my shawl. I grasped it and even without looking I knew what it was – the small white finger bone, encircled by the iron ring. On the top of the ring was a flat disc, and I could feel the faint lines of some letter or mark etched into it like the mark of a seal.

I felt like a thief. I should not have picked it up. To steal from the dead was almost worse than stealing from the living. I should take the bone back, return it to the grave and bury it once more, but even if I could have found the place again, I couldn't walk there. The last thing I wanted to do was keep it, but I couldn't just cast the bone away as if it was rubbish. What I held in my hand was part of a human being, a person, someone who had lived and been loved. It would be sacrilege to throw it away. The image rose up in my head of the girl at the *auto-da-fé* sobbing as she was driven to place the box of bones on the pyre, of her refusing to relinquish her grip on the box and them beating her until they had forced her to let go. I shuddered, and not simply from the chill of the icy rain.

I fumbled for the little leather bag I wore around my waist and pushed the bone and ring inside. I had no idea what I would do with them, but perhaps I could rebury them in the next graveyard I came across or lay them in the crypt of a church where they would be safe.

We lay in the gulley all night as the wind howled, the rain lashed down on us and the branches of the trees whipped and cracked all around us. Never had a night seemed so long or so dark. By morning intense pain and cold had left me barely able to move. My jaw had locked rigid, for I had been clenching my teeth so hard. As Vítor picked me up in his arms, I couldn't even open my mouth to acknowledge him.

I was dimly aware that it had stopped raining and the sun had already risen behind the trees.

Vítor carried me back to the end of the gulley and managed to raise me just high enough so that I could grasp the thick ancient roots of an oak tree, though my fingers were so numb I could scarcely hold on. Nevertheless, he was able to heave me over the lip of the gulley, and I collapsed on the sodden ground above. I no longer had the strength even to sit up.

Vítor heaved me into his arms and carried me back through the forest. Each time he stumbled a searing pain ran up my leg, making me cry out, though I tried to bite it back. Several times he was forced to set me down while he scouted around, trying to work out which direction the sea might lie in, but it wasn't until we heard the faint sound of the trumpet in the distance that we were certain we were walking towards the shore. However, the notes, far from reassuring me, only renewed my fear. How long would it take us to reach the beach?

'They will wait,' Vítor said in answer to my unspoken question. 'They won't sail without us. They know I came to look for you.'

He set me down on the ground. 'You rest here and I'll run to the beach and explain that you're hurt. I'll bring some of the sailors back with me to help carry you.'

'No!' I grabbed his leg. 'Don't leave me here. What if you can't find me again? What if some wolf or boar should scent me and attack before you can return? I can't walk, never mind defend myself like this.'

But it was not the thought of wild boars or wolves that terrified me. For some reason, in spite of all his kindness since, I could not forget that image of him standing over me in the gulley. I knew I was probably imagining it, I told myself I was, yet I could not shake off the feeling that he had no intention of returning for me.

He hesitated and for a moment I almost convinced myself

I was right, but then he scooped me up again and we struggled on. I roundly scolded myself for my doubts, and blamed them on the pain. People are like falcons, they lash out when they are hurt, believing everyone is their enemy, even those who are only trying to help them.

The beach was deserted when we emerged from the trees, save for some gulls picking over clumps of glistening emerald seaweed and stranded starfish washed up on the wet sand. Vítor stopped and stared out to sea.

'They're setting sail. The bastards are leaving without us!'

He lumbered over the sand and down to the shore, the wavelets lapping over his boots. 'No, no, come back! You can't leave us here!'

I felt as if a great black curtain was slowly closing around me. Hunger, cold, pain and fear finally engulfed me and I knew no more.

I swam in and out of consciousness as they laid me in the shore boat, and was carried over a seaman's shoulder up the rope ladder, passing out cold again when the ship's surgeon with the help of one of the sailors wrenched my knee back into place. And I was told it was the ship's surgeon who strapped my leg with wooden splints to support it as it healed. Marcos apparently declined to take any part in this procedure, saying he was a physician, not a common bone-setter.

Afterwards, though, Vítor, Fausto and Marcos behaved like lovelorn suitors, each insisting on mulling wine for me in case I should take a chill, pressing their blankets upon me and almost falling over one another to be the one to fetch me meals as I lay on my pallet. But all I wanted was to be left alone, and I was profoundly grateful to Dona Flávia when she insisted the three men joined her and her husband at the table for meals, leaving me alone in the passengers' quarters, though I know full well that she did not do it for my sake.

And during those few precious times when I was alone I could not help repeatedly taking the bone with its iron ring out of my scrip. The ring was a plain band of iron, flattened into a disc on the top on which a simple word been inscribed – *foi*. Was it a name? Was this a lover's ring? Who were they, buried out there in the wastes of that forest with no church nor shrine? Who had interred them there? Was it a kindness they had performed for the dead or a cruelty, a concealment of bodies that were never meant to be found?

Each time I touched that ring and bone I felt a strange sense of grief, as if I had lost someone I had known and loved, as if I had just watched them being laid to rest in a cold grave. It was a feeling of utter desolation, and more than that – a fear, a horror that some nameless force was about to descend upon me. I longed to cast the bone away, but even if I could have dragged myself to the ship's rail, I knew I could never have tossed it into the sea. The bone needed a resting place and because I had taken it, I must give it what it craved.

Eydis

Rouse – *the action of a hawk shaking its feathers.*

I know she is drawing closer. I sense it. The draugr senses it too. I take up our lucet again, our cord-maker, our power. It will lead her to us. It must.

Our lucet is fashioned from a piece of deer-horn, but it was not carved by our hands. It is an ancient thing. The Vikings brought it on their long-boats when first they ventured to this land. When its owner died it was placed in the grave with her. And there it lay for hundreds of years, until a storm washed rock and earth and grave away, and we found it, lying among the brown bones and a scatter of amber beads.

Though we were scarcely five years old we knew at once what it was, for our mother had taught us the art of plaiting cords for our clothes, just as she had taught us how to cook lichen and clean pots. But our lucets were carved from rough pieces of mutton bone, not smooth and polished as a sea-washed stone, not curved as proudly as a horse's neck . . . not a precious gift from the long-dead. We sensed even then our mother would fear to see it in our hands.

Now the cord I have woven twists from its twin prongs. It is long enough to reach the girl, but not yet long enough to pull her close. Each day I must add another finger-length to it. Each twist, each loop gently and slowly guides her footsteps to this place. Three strands of wool woven together to make a single cord – black to call the dead, green to give them hope, red to lend them strength.

I turn the stem of the lucet in my hand, twisting it always with the sun I cannot see but have never forgotten. And with each new knot, the cord tightens and tightens until she will feel it drawing her, and know it is the falcons calling her. Then she will come. She must bring them to us. For the dead who follow her are our only living hope.

Iceland

Ricardo

*Entraves or fetters – the equipment used to prevent a
bird of prey flying away, comprising the jesses attached
to the legs, a swivel and a leash with which to
tie her to the perch or block.*

It would just have to be that snivelling little wretch Vítor
who gave Isabela the news that the coast of Iceland had been
sighted, wouldn't it? I'd heard the cry go up from the watch,
of course, but they were always hollering orders at one
another in their own jargon with the sole purpose of trying
to make the passengers feel inferior, so that I had long since
abandoned any pretence of listening to them. But on this
occasion it turned out the incoherent bellows were because
land had been sighted, and Vítor came thundering down the
steps into our sleeping quarters to convey the glad tidings,
urging us to come and look, as if this was an uncharted land
and he had personally just discovered it.

I was the more annoyed because, for the first time, I had
actually begun to believe I was gaining Isabela's trust. There
is a moment in every scam when you know that you have succeeded in putting a halter on your victim and may lead them
to wherever you want to take them. At first they are wary of
you, then comes suspicion, distrust and even hostility, but
you must hold your nerve, persist. Gradually you will see they
are listening to you, pricking up their ears, sniffing the air, and
then they begin to edge diffidently towards you. They ask a

few questions which suggest they are thinking about the prospect. They give you a tiny inadvertent nod of agreement, a hesitant little smile, and this is the beginning of trust, but only the beginning, mind you. Move too fast at this stage and they will shy away, never to return, but offer soothing words, compliments about their good sense and judgement and you'll find them snuffling ever closer. Believe me, I have conned enough men and women to know the signs. And Isabela was almost there, almost willing to allow me to lead her.

It was imperative that I got her to trust me before we reached Iceland. If I didn't, it was all over. For her to come off that beach alive was bad enough, but to come off with an injured leg which meant she was confined to the safety of sleeping quarters where no *accident* could possibly befall her, was nothing short of a disaster, especially with Vítor and his companion sticking to her like birds to lime.

'Don't you want to see your first glimpse of Iceland?' Vítor urged. 'Isabela, won't you allow me to carry you up?'

'No, no. I can manage.' She brushed his extended arm aside.

For a moment I thought I glimpsed an expression of fear in her eyes. It was not the first time I had witnessed such a look since she had returned from the beach. What had passed between them that night? Had the bastard tried to force his oily little carcass on her?

Isabela levered herself to her feet, steadying herself against the bulkhead as the ship rolled. She limped to the bottom of the short flight of steps. Once more, Vítor put out a hand to try to assist her, but she pretended she hadn't seen it, and with grim determination hauled herself up the steps.

Over these past two weeks she had daily practised walking until she was exhausted. Even the ship's surgeon had told her to rest, and that was certainly a measure of the serious-ness of his concern, for it was rumoured he'd once told a man on his deathbed to shift his arse and stop lounging about cluttering the place up. But Isabela took not a jot of notice. She was going to walk without a crutch and splints if it killed her. And give the girl her due, she'd done it, though it was obvious her leg still pained her, not that she'd admit that to anyone.

Sometimes her stubbornness reminded me of my Silvia when she was working up to a fight, though Isabela was not the kind of woman who would shriek dockside obscenities and hurl her boots at a man, more's the pity. Sweet Jesu, how I missed Silvia. Without warning, the maggot-white, bloated face of that woman's corpse swam up before my eyes and I pushed it firmly back down again before racing up the steps behind Vítor.

To be honest, I had no idea what sight was going to greet me on deck. I hadn't given much thought to what manner of place Iceland was and I'd never had any desire to find out. Ask me to imagine parting a wealthy widow from her jewels and I would have no trouble in picturing such a scene in exquisite detail. But tell me to imagine a place I never really believed existed except in tales of drunken sailors and I could no more picture it in my head than I could see heaven. And, to tell the truth, since the day we set sail I'd never believed I would actually get as far as Iceland.

My plan, if you can call it such, was to somehow dispatch the girl long before we ever got this far and then to disembark at some civilized port and find a ship to carry me home. I'd thought it was going to be so easy – a ship tossing about in stormy seas, slippery decks, dark nights and a fragile young girl – it was an accident waiting to happen, so what could possibly go wrong? Iceland wasn't even worth wasting a stray thought on. And if I had been forced to think of Iceland at all, the image that would have occurred most naturally would have been that it was . . . well . . . icy . . . covered in snow, I guess. But somehow black was never the colour that came to mind when I heard the name.

Now I joined the others at the rail and stared as dumb-founded as they. Before us was a scene that might have been the gateway to purgatory itself. Towering columns and jag-ged shards of black rock rose from out of the cobalt-blue sea. Huge waves crashed against these pinnacles with such violence that spray was flung high into the air, so that it looked as if a pall of white smoke hung permanently above them. What I could see of the land itself was nothing more than a hunk of craggy black rock which jutted out into the sea, like a splintered jaw, without a single blade of grass or even a smudge of moss to soften it. The roaring waves hurled themselves into the cracks in the rock with such force that great plumes of foam exploded upwards and the white water streamed in waterfalls back down the stone and into the churning sea.

The air throbbed with the screams of seabirds. The gulls were much like those that used to drag me from my sleep in Belém with their raucous screeches, but others were some of the oddest-looking birds I'd ever seen, small black and white creatures with huge red, blue and yellow beaks covering most of their faces. The cook and a couple of the seamen were tossing weighted nets over the side trying to capture them as they bobbed about on the boiling foam as serenely as ducks on a village pond.

'Dinner, if you can stomach it,' the boatswain said glumly, as he joined me at the rail. 'Still, you'll be supping on shore soon and after a few weeks eating on this isle you'll think that puffin and ship's biscuit is the food of angels.' He laughed, evidently relishing the misery he thought lay in store for us.

'You're surely not going to try to land here?' I said, staring with horror at the fanged rocks and crashing seas.

The boatswain regarded me as if I was an imbecile. 'You'd best pray we don't get within spitting distance of that shore else it'll be us that's the dinner . . . for the fishes. No, the cap-tain's heading for a bay further round the cliffs, only a piss-poor village there but that suits the captain fine.' The boatswain lowered his voice. 'There's a few little trifles he wants to unload.' He tapped his nose and grinned.

It wasn't until almost dusk that we finally sailed into a long, narrow inlet, dropping anchor in the ghastly embrace of steep black cliffs which circled us on three sides and threatened any minute to clasp their long, bony hands and crush us. The sides of the inlet, though jagged enough to be scalable, assuming you didn't slice yourself to ribbons, were so high as to hide any glimpse of the land that lay beyond, and I guessed to hide the ship from anyone staring out to sea, unless he was perched right on the cliff edge. That's if there was anyone living on that godforsaken lump of rock, which I seriously doubted. But someone had been there. A small strip of white sail cloth had been lowered down from the top of the cliff and was fluttering in the wind against the black rock. It would have been easy to mistake it for a gull, if you were not expecting it to be there. But the captain evidently was. He had promised a gold coin to the first man to spot the signal, a pledge guaranteed to miraculously sharpen any man's eyesight.

A ruby-red sun was sinking into the sea, staining the water, as if blood was seeping from a corpse. Then out of the dazzling light, the dark outlines of two small fishing boats emerged from around the headland and made straight for us. As soon as they came close enough they tossed ropes to the ship and remained fastened up just long enough to be loaded with bales, boxes and barrels, all lowered down to them by the sailors, though not until after they had sent up several large bales of dried cod and a good heavy purse which the captain took himself off with the ship's master to count. I grinned to myself thinking of Dona Flávia's many chins wobbling in outrage had she been here to witness such nefarious goings-on. The old she-whale would probably have burst her corsets in sheer indignation. I was almost sorry she wasn't there.

It was dark by the time the boats slipped away, and we stayed at our anchorage for the night. It was too dangerous to navigate round these murderous rocks in the dark. I tried to get Isabela alone, but she insisted on eating her meal with all three of us at the table and afterwards it was impossible to shake the other two off. It was almost as if they too were trying to find a way to get her to themselves, but none of us succeeded in that.

At dawn we weighed anchor and sailed on for more than half a day, before finally docking in a small harbour at the mouth of a broad, flat river valley. The sailors had scarcely fastened the mooring ropes before six men scrambled over the ship's rail and bounded on to our deck without so much as a by-your-leave to the captain. For a moment I feared we'd been boarded by pirates, but seeing the sailors exchanging covert grins with one another, I gathered that they had been expecting this.

The men stood back to back in a little circle on deck, thick staves grasped tightly in their hands. They were ragged, sullen-looking fellows, but tall and tolerably well-favoured. All of them had light brown hair and eyes of such a similar shade of grey, I supposed them to be cousins at least, if not brothers. A few onlookers had gathered on the rickety wooden wharf, more it seemed because they had nothing better to do than because they had any real business concerned with our arrival.

For a few moments the sailors and the Icelanders simply eyed one another as if each side was daring the other to make the first move. Then a small man pushed his way through the little circle. He was so much shorter than the Icelanders, I hadn't even noticed him board the ship behind them. In contrast to the dull browns and greys of the Icelanders' coarse woollen clothing, this little clerk, for that is what I assumed him to be, resembled one of those ridiculous puffin birds, dressed in a black and orange doublet and massively padded breeches which only emphasized the scrawniness of the little legs that stuck out beneath them. The outfit was crowned with an over-sized green cap decorated with a huge bunch of lace, which he had to hold in place to prevent the sea breeze snatching it off like a mischievous schoolboy and tossing it into the water.

The captain gave an exaggerated bow, which seemed to please the little man, though from the sly grins of the seamen, it was plain they thought he was taking the piss.

'Woher kommen Sie?' the clerk demanded, but was met only with blank stares.

He decided to attempt another language. 'Hv . . . ' He coughed. The remainder of the word was plainly lodged in the back of his throat like a fishbone. 'Hvadan ert pú?'

The captain shook his head. 'We'll be here all night at this rate. Where's that brat Hinrik?'

The ship's boy who had christened Dona Flávia with pudding on our first night aboard was dragged forward by the cook. He stood trembling as if he'd learned long ago that the only reason any officer might send for him was to thrash him.

The captain laid a hand on the cringing lad's shoulder.

'Did you understand what the man said? Is he speaking Icelandic, your tongue?'

The lad nodded cautiously.

'Then tell us what he is saying, boy,' the captain snapped, barely able to contain his exasperation.

'He wants to know where we are coming from.'

'Portugal,' the captain said, looking at the clerk. 'PORT . . . U . . . GAL. We are Portuguese,' he added, his hand sweeping around the crew.

The clerk's face flushed angrily, though whether it was the captain's exaggerated tone or nationality he took offence at was impossible to say. He barked something at young Hinrik, who dutifully translated it.

'He says, only ships from Hamburg can trade in this port.'

'Port, is that what he calls it?' The captain gave a wry glance at the few squalid little wooden and turf huts scattered haphazardly along the edge of the shore in such disarray it looked as if some drunken giant had hurled them about as he lurched past. None of the crew was bothering to disguise their amusement.

The clerk sensed the mockery and puffed his chest up like an enraged toad, and muttered furiously to Hinrik.

The lad nodded gravely. 'He says, the port is new. Soon it will be as good as Lisbon . . . better.'

Nothing could quell the bellow of laughter that erupted from the sailors.

Hinrik translated the clerk's next furious diatribe.

'He says, what business have you here? It is forbidden to land cargo or take on goods. Not even fish.'

'Does this ship look like a stinking cod-boat?' the captain said. 'Tell that donkey's arse that I'm here merely to discharge passengers. Once they are safely ashore, I intend to sail for the isle of Guernsey where they welcome any chance to trade, no matter whose colours the ship sails under.'

Whatever Hinrik said to the clerk seemed to send him into a fit of near apoplexy. His gaze darted wildly about the deck like a fly trapped in a bottle.

'Passengers! What passengers, how many?' he demanded through Hinrik.

The captain gestured vaguely to where the four of us stood, surrounded by our bundles. The clerk gave a little squeak and scurried over to us. Hinrik hurried after him, eager to be of service. He was plainly enjoying his newly acquired power.

The clerk's Icelandic guard glanced at one another and promptly wandered off to engage certain of the sailors in furtive conversation. They were soon pulling small wrapped packages from beneath their clothes, clearly bent on engaging in their own little scraps of illicit trade while their master's attention was otherwise engaged. Barter is a language all its own that needs no translator.

'You,' the clerk pointed at Vítor. 'You look like a merchant. You cannot trade here. It is not permitted,' he said through Hinrik, as if we might have missed that point.

Vítor hesitated, then took a pace towards Hinrik and spoke in a low voice with several anxious glances towards the captain, who was in deep conversation with one of the Icelanders.

'I have something to tell this man, but you must swear on your life that you will not repeat what I say to the captain or any of the men. This is only for the clerk's ears. Understand?'

The boy nodded excitedly.

Vítor leaned closer still. 'Tell him I am a Lutheran pastor.'

Hinrik looked startled, but he did as he was told.

The clerk drew back and gaped at him, open-mouthed. 'A Lutheran ... from Portugal?' He could hardly have been more incredulous if Vítor had announced he was the ambassador from the lost African kingdom of Prester John.

'There are a number of Lutherans in Portugal,' Vítor said. 'But they have to remain hidden for fear of the Inquisition, who has declared them, that is to say, declared *us*, heretics.'

Hinrik grinned. 'He says you dress too brightly to be a Lutheran pastor.'

Since Vítor was clad in a tediously plain dark-green doublet, I thought the observation a trifle unnecessary coming from a man who was done up like the carnival king. But Vítor was as quick-witted and pert as a town whore for he already had an answer for that one.

'In order to escape the country, I had to look like a Catholic. The captain would never have given me passage if he'd known the truth – that I was fleeing for my life. I've come here to seek sanctuary.'

All of us were gaping at Vítor with as much astonishment as the little clerk. Could this possibly be true, or was it as fanciful as his tale about looking for sea monks? I'd never believed that one.

The clerk, still staring boggle-eyed at him, seemed to recall his duty and spoke earnestly to the lad.

'He says, why don't you go to Denmark or Germany where you would make a good living. In Iceland . . .' Hinrik trailed off and looked questioningly at the clerk, but the man was evidently unable to think of a single reason why anyone would seek refuge on the isle.

Vítor bowed his head. 'I long to serve God by spreading his word to those who have yet to hear it. I understand that there are many in Iceland who are not yet convinced of the truth which Luther preached.'

'They are not,' the clerk said with evident feeling. He glowered over at the people still staring curiously from the quayside. 'You will find no shortage of God's work to be done here, though I would not wager a dried cod's head on any of them having the wit to understand it.'

Hinrik glowered furiously at the clerk as he translated these words, but the clerk seemed blithely unaware that he was insulting the lad.

'You are also Lutherans?' the clerk demanded, glancing round the rest of us.

We shuffled and shrugged as if we didn't believe in anything much, certainly nothing we'd cause trouble over, which in my case was certainly true. I'd had quite enough of churches and priests in my youth. I'd been bored by the former, and beaten by the latter. Now I believed in leaving God to get on with His own affairs, and I devoutly prayed He would extend the same courtesy to me.

The clerk peered at Isabela. She looked terrified, and I wondered what she was going to tell him.

'Whose woman is she?'

I'd taken one pace forward, and I was just on the point of claiming her when Vítor leapt in.

'She's mine, my wife.'

The clerk did not appear to notice the darts of outrage all three of us shot towards Vítor. I saw Isabela open her mouth and for a moment I was sure she was going to deny it with the same fury she had displayed in the cottage before she went running off. But she seemed to think better of it.

The clerk nodded. 'Good for a pastor to have a wife with him to tend to his needs. These Icelandic girls who hire themselves out as servants cannot be trusted to have the running of a house. They need watching every minute.'

He added more, but Hinrik was sulking and folded his lips, refusing to translate what I assume were even greater insults concerning the character of his countrymen.

Without even the courtesy of asking permission, the clerk began a thorough search of our bundles, even Vítor's, for anything he feared we might be trying to trade. He was so intent on his task that he remained entirely oblivious to what was furtively changing hands between his own men and the sailors.

Hinrik, seizing his chance, clutched at Vítor's sleeve. 'Take me with you. I hate this ship. The captain is a wicked man. I am a Lutheran, just like you, a good Lutheran. That is why they beat me on the ship every day.'

'Don't lie to me, boy,' Vítor said, firmly pushing the lad's hand away. 'You only get beaten when you're lazy and clumsy, and from what I've observed, any punishment you've received has been richly deserved.'

Hinrik was not in the least abashed. 'But you need me to tell you what people are saying and you need me to tell them what you want.'

'He has a point,' I said. 'That popinjay of a clerk could have been asking us to marry his daughter for all the sense I could make of his gibberish. If they all talk like him, we'll probably end up buying a three-legged donkey when we wanted a plump roast chicken.'

'I seem to recall the cook saying the captain bought the boy from his father,' Vítor said. 'He will surely demand recompense to release the lad.'

Hinrik was looking beseechingly from one to other of us. 'I cost almost nothing to buy. And I can do everything for you. Fetch water, cook.'

'Don't push it, lad,' I grinned. 'I've seen you round a cooking pot, remember? If we let you anywhere near it we'll be poisoned, burned and scalded to death all in one night.' I fished out a few coins. 'I'm willing to offer that as my share for the boy. What do you say, shall we take the lad?'

After dithering like a couple of novice nuns, the other two men handed over an equal sum each and I went off to negotiate with the captain. Although he plainly wanted rid of the lad, he knew his value to us, and demanded an outrageous price.

I stalked away, making it plain that we had lost interest in the whole deal, but Isabela, bless her tender little female heart, pressed some money into my hand, though I suspected she could ill-afford it.

'We must buy his freedom. He's so wretched being at sea. It's a prison to him. This is his home. He should be here. Please try to persuade the captain to let him go.'

I allowed myself to be coaxed into returning, although I had every intention of doing so anyway. For it had already occurred to me that Hinrik might be just the solution I needed to solve a far more urgent problem than mere language. After some hard bargaining with the captain I negotiated a price which meant that, what with the sum Isabela had forced on me, my share wasn't needed, nor was half of Vítor's . . .

although I may have forgotten to mention that little detail to the others.

The clerk seemed determined to draw the search out for as long as possible, leaving every item in disarray on the deck, so that we were forced to repack them all over again. But finally, even he was satisfied, and with a stark warning not to sell so much as a single button, he herded us, together with a jubilant Hinrik, towards the gangplank.

Then, just as we were about to step ashore, he said something in an unnecessarily loud voice, a broad smirk on his scrawny face. He prodded Hinrik to translate.

The boy looked positively alarmed and it took several more prods before he would open his mouth.

'He says . . . he says he cannot stop you going ashore, but it is not worth you bothering. He says . . . you should sail back with this ship and return next year . . . but you won't, will you?' the boy added desperately.

I was already so infuriated by the lengthy search that it was all I could do to stop myself putting my boot up the clerk's arse and pitching him headfirst overboard.

'Why,' I inquired through gritted teeth, 'do you imagine we'd journey all this way simply to turn around again and depart with the ship the moment we land? Do you honestly think we've spent weeks on a lousy, stinking ship, eating pig-swill, and risking life and limb in storms, gales and every other horror the accursed sea can throw at us for the good of our health? Why the hell should we leave just when we've arrived?'

I suspected by the brevity of his speech that the boy only translated the last part of what I said, but it was evidently enough, for the clerk smirked triumphantly as if he had been *so* hoping we were going to ask him that question.

'He says,' Hinrik told us in a subdued voice, 'because it is law that no foreigners can remain on Iceland during the winter months. You can stay only for two weeks more. If you are caught here after that you will be arrested. And any man who gives you shelter will be punished.'

We stared at him, dumbfounded. Isabela gasped in shock.

The clerk made a curt incline of his head towards Vítor. 'I regret to say, that includes you and your wife also. You may be Lutherans, but you are still foreigners.'

The expression of sublime satisfaction on his face told us he was not actually regretting this in the slightest.

'You and your wife should take a ship to Denmark and there wait out the winter. You can return in the spring, if you still want to.'

He shrugged, as if to say he thought it most unlikely that anyone would elect to venture twice upon these shores.

We followed him down the gangplank in stunned silence. The news had badly shaken all of us. I had the distinct impression from the grins that the captain was exchanging with the ship's master that both of them had been fully aware of the law before they'd accepted the money for our passage, but what did they care? The only reason they'd wanted to carry passengers to Iceland was as cover for their real business of smuggling, and we had served their purpose well.

I was sorely tempted to tell the little clerk about the dried cod in the hold and what his own men had been doing behind his back, but I suspected I'd have a hard time proving where the captain had got the fish, and besides, for all I knew the clerk had deliberately prolonged that search to give his men the chance to trade and was taking a cut of the profits. I'd had dealings with enough sailors in Belém to know that you don't interfere in their business unless you want to find yourself floating face down in the sea with a knife in your back.

I glanced at Isabela. She had turned very pale, and little wonder. She had just two weeks to find her falcons. I had no idea how difficult a task capturing falcons might be, but even I was pretty sure two weeks was cutting it fine. More to the point, I had just two weeks left in which to stage her *accident*, and right at that moment I didn't have a single idea in my head about how to do that, especially as Vítor had now claimed her as his wife. I could hardly see him buggering off and leaving the two of us alone.

But I reminded myself that this morning's events had not proved a complete disaster. We had Hinrik, and every crusado we had spent on buying the boy, or should I say *they* had spent, was about to prove well worth it. Since we all now jointly owned him, and we all needed his services, it was the most natural thing in the world that I should travel with Isabela without it arousing any suspicion on her part. After all, we could hardly cut the lad into four, now could we? Of course, the drawback to my sweet little plan was that the other two men also showed every intention of coming with us for the same reason, but for the moment I could see no way to prevent that.

So there you have it, my friend – three men, a girl and an urchin boy, setting off for God knew where in that bleak wilderness. And the only thing I knew for certain was that in two weeks I had to be on a ship out of here, and that meant by then the girl would be dead and her body rotting somewhere in this purgatory. All I had to work out now was how to get Isabela away from the others. If I could just find a way to get her alone, then killing her would surely be easy.

Eydis

Birds of the train – *any captive bird used to train hunting hawks. Birds of the train might include pigeons, herons and kites. The birds were kept tied to a long line when they flew so that inexperienced falcons could learn to chase them.*

She has come. I hear her first footfall on the land reverberating through my bones, as if a herd of wild horses is thundering over my head. She steps from the cold, wild sea to the fiery earth, pulled by my cord. But she is not helpless, not my captive. It is her will that drives her on as fiercely as my will calls her to me. And the dead follow her, restless shadows slipping through the dark waves behind her. They come because of her. They come because they must, drawn to her as she is drawn to me. She can sense them like whispers at her back, but she has not yet found the courage to turn and face them. I knot another finger-length of cord on my lucet. Slowly, gently, she will be guided to us.

Ari comes slithering down into the cave. I know his footsteps well now, that careless bounding down over the rocks and boulders, as if he is invincible, as is always the way with the young, then the pause, the nervous hesitation, as he braces himself to come around the rocky outcrop, fearful of what he might see.

He slings the sack from his shoulder and pulls out the contents – wind-dried stockfish, a few strips of smoked mutton and a good measure of peas shrivelled until they are hard as stones.

'Fannar sent this,' he says, as if I need to be told.

We read the seasons by the gifts they bring us. The weeks of eggs and fresh lake fish have gone. Berries and herbs have been eaten and grow no more. Now we enter winter, when everything will taste of smoke. There will be weeks when no one comes to us at all, because the snow lies too deep, endless days when the wind howls across the mouth of the cave and time is measureless. Often in the past, through those long winds of solitude, Valdis and I used to wonder if every man and beast had perished up there in the frozen world, and we were the only two who remained alive.

Finally, when we fear the snows will last for eternity, they begin to drip, and the drips become streams, and streams become raging torrents powerful enough to drag great boulders as easily as grains of sand. Then come the hungry weeks of spring, when store cupboards empty, the animals bellow in vain for hay in the byres and fishing boats cannot put to sea. The people come, but they bring nothing but apologetic shuffles. They are ashamed to come empty-handed, but we can see the misery in their hollow cheeks and protruding bones. They swear they will bring us gifts when the first birds nest again. They keep their word, and so begins the time of eggs once more. Thus it has been since the day our mother brought us to this cave. But this year will be different – my sister is gone and I am alone with the nightstalker.

The boy's eyes dart sideways to the corner where the man lies. He knows it is dangerous to look, but he cannot help himself.

'I know why you fear him, Ari.'

'I don't fear any man,' he says, his chin jerking up like a child's.

'You should fear him. He is a draugr, a nightstalker.'

He flinches at the words, and hangs his head, but I can see he already knows this.

'It is what you feared he was. Who is he, Ari? What name was he known by in life?'

He does not answer, nor will he look at me. I wait. He will tell me in his own time. The young, like the old, cannot be hurried. Finally Ari raises his head. His face is as pale as ashes in the torchlight.

'I cannot be certain,' he says miserably.

'Tell me and I will know if it is true.'

'A while ago . . . I was working as a deckhand on one of the local fishing boats. One of our lads happened to look back at the land and saw the way the clouds were building over the mountain. The wind was still only a cradle-rocker then, but we could see the warning, a wicked storm was brewing. We hauled in the nets and got to shore as quickly as we could. But some of the foreign fishermen, they couldn't read the signs and kept on working their nets. The storm struck suddenly and it hit hard. Several of the foreign fishing boats were caught up in it, and saw that the safest course was to ride it out at sea well away from the rocks, but the men in one of the boats must have panicked and stupidly made a dash for the harbour. Likely they didn't know this coast. They came too close to the cliffs and the wind smashed the boat straight on to the rocks and broke her back. Nothing anyone could do but watch it happen.'

A spasm of anguish and guilt wrinkles Ari's face. It is hard to stand and watch men perish and know that had the bones which the gods cast fallen differently, it would have been you drowning in the waves.

'Was any man saved?' I ask him.

'Sea dragged them all down before any of us could even whisper a *Hail Mary* for them.' He stares into the flames of the fire. For a while he says nothing more, then he begins again.

'Next morning, when the storm had passed, there was splintered wood and rope from the wreck tossed up all along the shore, that and dead fish, not much else. It was as if the boat was an egg that had been stamped on. It made your guts churn to think of the power that could do that to great timber beams.' He shakes his head like a dog with sore ears, as if to rid himself of the memory.

'Nothing man can create can withstand the fury of the sea when she is determined to destroy it.' I glance back at the wreckage of the man in the corner. 'But what does this storm have to do with him?'

Ari's head also turns momentarily towards the man, but he averts his gaze. 'Every woman and child in the village was racing to gather as much wood as they could for the fire, before their neighbours snatched it. So it wasn't long before they came across the bodies of three of the drowned fishermen lying sprawled over the rocks, half-tangled in their own nets. Two more were washed ashore further down the coast. Five corpses in all. I don't know if that was all of the hands aboard or if the sea had taken the rest as her dues.

'The pastor came down to the harbour and told us to take the corpses up to the store cellar next to his house and lay them in there . . . though it wasn't so much a request as a command, as if we were his servants,' Ari adds indignantly. His loathing for Lutherans is plainly as deep as Fannar's.

'The gravediggers set to and started to dig a grave in the churchyard, but the pastor stopped them. Made them dig a mass grave outside the village on unconsecrated ground, waterlogged, wasteland it is, the kind you wouldn't even lay your dog to rest in. Said the men were Catholics, idolaters who shouldn't lie with good Christian folk. He could tell that from the crucifixes and amulets they were wearing.

'Once the bodies had been dumped into the pit which was already oozing with stinking water, he sent the gravediggers home and said he would fill in the grave himself that same night. It's my betting he was afraid that some in the village might secretly try to anoint the corpses with holy oil, or pray for their souls, even hold a service for them, so the pastor wanted to make sure they were buried quickly before anyone got the chance.'

Ari gestures towards the body of the man lying in the corner of the cave, but he studiously keeps his gaze turned from him.

'That's when I first saw him, or at least I thought I had. I would have sworn on my mother's life he was one of the corpses that I'd helped carry up to the pastor's store cellar. I mean, I had hold of the man's ankles and his dead face was in front of me all the time we were carrying the body up the rise. A man's features get burned into your mind, when you have to stare at him for that long.

'But a few weeks later when I was working on Fannar's land, I saw a man walking along the track. Right from the first moment I glimpsed him, I knew I'd seen him before, even though he was a foreigner. That's what made me take such an interest in him – I was trying to remember who he was. I was so sure I knew him that I was on the point of climbing down to the track to greet him.

'But the Danes got there first. Before I'd taken more than a couple of steps down the hillside, I spotted them walking towards him. I could tell from their jeers there was going to be trouble. They surrounded him and started beating him. So I ran for Fannar. By the time we returned he was unconscious. It was only when Fannar and I went to tend him that I remembered where I'd seen him before. Seeing him lying there, so near to death, was like seeing his drowned corpse all over again.

'But I kept telling myself I must have been mistaken. The man I'd seen was long dead and buried in a grave. I'd carried him to the pastor's house myself and I knew he was as blue and cold as any corpse could be. There wasn't a breath of life in him. So how could a man who was dead be striding, full of life, along a track? It was impossible!'

I do not ask the lad if he could be mistaken. I know with absolute certainty he is not.

'The pastor who buried him, Ari, what do they call him?'

'Pastor Fridrik.'

'Fridrik of where, Ari?'

The lad's brow furrows as he tries to remember. 'Borg . . . Fridrik of Borg, that's what one of the gravediggers told me. Said it was a pity he hadn't followed his father's example and murdered himself, for he was turning out to be just as miserable a bastard as the old man was.'

'So Fridrik has returned, has he?' I murmur to myself, but the boy hears me.

'You know him?'

'If his father was the farmer Kristján, then I know a little of the family, though not much of the son.'

'Was the old man as sour as they say?'

'I never spoke to him, but I knew his wife. She sometimes came to Valdis and me when her sons were infants for cures and charms. But each time she came we could feel more sorrow in her. She complained that Kristján treated her no better than a hired maid, even in his bed she was of no more worth to him than a brood mare, and she spoke the truth, we were sure of that. But every story can be told in many ways and we believed that Kristján wasn't entirely to blame. Even he must have noticed his wife was deeply in love, but not with him.

'We saw that she was set on a path from which there would be no turning back, and so it proved to be, for one day she ran off with her lover, Kristján's own brother, abandoning not only her husband but also her sons, who were still only children. It filled the gossips' mouths for weeks. Every man or woman who came here was chewing some new little gobbet of it. Kristján's humiliation made him a bitter man and any shoot of tenderness he might have had even for his own children withered inside him.

'Over the years we heard stories of his sons leaving the farmstead one by one as soon as they were old enough, unable to endure their father's violent temper. With no kin left to help him, and no hired man willing to work for such a brutal master, the farm fell into ruin and finally Kristján hanged himself in his own byre. As for Fridrik, all we know is that for a while he worked as a hireling, then one day he boarded a ship and disappeared. But that must be more than seven years ago . . . So now he is back from across the water and a Lutheran pastor . . .'

I lean forward. 'Tell me, Ari, on which day of the week were the corpses of the drowned fishermen found, can you remember?'

He stares at me, evidently puzzled by such a question. 'How should I remember that . . . ? No, wait, it must have been a Friday, for though we'd lost a day's fishing on account of the storm, we did no fishing the next day either, for no fishing boat'll put to sea on a Friday. That's how we came to be ashore when the corpses washed up and could carry them up from the beach, else we'd all have been back at sea . . . Why, what does it matter what day it was?'

'Because if a corpse is to be raised using the black arts, it must be on Friday night before Saturday dawns.'

Ari swallows hard. His voice is trembling a little. 'You think he was the man I saw drowned and someone raised his corpse? But how?'

'There are many ways to accomplish that. But if the corpse is newly dead, the sorcerer writes the Lord's Prayer on a parchment using the feather of a water rail for a quill and his own blood for ink and he must carve the troll runes upon a stick. Then he must lay the stick on the corpse, rolling it as he reads the prayer he has written. Gradually, the body will stir, but before it gains its strength, the sorcerer must ask the corpse his name. If the corpse regains his strength before the question is asked or answered, then the sorcerer will never be able to master it and the draugr will kill him.

'The draugr's nostrils and mouth will bubble with grave-froth and this the sorcerer must lick off with his own tongue and place a drop of his own blood in the corpse's mouth.

Then great strength will come upon the draugr and he will attack the sorcerer and wrestle with him. If the sorcerer wins, the draugr must do his every bidding, but if the draugr wins, he will drag the sorcerer back down into death with him. It is an extremely brave or an extraordinarily bitter man who would risk raising the corpse of an adult man like this one, who would have enormous power. Most sorcerers fear to raise anyone except children whose strength they can master. Whoever raised the corpse of the drowned fisherman must have had a good reason for needing a grown man to do his bidding.'

'Who?' Ari asks. 'Who would do such an evil thing?'

I am certain I know, but I will not tell the boy. It is the worst of crimes to poison the young with hatred.

Ari draws up his knees and clasps his arms tightly around them, staring into the flames of my cooking fire. 'I heard my grandfather speak of a nightstalker that was sent by a jealous neighbour to terrorize a blacksmith and his family. He arrived one night as a stranger seeking shelter. They offered him their hospitality for they didn't know what he was. But soon he made their lives a torment. He turned their winter stores of smoked meat rancid and the dried fish rotten. He caused every iron tool the blacksmith fashioned to crack, and every horseshoe he made to lame the horse it was nailed to until the whole neighbourhood was furious with the blacksmith and refused to bring their horses to him. My grandfather said the nightstalker kept the whole family constantly awake with his shrieking and singing of drunken songs, but he wouldn't leave. Then, when they finally realized what he was, the blacksmith and his brothers circled him with sharp knives so he couldn't escape, then they struck off his head with a great axe and burned the body.'

'I know that the draugr in this cave has been conjured to do far worse than break tools or spoil stores. It is not animals he has been sent to destroy, Ari, but men.'

It pains me to frighten the lad, but I must make him understand why I am about to ask him to undertake a task for me that will place him in such danger.

Ari moans and brings his fists up over his head. 'It's all my fault. I should have let him die on the track. The Danes were right to attack him. We must kill him now, before he regains his strength. Cut off his head and burn the body, like my grandfather said, that's the only way to destroy him.'

Ari struggles to his feet and pulls the knife from his belt.

'No, Ari!' I shout. 'No, don't hurt him. He must live.'

But the lad takes no notice of me. Although I can see he is terrified, I know by the hard set of his jaw he is resolved to see it through. He thinks it is the only way to undo the harm he has done. He starts across the floor of the cave, his knife raised high in both hands.

'If you spill one drop of his blood, Ari, we will curse you to the grave and beyond.'

He ignores me, and I know that even if I utter a curse it will not stop him. But just as he reaches the man, there is a great clicking and whirring. A dense cloud of black beetles rises into the air and buzzes around Ari, dashing their sharp wings against his face over and over again. He flails his arms wildly, trying to beat them away. The knife flies from his hands as he staggers blindly across the cave.

'Sit down, Ari! Sit and they will leave you.'

But so great is his panic that I have to shout twice more before I can persuade him to crouch down on the ground.

He kneels, hunched over, covering his head with his arms. The beetles fall back to the floor and scuttle back into the cracks in the rock.

Ari sits trembling for several minutes before he finally manages to find his voice again. 'Eydis, I . . . I don't understand. Why did you stop me? Why do you want this creature of hell to live?'

'We don't, Ari. We swear to you we would give our lives to

see him destroyed, but for now he must live. His spirit has left his body. If the body is destroyed while the spirit is absent from it, his spirit will remain among the living and there will be no way to banish it. Not even the sorcerer who conjured up the corpse from the dead will be able to send the spirit back to the other world. The spirit will be capable of doing as much harm as the draugr itself, maybe more. Until the spirit returns to the body, we cannot risk destroying the corpse.'

Ari raises his head, despair etched into his face. 'Then what can we do? Tell me what to do to put things right.'

'Listen to me, Ari, the corpse is growing weaker. Soon it will be too weak for the spirit to return. We must heal the body. We have a jar of the fox fat we need and the dried herbs, but there is one ingredient, the most important, we do not possess. We need to prepare some mummy.'

The boy looks blank, as well he might. The ingredient is too costly for a hireling like him ever to have seen, never mind used.

'Mummy is the render from a human corpse. It is one of the most powerful physics there is. The merchants bring a little in from Germany for the wealthy Danes, but it is costly, far beyond what most farmers could ever hope to pay, even if there were any for sale.'

A look of apprehension crosses the boy's face. 'You want me to steal some . . . from a Dane?'

'No, lad. Even if we could discover who had some on his shelves, we could not risk you breaking into the house of a Dane. You would be caught and hanged without question. No, we must make it ourselves. But to do that we must have a corpse, or rather the head of one, for it is the render from the head that is the most powerful . . . Ari, listen to me carefully, we need you to break open a grave. You must choose the grave of someone not too long dead, so that some of the flesh and brains will still remain. You must cut off the head and bring it to me.'

256

He gags and the blood drains from his face so swiftly I fear he is about to faint.

'Surely there must be something else that would heal him?' he begs. 'A root . . . a herb? It doesn't matter how rare it is, only tell me what to look for and I promise I'll search every mountain and valley. I won't rest until I find it.'

'Ari, believe me, I would not ask you to do such a thing if there was any other physic that would work.'

'But to open a grave!'

'If we cannot heal the corpse, then this man's spirit will continue to serve the master who conjured it. To go to such lengths to raise a draugr, Ari, must mean whoever did this is planning great evil. Who knows how many men, women and children this spirit will drag down into the grave before his work is finished?'

The lad nods, his brow creased in anguish. I can see he is steeling himself to the task out of guilt for what he has unwittingly unleashed. I loathe myself for putting him through this, but there is no other way and no one else I can ask.

'Ari, you must find the skull of a dog and place it in the grave so that it will placate the spirit of the man or woman and stop them seeking vengeance. But you must do this soon, Ari, time is running out. If we leave it too late . . .'

Ari lumbers to his feet and stumbles across to the passage.

'I . . . I won't fail, Eydis. I promise I won't fail,' he says, but he does not turn around and look at me.

'Ari, take great care. Don't let anyone catch you.'

The Lutherans care little for the dead. They say no Masses for their souls, neither do they anoint the corpses, nor sprinkle holy water on the graves. They do not even lay food or drink on the graves to welcome the spirits of the dead back on All Hallows' Eve. But if they were to discover anyone attempting to open a grave they would accuse them of stealing bodies for the black arts and would hang the man or drown the woman, even if there was no proof they had removed anything from the corpse.

Ari clambers out of the cave with the heaviness of an old man. It is as if his youth has vanished in a single breath.

Laughter crackles from my sister's lips, then stops abruptly.

'So, Eydis, now you make a grave robber of the boy. My master would be proud of you. He has a great talent for dark arts. He has studied long and hard to acquire his knowledge and he will use all he has learned, you can be sure of that, for he has a passion, my master, a hatred burning him up. Ambition, all-consuming ambition is a goblet of acid that he daily drains to the last scalding drop. He would be delighted that you are going to such lengths to help him achieve what he desires, that you are taking such pains to cure my corpse.

'But, Eydis, you must have realized that all your tender efforts will be wasted. I won't return to my own corpse. I like being in Valdis's body. I feel so close to you, my sweet sister. It is lonely being dead, so lonely. Can you imagine what it's like lying down there among the bitter, angry dead, in cold black water, the grave mould slowly creeping across your tongue? I won't go back.'

The moon is rising. Death is riding. Eydis, Eydis. He chants the words like a mocking child.

I try to ignore the taunt, though the tone of the sing-song voice makes my flesh crawl. 'Fridrik raised you. He placed his bitterness on your tongue and his hatred in your mouth. But understand this. However strong you are, we are stronger. We will not let you live in her. We will not let you use her to destroy countless innocent lives.'

Eydis, Eydis, sister mine, the grave is cold, but we shall lie together and you shall kiss my rotting lips all through the days of the dead and into the darkness beyond.

He laughs, and I feel a strange tingling between my thighs and fingers rubbing my breast, though no hands are touching me.

My sister's head rears up towards my face, and her dead lips part. 'Caress me, Eydis. Kiss your master.'

I turn my head sharply away, but I cannot restrain the hands that are invisible. I cannot stop the fingers probing me, stroking me, for it is like trying to push away an icy wind. I roll myself into a ball, trying to repel him with my mind, but I cannot escape from his loathsome touch.

'You will surrender yourself to me, Eydis. Sooner or later, you will let me enter you too.'

Chapter Nine

The king of Persia once owned a white falcon worth more to him than his own palace. He cast the falcon after a crane, but when he drew close to where his bird had made the kill, he discovered that the falcon had slain an eagle instead of the crane. To honour his falcon's courage and valour the king had a lavish dais erected for her to perch on and placed a miniature golden crown on her head, then he ordered that the falcon's head be struck from her body, because she had killed her sovereign lord.

In the same manner a king of England cast off his falcon, but before the falcon could seize its prey, a wild eagle, king of all the birds, stooped down upon it. The falcon dived to the ground and hid itself among a flock of sheep, and when the eagle thrust its head into the flock to find the falcon, the falcon struck the eagle hard on the head and killed it. All the knights and noblemen who rode with the king cheered and praised the brave little bird. But the king of England, hearing their praises, had the falcon hanged as a salutary lesson for anyone who might dare to dream of rebellion against the Crown.

Isabela

To mount a horse like a falconer – *a falconer always mounts from the right side and with the right foot, because they hold the bird on the left fist.*

I couldn't believe what Hinrik was saying – we were allowed to stay here for only two weeks. I had just fourteen short days in which to capture the gyrfalcons! Surely, the boy had made a mistake. He'd used a wrong word. He meant *months* not *weeks*. But he was adamant, and I could see by the grin on the face of the official that it must be true. The man would hardly have advised us to go home otherwise. It was all I could do not to howl aloud with frustration and misery, but I couldn't afford to let myself sink into despair.

I swallowed hard and tried to think. When my father and I had gone to the plains in Portugal to trap migrating hawks and falcons we had caught a dozen in just a few days. I only had to capture a pair. I must surely be able to do that in two weeks. And in any case I couldn't afford to stay here longer than that. With every day that passed the shadow of the pyre crept closer to my father. Even before the year was up, weakened by hunger, he could die of prison fever in those fetid dungeons. And what if they were torturing him, trying to force him to confess to killing the falcons, trying to make him betray others . . . No, no! Even two weeks was too long. I had to find those birds now – at once.

As we walked away from the quayside we clambered up on to the rough track that wound between the little turf huts. Racks of dried fish lined the upper slopes, but their rotting guts paved the path, along with mutton bones, offal and every kind of excrement, which was trodden into the dirt. The smoke from the cooking fires stank of burning dung, charred fish bones and scorched seaweed. It made my eyes sting. Vítor, Marcos and Fausto were all holding kerchiefs over their noses and looked as if they were about to vomit, but Hinrik was grinning and sniffing the air. To him it must have been the smell of home, but I remembered the stench of another fire, a fire that smelt of burning flesh and death. I shuddered.

Then I heard it. *Krery-krery-krery* – it was the cry of a hunting gyrfalcon. I frantically scanned the skies. Only gulls wheeled over the dark blue water. But even as I strained to find the call again above the screams of the seabirds, I knew I wouldn't hear it. The cry of the falcon had come not from the skies, but from somewhere deep inside me like a second heartbeat, or a tiny bubble of memory that rose and burst in my head. I gazed out across the bay towards the distant mountains, their tops hidden in the swirling grey clouds. Somehow in that moment I knew that's where I must go. If the white falcons existed anywhere on this island that is where I would find them. But it would take days to walk there – days I did not have.

Fausto clapped a hand on Hinrik's shoulder. 'Now, my lad, you can start earning the money we paid for you by finding us a decent inn for the night. Even in this goats' byre there must be one that doesn't stink like a piss-pot and serves a good supper. My belly is howling for some fresh, juicy meat after all that dried-up old salt pork.'

Vítor pushed the boy aside. 'No, we can't seek lodgings here. That clerk will be watching every move we make, or at least his spies will.' He jerked his head behind him, to where three men stood in the shadow of a hut, their gaze fixed on us.

'And there was me thinking that now you'd confessed to

264

being a Lutheran, you and that popinjay were best friends, or was that another of your lies?' Marcos spat out the words loaded with venom.

Vítor shrugged. 'Obviously, I had to tell him something. I couldn't very well say I'd come here to map this island, he'd have me arrested as a spy.'

'In that case I'm sorry that I didn't tell them,' Marcos said. 'He would have entertained us like kings if we handed him a spy.'

'Or arrested you as accomplices,' Vítor said with a granite smile. 'I think you will find they don't trouble themselves with minor inconveniences like evidence before they hang a man on this isle. You should be grateful to me, at least it got him on our side long enough to let us land.'

I knew from the weeks aboard the ship that quarrels like this could occupy them for hours, but for once I was grateful. The men were so busy glaring at one another that I could slip away unnoticed. I had already seen a man ambling across the track ahead of us on a tiny, shaggy horse, leading half a dozen small horses who crowded behind him, their bodies pressed tightly together and their heads resting on each other's backs. If I could ride, I could reach those mountains in a quarter of the time it would take me on foot.

I moved closer to Hinrik, and lowered my voice to a whisper. 'That man, do you think he would sell me a horse? Can you ask him?'

As I hoped, Vítor, Fausto and Marcos were so busy snarling at one another that they didn't even notice the boy and me walking off. The horse-owner glanced at me several times as Hinrik explained what I wanted, but his face told me nothing of what he might be thinking. Finally he waved his hand over the small herd, inviting me to choose. I had already studied the stocky, shaggy little beasts and pointed to a pretty honey-coloured mare, which, unlike some of the others, showed no sign of lameness. I urged Hinrik to hurry and negotiate a price, but it seemed that no business was ever done in haste in Iceland. Finally, the horse-owner seemed satisfied, and I was just about to claim my beast and mount when to my dismay I saw the others hurrying towards us along the track.

'Well done, my lad,' Fausto said. 'Horses – just what we need, since Vítor is so determined on not letting us rest here.'

He glared resentfully at Vítor. Then he stared in dismay at the little horses. Not one of them was bigger than thirteen hands and he was a tall, broad man.

'Ask this man where he keeps his larger mounts. Those couldn't carry us more than a mile.'

Hinrik answered without bothering to translate. 'They can carry you easy for miles at the *tölt*.'

'At the what?' Fausto said.

Hinrik wrinkled his nose as he struggled to explain. 'You know, fast. Not as fast as a gallop . . . but you will not be thrown about like a trot.' He shrugged at our blank faces. 'You will see. You want to buy five more, one for the packs and for me too?'

'Of course for you too, you little maggot,' Fausto said. 'We paid good money for you. You're coming with us. We want our money's worth.'

Our bundles were stacked in a heap, together with some wind-dried fish and a small iron cooking pot which had been much patched and repaired. The owner was reluctantly persuaded to load the beast for us, but not until he received yet another coin for his trouble. He laid two fresh turfs on the horse's sides and over these tied a flimsy wooden frame, studded with pegs, fastening it under the creature's belly. Then, using lengths of wool knotted like fishing nets, he wound them round the pegs and over our bundles.

As the man worked, Fausto peered dubiously at the frame. 'This wool won't hold for long. Have you nothing stronger? Rope?'

The Icelander briefly lifted his head, frowning up at the

266

seabirds drifting in the grey sky, as if he thought the question had come from them. Then he resumed his work, knotting the strands of wool so slowly that it seemed it would take the whole winter for him to finish.

A crowd of adults and children had gathered a little way off and stood silently watching us, their eyes following our every move, like a clowder of wild-eyed cats hungrily watching a flock of sparrows. With a groan of frustration at the slow pace of the Icelander's painstaking work, Fausto elbowed him aside and seized the strands of wool, winding them rapidly several times in a loop over the frame and under the horse's belly.

'Come on, let's go while we've still a chance of reaching the next village before dark. I've no desire to spend the night sleeping in the open in this purgatory.'

Fortunately my skirts were full enough to allow me to straddle my mount, though it had a very broad back for such a short creature. But the moment I was in the saddle, my horse tried to throw me off and was only stopped by the owner grabbing her head. I moaned, rubbing my knee which was throbbing from where I'd gripped the horse's sides to prevent myself falling.

'He says she is called Gilitrutt after the troll-wife,' Hinrik said, grinning. 'Let your legs hang. If you squeeze her it will make her bolt. Do not pull on the reins. It makes them gallop.'

'Then how am I to bring her to a halt, if I can't rein her in?'

Hinrik shrugged. 'She will stop . . . when she wants to.'

The rough track that led away from the village was only wide enough for us to ride single-file, although the horses seemed desperate to walk next to one another and kept trying to squeeze past rocks to get closer together. The boy rode ahead, followed by Marcos and Vítor, who was leading the packhorse behind his own mount. I came next and, behind me, Fausto brought up the rear.

Hinrik led us between great towering mounds of dark soil and rock piled in haphazard layers, like carelessly heaped slices of bread. Broad streams, teeming with swan, duck and grebe, meandered across the valley floor, their waters riffled by the stiff breeze into little peaks and troughs, like a newly ploughed field. Great cushions of grey moss snuggled around the base of jagged black rocks that stuck out of the ground like rows of shark's teeth, and between the patches of dark, wiry grass were vivid splashes of a strange pink plant I'd never seen before. At the base of the hillsides long stretches of marsh pools shone like broken fragments of mirrors as the light caught them, and white-tufted cotton grass swayed in the wind. Ahead of us in the distance a huge rounded mountain rose into the grey afternoon light, as if it was a sleepy giant curiously watching us tiny creatures crawling towards it.

I heard a deep, croaking *pruk-pruk-pruk* above me. A pair of ravens was circling round the black rocks up on the hillside, their wings outstretched, gliding on the wind for the pure joy of flying. Suddenly I saw this was not the entrance to purgatory at all, but to heaven. It was the most wildly beautiful place I had ever seen. I half-turned, wanting to share my excitement with my father as I had done so many times when I was a little girl, when he took me with him to trap the wild falcons. But even as I opened my mouth, I realized with a sickening jolt that he was not riding behind me, but lying in a dark dungeon deep beneath the earth. I gazed up at the sky, desperately hoping to hear that cry or see the familiar outline of the gyrfalcon circling above me, but there was no sign of the birds.

I was so intent on searching the skies for the falcons that at first I didn't see what was happening, until shouts and curses from the men jolted me back. The packhorse which Vítor had been leading behind his own mount had stopped and was jerking its head, trying to pull away from the leading rein. The pack which Fausto had helped to tie to the beast had slipped sideways, so that now all the weight of our bundles and the iron cooking pot hung on her left side. The horse flopped down in the track and tried to rid herself of the irritation by rolling on her back and thrashing violently.

Vítor dismounted and, flinging his reins at Marcos, marched back to try to pull the packhorse up on to her feet. Marcos dismounted too and, holding tightly to both horses, led them forward, looking wildly around for somewhere he might tether them, but there was not a tree or a post anywhere. Hinrik, who had been riding ahead, was plainly oblivious of the commotion behind him and had disappeared around one of the mounds of soil.

Vítor glanced up at Marcos. 'Hurry up and give me a hand. We'll have to get this pack off her before we can get her up.'

He tugged at one of the knots in the wool, but it only seemed to make it tighter. Exasperated, he pulled out his knife. 'I'll have to cut it.'

Up to then I had kept my seat, but I saw the most useful thing I could do now would be to dismount and help to hold the beasts while the others freed the packhorse. Behind me, Fausto was still mounted too. I half-turned my head and saw his horse drawing level with mine.

'Can you hold her while I dismount?' I handed him the reins and, seizing a handful of the horse's mane, I leaned forward, about to swing my leg over its back, when I felt something hit my horse's flank, as if someone had kicked the beast hard. She whinnied and sprang forward off the track. Fausto dropped the reins, but before I could grab at them, the horse galloped away with me frantically clutching at her mane. I had lost the stirrups and was desperately trying to keep my seat by gripping her sides tightly with my legs.

Hinrik's warning flashed through my head. I knew that by pressing the horse's sides I was only encouraging her to go faster, but I couldn't help myself. I was only holding on to her mane and I was terrified that if I relaxed my grip with my legs I would be thrown straight on to those sharp, jagged rocks.

As we dashed forward, I coaxed and pleaded with the horse to stop, but she took no more notice of me than she would a fly. I crouched low across her neck, groping for the swinging reins with one hand while I twisted the fingers of my other hand tighter into her mane. I was dimly aware that the ground right in front of us looked flatter and smoother and the vicious black rocks had given way to pools of water. Perhaps I could manage to slide from her back. I would be bruised, but at least I wouldn't smash my head open on the stones. I felt again the twinge from my injured knee and almost before I'd thought about what I was doing I began to shift my weight to the other side. I couldn't afford to fall on that leg again.

Without warning the horse staggered, her back legs buckled beneath her. The violent jerk dislodged the precarious hold I had on her and I found myself sliding sideways and backwards. I landed in something soft and at the same moment the horse lashed out wildly with her hooves, kicking and bucking as she tried to free her legs from the sucking mire in which she was caught. I rolled over, covering my head and trying to protect myself. I felt the rush of wind as her hoof passed within a hair's breadth of my head. Then, with one tremendous heave, she had freed herself and was gone.

My relief lasted barely half a breath. For in the same instant I discovered I was unhurt, I also realized that I was sinking. I was lying sprawled in a pool of warm black mud, but as soon as I tried to push my arms down to prise myself up my hands disappeared into the ooze. I scrabbled around, trying to feel something solid to push against, but there was nothing. Each time I moved, more of the thick, sticky mud welled up over my body and legs, pulling me in deeper. I was in the grip of a giant. I tried to pull one arm free, but dragging it up through the sucking mud was like trying to lift a blacksmith's anvil in one hand. Blind panic engulfed me and I screamed.

As I twisted around I saw a tall woman standing a few feet away from me. Where she had come from I had no idea, but she looked as old as poor Jorge. For a moment she just looked at me, then turned away and began to pick her way around the edge of the mire. I shouted at her to help, but she didn't even glance in my direction. I yelled again, certain that she was just going to walk on and leave me to drown.

She halted at the edge of the bog and swiftly untied a long, coarse apron from her waist, then she knelt down and flicked the apron towards me like a whip. I suddenly realized what she was trying to do. I tried to lift my hand to catch the end of it, but I couldn't pull it from the mud. The edge of the cloth fell near my face, but I couldn't grasp it. The black mud bubbled against my lips, and in terror I tried to arch my head up and away from it, but that only made me sink deeper.

She pulled the apron back and I could see she meant to throw it again. I heaved my arm up with all my remaining strength and, with a pop, my hand shot free of the mud. But the movement cost me dearly, for even with my head thrown back as far as I could, the mud was oozing into my mouth and nose. I was trying to hold my breath, but my lungs were bursting with pain. I was dimly aware of a cry and felt the edge of the apron whip across my face. I flayed around blindly with my fingers, and then I felt the blessed solidity of the cloth. I clutched it as hard as I could and felt the tension on the cloth as she gently began to tug it towards her. By pulling against the cloth, I managed to wrest my head a few precious inches out of the mud, and lay there coughing and choking.

The woman began to pull steadily. For all her great age she was surprisingly strong, but my hands, slippery with mud, kept losing their hold on the apron, and she was forced to stop until I could struggle to grasp it again. I had not moved more than an inch or two. I was utterly exhausted. My limbs felt like jelly. I didn't care any more. I just wanted to let go, sink down and down into the soft, warm mud and sleep for ever.

Marcos came running up behind the woman. He stopped a little way off and froze, staring wildly as if he was at a loss to know what to do. The woman half-turned her head and beckoned to him. Still he stood there as if he couldn't remember how to move.

'Marcos, help me! Please . . . help . . . me!'

The sound of my voice seemed to jerk him into life and he ran forward and crouched down next to the woman. She thrust the end of the apron into his hands.

'Twist the cloth around your wrists,' he called to me urgently.

I tried, but my fingers felt like sausages and every movement buried my arms deeper. When he saw that I had grasped it as well as I could, Marcos began to pull. I felt as if my arms were being dragged from their sockets. I willed myself to grip it, even though I knew it was useless.

'It's no use . . . I can't,' I wailed.

'You must, you're nearly there. Hold on, Isabela. Just hold on!'

Then, with a rapid slither like a newborn lamb sliding out of a ewe, my body burst from the mud and I felt hands clutching my arms and hauling me on to firm ground.

I lay on the grass, too weak even to sit up, mumbling my thanks to him over and over again. I looked around for the woman to thank her too, but she was nowhere to be seen.

'Are you cold?' Marcos asked anxiously, and I realized my teeth were chattering, but it was from shock not cold.

'Mud was warm.' The strangeness of that had only just occurred to me.

'It must be that little brook. There's steam rising from it. Come on, try washing some of that mud off in there.'

He had to support me the few yards to the shallow stream,

for my legs repeatedly gave way beneath me as if every drop of strength had been sucked out of my body. I touched the water gingerly. It was blissfully warm. I slipped into it and lay on hot stones on the bed of the stream, letting the water gently trickle over me.

Finally, when I felt strong enough to move again, Marcos helped me out and wrapped his own cloak around me, though it was so long I had to loop it over my arm. I glanced back towards the track. Vítor and Fausto were picking their way towards us around the black rocks. The two men were making slow progress encumbered by our packs, the cooking pot and stockfish, which they now had to carry upon their own backs.

Before they could reach us, I grabbed Marcos's arm and whispered urgently, 'I think Fausto deliberately kicked my horse and that's why she bolted.'

'But why on earth should he want to make your horse bolt? His foot probably nudged your beast by accident. It's hard to know where to put your legs on those brutes, especially when you're the size of that gangling lump Fausto. He could practically straddle that horse and still keep both feet on the ground.' Marcos smiled at me in a pacifying sort of way, as if I was a small child who had complained a playmate had shoved her over in a game. 'Those horses crowd together and lean on one another's flanks every chance they get. They're doing it now. It's little wonder he bumped you.'

He pointed to where Hinrik was riding back towards us, leading one of the other horses. The rest were following, pressing themselves so tightly together that it seemed as if they were one beast with twenty legs. My own mount, the wretched little troll-wife, was trotting calmly back towards her companions as if nothing had ever alarmed her, deftly skirting the rocks without once breaking her gait.

'You look as bedraggled as a street urchin,' Fausto said cheerfully as he drew close. 'But no bones broken, I hope.'

'Do you?' I answered coldly.

A vaguely startled expression crossed his face. But before he could reply, Hinrik trotted up.

'There is a *bóndabær* . . . farm . . . not far. We can sleep there.'

'You know the farmer? Are you sure he will give us hospitality?' Vítor asked him.

The boy looked mildly surprised. 'I do not know anyone in these parts. But it is the custom, if a stranger asks for shelter, he will be given it.'

Vítor turned to us. 'If the boy speaks the truth, then I think we should avail ourselves of the hospitality while it is still permitted for us to do so.' He lowered his voice. 'Let's sleep under a solid roof while we can, for if we find ourselves still in this land in two weeks' time, then we'll be forced to fend for ourselves out in this.' He swept his hand towards the distant mountain peaks, suddenly dark and menacing in the fading light.

'And will you still be here in two weeks, Lutheran?' Marcos asked sharply, but Vítor ignored him.

Hinrik, without even asking us if we wanted to remount, turned his horse's head and began threading his way over the springy turf and through the rocks. The rest of the horses turned as one and followed, leaving us no choice but to trail after them.

My knee was really aching now. I wrapped Marcos's cloak more tightly around me, but my sodden garments clung to me, chilling me to the bone. It wasn't just my wet clothes that made me shiver, though. Marcos was too kind and generous to see it, but whatever he said, I knew Fausto had tried to get my horse to throw me. The ground was littered with sharp rocks. If I had fallen from a galloping horse on to any one of those I would have been killed or badly hurt.

I felt someone's eyes on me and glanced over my shoulder in time to meet Vítor's fixed gaze. His stare was cold and intense and I felt as if he was trying to read every thought in my head. I still could not bring myself to trust him. For all that he had rescued me in the forest that night, I could not rid myself of that image of him standing over me with a stick raised menacingly above my head.

But it made no sense. As Marcos said, why should either man want to harm me? They couldn't have discovered who or what I was. If they had known, they would have told the captain of the ship that I was leaving Portugal illegally, and doubtless he would have been only too happy to chain me up until I could be returned, or sell me as a slave or even simply throw me overboard. They couldn't know who I was, so why should either man want to do me harm? Yet I could not shake off the feeling that that was exactly what they intended.

And it wasn't just my own life that they had threatened. If I was killed or badly injured and I couldn't return with the falcons, my father, my whole family would go to their deaths believing I had deserted them. And if my father, a Marrano, was executed for killing those royal birds, they would use the outrage of the people to round up others. How many other innocent lives would end in the flames? How many more sobbing girls would place a box of bones on the pyre? How many Jorges would die in agony, their mouths bound so tightly they couldn't even scream? Suddenly the enormity of what rested in my hands almost made me vomit with fear.

I had to get away from these men, and soon, before either of them could try to harm me again. My mistake before had been to involve the boy, Hinrik. This time I would have to do it alone.

Eydis

Mantle – when a falcon spreads her wings and her tail, and defensively arches over her food to protect her kill from other birds which might snatch it from her. If a falcon without a kill adopts this sitting position it is a sign she is irritated or feels threatened.

I lift the piece of black bog oak in my hands. It is an old friend, a friend I both respect and fear. The wood is oval like a giant egg, but it has been sliced down the middle and hollowed out, the hollow polished until it gleams in the firelight. It is a black mirror in whose labyrinthine depths the spirit wanders freely to see what it already knows but cannot yet give form.

I gaze unblinkingly into the black centre of the hollow. At first I see nothing but my own smoky reflection, but I know that I must sink beneath its surface, allow my sight to be pulled deeper and deeper into its heart until the hollow becomes bottomless, timeless, eternal, until I can see into the eighth day.

I am staring down a long, dark tunnel. A girl is standing at the far end. She is gazing towards me, as if she senses I am there, but cannot quite see me. She knows where she must go. But something has changed. A man is standing behind her. He is not one of the dead who follow her. He is alive and he is coming close to her, too close. He means her harm. She knows it and she is afraid. She turns away from me. Her fear is driving her, separating her from me, as a dog cuts out a single sheep from the flock. She is in danger, mortal danger. Even as I try to call out to her, she vanishes.

Someone is walking ahead of me. But it is not the girl. I recognize him. It is Ari. He is walking towards a farmhouse. It is the darkest hour of the night, and a chill wind is rolling down from the mountains. His step falters. He stops. He knows that something is terribly wrong. The farm dogs are howling, not barking excitedly at his approach, but whimpering in terror. They know him. He feeds them. They love him. At any hour when he approaches the farm, they recognize his tread, smell his scent on the wind and come running to leap up and lick him. But tonight they are cowering, trying to hide. They shrink from the house as if even to brush its walls terrifies them. All, that is, save one. This dog is screaming and jerking convulsively where it lies helpless on the ground. Ari can see at once that its back is broken.

He moves to try to help it, but he never reaches the poor creature, for his gaze is drawn instead to the door of the farmstead. Since the days of the Vikings, men have constructed such doors to withstand the onslaught of sword and spear. It is a craft learned from their fathers and their fathers before them. But now the stout timbers have been smashed open with such force that only a few splinters of wood dangle uselessly from the hinges and one of the great doorposts has crashed to the ground. Silence, as icy as a winter's sea, flows out from the dark passageway beyond. Ari is terrified, but he forces himself to climb through the splintered wood.

He edges warily down the passageway as if he is in a stranger's house, though he knows this place as well as he knows his own flesh. He creeps into the great hall beyond. Three oil lamps burn on those few wooden pillars which still remain upright. Their light is thin, flickering like candles on a tomb, and he knows at once that this is a grave.

The wooden beds are shattered as if great boulders have been hurled at them, but it is not rocks that have been thrown across the room, but bodies. Ari finds little Lilja lying in a twisted bloody heap at the base of one of the pillars. Her head is crushed as if it had no more substance than a snail's shell. Her sister Margrét's face is frozen in agony and terror. Her belly has been ripped open, her guts torn out. Unnur, her mother, is dead beside her daughter, her chest crushed in an embrace so powerful that the broken pieces of her ribs are protruding from the mangled flesh. Her sightless blue eyes stare up at Ari, even in death beseeching him for mercy that was not granted.

Ari is retching now, sweating with shock and fear. He is praying desperately that one man at least has survived, just one. But then he sees him, Fannar. His head has been torn from his shoulders, and lies, eyes still open, between his legs. He still grasps his axe in his hand, but the blade bears no blood. How could it? What chance did he have, what chance did any of them have against that monster?

Ari flees from the stench of blood. He hurtles back down the darkened passageway, desperate to get out of the house of death, as if somehow he will find life waiting outside.

I see him emerge from the broken doorway. I move towards him, wanting to comfort him, but I see the terror spreading across his face. My arms are spread wide, but he backs away from me, pleading, sobbing. I taste my cold, fetid breath. I feel the grave mould creeping across my face, eating into the skin. My lips curl into a snarl and I feel the strength pounding through my hands like rivers of fire. I know I am going to crush him as I crushed Unnur. I know I am going to rip his limbs from his body as I twisted Fannar's head from his shoulders. I know I am the draugr and I will destroy them all!

It takes all my strength to tear my gaze from the dark mirror and send the wooden hollow clattering to the cave floor. As my mind returns to the cave, dark laughter rolls around its walls. I look down. Valdis's mouth is open wide, her head thrown back.

'What did you see that frightened you so, my sweet sister?

278

Could you see me, Eydis, Eydis? I think you did. You are growing fond of me, I knew you would. Let me in. You can't close your mind to me for ever. It weakens you to try. Sooner or later I will creep in. I will slip between your sleeping and your waking. I will slide into your dreams. You will grow weary and careless, you know you will. It is only a matter of time, my sweet Eydis, and I can wait, oh yes, the dead are well schooled in the art of waiting.'

I try to close out the words. I have to take more care. I am sickened by what I have seen in the black mirror. I knew that the draugr would use us if I could not drive him back into his own body, but to see the shadow of it, taste the foulness of the grave in my mouth, see death in my hands – that goes beyond knowledge, it enters the very soul. And it will happen exactly as I have seen it, if I cannot find a way to stop him.

And Fannar and his family will only be the beginning of the destruction he will wreak across the land. In his hatred and jealousy of the living he will kill as surely as a cloud of poison gas. With each slaughter he will grow in strength. With each drop of blood he spills, his craving for murder will increase. And no one, not even the man who raised him, will have the power or strength to stop him then.

I did not mean to see Fannar's fate. Heidrun is right, I have allowed my powers to wither. Having to fight, both sleeping and waking, to close my mind to the draugr takes all that strength I possess. When my spirit is inside the black mirror I am vulnerable. I cannot defend myself against him. I know that now. I dare not risk using it again when I am alone with him.

But the girl is in danger. If she does not reach the cave, if she cannot bring the dead here, then all is lost. I have to try to protect her, to make her turn back to me.

The cave is growing warmer. The heat makes me drowsy, but I must not surrender to sleep, not yet. I push myself to my feet and cross to my stores, moving aside jars and bundles until I find what I seek – fern seed to make the girl invisible to evil spirits; dried blood-red rowan berries to summon the spirits of the dead to battle. I take a few flakes of precious salt and mix it with the water from the hot bubbling pool, stirring it three times with my little finger as the sun turns. I reach for my horn lucet which hangs from my waist and dip the cord which dangles from it three times into the salt water. Then I loop and knot, loop and knot, fastening the rowan berries and fern seed deep inside the heart of the cord.

'The black thread of death to call the spirits from their graves. The green thread of spring to give them hope. The red thread of blood to lend them our strength. As we turn the cord towards the sun, so we turn the eyes of dead towards the living. Rowan, protect her. Fern, defend her. Salt, bind her to *us*!'

Valdis's head twists up to gaze at me from eyes that are all black. 'You could plait a cord as long as the ocean is deep and you won't reach her, my sweet sister. What feeble charms and powers you think you possess cannot reach beyond the walls of the cave. That is why they chained you up in here. That is why they bound you in iron to make you powerless and stop you reaching out to them. You can no more protect the girl than you can bring her here. You are weak, Eydis, Eydis. Accept it, accept me. Let me join myself to you and I will give you power to take vengeance for what they have done to you. I will give you the strength to destroy them all!'

Chapter Ten

The lord of Sassay was granted the right to hunt throughout the diocese of Evreux with a pair of male and female goshawks together with six spaniels and two greyhounds. He was permitted to carry his goshawks into the church of Our Lady of Evreux and could set them to perch on the main altar at whichever position was most convenient to him. So that his day's hunting was not interrupted, he could order Mass to be said at any time that pleased him and the curé of Ézy could say the Mass at that church whilst wearing his hunting boots and spurs and with a drum beating instead of music.

The lords of Chastelas were granted the privilege of taking their place among the canons of the church of Auxerre carrying their sparrowhawks on their fists, wearing their swords as well as their surplices, carrying the amice (priestly stole) on their arms and sporting a hat covered in feathers. And the treasurer of this church could assist at Mass while carrying a sparrowhawk on his fist, a right he demanded because the treasurer of the church at Nevers had also been accorded this prerogative. For the hunting bird was deemed to be a bird of noble blood and therefore could no more be denied its place at the high altar in the church than could a lord or a king.

Isabela

Truss – *when a falcon seizes the quarry in the air and flies off with it.*

I was just beginning to think that Hinrik had been imagining the farmstead, when we crested a low hill and the horses ambled to a halt. Hinrik swivelled around on his horse's back and pointed ahead of him. I could see nothing except some turf-covered hillocks, but then I noticed that a thin plume of lavender smoke was meandering from the top of one of them. As we drew closer, a wooden door became visible in the side of the hillock. Great boulders formed the base of the walls of the strange house, but higher up they seemed to be fashioned from nothing more solid than sods of earth pressed between thin strips of turf. Hinrik, sliding effortlessly from his horse, marched up and hammered with his fist on the great wooden door. The boom echoed back at us from out of the hillside.

The horses moved restlessly as we waited. Vítor was grasping the hilt of the dagger in his belt, though he had not drawn it from its sheath. From the stance of the others and the tension on their faces, I guessed their fingers had also strayed close to their knives. The wind cut through my wet clothes and I had to clench my teeth to stop them chattering.

Eventually the door was flung open and a man ducked out, closely followed by a small woman with a half-naked toddler balanced on her hip and a runny-nosed boy of about four or five clinging to her skirts. Hinrik spoke rapidly to the man whose gaze flicked over each of us in turn as he listened to the boy in silence.

Finally he took a step towards us. 'Gerðu svo vel!' The expression on his face was grim.

Vítor and Fausto glanced uncertainly at each other, their hands still on the hilts of their daggers. I tried to smile at the woman, but she merely stared sullenly at us, her shoulders hunched, wary. Her free hand crept down and grasped the shoulder of the little boy who peered around her legs, as if she was frightened we would snatch him away from her.

'He says to enter,' Hinrik said.

The man's expression was hardly inviting, but Hinrik stepped confidently through the door, and rather more cautiously we followed. We squeezed through a small, narrow passageway until we emerged in a long room smelling of acrid smoke and damp. This hall must have occupied the whole length of the mound we'd seen from the outside. Wooden panelled berths were ranged down either side and heaped with patched wool blankets and old fox-fur skins which had lost most of their hair and stank. The roof was held up by several stout wooden posts placed at intervals down the length of the hall, and tiny cracks of light filtered down between the sods which covered the roof.

I couldn't believe the blackened walls were just made of sods and touched one to find out. It really was earth, and wet earth too, blackened with mildew. The floor was covered with ashes from the fire as well as numerous fish and animal bones which had been stamped down into it to make a hard surface. A long fire pit had been cut into the middle of the floor, on which a couple of cooking pots bubbled. The smoke wandered out through a vent in the cobwebbed roof ridge, which was also the only source of daylight. A few stone lamps were fixed to the wooden posts, and from the dim mustard light and stench of stinging smoke coming from them I guessed they were burning fish oil.

The farmer motioned us to sit with a grunt and a jerk of his head, but we could see no chairs.

'You sit there on the beds.' Hinrik gestured towards the berths. 'No!' he yelped as I attempted to do so.

'Men sit this side, on the port side, women must sit on the starboard of the *badstofa* . . . the great hall.'

I crossed to the other side and hesitantly sat down. The mattress crunched beneath me, releasing a smell of mouldy hay and dried seaweed. Opposite me on the men's side, a wizened old man was hunched in the corner of the bed, a heap of patched and tattered woollen blankets pulled up to his chin, saliva dribbling continuously from his mouth on to the corner of the blanket. His red-rimmed eyes peeped fearfully over the top of the bedclothes, and his hands shook as he pulled the edges even higher up over his face.

We all stared awkwardly at one another in a silence that no one seemed to know how to break. The woman brought us beakers of watered-down milk, which Hinrik informed us was called *bland*, at least that's what I thought he said. Even across the dimly lit hall I could see the expressions of distaste on the faces of Marcos and Fausto, though if Vítor also hated it, he was disguising it well.

The fishy steam from the pots, the smell of damp wool, musty earth and the smoke from the dried cow's dung burning on the fire, created such a fug that I could hardly breathe. I almost longed to be back out in the cold air again. I was desperate to change out of my filthy, wet clothes, the skirts of which were beginning to steam at the bottom from the heat of the fire, though none of the Icelanders took any notice of my state. But there didn't seem anywhere private I could strip off and I couldn't bring myself to ask Hinrik.

The woman ladled the contents of one of the bubbling cooking pots into wooden bowls fashioned from staves and hoops, with hinged lids. These eating bowls were nearly as heavy as my mother's cooking pots. We ate still sitting on the beds, grateful for the food to give us something to do other than stare at one another. I discovered I was ravenously hungry, but the food was almost as tasteless as the watered milk: dried cod, softened only a little by boiling in water, and flavoured with a sour white butter. I saw the woman watching me anxiously as I ate and I immediately felt guilty. I beamed at her, trying to look as if I was relishing every mouthful.

The meal seemed to be the signal to talk, at least for the men, with Hinrik translating. The farmer asked nothing about what had brought us to Iceland, but he wanted to know about life in Portugal, how many horses we had, how many cattle, what crops we grew. He seemed baffled when the men told him they lived in towns and had no need to farm.

All the time they were talking, I was barely listening. There was one thing I was desperate to learn, but I dared not ask directly for fear of arousing suspicion. Try as I might, I couldn't think how to work the conversation round, so in the end I just blurted out the only thing that came to mind.

'Hinrik, I've heard that the wild animals on this island are white as snow, because it is so cold. Is that true?'

The Icelanders stared open-mouthed at me as if amazed that I was addressing them. Hinrik thought for a moment, frowning, then answered without bothering to translate the question for the farmer.

'Dogs . . . no, like dogs . . . foxes! They are white in winter. And great white bears, sometimes they come from Greenland on the ice. They must be hunted. White bears kill even a strong man with one blow.'

'And birds, white birds, do they come here?'

Hinrik laughed. 'Ptarmigan? Not down here, but up in the mountains there are more than there are gulls at the shore. Good eating, if you can catch them.'

'I heard stories of a falcon, a white falcon. Is it true, does such a bird exist here?'

The boy shifted uneasily, then muttered something to the

farmer. A long discussion followed and I could barely contain my impatience.

'What's he saying, Hinrik?'

'He says where there are ptarmigan on the ground to eat there will always be white falcons in the sky above. They follow them. They are sisters. Strange sisters, for ptarmigan are worth nothing, but the falcons are worth sacks of gold. He says the Danes would sell their own wives and children for them. Two hundred white falcons they took last year. The hunters have to pay much money to the Danes for permission to capture the birds . . . He says how can a wild bird belong to any man? The falcons belong only to the sky. It is as crazy as a man saying he owns the fire in the mountains or the rain that falls.'

The farmer spoke again and whatever he said made Hinrik laugh. He turned to Marcos, Vítor and Fausto sitting beside him on the bed.

'He says he hopes you have not come here to steal a white falcon. Last year, there was a boy from Bolungarvík. The Danes caught him with a sack. He swore inside was a white ptarmigan. But they opened the sack and pulled out a white falcon. The boy said he must have grabbed the wrong bird when the falcon attacked the ptarmigan. But they did not believe him. So . . .'

Hinrik put his hands round his throat in the manner of a noose. Lolling his tongue out and crossing his eyes, he made a gurgling sound which caused the farmer's little son to giggle so much he almost tumbled off the bed.

My three companions laughingly assured him they would attempt no such crime, but Vítor's smile faded rapidly and he stared at me, frowning as if he somehow knew why I had raised the question.

'I was just asking,' I said hastily, 'because I'd love to see one of these birds flying. I've heard they are beautiful. Are there any nests in these parts?'

'Not here, they nest in the north. When it is summer the hunters climb the rocks to take the chicks. Many men die. You know where a white falcon nests on a mountain, for the bones of the hunters lie at the bottom.'

The conversation drifted away to hunting. The woman fetched a leather bottle and poured a measure of thick liquid into beakers for each of the men. Whatever it was, they seemed to relish it much more than the *bland* and soon their eyes began to shine in the firelight and laughter came easily and grew louder, as they reclined and drank deeply whenever the woman refilled their beakers – all, that is, except Vítor, who had taken one sip and no more.

The more the farmer drank, the wilder his tales of his hunting prowess became. Through Hinrik, he regaled the men with stories about the wild horses he had captured, of the white bears he had fought and the foxes he had killed for their valuable pelts. He even told us that once, when he was a boy, he and his friends were tracking a huge fox which tried to escape them by crossing a great river of ice. This frozen river was criss-crossed by crevasses and ravines that were so deep and slippery that if a man tumbled into one he would never be able to clamber out again and would die of starvation, if he didn't freeze first. His friends were too scared to venture on to the ice for they all knew of men who had fallen to their deaths down those treacherous crevasses, but the farmer was determined to get that fox, so he fearlessly went on alone to capture the beast and lived to tell the tale. He thumped his chest with pride as he recounted this story. He sounded just like the nobles at Sintra when they returned from their hunting, always full of impossible tales of courage and daring. I listened only because I was desperately hoping that when he'd drunk enough the farmer might speak again of the white falcons, but he didn't.

I could not afford to wait till summer to take an eyas from its nest like the hunters, though I knew that would be the easiest way to capture a bird and give me the best chance of bringing it back alive. It would be too late to save my father by then. I would have to try to trap a pair of adult birds as they searched for their prey. Follow the ptarmigan, like the falcons. But where would I find the ptarmigan? And how would I recognize them? I'd never seen one before – was it as small as a swallow or as large as a duck? But I dared not ask more. I had already shown too much interest.

I rose as cautiously as I could and slipped across to the passage. Vítor's head jerked up.

'I need to relieve myself,' I muttered.

I felt my way down the damp, narrow passage. It took all my strength to heave the great wooden door open, but outside all was quiet. Not a spark of light showed anywhere in the cold, clinging blackness. If I took more than few steps from the house, I would never find it again. I edged along the rough stones of the wall, hoping that my eyes would accustom themselves to the darkness. If I could take one of the horses, while the men were all occupied inside, then I could put as much distance as I could between myself and them, before anyone realized I was gone. The horse would surely be able to find the track even if I couldn't. I had no idea where our packs had been stored, but if I couldn't find them I would have to go without them. This might be the only chance I got.

The wall seemed to go on for ever, but eventually I came to the end and I stared out into the darkness, listening for the crunch of horses' hooves as they shifted in the coarse grass, straining to hear the snorting and whining they make when they smell a human approaching, but I could hear nothing except the wind stirring the dried stalks and the sharp, insistent cry of some bird or animal I didn't recognize.

Perhaps the horses had been stabled in the byre at the other end of the house. I thought I had glimpsed one earlier. I groped my way back along the wall, trying to find the door which would tell me I had reached halfway along. Then suddenly my hand connected with something soft and warm. I stifled a cry as I stepped backwards.

'Isabela, so there you are! Can't see a bloody thing.'

The voice was slurred, but it was still recognizable. My stomach contracted. It was Fausto, the man who only a few hours ago had tried to kill me.

'What do you want?' I could hear my voice shaking.

'You . . . looking for you. Wanted to speak to you alone. Tried earlier today . . . but you galloped off.'

If I yelled for help they'd never hear it deep inside that hillside. I tried to keep calm.

'It's cold. I'm going back inside. Whatever you have to say you can say it in there.'

'You're not going back inside.' He stretched out his arm, barring the doorway.

I couldn't push him aside. He was twice my weight and size. I could try to run. Once I was out there in the darkness, he'd never be able to find me, but suppose I stumbled into another bog? I shivered.

I fought to keep the panic from rising in my chest. 'What do you want with me?'

'Come with you, of course. I know you've no intention of going back in there. You're going to look for them, aren't you?'

'What . . . look for what?' I stammered.

'White falcons.' He lowered his voice to an exaggerated tipsy whisper, though there was no one to hear us. 'That's why you were asking the lad about them. First night on the ship when I told you about the eagles . . . could tell that you knew more about falconry than you were admitting. That's why you came here, isn't it?'

A wave of cold nausea rose in my throat. 'I don't know anything about birds . . . I came here to join my husband.'

He chuckled. 'Come on, a husband who didn't trouble to

come to the ship to meet you? A husband who sent you no papers? If you were married to a Dane, you'd not have to leave here for the winter. I saw the look on your face when you heard you only have two weeks. There is no husband, is there? You can tell me.'

He attempted a clumsy pat on my shoulder. I shrank back.

'We all have our little secrets, Isabela. Don't you worry, I won't breathe a word. Ssh!' He leaned over me, pressing his finger to his lips. 'Trust me, Isabela, I can help you get those birds. That farmer seems to think they're worth a few escudos, and I'll let you into a little secret of my own. I could do with a little gold right now.'

'What happened to the diamonds? I thought you were planning to get rich finding those?'

'There are no diamonds here.'

'Then why come to Iceland?'

He deflated like a pierced bladder and slumped dejectedly against the wall. He was more dulled than actually drunk, his movements slow and clumsy. If he made a grab for me I might be able to dodge him. I tried to ease away from him a little, bracing myself to run as soon as he was off guard.

'Planned to go to Canada to search for diamonds, but I was . . . had to leave Portugal in a hurry. Costs a lot to get passage to Canada. Long voyage. Couldn't raise the money I needed in time.'

'Why did you need to leave so quickly?'

'Killed a man.'

He must have heard my gasp of fear.

'Not murder, nothing like that.' He seized my arm so suddenly I didn't have a chance to pull away. 'It was an accident . . . swear to you.' He drew a deep breath and shook his head as if trying to clear the mist from his thoughts. 'So happy that night. Can't believe it all changed in the time it takes to draw breath . . . festival for Our Lady of Light in Sampaio. My friends and I, we just went to celebrate, same as everyone else. After the procession, people were drinking and eating in the streets. All the women were dressed in their prettiest dresses. My friend started talking to a girl, flirting with her. Everyone does it. It's what festivals are for. Bit of harmless fun, that's all. But her fiancé saw them together. He got jealous and shoved my friend away.

'You know how it is, punches were thrown. All the lads started to take sides and join in. It was just fists at first. Then I saw one man draw a knife and come up behind my friend. I threw myself at him. There was a struggle. The next thing I knew a young man was lying on the ground, blood pouring from his guts. I was horrified. I started to back away, but someone yelled that I'd done it, and when I looked down, I saw my own hand was covered in blood. I ran then. I got away, but later I discovered the young man had died and, worse still, he was the son of a noble. His father was determined that he would settle for nothing less than the blood of the man who killed his son. No choice. Had to get passage on the very first ship I could find.'

After the events of that afternoon I found it only too easy to believe that Fausto had killed a man, but I did not believe it was an accident, any more than him kicking my horse had been.

Fausto was still gripping my arm. My fear spun into anger.

'So you didn't intend to come to Iceland to look for diamonds. That story you told us on board the ship about India and the eagles carrying up the diamonds from the ravine, that was a lie too, wasn't it?'

'No!' he said hotly. 'It's completely true, I swear.' He shuffled uncomfortably. 'But it wasn't exactly my story . . . a merchant told it to me. But I do know all about diamonds. I worked for a jeweller who set precious stones into necklaces, earrings, brooches and buckles for the wealthy. My master taught me how to read a stone, to assess its colour and weight, how to look for flaws and determine when and where it was cut. I can tell you what any stone is worth. If I can reach Canada, I can find diamonds. I can make a fortune. I just have to find the money to get there.

'And if those birds are as valuable as that farmer seems to think . . . Look, this is a dangerous place for a woman alone. You can't do this by yourself. But I can take care of you. We can find those birds together and I can help you sell them. That's something I do know about, persuading men to buy . . . and there's something else . . . something I must tell you. You see, the truth is –'

'The truth is what, Senhor Fausto?'

Fausto spun round. The figure standing in darkness behind him raised the little fish-oil lamp, shielding the fragile flame from the wind with his hand. Although the light was feeble, it deepened the hollows under his cheekbones and made caverns of his dark eyes, so that his head looked like a pale skull suspended in the darkness.

'Vítor!' Fausto snapped. 'What the devil do you mean, sneaking around eavesdropping on private conversations?'

'I merely chanced to overhear your last remark, Fausto. I was, in fact, in search of the young lady. She had been gone so long I feared she might have met with an accident or was unable to find her way back. It was foolish of you to venture out here without a lamp, Isabela. The ground is treacherous enough by day, but at night you could blunder into any kind of peril and no one would hear your cries for help.'

He reached his arm round Fausto and extended his hand to me.

'Come, let me escort you safely back inside into the warm.'

I hesitated, not knowing which of the two men I feared more at that moment, but at least if Vítor was taking me back inside, he could not be intending to harm me, for now at any rate – not even he would be stupid enough to attempt to do so in front of a witness. Reluctantly I placed my hand on his and allowed myself to be drawn past Fausto.

Vítor's thin, spidery fingers were even colder than my own. He glanced back over his shoulder as we squeezed down the musty passageway.

'Isabela, let me offer you a word of caution. You would be well advised not to trust Senhor Fausto. I fear that he and the truth are not well acquainted. Such men wear a cloak of courtesy which often conceals a dagger of malice. You should try to avoid him as much as you can until we are able to rid ourselves of him.'

We are able to rid ourselves . . . So he intended to attach himself to me, maybe even get rid of Marcos and travel alone with me. It was almost as if Vítor was really starting to believe I was his wife. Was he planning to make it so? I had no experience of being wooed, but even I was sure that what I saw in Vítor's eyes was certainly not love.

And as for Fausto, had he told me that story about killing a man to let me know that he was capable of murdering me too? Had he been about to make a more explicit threat before Vítor interrupted him? If I had not been certain before, what had just happened outside had me convinced that I must get far away from both of them as quickly as I could.

I lay huddled uncomfortably on the bed. The dried seaweed and mouldy straw which filled the pallet crunched deafeningly in my ear every time I or the woman and her children moved, releasing a sickening stench. I was determined to keep awake, but there was little danger of falling asleep. The three men lay hunched under the threadbare blankets and furs in the opposite bed stalls, with Hinrik, the farmer and his old father. I couldn't see their faces, but I sensed that while the others might be snoring, Vítor, like me, was still lying awake.

The blood-red glow of the embers in the fire pit drew my gaze back to it. There was a whole landscape in miniature contained in that smouldering, blackened pit – rock-strewn valleys and mountains, with veins of fire running through them, dark caves and white ash peaks. As I stared into its depths, I could almost feel I was walking through those rocks, climbing the side of that mountain, sliding into the cave.

Krery-krery-krery!

I started up on one elbow, staring about the hall. The cry was so close that it was as if I was again in my father's mews. But surely the farmer was not keeping a gyrfalcon hidden in his house, after all he had said about the dangers?

Krery-krery-krery.

It was fainter now, but insistent as if it was screaming from a distant mountain, yet was determined its cry be heard. But where? Hinrik had said there were no falcons in these parts, and besides, the white falcon did not hunt at night.

I half-sensed a movement, and turned my head back to the fire pit. An elderly woman was standing in front of it. In the owl-light of the hall I couldn't see her clearly, only the shape of her blocking out the fire beyond. Was she wife to the old man in the bed? She was holding a little child by the hand, trying to push her behind her own body. She raised her other arm over her face, cringing, as if trying to ward off a heavy blow. Then, as if the blow had fallen, she crumpled into the darkness of the earth floor and was gone, leaving behind her only a cold, damp breeze which lifted a tiny flake of white ash in the fire pit and sent it soaring into the shadows above. Had I just imagined her there? Without knowing why, my fingers reached for the white finger bone hanging in the bag around my neck.

Krery-krery-krery.

I could barely hear it. It was only the breath of the scream, not the cry itself. But it was enough.

Ricardo

Summed – *when a falcon has fledged and grown all her flight feathers, or has grown new feathers after the moult, and is ready to fly.*

I woke with what tasted like a beggar's armpit in my mouth, and my head ringing like a blacksmith's anvil. It took a few moments to realize where I was, and even longer to work out that I was lying with someone's foot halfway up my arse and a hairy arm draped across my head. I struggled out of the tangle of groaning bodies, balding furs and musty blankets.

There was no sign of Hinrik, but the old man snored on in his corner of the bed, propped upright just as he had been last night. Even his own farts didn't wake him. The farmer's wife was stirring a great pot over the fire, and shot us a look of disgust that would have outdone even my Silvia's scathing glances, and, as all the saints know, Silvia could floor a man at twenty paces with one of her withering looks.

As her husband and my two companions struggled upright, she silently handed each of us a bowl of what looked like grey glue, so thick and glutinous that I was certain it could never be coaxed from the bowl. I managed a couple of spoonfuls before the whole mess tried to crawl its way back up my throat again. I dashed out of the hall and only just made it through the door before my breakfast made its bid for freedom.

I leaned weakly against the turf wall and drew in great gulps of cold air. What the devil had been in that drink last night? I didn't remember a thing, except for a dim memory

296

of hating Vítor for some reason, but then that didn't tell me much. I'd loathed the man since he first set foot on the ship.

Hinrik sauntered around the back of the house. He grinned when he saw me. 'It was a good night, yes?'

I groaned and rubbed at my eyeballs which were as swollen and raw as if they'd been skinned. How had he managed to sleep in that fug of smoke and look so lively in the morning? The impudent puppy plainly found my misery hilarious. I would have kicked his arse just to remind him I owned him, if I could have trusted myself to do it without falling on my own backside, but the lesson would have to wait until the ground stopped tilting.

I stumbled over to a trough and dashed some water on to my face. How it hadn't frozen, I don't know, for it was far colder than ice. I can only guess that it was so thick with slime and dirt that nothing would make it freeze. Every animal on the farm seemed to have pissed in it, but at least the cold cleared my head a little.

Vítor emerged from the doorway. 'Have you seen Isabela?' he demanded as I walked back towards the house.

His face was the colour of a squashed slug and he seemed to be holding his head very stiffly as if it was thumping as much as mine, which was at least some consolation. But it couldn't have been from the drink, for he'd taken hardly any last night, though sleeping in that fug was enough to make anyone bilious.

'Isabela, where is she?' he repeated impatiently.

'Isn't she inside?' I said, staring around vaguely.

I couldn't recall seeing her since I'd woken, but then it had taken all my concentration just to get my limbs to move in a vaguely co-ordinated fashion.

'I'd hardly be asking you if she was,' Vítor snapped. 'Hinrik, have you seen her?'

'She's gone. She took some smoked puffin meat. The breakfast was not cooked then. Too early.'

Vítor leapt forward and seized Hinrik by the shoulders, shaking him till his teeth rattled. 'She's left? All by herself? You stupid half-wit, why didn't you wake us? Why did you let her go?'

Hinrik was goggle-eyed with fear. I dragged Vítor off the boy and both of them stood there panting. The lad looked on the verge of taking to his heels.

'You saw what happened yesterday,' Vítor yelled at him. 'She doesn't know how to look after herself in this place.' He took a deep breath as if he was making a great effort to regain control. 'How long ago did she leave? Which way did she go?'

Hinrik was watching Vítor apprehensively as if he thought he would launch another attack at any moment.

'Before the sun was up. She went . . .' The lad tentatively gestured along the track which led in the direction of the mountains.

'Did she say *where* she was going?' Vítor demanded impatiently, looking as if he was about to try to shake the information out of him again. 'Didn't you ask?'

'Look, we're wasting precious time standing around here,' I said. 'Let's just saddle up and go after her as quickly as we can, before she gets herself into any more danger.' I turned to the farmer who was stumbling out of the door, his face as crumpled and creased as a whore's petticoats. 'Hinrik, ask him to bring us our horses, will you, quick as he can.'

Hinrik translated and the farmer spat on to the ground and muttered something. Clearly the drink had left him with a foul hangover.

'He says fetch them yourself,' Hinrik said.

I felt my own temper rising as fast as Vítor's. 'Then where are they?'

'He says back with their owner by now.'

'But we *are* the owners,' Vítor said indignantly. 'We paid a great deal for those beasts.'

'How are the horses to know that?' Hinrik giggled, then, catching sight of Vítor's face, abruptly stopped himself.

'Tether does not hold them,' he said. 'He says you should have taken them to the stone fold and hobbled them. Horses return home first chance they get. Everyone knows that.'

Vítor railed furiously at the lad and followed it up with a hard clout across the boy's head which, thinking he fully deserved it, I made no attempt to prevent. But finally, even Vítor could see that no amount of shouting or raging was going to recover the animals. In the meantime, as I reminded him, Isabela was getting further away.

We assembled our packs, abandoning all but the essential items we could carry on our own backs, and set off in pursuit of Isabela, with Vítor still muttering that the farmer had probably stolen our beasts himself and was hiding them somewhere until we were safely out of sight. If he hadn't been so anxious to find the girl, he said, he would have searched every inch of the place and would most assuredly do so when he returned. There was only one consolation in all this, and that was that Isabela had apparently been forced to depart on foot as well, so that I was sure it wouldn't be long before we caught up with her.

The Jesuits were not joking when they said this would be like a pilgrimage. Climbing up the steps of some monastery on your knees would be less painful than marching over that terrain. I'm used to city streets, not dirt tracks, and when I wasn't sinking knee-deep in freezing mud, I was barking my shin on a rock, or flaying my legs on thorns. One of the sailors told me that when Satan saw that God had created the world, he was jealous and demanded the right to create just one little piece of land himself. He laboured hard for a week, throwing into it all the skills he had to create a piece of hell on earth, and the country he made was Iceland. Never was a truer story told.

After several hours of walking, I was almost at the point

of refusing to take another step when we heard laughter and raised voices carried towards us on the wind almost at the same time as we saw the men ahead of us on the track. All four of us hesitated and peered warily ahead to see what might be amusing them.

When you live by your wits in the streets of Belém or Lisbon, you learn to read a crowd. Not that this was a crowd – I could dimly make out three, maybe four, figures – but still it becomes second nature to peer round the door of a tavern or pause before entering a square. You sense, just by the way people are gathering, that trouble is bubbling up like foul water in a ditch. Then, unless you are itching to get your nose smashed or a dagger in your back, you know it's time to slip quietly away before anyone notices you. I'm fond of my face and want to keep its features exactly as God made them.

But there are some men who have the brains of bulls. Wave anything in front of their squinty little eyes and they'll charge at it, without even bothering to look to see if they are making straight for a spear. Vítor, instead of turning away, simply quickened his stride.

I ran a couple of steps and grabbed his arm, pulling him round.

'This way,' I whispered. 'Quickly, take cover behind those rocks. If we cut across behind this rise we can avoid them and rejoin the track further up.'

Vítor jerked his arm away. 'They've got hold of someone. It's obvious they mean mischief,' he added as a cry of pain cut through the bellows of raucous laughter that drifted back towards us.

'Exactly,' I said. 'So let's avoid a fight and go round them. We can't afford any delays if we're to catch up with Isabela. Besides, we don't even know if they're armed, and there are only three of us.'

But at that moment we heard a shout. It was a woman's voice and she was yelling in our own tongue.

'That *is* Isabela,' our companion shouted.

In a trice he was throwing off his pack, and with his hand already drawing his dagger, he had sprinted past Vítor and me down the rough stony track with a bellow loud enough to make one of the men turn round. Vítor and I struggled to disengage our own packs, tossing them over the rocks on the edge of the track before we followed him.

Isabela was pinned down on the grass by three youths. One of them, his face covered with the red pimples of adolescence, was kneeling astride her, trying to yank up her skirts, and a second was standing on one of her wrists, holding her to the ground while she fought desperately with her free hand to fend off her attacker.

The third youth had wheeled round to face us, a short-bladed knife in his hand.

'Let her go,' I demanded.

'Hvem er du?'

I'd no idea what he said, but there was no mistaking the insolent tone. I looked round for Hinrik, but the wretched little coward was nowhere to be seen. I only hoped he was hiding and hadn't run off, not that I would blame him after the way Vítor had yelled at him.

A squeal from Isabela, as the bastard ground her wrist hard into the ground, recalled me to the point.

'Leave her alone!'

'Hun er Katolik.' The youth pushed his cabbage face close to mine. 'KATOLIK!' He stepped back and jabbed the knife upwards.

'Skrub af, gamle! Eller skal du ha' taesk?'

I may not have understood the words, but I all too nearly got the point. I think, roughly translated, he was inviting me to leave before I got a knife between my ribs. The ill-mannered youth looked back at his friend who was kneeling astride the writhing Isabela and gestured impatiently at him with his blade.

'Skynd dig nu, eller lad mig komme til.'

There's one thing I've learned about fighting – if you really can't avoid it, then make damn sure you get your blow in first. As the youth turned his knife and, more foolishly, his attention away from me, I grabbed his wrist and twisted. The knife flew out of his hand and at the same time I brought my knee up hard into his balls. It's a girl's trick, I know, but I make no apologies, for believe me it works most effectively and, unlike a punch, avoids any risk that your opponent will be able to deliver a counter-blow to your own jaw. He yelped as he sank slowly to his knees and rolled on to his side, clutching himself between the legs, his eyes screwed up in pain.

My two companions must have launched themselves at the two youths holding Isabela, for when I looked up I saw that the youth who had been standing on her arm was now crouching on the grass holding his face as the blood ran from between his fingers, whilst Vítor had grasped the lout who was straddling Isabela by his hair and was holding the point of his dagger at his throat. Isabela winced as she massaged her bruised wrist, but was unable to move because of the lad still kneeling astride her.

The youth I had kneed was struggling to rise again, so I stamped as hard as I could on his foot, just to give him something else to whimper about, then helped Vítor drag his prisoner back off Isabela. I lifted her to her feet as she struggled to straighten her skirts. She wasn't sobbing as most women would have been, but her face had blanched and she was breathing in noisy little rasps.

I'm no saint, as you have possibly deduced by now, but rape is the one crime I despise. Whether it was what the bastards had tried to do to her, or Isabela's refusal to give way to tears, I don't know, but I suddenly felt an overwhelming tenderness towards her. Not that I would have admitted that to anyone, you understand.

Vítor still held the kneeling youth tightly by the hair, but he moved the knife so that the point of the blade was pressing into the young man's closed eyelid. A knife in the eyeball was a rather nasty touch, I thought, but nevertheless it was certainly effective for none of the youths was daring to move.

'Collect up their knives,' Vítor ordered.

I did so. Two were plain but serviceable. The third had an exquisitely carved bone handle and I discreetly slipped it into my belt under my cloak.

When I had led Isabela far enough away from the youths for them not to try to grab her again, Vítor released the man he was holding.

'Take your two friends and go.' He pointed out across the rough pasture in a direction which would take them well away from the track. 'Go! Go!'

The three youths hesitated, their pride evidently smarting worse than any injury we'd inflicted. I could see they were itching to fight, but finally realizing we were armed and they were not, sense got the better of them and they limped off in the direction Vítor had indicated.

As they moved away, the youth whom I had kneed in the balls turned around, his face twisted in hatred.

'Vi kommer igen, og naeste gang slaar vi dig ihjel!' He drew his finger slowly and menacingly across his throat, and spat on the ground as if to seal the promise.

I watched them walk away, then turned to Vítor, grinning. 'I may have misunderstood, of course, but I get the distinct feeling he wasn't inviting us to share a flagon of wine with him. Now, you see, this is where it might have helped if you had told him you were a Lutheran pastor, Vítor, instead of threatening to put that poor fellow's eye out with your knife. Do remind me to give you some lessons in diplomacy some time.'

Vítor scowled, but before he had time to reply Isabela came up to us. She was still nursing her wrist, which was grazed and bore the scarlet imprint of the man's shoe. She did not look at any of us, but held her back very stiffly.

'I would like to thank you all for your assistance,' she said, as if she was some noblewoman about to toss us a coin apiece for moving some furniture for her. 'But it was quite unnecessary to put yourselves in danger on my account.'

Her performance was magnificent. I could have kissed her!

She glanced over to where the three lads could still be seen in the distance. 'Did they mean . . . do you think they will return?'

'I'm sure they'll try,' I said, 'and if they're anything like the louts I've encountered before, they'll probably bring a rabble of friends back with them. So I suggest we collect our packs and get out of here . . . Hinrik! It's safe, they've gone. You can come out now, you little canary.'

The top of a tousled head raised itself from behind a nearby rock, and gradually the rest of the lad emerged, some-what sheepishly, and edged towards us, keeping, I noticed, well out of arm's reach of Vítor. He studiously avoided look-ing at Isabela.

'Did you hear what the youths were saying?' I asked him.

The lad nodded. 'They were Danes. I only know a little Danish . . . but I think . . . he is going to kill you.'

'I think we'd managed to work that one out for ourselves. Anything else?'

The lad hung his head, then, barely raising his hand, pointed vaguely in the direction of Isabela.

'Katolik – Catholic . . . That is why . . .'

There was an uncomfortable silence, broken by – you've guessed it – Vítor, who cleared his voice as if he was about to deliver a sermon.

'Isabela, you must see from this incident that you cannot travel alone. We must stay together.' Seeing Isabela about to protest, he added more firmly, 'No traveller, man or woman, should cross this land alone. There are too many hazards of

304

which the foreigner can know nothing. Remember the accident you had yesterday? If there hadn't been someone on hand to help you, you would have most assuredly drowned.'

At the mention of the incident yesterday, Isabela darted a piercing glance at me, as if to say she knew full well it wasn't an accident. But nevertheless, visibly shaken, she consented to walk with us, or rather, she didn't refuse.

We continued along the track at a much slower pace than before. Isabela was plainly making for the mountains in pursuit of those birds of hers. With every step we took, I could see her scanning the hillsides and the air for them. I even found that I was beginning to do it, though I'd no idea what I was looking for, except that obviously it wasn't those black things flapping about and cawing, which was all I could see.

I was certain that at the first chance she got, Isabela would slip away from us again, just like those wretched horses. I had to convince her that I would help her find what she was looking for. I'd convinced women before that I was madly in love with them or that I could make a fortune for them. It was all about trust, after all. Get someone to trust you, and you can persuade them of anything.

I watched Isabela striding ahead of me up the track, her eyes fixed on the sky. I sighed. I could make her trust me if I really wanted to. I'd done it a dozen times before and to women far more astute in the ways of the world than she was. So why every time I approached her did I find myself doing it with all the finesse and skill of a half-witted dung collector? Was it because I knew in the end there was only one reason for me to win her trust, and that was to get her alone and murder her?

Yet if I didn't bring about her death, if she returned to Portugal with those birds, then I would be forced to spend the rest of my life in exile. I had a simple choice. I could either kill her and enjoy a life of luxury in my own homeland, or I could spare the life of this wretched girl who meant absolutely nothing to me, and drag out my remaining days in poverty and misery. There was no contest. Isabela had to die. So why was I making this so hard for myself?

Pull yourself together, Ricardo, and just do it! Do it and get it over with once and for all!

Eydis

Bating – *when a hawk becomes angry or agitated, flapping its wings wildly and flinging itself off the perch or fist, often resulting in it hanging upside down from its straps or jesses.*

'I've brought what you wanted,' Ari shudders, as he hands me a sack.

I will not open it in front of him. It would be cruel to make him look at it twice over. Time enough to prepare the head once he has gone.

'I took it from . . .' He gnaws at his lip. 'I meant to take it from the mass grave where all the other foreign sailors had been buried, but I was afraid of arousing the anger of so many dead men, and strong men at that. I was afraid they'd drag me back down into the grave with them.'

Beneath her veil Valdis's lips move and a mocking voice fills the cave.

It is lonely in the grave, Ari. It is dark in the cavern, pressed down by stench and decay. Your eyes are blinded in the endless night, Ari, in the endless night.

Ari shrinks back in terror.

'Stop your ears against him, Ari. It is dangerous to listen to him. He will poison your mind with misery. The dead are jealous of the living and that makes them cruel.' I try to pull him back to the purpose. 'You said that you did not take this head from the sailors' grave. Where then?'

Ari is still staring fearfully at the body of my sister, but finally he manages to wrest his attention back to me.

'There was an old woman, died of the spring hunger for

307

she'd no family to care for her. There was no marker on her grave, but I could still see the scar on the earth. I stole the sexton's spade and used it to separate the head from the body. That was right, wasn't it, Eydis? The corpse can't rise if the spade that buried it is used to cut off the head, can it?'

'You did well. But did anyone see you?'

Ari squats down, warming his hands over the flames of my cooking fire, although to me it feels warmer than ever in the cave.

'No one, I'm sure of that. I took one of the farm dogs with me and I left him on the track that leads to the graveyard. He's a good watchdog, he can hear a mouse running a mile away. I knew he'd bark at once if anyone approached. There was a moon, so I could see well enough to dig, and I only had to uncover one end of the grave, and then used my hands to feel for . . .' He gives another convulsive shudder, pressing his fist to his mouth as if to stop himself retching. 'Feeling is better than seeing. Once you've seen a thing, you cannot shut it out from your dreams . . . then I placed the dog's skull in the grave, just like you said.

'But I knew if they saw the ground had been disturbed they'd dig the body up, and then they'd see the head was missing. They'd question everyone. So when I filled the hole in again, I scattered some scraps of meat over it and let the dog loose to hunt for them. If they notice the fresh soil, they'll see all the paw marks and think it was just a stray dog or fox churning up the earth, digging for bones.'

'You are a bright lad, and a brave one.'

I am impressed at his resourcefulness. I know how much I have asked of him. He has risked his life to bring me what I asked and not many men twice his age would have the stomach to open a grave.

He gestures towards the sack. 'Are you sure this will keep the nightstalker's corpse from dying?'

'It is the only thing that can.'

'And his spirit will return to his body as soon as it has healed?'

Valdis's head swivels sharply towards him. 'Eydis has been lying to you, Ari. She knows I won't go back into that corpse. She hasn't the knowledge or the power to make me return. Why would I go back? We all know why she is so anxious to have me return to that body, because the moment I do, she will attempt to destroy me. Not that she would be able to, but I don't intend to let her try. Don't you see, you risked your life for nothing, you stupid little boy? All you've done is useless. Did you really think a woman could master me? She didn't raise me from among the dead. No one may command me.'

Ari has risen to his feet. He is staggering back away from Valdis, his arms raised protectively in front of his face as if every word the mocking voice utters is a hammer blow.

'Go!' I shout at Ari. 'Get out of here now!'

Ari turns his face to me, a mask of fear and anguish. 'I can't . . . I don't know what to do . . . I can't leave you alone with that. It's my fault. It's all my fault. I should have left him to die on the road. I should have left him floating in the sea. I'm sorry . . . so sorry.'

'Ari, you must trust me. It will come right. But now you must go from here and leave me to work.'

'Yes, go, Ari, go!' the voice mocks. 'And when you return you will see I have mastered her. It will be my voice coming from her lips. You will see, little Ari. You will see what mischief you have done, what terror you have unleashed, and there will be nothing you can do to stop it. Every day my spirit grows stronger and soon I will spew out over this land, like a river of molten lava. Think about that, little Ari. Think about all those who I will destroy. Where should I start, do you think? With your mother, your sister?'

'Get out of here, Ari,' I shout at him. 'You must trust me.'

He runs, clambering up the rocks and out through the slit

with such haste, a shower of stones clatters back down into the passage. But the mocking laughter pursues him.

I stir the embers in the fire and add several pats of dried dung from the heap. I need a good steady heat for the next three days; the flesh and skull must dry out completely before I can grind them into powder. Though I am desperate to finish this as quickly as possible, it is not a task that can be rushed.

I worry that the head might have little flesh on it now, if the woman died last spring. Gingerly I peel back the edges of the sack. Long grey hair still clings to her pate. The head stinks and oozes with the slime of decay, but enough flesh still adheres to the skull to prepare the physic I need.

'Forgive me, Mother, that I disturb your rest. Forgive me, Mother, that I take your bone. Forgive me, Mother, that I steal your flesh. I take from the dead, to return to the dead one who should not have been called forth.'

I lower the head as reverently as I can into a clay pot and cover it with a thick layer of hay torn from my pallet, then set it close to the glowing embers, so that the heat will warm the pot and mummify the contents. The head must dry, but not burn.

A shriek of laughter erupts from my sister's lips. 'You're wasting your time, Eydis, Eydis.'

His voice grows more powerful as he becomes accustomed to my sister's mouth. Her tongue moves as if it is his own. His foul breath vibrates in her throat. But it is my feet which tread on Fannar's mutilated corpse; my reflection I see in Ari's horrified eyes as I lumber towards him. The monstrous shadow falling across the threshold of a thousand dwellings. The screams that tear my soul into a million burning shreds. The awful, chilling silence.

I force myself to fight the images, drive them from my head. If I even once allow that terror to engulf me he will possess me as surely as the raging sea drowns the land. I will not surrender to fear. I am the stronger. I will be the stronger.

The creature is silent now. He is trying to read my thoughts. I can feel his spirit prowling round me looking for a way in, trying to guess what I am planning to do. But he dares not enter me, not yet. He fears that if he does I will learn his name and I will use it. He knows he must wait until I am weaker. We are both waiting, watching for our moment, our one chance to overcome the other, and there will be only one chance.

The foul steam rises from the clay pot and spirals up into the roof of the cave. An old woman, her cheeks hollow with hunger, her lips withered with age, hangs in the vapour of her own head. She stares out through the smoke at me, surprised, fearful even, as if I am the shadow on the wall of her childhood.

'There is nothing to fear, Mother. You are the first, the first to be summoned to the door-doom of the dead.'

'You are the last, Mother, Mother,' the harsh voice mocks. 'You are old, feeble. Do you really imagine you can command me? Mother, Mother, will you return to the grave with me? I should enjoy that. I will tear your skin from your wizened old back slowly, slowly as if I was peeling a plum, and you will feel the agony of it every hour, except that no hours pass in the grave. Time will run out, but torment never will.'

The old woman's mouth opens wide in terror.

'We will not let him enter your grave, Mother,' I tell her. 'Others are coming, you will not be alone.'

'But they will not come in time, Eydis, Eydis. The mountain is stirring. The pool is answering.'

The draugr raises Valdis's head and blows through her dead lips, a violent gust that shatters the ghost of the old woman, tearing the grey shadow of her into a hundred pieces and sending the wisps of vapour swirling up into the darkness above.

The old woman cannot stand against him alone. I grasp the iron ring about my waist, cursing it, cursing those who have bound me. I cannot reach out beyond the cave and bring the dead here. I can only call the girl, and if she does not come soon . . . The pool is answering, just as Heidrun said it would. The water is growing hotter, the heat building in the rocks under my feet and in the air. With every passing day, the steam hangs a little more densely over the pool. Bubbles of gas are popping from it, as if the great monster beneath it we have always feared is finally wakening. Soon the water will begin to boil. I know what that will mean for me, trapped here in the cave, unable to escape the scalding steam.

My grandfather often told us of a lake he used to swim in as a boy. The water was so warm that he was able to swim even when the snow lay thick upon the ground. The lake sides were very steep and they said that it was so deep in the middle of the lake that no one had ever been able to reach the bottom and whatever was lost in there could never be found. Some said the lake reached so deep that those in hell could look up and see the blue of it and imagine it was the sky.

One day, my grandfather and his friends had been swimming naked as usual, diving and chasing one another like seals. He had clambered out and to dry himself he had begun to kick about a calf's bladder which he had fashioned into a ball. All his friends climbed out too to join in the game, all that is but one of them who had swum further out than the others. He was swimming back towards the shore when he began to scream, thrashing about in the water. His friends laughed, thinking he was playing the fool, but then they saw his face and arms were scarlet, and blistering.

My grandfather ran to the edge and prepared to dive in to rescue his friend, but just in time his companions grabbed him and pulled him back. Seeing the dense clouds of steam rising from the surface, my grandfather bent down and touched his finger lightly to the water. He drew it back with a shriek of pain. The water was scalding hot. His friend was being boiled alive.

But that was only the beginning, only a warning of what was to fall upon them. For fire and rock exploded from the mountains of Hekla, Herdubreid and Trölladyngja. Great torrents of red molten lava rushed down the mountainsides and into the valleys, hot ash and smoke shot into the air poisoning the land and suffocating people and animals alike. I know this. I have seen the bones of those who perished piled up like great scaffolds on the wasted lands.

My family survived. But the day the lake boiled, the skin was burned from my grandfather's finger, a burn so deep the finger withered up, blackened and useless until the day he died. Every time he looked at it, he felt again the searing agony of body and heart. And now I realize that the monster in our pool is far more terrible than even the one Valdis and I feared as children. My grandfather could run from his burning lake, we cannot.

And when our pool boils, nothing will be able to survive in this cave, not the mice or the beetles, not the corpse and not me. If I cannot escape this cave, I will die in agony, scalded alive, like the boy in the lake. But I cannot leave Valdis. I swore I would take her body back to the river of ice so that her soul can be released to fly, I promised her. But if the draugr is not gone from her by then, I cannot take her from this place and release that monster into the world to destroy and murder. I will not leave her alone with that creature. I never left her side in life. I cannot abandon her in death. I will die in here as she has, chained to this rock. I press my hands together to keep them from shaking at the terror of it. Will I have the strength to do it?

I stare into the embers of the fire as the clay pot bakes. Three days before I can even begin to heal the draugr's corpse. Three long days and nights of waiting. But how long will it be before the monster in the pool starts to roar. Weeks? Days? Hours? Minutes? How long can I survive in the cave as the water boils and steam rises ever more densely? I need time, enough time to find a way to send his spirit back, but however desperately you plead for it, time is not always granted. The water that drips from a leaking bowl will not run back into it again.

Chapter Eleven

Hausse-pieds, *teneur* and *attombisseur* were the names given to the three falcons cast off one after another when their master was hunting a heron.

Hausse-pieds, 'raised feet', was the first falcon. Her role was to rise above the heron in the sky, then harry and distract it.

Teneur, 'holder', was the second. Her task was to stoop on the heron in the air and grasp it or 'bind to' it.

Attombisseur, 'the one who causes the fall', was the third. She brought the heron down to the earth and killed it.

Isabela

Wait on – when a hawk soars high above a falconer and the dogs, waiting for the game to be found and flushed out of the cover so that she can stoop on it.

'Where are you running off to now, boy?' Vítor shouted, as Hinrik clambered up a ridge towards a great heap of small stones that had been piled up there.

Hinrik carefully added his own stone to the top before clambering back down. He stood in front of us, his bandy legs astride, looking at each of us expectantly. Then he squatted down, picked up another stone from the track and handed it to me. 'You must all pay a stone or you will have bad luck.'

'What is this nonsense, boy?' Vítor snapped. Hunger and tiredness were making us all irritable.

'First time you pass a *gröf* . . . a grave like this with stones, you must add a stone to it.'

'Whose grave is it, lad?' Fausto asked.

Hinrik shrugged. 'Witch or wizard. They must be very powerful to be buried out here. They will curse you if you do not give them a stone. You must do it,' he added anxiously.

Vítor snorted. 'I'm certainly not going to make any offerings to witches. That's blasphemy, boy.'

'Oh yes, I was forgetting you're a strict Lutheran pastor now, aren't you, Vítor?' Marcos said.

'You know very well I am not a Lutheran,' Vítor said, his voice crackling with ice. 'I am here to map this island.'

Marcos and Fausto exchanged looks which plainly said neither of them believed a word of that.

'Then why didn't you stay at the coast? Isn't the shore where map-makers usually start?' Fausto said. He bent down and selected a stone from the many that lay scattered about, fallen from the steep peaks above us. From the expression on his face, I half-thought he was going to use it to batter Vítor.

It was hard to say which of the two men disliked Vítor the more, for both took every opportunity to goad him as well as each other. Over the last few days, struggling to survive out in the open, hunger and exhaustion had only made their tempers worse. Fausto and Marcos were forever snapping and snarling at each other and at Vítor. Of the three, only Vítor never seemed to lose his chilling self-control, which only made me more wary of him.

'The coast is already well mapped, Senhor Fausto, as you would have seen if you had taken the trouble to show any interest in the navigator's work while we were at sea, which I can assure you I did. But my masters are interested in the interior of the island, the mountains to be precise, of which few details are given on the charts. Why do you imagine we are travelling in this direction?'

'And who are your masters exactly?' Marcos said.

Vítor allowed himself a half-smile. 'I, unlike some, am known for my discretion. I was chosen for this task because I could be relied upon not to gossip about their business like some market crone.'

'Anyway,' Fausto said with the tone of a petulant child, 'who says we're travelling this way for your convenience?'

'An excellent question, Senhor Fausto, and one I've been meaning to ask you. I have patiently explained why I wish to venture into the mountains, not that it is any concern of yours, so perhaps you would care to enlighten us about your reasons.'

'Diamonds,' Fausto said brazenly, without the slightest hesitation or embarrassment. 'Where else would they be found except in the mountains?' Then he suddenly seemed to recall that I was standing there listening. 'Isn't that so, Isabela?'

His eyes met mine. There was something in that tone and look that went far beyond asking me not to expose his lie. It was almost a threat, warning me to keep silent. He offered his hand to me with a slight bow.

'Come, Isabela. Shall we cast our stones together to appease the old witch? We don't need any more ill luck, we already have an albatross trailing after us as it is,' he said, glaring at Vítor.

I shrank away from him. Did he really think I would be so foolish as to clamber up on that ridge alone with him? I could see exactly what he was planning. If Fausto succeeded, the witch wouldn't be the only corpse lying under a pile of stones. Ignoring Hinrik's frantic pleas, I turned and walked on up the ravine. I knew the men would follow. No matter what I did, I couldn't lose them. The more desperate I became to get away, the more determined they seemed to keep me close.

The land had grown more strange and wondrous the further we had travelled from the coast. Once we passed a great flat plain dotted with pools with raised clay sides like little washing tubs. All around them the earth was stained every colour that you can imagine – vivid blue, gentian and red, green, yellow and ochre. I thought at first the wool and cloth dyers had been at work there, but when we walked up to them we saw that the pools contained not water but boiling mud that glooped and bubbled like a thick soup on a cooking fire. Then suddenly behind us a jet of pure, clear water shot high into the air straight out of the ground and fell to earth again, leaving behind nothing but a cloud of steam. As we walked further, we came across more pools of boiling mud and found to our horror that the earth was falling away beneath our feet with every step. Terrified of plunging down, we ran for higher ground.

But the hills and high ridges were not without their hazards either, for we often had to cross wide rivers of loose shale that threatened to sweep us down the hillside. Hinrik showed us how to drop on our hands and knees and dig with a stick a few inches beneath the shale to find the firm rock on which we could crawl across. I copied him and Fausto followed, but Vítor and Marcos were still vying with each other and neither would humiliate himself by kneeling, until Vítor, trying to walk across it, slipped on the loose stone and was carried halfway down the hill by it before he could stop. He soon learned to crawl then. But it was slow, painful work and our knees and hands were cut and bruised by the end of it.

Each time I could safely drag my gaze from the ground I was searching the skies for the falcons, but though I saw many waterfowl winging their way between the rivers and lakes, and even a tiny merlin, I didn't see a single white falcon, nor its prey the ptarmigan. Whenever I could safely do so, out of earshot of the others, I asked Hinrik where the ptarmigan were. Had he seen any? When did he think we would see some? The poor lad began to look alarmed every time I approached.

'They are not here,' he said wearily each time. 'I told you. In the mountains. High in the mountains.'

'But if you see one you will show me at once,' I begged him.

'I can show you duck. They are good to eat too.'

But we didn't catch any duck either.

All the time we were walking, and when we sat around the camp fire at night I was constantly planning how I might capture a wild falcon, for I knew I might only get one chance. If I could find them I wanted to take two sore birds, those in their first year of life. They were easy to distinguish because before they went through their first moult their plumage was much darker. But after the first moult it was much harder to tell the age of a falcon from a distance. If I captured one that was too old, the chances were it would not survive the long sea journey home and all this effort would be for nothing. But perhaps I would have no choice but to take whatever I could.

I knew how to take passage birds, those birds migrating south in the autumn. Ever since I had been old enough to sit still, my father had taken me out to the plains in Portugal to wait for the kites and harriers, eagles, buzzards and falcons to arrive. There he built elaborate hides out of sods and set up nets and poles with live pigeons as bait, wooden falcons as decoys, and tethered shrikes that would give warning of the approaching bird of prey.

We would wait in silence in the hide from dawn until dusk, never taking our eyes from the shrikes. 'Patience,' said my father, 'is the most important skill a falconer must master.' When the shrikes became agitated my father would know exactly which bird of prey was approaching. If they bated and flapped on their perches, it was a buzzard. If they ran out of their hiding places with cries of alarm, it was a sparrowhawk or falcon, and if they moved slowly, a kite, eagle or harrier. If the approaching bird was one my father wanted, he would release a tethered pigeon, and once the hawk had fastened on to it, he could pull them both into his net.

But I could not set traps like my father. He knew exactly which route the migrating hawks would take. He could wait in the certainty that, sooner or later, they would come. I had no idea where the white falcons were.

There was another way he had shown me once when he had helped a man recapture a falcon that had returned to the wild. That required only a long line to which a pigeon or other prey was attached, but that method depended entirely on luck. You had first to find your bird and then hope that it would fly at your prey. If the bird was hungry enough and prey was scarce, your chances were good, but if the white falcons were following a flock of ptarmigan, it would take more than luck, it would take a miracle, and I was no longer sure which God I should beg for the miracle now.

When those Danes seized me and forced me to the ground, did I pray then? I shuddered as I remembered it, feeling again the weight of the man on top of me, crushing me, the stench of his sweat in my nostrils, the sheer terror of being pinned down, unable to move. *Katolik! Katolik!* they kept shouting at me. I didn't need Hinrik to tell me what that meant. But I wasn't a Catholic, didn't they know that, couldn't they see? I was seething with rage and the burning injustice of it.

I know it was foolish. In the end it doesn't matter why a man rapes you. Rape is animal lust. Rape is foul. Rape is the desire to hurt and destroy, because a man has that power. Yet the fact that they were doing this because they believed I was a Catholic was the only thought I could hold on to in my terror. If they had attacked me because I was a Marrano, a Jewish pig, would that have made it easier to bear? I knew it would not, and yet I could not stop hating them for calling me a Catholic.

For the first time since my father's arrest, I felt in my heart a truth that I had only up to then grasped in my mind – I was not a Catholic. They were my enemies. What I had once believed, I now despised with a loathing that filled my frame with fire. It was that attack which had made me understand it, truly feel it. I was like one who has been drugged for a long time and suddenly wakes to sharp, raw pain.

We made camp not long after we passed the witch's cairn, higher up the steep ravine whose entrance she guarded. The sun was already setting below the rocks though it scarcely seemed any time at all since it had risen. Even at midday it barely managed to struggle over the back of the mountains, and it was as cold as its own reflection in the bog pools.

We built a fire on a mossy ledge beside a raging river which had cut deep into the hillside. Great rocks were strewn either side, some balanced upon one another. There was a little hollow under one, which had evidently been worn down by sheep pushing their way under the boulders in search of shelter from the wind and rain.

Fausto yanked up a small wiry bush and, using the stiff stems as a brush, cleared out the hollow of sheep's droppings, carefully assembling them in a heap for fuel. We were all learning fast to hoard anything that would burn.

'You can sleep in here, Isabela, it's just big enough for you and it'll shelter you from the wind.'

'Let Hinrik have it, I prefer to sleep by the fire.'

It was not just because Fausto had suggested it that I refused. Nothing would have induced me to crawl under that huge rock. It felt too much like the nightmares that stalked my sleep.

Ever since we had left France, I had dreamt of that forest, and in Iceland, a land without trees, the nightmares had become more vivid than ever, but they were never quite the same. In some dreams I would be running, fleeing for my life. In others I was trying to hold on to a child, fighting desperately to keep the little one safe, shielding a baby with my own body, pleading for its life. But all the dreams ended in the same way with violent, savage death and then silence, a terrible dark and lonely silence which chilled and haunted me even in my waking hours.

Marcos hunkered down next to me, trying to warm his hands over the tiny fire which Hinrik had managed to get burning with a flint and iron.

'Fish again tonight?' he asked dismally. 'If you can call it *fish*, more like eating old shoe soles. I never thought I'd say this but I'm actually starting to crave ship's biscuit, at least the weevils gave it some flavour.'

I rummaged among our pitifully few stores. The smoked puffin was long gone, and there was precious little dried cod left.

I drew out what remained and showed it to them. 'Fish is better than nothing and tomorrow there will be nothing, unless we find something to stretch this out tonight.'

'Since you were complaining about the food, Senhor Marcos, I would suggest that you and Senhor Fausto go and find us something else to eat,' Vítor said. 'And you, boy, make haste and find us some more fuel before this feeble little fire dies away entirely.'

Fausto threw the stems he'd been using as a brush on to the fire, where they blazed for a few moments before collapsing into ash. 'And what exactly will *you* be doing, Senhor Vítor, while we're all toiling away to keep your belly stuffed and your bony arse warm?'

'I'll stay with Isabela and try to keep the fire going. Someone has to stay with her. It will be dark soon. It isn't safe for her to be left alone.'

'No!' The word burst out of me in a shriek before I could stop it. The last thing I wanted was to be left alone with Vítor. 'Let Hinrik stay with me and we'll both collect fuel. You three go. As you say, it'll be dark soon and you'll all need to search if we're to have any hope of finding anything to eat. Marcos, you said you studied herbs. There must be some kind of plant growing here we can eat.'

'Herbs won't fill our bellies,' Fausto said before Marcos had a chance to reply. 'Good strong meat, that's what we need. I was always rather good at setting snares when I was a boy. I promise you shall dine like a queen tonight, fair Isabela.' He swept off his cap in a low bow, and bounded away down the hill. 'Look after her, lad, don't let her out of your sight.'

With a great deal less enthusiasm Vítor and Marcos set off too, Marcos taking care to go in the opposite direction to the other two.

Hinrik began to feed the fire with sheep's dung, absently dropping them in one at a time, as if he was feeding scraps of meat to a puppy. He was grinning to himself, obviously enjoying some private joke.

'What's funny?' I asked.

'Senhor Fausto is in love.'

I smiled. 'If he is, it certainly isn't with Vítor, or Marcos, come to that.'

'With you. He always tries to get you alone. He always tries to get near you when you walk. He watches you when you are sleeping. I have seen him. He loves you.' Hinrik chuckled.

A cold fist clutched at my belly at the very thought of him watching me while I lay asleep and helpless.

'No, believe me, Hinrik,' I said fervently, 'you couldn't be more wrong.'

I stared at the hollow under the balancing stone. Why had Fausto urged me to sleep in there, under that great rock? What was he planning now? I would never be able to sleep again, not as long as he was anywhere near me. I glanced up at the hill top. How long would it be before the men returned? If I could just get as far as the top of the hill before they came back, once I was safely out of sight I could hide and then . . .

'Why don't you go and see if you can find something else to burn, Hinrik?'

The boy shook his head. 'Senhor Fausto said I was to stay with you.'

'I need to stay with the fire to keep it burning. If I leave it, it'll go out, but we need more fuel, lots more fuel. Hurry now, it's nearly dark.'

'Not unless you come with me. I do not want to go alone . . . the witch.' His face was screwed up in anxiety. 'They rise from the grave when the sun sets. You did not give her a stone. You should have given her a stone. She will curse us. You see, nothing will go right for us now.'

The shadows were deepening in the ravine, the great boulders assuming almost human shapes in the twilight. In that place, I could believe anything was possible. Why hadn't we done as Hinrik had asked, even if it was to reassure him? I didn't need any more bad luck. I was running out of time. How many days had passed since we landed? I was losing count. A week? No, it couldn't be, not yet! Please God, not yet!

'Hinrik, are we near the place of the white falcons? How far is it to the high mountains? How many days?'

The boy hunched away from me. 'You must not talk of them. Not in this place. It will call the witch's curse.'

He refused to say more. In the end we searched for fuel together, never straying out of sight of the guttering yellow flames. We heaped our finds near the fire to dry them – more dung, dried woody roots and stems from bushes and the dried bones and skull of a sheep that must have fallen from the rocks and broken her legs. Hinrik insisted on dragging them to the fire, saying his mother had often burned bones for fuel.

But as soon as I smelt the stench of the burning, I could only see the girl standing in the flickering torchlight of that sultry Lisbon night with the pitifully tiny casket of bones in her arms. I could hear her sobbing as the casket burst into flames on the pyre. Her mother . . . ? Her father . . . ?

Hinrik stiffened at the sound of footsteps on rocks as Marcos stumbled back towards our camp. He tossed a small heap of woody plants down beside me.

'Is that for the pot or the fire?' I asked.

'All I could find,' Marcos said morosely.

Before I could ask him what the plants were, Vítor reappeared, closely followed by Fausto, who threw himself disconsolately on to the ground beside the small fire, and stared into the flames, his fingers savagely plucking at the grey, wiry grass. Marcos glowered at the pair of them.

It was obvious from Fausto's empty hands and stony expression that he'd caught nothing. So there was really no need for Marcos to comment, but he did.

'So where's this sumptuous supper you promised us, Fausto?'

The light from the flames flickered across Fausto's face, showing the muscles tighten as he clenched his jaw.

'There's nothing to trap in this cursed land.'

'Yet according to you we were going to dine like royalty tonight.'

'So what game have you brought us for the pot?' Fausto retorted. 'I don't smell it cooking, or was the boar you slaughtered with your bare hands too massive to carry back?' He prodded the bundle of withered herbs which I was sorting through. 'Is this what you brought back? Not even sheep could eat this. What is it anyway?'

'Herbs, but if you don't want to eat them . . .'

'Yes, but what kind of herbs? On the ship you told us you were a physician, come here to look for new herbs for cures. I can't say I've noticed you take any interest in the plants as we've been tramping through this wilderness. And for that matter I haven't seen you do any physicking either. When Isabela hurt her knee it was the ship's surgeon who attended to her, not you.'

'That was a job for a bone-setter. I am no common bone-setter. A physician doesn't deal with such matters.'

'So you'd let a woman suffer in agony rather than soil your hands, would you? You know what, if you are a physician, prove it.' Fausto plunged his hand inside his scrip and drew out a couple of handfuls of wizened red berries. 'I found these. I have no idea whether they're poisonous, but if you're as knowledgeable with herbs and plants as you claim, you'll know whether or not these are safe to eat.'

'Why don't you eat them and find out?' Marcos growled. 'Then with luck we'll only have four people to divide that fish among instead of five.'

'I've got a better idea – why don't you eat them?'

Fausto flung himself on Marcos, seizing him by the front of the doublet and trying to cram the berries into his mouth.

'Stop it!' I yelled. 'Leave him alone. Those berries might kill him!'

Vítor rushed over and tried to prise Fausto off, but even so it took several minutes of Marcos pushing and kicking, and Vítor tugging, before Fausto could be persuaded to let go. All three men collapsed on to the ground, panting. Marcos spat out the berries still in his mouth, and rubbed his bruised lips. It was clear that neither man was in any mood to apologize.

I began to gather up the withered herbs that their flaying feet had scattered, more to break the paralysing silence than with any intention of using them. But as I reached for one plant that Marcos had dragged up by its root, I caught a whiff of something that was vaguely familiar. I examined it more carefully, and sniffed at it again.

'I'm sure this is valerian. The root smells like old leather when it's freshly dug up, but more like stale sweat when it's dried. My father uses it to cure . . .' I stopped myself just in time. 'As rat bait.'

'Then it's poison!' Fausto clambered to his feet.

'No, no,' I said quickly. 'It just draws the rats. They love the smell. But every apothecary has the dried root of this on his shelves. It's a healing plant, it eases pain, but it will make you fall asleep.'

'So that was your little plan,' Fausto said triumphantly, as though he had unmasked a plot to murder the king. 'What were you going to do, put it in the pot, then refuse to eat any yourself? What then, rob us?'

Without warning he sprang at Marcos again, pulling his knife from his belt as he did so. Marcos leapt to his feet, but he didn't move quickly enough and found himself backed against a rock, with Fausto's dagger pointing directly at his heart. Hinrik took refuge behind a boulder. Vítor scrambled to his feet, but eyeing the dagger, this time made no move to intervene.

'I didn't know what it was! I swear!' Marcos protested.

'But you said you were a physician,' Fausto yelled. 'So you should know, that's the point. If you are not a physician then tell us who you are.'

He jabbed the dagger towards Marcos, and for one dreadful moment I thought he had thrust it in. I ran at him and grabbed his arm, trying to pull the dagger away.

'How dare you of all people accuse Marcos of lying,' I shouted. 'You've no right to question him!'

Fausto pushed me away with his other hand. 'I've every right to find out what kind of man we're travelling with, for all our sakes. He's obviously got something to hide.'

'I think you had better do as he says, Senhor Marcos,' Vítor said quietly. 'I am sure you can explain yourself. And Senhor Fausto, I suggest you stop waving that dagger about before someone gets hurt. If, as you surmise, Senhor Marcos is not a physician, then you will have no one to tend you if you manage to stab yourself in a tussle, and that could lead to a very painful and lingering death out here miles from any assistance.'

Fausto hesitated, then with obvious reluctance lowered the knife, but he did not sheath it.

'Go on then,' he growled at Marcos. 'What are you waiting for? Tell us.'

Marcos was breathing heavily and his hands were trembling, but he tried to laugh it off.

'There was really no need for theatrical gestures; I have nothing to hide from my fellow countrymen. I couldn't divulge my real reason for coming here to any on the ship, nor to that man who searched us. But none of us is in a position to report each other to the Danes, are we? We all have our reasons for being here, which we would not want to make known to them.' He raised his eyebrows, challenging Vítor, but his face gave nothing away.

329

'The truth is I came here looking for the white falcon. I hoped to capture one of these birds and smuggle it back to Portugal.'

I must have let out a cry for Marcos turned to me.

'Yes, I know how dangerous it is. I realized that even before Hinrik here told us the night we spent with the farmer, but you see, I'm desperate enough to take that risk. I'm heavily in debt.'

Fausto shot a startled glance at me, but Marcos appeared not to notice.

'A friend of mine, a friend I trusted with my life, came to me to borrow a great sum of money. He needed it, he said, to buy a farm. He was in love, but the girl's family wouldn't consent to the wedding unless he could provide her with land and a respectable living. They were threatening to marry her off to a wealthy old man who had asked for her hand. He showed me the farm. It was good land, well stocked with mature vines and olives, as well as pasture. The girl was as terrified of being married off to the old man as my friend was of losing her. He assured me that once he had the girl's dowry he would repay a third of what he borrowed from me, then another third each year until the debt was repaid.

'I had nothing like the sum, but I was able to borrow it on my good name, for people knew me as a respectable notary and I was trusted by wealthy men. But it seems my friend was less than honest with me. He was in the habit of gambling and had even stolen from his employers. He laid the money I had given him on the fighting cocks, in the hope of making a fortune and replacing the money that he'd stolen before the loss was noticed, but he lost it all.

'If I can't repay the people I borrowed from, my reputation will be ruined and so will my livelihood, for no one will come to me if they think I can't be trusted. I don't know how to find enough money to repay them, but if I could get my hands on just one white falcon and sell it I could pay all those I owe and more besides.'

Fausto's gaze darted to me again before he turned back to Marcos. 'And just how are you intending to capture these birds? You don't appear to have brought any nets or traps.'

'It would have looked a little suspicious if I had, wouldn't it? You saw how thoroughly that little clerk searched our bundles. If he'd found nets and traps, I don't think even he would have believed they were for capturing flocks of wild plants.'

Fausto's mouth twitched in a smile he couldn't suppress. But Hinrik wasn't laughing. He edged forward, his face pale under the sea-tan.

'No, Senhor Marcos, you must not try to catch the birds. The Danes have spies everywhere. They will catch us and hang us.'

Marcos grasped his shoulder and squeezed it gently. 'They won't catch me, lad. And if they do, I will tell them you knew nothing of it.'

Hinrik shook his head at what he appeared to think was the sheer stupidity of the foreigner. 'They hang everyone, even little boys if they are caught with their fathers. The girls and women, they tie their hands and feet then they throw them from a high cliff into the lake to drown. My mother . . . I watched her . . .'

He scrubbed angrily at his eyes, then turned and pointed down the ravine in the direction of the witch's cairn, though it was too dark now to see it. 'If you try to take a falcon she will make sure you are caught. Nothing will go right now.'

I rose and bustled across to the gently bubbling pot, hoping that food might dispel the boy's fear. But what was in that pot was not likely to cheer anyone. I found a handful of withered thyme among the valerian Marcos had plucked, though I suspected he didn't recognize that either. Its leaves were hairy, unlike the thyme at home, but they still had that faint familiar smell of summer, like a wisp of perfume that you catch just for a moment when you crush an old dried rose petal. But it was only a shadow of the plant I knew which thrived under the hot sun of Portugal, and did little to add flavour to the dried cod.

There was not the brittle spark of a star or a sliver of moon tonight to illuminate the distant mountains. A thick blanket of darkness lay across the land. The tiny pool of blood-red light from the fire was like an island in the black ocean that we heard and sensed moving around us, as the wind stirred its waves of grass and the creatures in its depths shrieked and called unseen.

Was it really possible that three of us were here on the same quest? I hadn't believed Fausto's story and I wasn't at all sure I believed Marcos. Had they both mentioned the white falcon because they knew that was why I had come here? If they were lying, then why were they really here, and more disturbingly, why were they so intent on keeping me with them? But if they were both telling the truth, if they were both searching for the white falcons, what would happen if I did catch one? Surely they would try to take it from me. To try to find a pair for myself was hard enough, but if all three of us were going after the same rare quarry . . .

I glanced over at Hinrik sitting hunched miserably as close to the fire as he could. If the poor boy had been forced to watch his own mother thrown from a cliff, he certainly wasn't going to help me find those birds, and I couldn't blame him. I shivered, feeling again my lungs screaming in pain as they fought for air when I was drowning in that bog. If Marcos had not been there to pull me out . . . No, I mustn't even think about getting caught. I must not get caught.

We huddled round the fire spearing the meagre pieces of dried fish from the pot with the points of our knives and chewing the boiled pieces. I have never attempted to eat sheep's wool, but I imagine the texture would not be unlike that fish, and would taste much the same too. We chewed and chewed until the mouthful was softened enough to swallow. Only hunger made us persist.

If we couldn't even find food now, how would I survive the winter? If I didn't return to a port and find a passage on a ship I would be trapped here as an outlaw, unable to seek shelter in any man's home. But of one thing I was certain: whatever it took, whatever it cost me, I would not leave without the falcons. I couldn't come all this way to give up now, knowing it would mean my father's certain death.

Even now he was lying in the Inquisitor's jail in Lisbon, deep in the earth. Were they hurting him? Torturing him? Did he have food in his belly tonight or clean water to slake his thirst? I felt suddenly guilty that I had complained about the tastelessness of the fish. My father and many like him would have been glad of just a fragment of what I'd forced down my ungrateful throat. I had the clean cold streams to drink; I had sweet fresh air to breathe, while they lay in dungeons so fetid that every breath they drew in choked them. And my mother, where was she, and what was she eating tonight?

'Listen!' Vítor whispered urgently. 'There's someone moving about out there. Scatter. Hide yourselves.'

We scrambled behind rocks, and crouched low. I was thankful for the darkness that concealed us, but also cursing it for I could see nothing and was terrified I had put myself directly in the path of whoever was moving towards us.

Someone called out softly and we held our breath, not daring to move. There was a muttered exchange in words I didn't understand. It sounded as if there were two men close by.

'Who are they, boy?' Vítor whispered to Hinrik.

'Icelanders. They say they are friends.'

'We have no friends here,' Vítor said.

The same young voice called out again.

'He says they've come to help. He says we must hurry! We must come now.'

None of us moved or made a sound. I cautiously peered around the rock. Two men were standing beside the fire. I couldn't see their faces.

'Stay here,' Vítor whispered fiercely. 'Not you, boy, you're coming with me.' He grabbed Hinrik by the back of his jerkin and pulled him out from behind the rocks. They took a few paces towards the fire, Vítor's fist clenched tightly around the hilt of his dagger.

'Who are you?' he demanded.

The younger of the two knelt down and, as if to show he was no threat, warmed his hands over the glowing dung. The firelight lit up his smooth cheek and the red-gold of his hair. He spoke rapidly and quietly. Hinrik whispered back. Vítor shook his shoulder to remind him to translate.

'He says his name is Ari. The man is Fannar. He has a farm two valleys from here.'

'What do they want with me?' Vítor demanded.

'He asks if we have a girl with us and two other men.'

Hinrik seemed to be on the verge of answering this question himself, but Vítor jerked him backwards.

'Tell him no. Say there are just two of us.'

Ari frowned, looking round at the rocks as if he could see me hiding. The older man, Fannar, bent his head close to the lad and they muttered together.

Ari turned back to Hinrik, gesticulating as he spoke.

'He says Danes on horseback are tracking three men and a girl who attacked their sons. When they catch them they will tie them to the horses and run them back. It is what they always do. Most die before . . .' Hinrik was plainly so terrified he could not bring himself to translate what would happen to us, if we survived long enough to reach a town.

'Tell them if I see these people, I'll warn them.' Vítor was still giving nothing away.

Ari sighed, plainly exasperated by the game, and spoke again to Hinrik.

'Ari says if he can find you, the Danes can too. They are fools, but not dead fools. They can see the glow of a fire in the dark and smell smoke and fish cooking. They know only an outlaw would be camping out at this season. If we want his help, Fannar will give it.'

'And why would this Fannar risk his own life to help strangers?' Vítor asked.

'Fannar hates the Danes and they say . . .' Hinrik hesitated, exchanging glances with the older man, 'He has heard the girl is of the old faith.'

'And he is of the old faith, the Catholic faith?' Vítor said carefully.

Marcos suddenly stepped into the circle of firelight. 'What are you playing at, Vítor? The three of us can't fight off armed men on horseback. These men are offering to help us.'

Vítor tried to say something, but Marcos took a step forward, pushing him aside and addressing himself to Hinrik. 'Tell them we're the ones the Danes are hunting, but we didn't attack them, they were trying to rape the girl.'

I rose from my hiding place and edged forward a few paces. 'It's true. They were only trying to help me.'

When Hinrik translated the older man nodded and grunted, as if he had guessed as much, then spoke to Hinrik, gesturing to him with an impatient wave of his hand to tell us.

'Fannar says those boys are evil. But what can you expect with such fathers? But it is not safe here. He says he will hide us until the Danes have moved on. But we must come now. We —'

Fannar grabbed Hinrik and clapped a broad, meaty hand across the lad's mouth. The boy struggled until Fannar whispered something, then he stood rigidly still. Ari motioned us to be silent. We all stood still, listening.

'Hestur!' Ari whispered.

Just at that moment I heard it too, drifting up from the bottom of the ravine, the unmistakable ring of horses' shoes striking stones and the creaking of leather. Before any of us could move, Ari had tipped the contents of the pot over the fire, extinguishing the flames with a hiss of fishy steam.

I felt my hand grabbed by someone in the darkness. For a moment, frightened it might be Fausto or Vítor, I resisted, but then realized it was Ari. He was pulling me between the rocks, as if he could see exactly where we were going. I was running blind, stumbling and slipping. I didn't know if the others were following or not. All I could do was cling to Ari's hand and trust him. The ravine was filled with the sound of hooves, shouts and yells as the riders urged their mounts up the steep track. But we did not stop to look back. We ran for our lives into the darkness.

Ricardo

Haute volerie – *'the great flight', when the quarry bird such as a kite, raven, crane or heron climbs high into the air and the falcon tries to fly above it to stoop down on it, resulting in a great aerial battle of life and death.*

The world was suddenly plunged into darkness as Ari extinguished the fire. I couldn't even work out which was up or down, but when I heard the horses' hooves clattering over the stones, I wasn't going to stop to find out. It sounded as if there was a whole army down there. I turned and fled in the opposite direction to the shouts below. Stones were kicked down as someone scrambled up the rocks ahead of me. It's not often a fellow has reason to be grateful for dirt being kicked in his face, but at least it meant I could follow the trail. I just hoped they didn't dislodge anything bigger.

A broad, heavy hand suddenly clamped down on my arm and hauled me into the shelter of some overhanging rocks, nearly dashing my brains out on the stone. I yelped, but another hand shot over my mouth to silence me. We huddled together, crouching in the darkness, listening to the sounds of one another's rasping breath and the roar of the river as it galloped down the hillside. We were all straining to hear if the Danes were following us. We could hear them blundering about below us, but their voices did not seem to be getting closer.

Fannar whispered to Hinrik who in turn relayed the message to us. 'He says he will go ahead to guide us. We must follow one after another, but keep close. Hold on to the person in front until he says it is safe to let go. If we fall off the track, we will fall a very long way down. Come.'

'No, wait. I think someone is missing,' Isabela whispered urgently.

In the darkness it was impossible to see who anyone was, but we each whispered our names and realized that it was Vítor who was not with us.

The Icelander muttered something that I'm sure was a curse or two.

'You don't think Vítor would tell the Danes . . .' Isabela began, but trailed off.

Fannar whispered to Hinrik in a gruff voice.

'He says he will go back to look for Vítor. Ari will guide us to the farm.'

Before any of us could stop him, Fannar was gone, sliding back into the darkness.

There was a pause, then we heard voices.

'That's Fannar talking! Have they caught him?' Isabela asked.

I could hear the fear in her voice. I reached out and took her hand. It was as cold as marble. I chafed it gently to warm her, but she jerked it away as if I'd burned her.

Hinrik had crept a little way out of the overhang to listen. He came scuttling back on all fours, as silently as a spider. 'He tells them the fire they saw was his fire. He was searching for lost sheep and got hungry so he cooked himself some supper.'

'Do they believe him?' I whispered.

'If they do, they'll ride on and Fannar can look for Vítor, if not . . .' He did not need to finish the sentence.

With Ari leading we trailed up the mountain track. I was holding on to Isabela as we stumbled through the dark, edging round great lumps of rock on one side of the gut-churningly narrow path, with nothing but a yawning black abyss on the other. As we climbed the wind grew stronger, buffeting us as if it was trying to push us off the track. I pressed my free hand against every boulder I could feel on the side of the path, in the desperate but vain hope that I would be able to grab hold of something solid if I slipped.

Occasionally one of us would kick a stone and we'd hear it fall away in the darkness, rattling and bouncing down the steep hillside in a drop that seemed to go right down into hell itself. I asked myself a dozen times how on earth I had come to be wandering blindly along a path in the pitch dark, following a mountain goat of a boy I'd never met in my life before, when every step I took could see me plunging down to certain death. Was Ari even human? Maybe he was a demon or one of those trolls Hinrik talked about. How would I know? All I did know was that I had to be as mad as a mooncalf to be putting my life in his hands.

And yet, as I felt the warmth of Isabela's back, the flexing of her muscles beneath the cloth, smelt that strange, sweet perfume of her hair, I found myself willing to be led anywhere.

Finally, to my immense relief, I felt the track beginning to descend, but I quickly discovered a new hazard, for it seemed to be far easier to slip walking down. In front of me Isabela was limping badly. If my knees were protesting at the slope, her weakened leg must have been giving her agony, but she didn't so much as let out a squeak of pain or ask to rest. That girl had more spirit than a vat of brandy.

But soon we found ourselves walking on a flatter, smoother track. Every now and then the moon would peer round the curtains of cloud at us, like some inquisitive old lady determined to see who was passing along her street. Its silver light appeared just long enough to reveal that we were in a high valley, with the sharp ridges of mountains on either side, before darkness closed in again.

God alone knows how far we walked. Now that we were no longer in single file, Isabela was walking at my side. Several times she stumbled, and in the end I put my arm around her to help her along, and though she resisted at first, eventually, limping and exhausted, she leaned into me. If she hadn't been with us I'd have collapsed in the grass and refused to take another step, but I had to keep going for her sake. I could hardly let her think I was weaker than a woman. Besides, that little mountain goat, Ari, was still bounding along as if he'd just been taking a summer's evening stroll around town. He might not have looked like a troll, but he certainly wasn't human. No normal man could ever have that much energy. There are times when a fellow could really loathe the young.

Fannar and Vítor arrived at the farmstead not long after we did. Fannar's wife, Unnur, had just served us with some kind of broth that tasted of nothing but smoke, when they stumbled in. Fannar was in high spirits. Apparently he had managed to convince the Danes that he was alone, and they had finally ridden off. Vítor who, so he claimed, had lost his bearings in the dark, had hidden nearby, emerging only when he heard the Danes ride away.

Fannar's wife, a dumpy little woman, looked thoroughly alarmed when the story was recounted, clearly not believing even the Danes could be so foolish as to think a farmer would go looking for sheep at night without dog or lantern, but Fannar thought it was a huge joke.

'Fannar says Unnur worries too much,' Hinrik told us. 'The Danes think Icelanders are so stupid that they believe nothing is too crazy for us to do. He could have told them he was fishing for whales in the stream, and they would have asked him how many he had caught.'

Hinrik and Fannar clearly thought this was hilarious, as did Fannar's two daughters, Margrét and Lilja, but his wife bit her lip and went to the cooking pot to ladle out more broth, the frown deepening on her face.

*

I must have fallen asleep where I sat out of sheer exhaustion, for when I finally managed to prise my eyes open it was morning and the hall was almost deserted save for Unnur and Hinrik. Unnur seemed to have been waiting patiently for me to wake, for as soon as I stirred she thrust a bundle of unsavoury-looking rags at me. I prodded the cloth dubiously.

'What is this for?' I asked, pronouncing the words slowly and loudly. 'Cleaning?'

I mimed polishing one of the wooden bowls, though nothing in the house looked as if it had ever been cleaned. Everything from the floor to the rafters, including Fannar's wife, seemed to have been smoked to the same shade of grey-brown.

'Unnur wants you to put them on,' Hinrik explained. 'If you are seen in your clothes, everyone will know at once you are a foreigner.'

Unnur said something, and Hinrik sniggered. 'She says you look like an erupting volcano, with your white, black and red.'

That was some cheek coming from a woman who was dressed like a bog.

'She asks how you can work with all that padding in your jacket and breeches.'

'And can you give me one good reason why I should want to work?' I said.

Hinrik translated this for Unnur and she stared at me in disbelief, as if I had asked her why I needed to breathe.

I sighed. I could tell it was pointless trying to explain that the voluminous slashed and padded clothes were intended as a proclamation to all the world that the wearer had no need to soil his hands with manual labour. But when I looked down at my doublet, even I was forced to concede that my clothes weren't exactly shouting 'man of substance' any more. Several nights of sleeping rough, the fight with the Danes and then blundering across the hills and valleys in the dark to evade the horsemen, had covered my breeches, hose and doublet in thick, greenish mud. The fabric had been ripped in nearly a dozen places, so that half the padding was falling out, and most of the trimming and a part of one sleeve had been torn away. I hadn't seen a mirror since I had left Portugal, and for once I was glad to be spared the sight of the ruin I had undoubtedly become.

Seeing that Unnur was consumed with curiosity about what garments I wore underneath my clothes – at least I hoped that was why she was watching me with a fascinated expression – I removed my outer clothes and pulled on the plain brown breeches and shirt she offered. They stank as if they'd been stuffed up a chimney for years, and the cloth was so rough that within minutes I was scratching and chafing, though it didn't take me long to realize that it wasn't just the coarseness of the cloth that was making me itch.

'Unnur says you can go outside,' Hinrik said. 'But do not go far from the house, and if we hear the dogs barking, we must run inside and hide. She will show us where.'

Unnur led Hinrik and me out of the hall into a passageway so narrow that we could only walk down it in single file. She opened another low door.

'This is the store chamber. If anyone approaches the farm we must hide in this place until one of them comes to tell us it is safe to come out,' Hinrik told me.

The only light in the room filtered in through the open door from the passage. A few barrels, a loom and several small chests stood in the centre away from the damp earth walls. The cold air rolled up from the muddy floor. I shivered. I hoped none of Fannar's neighbours would decide to come calling for dinner. I didn't fancy spending even a few minutes in there, never mind several hours.

'Does she think the Danes will come here?' I asked Hinrik.

'She says if they suspect Fannar was not telling the truth, they will. She does not think they are as easy to fool as her husband believes.' Hinrik darted an anxious glance up at me. 'I think she is right.'

I had no sooner ducked out of the low doorway into the blessed fresh air than Vítor grabbed my arm without so much as a by-your-leave. 'I need to talk to you. Come with me.'

He strode around the side of the turf building, where we couldn't be overheard, dragging me with him. I was sorely tempted to shove him off and walk away, but curiosity got the better of me.

'Isabela,' he announced, 'is still alive.'

'Why shouldn't she be?' I asked him, startled by the oddness of the statement. Then I looked round in alarm. 'Has something happened to her?'

'No, but that, my friend, is precisely my point. We both know something *should* have happened to her by now, but it hasn't, has it?'

I shook off the grip he still had on my arm. 'Vítor, I thought you were a tedious little turd the first moment I clapped eyes on you, but now I'm convinced you are not merely tedious, you have the brains of a senile goat. I haven't got a clue what you're talking about, and I rather fear, *my friend*, that you haven't either.'

'Then let me make it plain for you. The girl you were sent here to kill still lives.'

Suddenly the breath seemed to have been sucked out of my lungs.

'Kill . . . I . . . I beg your pardon,' I stammered, trying to regain control. 'Do I look like a murderer?'

'No,' Vítor said, with chilling calmness. 'You don't look like a murderer, which is exactly why you were chosen, but you *are* a murderer, aren't you? Silvia. I believe that was her name.'

The ground seemed to be buckling under my feet. I must have looked as if I was about to pass out for Vítor grabbed my arm again, but this time as if he was trying to hold me up.

I swallowed the acid that was rising in my throat and took a deep breath.

'I am very much afraid, Senhor Vítor, that you have me confused with someone else. I don't know who you think I am, but –'

'I *know* the name by which you were christened in the Holy Church was Cruz. I *know* that you were arrested for attempted fraud, and taken to the tower of Belém. And I *know* that you were advised by two of my most respected brothers to embark on a sea journey for the good of your health, or in your case one might say for the good of your life, for if you'd refused their generous offer, you would by now have joined your lover in her sepulchral embrace.'

I gaped at him. How the hell did he know all this? I tried to laugh as if this must be a joke, but only succeeded in producing a squeaky giggle which might have been emitted by a nervous maiden aunt.

'I regret to say I have absolutely no idea what you are talking about, Vítor. I thought our companion was the biggest liar in our little band, but you make him sound as truthful as a nun in confession. First you told us you were collecting sea monsters. Then you were a Lutheran pastor. What was it after that – oh yes, I remember, you were supposed to be mapping mountains. And now – just who are you claiming to be this time, a prison guard?'

'A Jesuit,' he said softly. 'Like my two brothers who visited you in the tower of Belém. My sole purpose in coming here was to ensure that you carried out your part of the bargain you made with them. Come now, Cruz, there's no need to look so shocked. You didn't really believe that we would simply take your word for it that the girl was dead, did you?'

Vítor gave a mirthless chuckle. 'You were, after all, arrested for fraud, and it wouldn't be the first time in your illustrious career that you have spun, shall we say, a web of untruths. You might have allowed the girl simply to run off, as she so nearly did that night in France. Then you could have returned to Portugal to claim your reward, swearing that you'd disposed of her, and leaving us with the potential embarrassment of her somehow finding her way back to Lisbon.'

'Such an idea never crossed my mind,' I spluttered indignantly.

I was outraged. They had sent someone to watch me as if I couldn't be trusted. This Jesuit had deceived me, lied to me, lied to us all. Map-maker, collector of curios, persecuted Lutheran. How could he sit there and blatantly tell us such tales, without so much as twitching his eyelid? I mean, surely you are supposed to be able to trust a priest to tell the truth.

Vítor, if that was his name, though doubtless he lied about that too, was studying me with disdain as if my face was some kind of fake document he was examining.

'It would seem that my brothers were wise to send me to watch over you. You were sent here to arrange an accident for Isabela. But, though you've had countless opportunities to dispatch her, she is still very much alive and, if I am not mistaken, still determined to find those falcons. Worse still, I think you are beginning to fall in love with this girl.'

It was hearing those words – *you are beginning to fall in love* – that really made me smart, because for one brief moment I wondered if it might just be true. I had whispered the word tenderly and passionately to a hundred different women, especially my poor Silvia. But up to now the word *love* had been as empty as a discarded nutshell, just something to be tossed away with a thousand other casual phrases. Now, for the first time, the word seemed to contain a tiny kernel of something that I couldn't quite identify. Could I be falling for the girl? No! It was pig's dung. I was just suffering from the shock of finding out who Vítor was, that was all. Sweet Jesu, I certainly wasn't going to tie myself up in all that nonsense with any woman. Lust always, but never love, that's my motto.

345

Vítor glanced around again to reassure himself we were still alone. Then he took a step closer to me. 'Isabela may appear to be a helpless, pretty little girl. I can see why men would want to protect her. But let me remind you again. She is not an innocent little virgin, she is a Marrano, a vile Jew, a heretic who is already condemned to the eternal fires of hell and you are sworn to send her down into those flames.'

'Let me get this straight,' I said coldly. 'You're now claiming to be a Catholic priest. And if that is true, you, a priest in holy orders, are telling me I must damn my own soul by committing murder.'

Vítor arched his brows as if in mild surprise that anyone should object to this. 'You have already damned your soul with one murder. I hardly think another will make much difference. Besides, all sin may be forgiven, if confession is made of it in all contrition. The more so, if it is committed in defence of the Holy Church and to the greater glory of God. I could absolve you of the deed within the hour if you're afraid you might die before you return to Portugal. I would willingly absolve you too of the murder of your lover, Silvia, if you were to confess to it. Indeed, many would say ridding the Church of one of her enemies might be considered apt penance for the crime you committed in lust and anger.'

'How many times do I have to say it? I did not murder Silvia. No one did. She's still alive. And if killing this girl is such a pious act,' I spat, 'I'd hate to deprive you of the opportunity of cleansing your own soul. Why don't you kill her? You've come all this way. You may as well make certain. After all, if it's so important to the Church that she dies, they might even make you a saint for doing it.'

Vítor folded his hands as a monk slides his hands into his sleeves. 'I am a consecrated priest, a man of God. The Church cannot shed blood.'

'But you can order others to do it for you,' I said savagely.

But Vítor's tone remained unnervingly calm. 'The Church orders nothing. When the Church has assisted heretics to see the error of their ways and confess their wickedness, they are released to the State. It is the State who pronounces the death penalty on them and the State who executes them, as you are in grave danger of finding out at first hand.'

He spread his hands wide. 'It's entirely up to you whether or not you choose to kill the girl. I am only here to bear witness. My duty is to carry the news back and to assure the Grand Inquisitor that nothing and no one will remain to adversely influence the young king's innocent mind and beguile him into undoing the holy work of cleansing Portugal when he comes of age. I am not ordering you to do anything. Alas, I don't have that power, I am merely a priest.' Vítor pressed his hand to his heart and humbly inclined his head. 'It must be your choice, your decision. Like all priests, I am merely here to serve you. Think of me as your conscience, there to whisper softly in your ear when I see you on the verge of doing something foolish, something you will live to regret bitterly. I am here to remind you what your fate will be if you make the wrong decision and, of course, to see you return safely to Portugal, to face the consequences of any decision you make.

'But I hardly think my gentle counsel will be necessary. Can you imagine what might happen to you if you return to Portugal having deliberately aided a heretic to escape? I cannot believe that a man like you would willingly subject himself to weeks of agonizing pain and an ignominious death, simply to save a Jewess you barely know. Besides, when she returns to Portugal with or without those birds, eventually she will find herself burning on a pyre. The king might spare her this year, but she won't have many years of liberty, that I promise you, for the Inquisition will not rest till every last Marrano is dead. Wouldn't it be kinder, more merciful, to ensure she did not return to such a fate? An opportunity to dispatch the girl may arise sooner than you think, Cruz. I suggest you think over what I have said and prepare yourself to take full advantage of it.

'And while you are making up your mind, Cruz, you should remember this – you may believe that you were ill-used in the tower of Belém, but I can assure you those who have fallen into the hands of the Inquisition would think your incarceration was a year spent in paradise compared to the tortures inflicted upon them. There is the *strappado* which dislocates their limbs, or the roasting of their larded feet over a fire, or the water poured over a cloth on their face, forcing it down their throat until they are convinced they are drowning. You see, the Inquisitors love their little games.

'Can you imagine how cruelly that fragile young girl will suffer in the dungeons of the Inquisition before she dies? If you love her you would surely want a swift and unexpected death for her, so that she has no time to dread it. Silvia's death was quick, wasn't it? How long does it take to strangle a woman, Cruz?'

I was woken unceremoniously as several feet trod on me at once. I cursed and turned over, determined to burrow back into sleep, until I realized that everyone was scrambling out of the communal beds and pushing their feet into their shoes. The fire in the hall had died down to a faint ruby glow, and only two small dish-shaped oil lamps burned on the upright beams, which hardly gave enough light for me to see my own hand.

'Is it morning already?' I groaned.

'Dogs outside are barking,' Hinrik said.

'What of it?' I mumbled. 'Dogs bark at their own shadows. Maybe they saw a fox.'

'They are trained only to bark at men.'

Unnur hurried Isabela and her own daughters out of the hall ahead of her, pausing only to give her husband a brief but desperate hug. Fannar turned and addressed the three of us in low urgent tones.

'Wait, Hinrik, come back and tell us what he's saying,' I called.

Hinrik had started to follow the women towards the hiding place in the store room. He hesitated, then reluctantly slunk over to us, his eyes wide with fear.

'He says you have claimed the protection of his *badstofa* . . . It is his duty as a host to defend you . . . As guests, it will be no dishonour to you if you go with the women and hide, but if you wish to stay and fight as brothers . . .'

Seeing the grim exchange of glances between Fannar and Ari, the blood started to pound in my head and I felt my chest tighten. They were in earnest and they were afraid, which was nothing to what I was. For a moment or two I was sorely tempted to run after the women, but Ari began to hand out heavy staves and axes, and before I knew it I found myself grasping an axe. I was grateful for the stout wooden handle to hold on to, but in truth I had no more idea of how to wield an axe than shoe a horse. I just hoped I could swing it around a bit and do some damage to the right people, without chopping my own leg off in the process. But what would these unwelcome guests be armed with? We could already hear horses' hooves clattering into the yard.

'Komdu! Komdu!' Ari whispered, beckoning frantically to us to follow him.

He led us out into the narrow passage and through a door on the opposite side to the store room. We crowded in and found ourselves standing in a cow byre, stinking of dung and piss, where half a dozen cows and a couple of calves lay on a thick layer of straw and dried bush twigs. The beasts rolled their eyes back and scrambled clumsily to their feet, lowing in agitation at the sudden appearance of five men in the middle of the night.

Ari motioned to me to help him lift a beam and lower it

into two iron brackets either side of the door we'd come through, to brace it shut behind us. Then he whispered to Hinrik, gesturing to a low, wide door on the opposite side of the byre. All three of us pressed our heads close to Hinrik. He was shaking and cringing at each new sound that echoed from the courtyard.

'He . . . he says crouch down. Keep very still and quiet. When he opens that far door . . . we must . . . must push the *kýr* out and creep out between them so they hide us.'

Outside in the yard, men were calling to one another as they dismounted and yelling at the dogs which were still barking. Then came a thundering at the main door, as if someone was pounding on it with the pommel of a sword. I gripped my axe more tightly and glanced at Ari, but he motioned us to keep still.

We heard the grate of the door as it opened, a man barking questions and the lower tones of Fannar answering. There was a thump as if someone had been shoved hard against a door, followed by the clanging of metal and more shouts as the men pushed their way down the narrow passage. The great hall must have run directly behind the byre, for though noise was muffled by the earth wall, there came the sickening sounds of wooden panels being ripped off, beds being torn apart and objects being hurled aside. The men were tearing the place apart.

Someone rattled the handle of the byre door which led into the passage, then barged against it, but it held.

Ari's head swivelled towards the opposite door. He held up his hand, signalling to us to wait. We crouched rigid. Hinrik was grasping a stave in both hands, his eyes closed, but his lips were moving soundlessly as if he was muttering some desperate prayer over and over again. For once, I was almost tempted to pray too, except that the name of every saint I'd ever known seemed to have vanished from my head. My palms were so slippery with sweat that I was sure the axe was going to slide from my grasp the moment I stood up. Then we heard the men fumbling with the latch on the outside door and moments later it swung open.

Ari leapt to his feet, shrieking and waving his arms like a man possessed. The cattle, with bellows of fear, reared and turned, charging at the open doorway. It was probably as well we couldn't move as quickly as the beasts for we would have been crushed between them in their panic to squeeze out through the gap. One of the men standing outside was knocked over by the first animal and we heard his screams as the others' sharp hooves trampled over him. The second man managed to jump back in time as the cows thundered past him.

We ran after them. Ari swept his cudgel sideways as he burst out of the doorway and succeeded in catching the second man full in the face. He crumpled to his knees, falling across his companion who was lying bleeding in the dirt, moaning helplessly as he tried in vain to lever himself up on crushed and broken limbs.

Ari began to run towards the back of the farmstead, but as we rounded the corner, two men sprang towards us from the darkness, swords flashing. Hinrik raised his stave, but the sight of the sword seemed to unnerve him completely. He dropped the stick and fled.

One of the Danes came straight for me. He raised his sword and swept it down. I dodged back, but the blade passed so close to my face I felt the wind of it as it whistled by. I lifted the axe high in both hands, but in that same instant I knew I had made a terrible mistake for I'd left my body completely unprotected. As if in the slowness of a dream I watched the point of his blade thrusting towards my chest and I could do nothing to defend myself. Then, just as the swordsman lunged forward, his leading foot slipped from under him in a patch of cow shit, and he landed on the ground with a cry of pain as his legs splayed wide. It was nothing to the scream he gave moments later as my axe blade sank into his skull. Scalding blood splattered on to my hands and face.

I glanced down. The other Dane was also lying there bleeding into the mud, though which of the others had killed him I had no idea. I briefly contemplated trying to wrench the axe out of the man's head, but almost vomited at the thought, so I snatched the sword from his still twitching fingers and fled into the darkness.

We ran a little way off and took shelter behind some low bushes. Some of the Danes were carrying burning torches and by their light we could see the dark figures of men milling around the farmstead and hear them bellowing to one another. But it was too dark to make out their numbers. The cries and shouts redoubled. Someone, it could have been Fannar, was running from the house. I only glimpsed him for a moment or two before he vanished into the darkness.

Then we heard a familiar but desperate cry. I could make out the slender outline of a lad struggling between two Danes who were dragging him towards one of the horses.

'They've got Hinrik,' I whispered.

'If he stays calm he might be able to convince them that he is just a simple farmhand,' Vítor said.

'I don't think there's much chance of him staying calm.'

The lad was shrieking for help and even as we watched, we saw them tying his wrists to a long length of rope which they evidently meant to fasten to the horse.

'If they leave him to search the building, we might be able to creep over and cut him loose,' I said.

But before I could even think of a way to reach him, a horse came galloping round the corner of the building, the smoke and scarlet flames from the rider's torch streaming out behind him like a banner. As the horseman passed the entrance to the byre, he tossed his blazing torch into the straw. The flames ran swiftly across the floor, then roared upwards as the whole byre ignited at once.

'Look at the roof,' Vítor whispered. I followed his finger. Behind the byre, flames were starting to curl up through the turf roof of the hall. Dense smoke rose into the air as the turfs smouldered from the heat beneath.

Beside me in the darkness, I heard Ari cry out in horror.

'They've fired the whole building,' I breathed. 'They must have set the hall ablaze from inside.' A terrible chill went through me. 'Isabela and the women are in the store chamber. The fire will spread along the beams. They'll be trapped. We have to help them.'

'The Danes are waiting for us to do just that,' Vítor said. 'The moment you go out there you will be captured just like the boy.'

'But we can't just leave her. We have to get her out.' I started up, but someone grabbed my arm and twisted it, forcing me to the ground.

I felt a knee in my back pressing me down. Vítor bent his mouth so close to my ear I could feel his hot breath on my skin. 'They won't let you get within shouting distance of the farm. We need an accident, remember. Think about it. Her blood will be on the hands of the Danes, not yours. I have made it easy for you.'

I was struggling to fling Vítor off, but with the full weight of his body pressing down on my back, I was as helpless as a trussed chicken.

Fausto scrambled to his feet. 'I'm not just going to sit here and watch her die, not my Isabela. I won't. I have to try, I have to!'

Ari tried to grab him and pull him back down behind the bushes, but Fausto shook him off and the next minute he was running back towards the farmhouse, crouching low, trying to keep to the shadows. The flames from the burning house were now so high that they bathed the whole meadow around it in an eerie red glow. We could feel the heat from it even where we lay. We could see the dark outline of Fausto running towards the back of the building. It looked for a moment as if he was going to reach it, but the Danes must have had men watching.

A cry went up which carried even over the roar of the flames. Two men came galloping around the side of the building towards Fausto. We saw the glints of their blades, blood-red in the firelight, as they raised them. They drew level with him, one on either side. Fausto raised his staff and swung at one of the riders, but the second rider thrust his sword into his back at full gallop. For a moment Fausto was thrown clean off his feet with the force of the blow, his back arched in agony, and then he crumpled and fell without a cry.

As Fausto was slain, the farmstead, as if it could bear no more, surrendered itself to the ravenous fire. With a thunderous crash the roof caved in and flames shot high into the air. Red and golden sparks from the burning turfs and hay drifted over us in the dark sky, falling to the earth like rain.

I stared at the inferno, numb with horror. I couldn't take it in, but even as I watched, unable to speak or move, I knew that nothing . . . nothing could remain alive inside that tangle of burning wood and flames.

Eydis

Imp – to mend the broken feathers of a hawk. A wooden imping needle, whittled from a piece of twig, is inserted in the hollow shaft of the broken feather, to which a previously moulted feather can be glued, enabling the bird to fly.

The corpse is healing now. I watched and waited for three days, turning the pot containing the severed head in the embers of the fire, until the flesh and bone were dry enough to pound to pieces. I knew they sat with me in the shadows, the old woman and Valdis. As mourners we waited, we watched not to see life depart, but restored. The draugr watched too, and he is afraid. I can breathe his fear.

I ground the old woman's skull into a fine powder in my mortar and pestle. I mixed it with the fox fat, blessing the hunter who had brought me a jar of it as an offering. Dried primrose, burnet, root of bistort and seeds of lupin, these too. And when all was infused into the fat, I spread the ointment on the wounds of the corpse, anointing also his lips and tongue, his nostrils, ears, hands, feet and genitals. Now his skin is flushed with blood and his chest is rising and falling. But he does not open his eyes or stir. How can he? For the spirit which animates the body remains inside my dead sister, mocking me through her lips, watching me through her eyes.

A spasm of pain shoots through my head, and for a moment I can see nothing. As it subsides, I know it is the girl. I feel her terror. I feel the cold breath of all those who follow her, like a mountain stream running through my fingers. Valdis's head turns towards me. The black eyes search mine, trying to find a way into my thoughts. The draugr knows that something is wrong. He knows I am losing her.

I take up my lucet and weave the cord as rapidly as my fingers can move.

'Rowan, protect her. Fern, defend her. Salt, bind her to us!'

His laughter rolls around the cave, but I will not be silenced.

Ari is scrambling down the rocks. I know his tread well by now, but he is not alone. Others descend cautiously, cursing in foreign tongues as their feet slip or they bang an elbow on the sharp rocks. I pull the veils over our faces and retreat to the shadow of the far corner of the cave to wait.

Ari leads two men into the cave. They gaze around them in clear amazement. The taller of the two bends down and touches the rock he is standing on as if to assure himself it really is warm. He is a handsome man, with thick black hair, a straight, elegant nose and eyes of such startlingly deep blue that he might have plucked them from the sea. The smaller of the two is pale beneath his dark stubble, and his dark eyes move restlessly around as if he is trying to memorize every detail of the cave. Like Ari, both men are covered in mud and splattered with blood, though it is not their own.

I step from the shadow as Ari gestures to me. Looks of utter horror and revulsion pass across the two men's faces. They gaze open-mouthed at me. A throb of shame runs through me, as if we are girls again being stared at by mocking children. The Icelanders who come to the cave have known us all their lives and their faces no longer betray the disgust they feel. Until a stranger reminds us, it is easy to forget that we are not like other women.

'Eydis, this is Vítor and this is Marcos.'

The taller of the two, the one named Marcos, makes a gallant effort at a bow, though he cannot tear his gaze away from me. The other, Vítor, makes no effort to acknowledge me, but watches me warily as if I am some loathsome creature who might savage him.

'They're foreigners, fell foul of the Danes, and Fannar was hiding them. But the Danes raided the farmstead looking for them and burned it to the ground. There was another lad with them, Hinrik, but the Danes caught him and took him off with them. I'm sorry, Eydis . . . I didn't know where else to bring them.'

'Does this Hinrik know about the cave?'

'I never told him, and Fannar and Unnur would never speak of you or the cave in front of strangers.'

'And Fannar and Unnur, and the girls, where are they?'

Ari hangs his head miserably. 'I don't know. I thought I saw Fannar running from the house, but I lost track of him in the dark. The women took refuge in the store room, but . . . the fire . . .' He shakes his head as if trying to dislodge the image from his mind. 'Now that these men are safe, I'll go back and search for the bodies. Bury them. They deserve that much at least.' His fists clench. 'Unnur was a good woman and I'll not leave her or her children for the foxes and the ravens to pick at.'

'You cannot return yet,' I tell him as gently as I can. 'The Danes will question this Hinrik and will show no mercy. It will not take them long to discover who has escaped them. Even now they will be searching for the three of you. If you leave here you will be caught. You might even be seen leaving the cave and lead them straight here. Patience, Ari. You must rest and take some food so that your wits are sharp when you return to the light.'

'I can't rest! What if Fannar is lying hurt somewhere? He'll think I've abandoned him.'

'He knows you, Ari. He trusts you to protect his guests, even before the lives of his own family. That is the old way, the code of honour he has always lived by.'

Ari will stay. Like a faithful dog, he will carry out what he knows to be Fannar's wishes, even if it costs him his life. But he is young and headstrong. The frustration will gnaw at him until he cannot bear it. No matter what the danger, I will not be able to contain him for long.

We sleep fitfully, eating when we wake, then sleeping again. Though Vítor sleeps soundly, several times I notice Marcos lies awake staring miserably up at the flame of the lamp, the glitter of tears in his eyes. Several times I rise quietly to anoint the corpse of the draugr.

And each time I rise I knot a few more lengths of the cord. Her footsteps have fallen silent. She is drifting, tossed like a gull on the wind of a storm. Without the girl, the ghosts will not come to help us. The mountain is calling and every day the voice of the pool grows stronger, the monster beneath more restless. The great black beast of death stretches his leather wings.

I wake again to see Ari returning from the mouth of the cave. He holds up his hand as if swearing an oath.

'I haven't been out. I just went into the passage to look up at the cave entrance to see if it's morning or night. It's dark again. A whole day gone.' He kicked a stone savagely. 'How can you bear this? How can you even tell whether it is day or night, or how many days have passed?'

'We sleep when we are weary, eat when we are hungry. We are not governed by the moon or mastered by the sun, schooled by the rain or herded by the wind. When we first came here we ached to feel the sun again, to see the first snow fall in winter and run in bare feet on the new spring grass, but eventually we came to learn that there is a kind of freedom in being outside the rule of time.'

'Don't you long to leave this cave? I couldn't bear to be shut up here alone for days on end, never mind for years. I'd go mad.'

'Madness is an escape which is not as easy to accomplish as you might think, Ari. But you will not be here for years, not even for many more days. We will hide you here for as long as we dare, but there is another danger greater even than the Danes. The pool is –' I hold up my hand. 'People are climbing up the mountainside towards the cave.'

Ari darts towards the two sleeping men and shakes them awake. He gestures to them and they spring up, one grabbing a sword, the other a staff.

'Ari,' I whisper urgently. 'Follow the ledge beside the pool. We have not been able to go far along it, because of our chains, but we were told it leads to a second cave. Take care not to slip; the water has grown much hotter since you were last here.'

Ari nods and beckons to the two foreigners to follow him.

'Eydis, Eydis,' the dark voice murmurs. 'You are wasting your time. You can't hide those men, those Papists. Don't you think I will sing out and tell the Danes exactly where they are? You can't silence me. The Danes will kill them and they deserve to die, you know that, Eydis. They're going to die.'

I close my eyes and concentrate on trying to sense who is approaching the cave. Feet are scrambling on the stones above. Familiar voices call out softly.

Fannar comes round the side of the rock carrying his younger daughter, Lilja, in his arms. Three women crowd in behind him, his wife Unnur, their elder daughter Margrét and a girl.

I know her face. I have seen her standing at the end of the tunnel in the black mirror. The blood pounds in my head. It is the girl I have been waiting for. The cord has drawn her here at last. She has come! She has come to us. I can scarcely take my eyes from her. I see the shock in her face as she catches sight of me, but there is no disgust in the look, only sorrow as she stares at the iron band around my waist.

Fannar lays his daughter carefully down on the floor of the cave. There is a deep cut to her shin, which is bruised and swollen. Fannar tenderly smoothes her tangled hair. He has suddenly turned into an old man, his face drawn, his hand trembling with fatigue.

'Eydis, we have . . .' he begins.

I shake my head. 'Save your strength. Ari has told me what happened.'

Despite his exhaustion, Fannar's eyes light up with hope. 'Ari has been here? He is safe? And the three men, the foreigners, did he speak of them?'

'See for yourself, Fannar.'

I drag my chain to the ledge and call out the news of Fannar's arrival. Moments later I hear the men edging back along the ledge towards us.

'Slowly, slowly, do not slip!' I warn.

Ari is moving far too hastily in his anxiety to see Fannar. My warning goes unheeded. Ari springs from the ledge and grasps Fannar in a great hug, both men clapping each other on the back and swearing that each believed the other dead.

Marcos, when he steps rather more gingerly from the ledge, stares around in bewilderment, then a look of utter joy fills his face and he runs to the girl, clasps her waist and, lifting her off her feet, whirls her around.

'Isabela, Isabela!'

She is startled and quickly wriggles from his grasp. So that's the way of it, he loves her, and she doesn't know it.

Vítor steps unhurriedly down. He too is smiling, but the smile does not reach his eyes. It does not take the gift of second sight to tell he is not pleased to see the girl.

Fannar greets both men warmly in turn. His relief is plain to see. Then his expression turns grave again.

'Where is Hinrik and the other man, Fausto?'

'The Danes arrested Hinrik,' Ari says. 'He was alive . . .

when they took him. Maybe they'll let him go,' he adds, but there is no conviction is his tone. 'Fausto is dead. He went back to try to help the women when the fire started. I couldn't stop him. The Danes cut him down with a sword as he ran across the yard. He would have died instantly from such a blow.'

Fannar shakes his head sorrowfully and makes the sign of the cross.

Ari turns to Unnur. 'But how did you escape the fire?'

Unnur is as drained and wretched as her husband. Her face and clothes are streaked with mud and soot. But she moves to her husband's side and pats his arm fondly.

'Fannar taught me what to do, if ever we were attacked. There was always the danger we might be, with Father Jon . . .' She hesitates and glances warily at the foreigners, even though from their blank expressions it is plain they cannot understand her.

'There was a place at the back of the store room where the wood which held up the turfs on the roof could be lifted off, like a trap door, but it was hidden from view, unless you knew where it was. Fannar said if ever we were attacked, the girls and I must lock ourselves in the store room. He would try to stop the attackers entering the *badstofa*. He said that if he appeared anxious they should not go in there, that would be exactly where they would go first. And they did.

'When we heard them smashing up the hall, we broke open the hole in the roof and crawled out, before the fire could take hold and spread to the store room. We had arranged a place long ago where we would go and wait for Fannar to come and find us, if he could. We waited and waited, but he didn't come. I thought he was . . .' She breaks off, unable to bring herself to utter the word.

Fannar puts his arm about his wife. 'The Danes were still searching. They were between me and where I knew my wife would be hiding. I was afraid that if I tried to reach her and was seen, I might lead them straight to her. They kept searching for most of the next day. Only once it got dark again did they give up and I was able to go and find her.'

Unnur suddenly bursts into tears, sobbing on her husband's shoulder. 'Our home . . . everything . . . all gone . . . destroyed . . .'

Their elder daughter, Margrét, begins to sob too, but little Lilja stares blankly into the flames of the cooking fire, as if her mind has frozen out all that has befallen her.

Fannar pats his wife's back awkwardly as if he's never seen her cry before and doesn't know how to stop her. Women like Unnur have too much pride to shed tears in their husbands' presence. But she has suffered much in the last two days, and hungry, frightened and exhausted, she can no longer hold back her grief.

'It's hard, I know, but homes can be rebuilt, Unnur,' I tell her gently. 'Fannar and your daughters are alive and safe, in the end that's all that matters.'

She nods and tries to smile through her tears, wiping them away on her torn sleeve.

'Now, Ari, find some spoons and let Fannar and his family eat while I tend to the child. I don't have eating-vessels for so many, so you must all eat from the common pot, though that will be no hardship if you are hungry.'

While they eat, I fetch some water I have already set to cool and prepare to wash Lilja's shin, but though she is normally an obedient child, the terror and shock of the last two nights have made her fearful of everything. She curls up in a ball and will not let me touch her. I sense someone standing beside me. It is the girl, Isabela. She crouches down by the child, holding out her arm to her. There is an angry red line across it, which has blistered badly. She must have been struck by some burning wood as she escaped the house. Isabela takes the bowl of water and the cloth from me and gives them to Lilja, miming that she wants the child to bathe her arm.

Lilja stares. Slowly she picks up the cloth and dabs at the burn. Isabela does not flinch, though the slightest touch of the cloth must hurt her. She holds her arm steady, smiling encouragingly at the child.

I fetch some of the mummy ointment and tell Lilja to gently coat the burn with it. It will heal them both as well as it has the draugr. But that is not why I do it. The bones of the old woman are in that ointment, the first spirit of the doordoom of the dead. I must make a connection, a bond, a cord, between the old woman and the girl. Only then, only if we can all join one to another, will we be strong enough to stand against him.

Isabela gestures to Lilja's shin and the child stretches out her leg towards her trustingly, allowing her to tend the cut, which she does with great gentleness and sureness. She is plainly well accustomed to caring for wounded creatures. She sniffs at the ointment, and dips her little finger into it, licking it. She nods to herself as if she recognizes the ingredients and approves of the mixture. As she returns the jar to me, our hands touch.

In that moment I see a great cloak of white feathers envelop her, like the cloak the goddess Freya used to turn herself into a falcon. It is only there for an instant and then it vanishes. But something remains behind. A host of shadows suddenly crowd at her back. I hear cries, screams, then a silence so deep it is as if every sound in the world has been obliterated. The shadows dissolve.

Who are these ghosts she has brought here? Evil and terror surround her, like dark water swirling about a rock. The draugr feels it too. Valdis's head swivels towards her under the veil. The draugr fears this foreign girl. He senses this fragile child holds the power to destroy him, when not even a blacksmith has strength to overcome him.

But Isabela has felt nothing. She slips an arm around Lilja, pulling her close, so that the child's head rests on her shoulder.

She smiles wearily at me. She does not know what she has brought to us. She does not understand why we have drawn her here. She thinks only of the white falcons, and her hunger for them is so all-consuming she will not listen to the shadows. She will not look at them. But she must, she must.

Fannar shuffles across to where we are sitting, and squats down next to me. His hands rest limply on his knees.

'Eydis, we have nowhere to go . . . I know our neighbours would offer us shelter on their farms, but our presence would only bring trouble to them. Besides, the Danes may have already raided them too. I know you don't have enough food to feed us all for long . . . we could hunt for birds, but that means going out in the daylight and I daren't risk that yet. But Ari and I will go out after dark and steal what we can, even a sheep if we must. We will repay our neighbours for what we take from them when we are able. But we can find food for us all . . .'

'Fannar, you know that you are welcome to stay as long as you need and share whatever we have, but you will not be safe here for long. Do you not feel how much hotter the cave has become since your last visit? You are sweating, so are we all.'

'I hadn't noticed. I was so thankful just to get here safely.' He runs his fingers distractedly through his grizzled hair. 'Now you mention it, I suppose it is a little warmer. But what of it?'

'Look at the pool. See how it is bubbling, how dense the steam that rises from it. The water is too hot to touch now. The rocks beneath us are growing warmer every day. Soon the steam from that pool will be scalding. Anyone remaining in the cave will be boiled alive. I know you have troubles enough, Fannar, but you must be prepared for the day when you will have to leave this cave, and quickly. It might be weeks yet, but it could be as soon as tomorrow.'

Fannar gnaws his lip. 'There are other caves.'

'The rivers of fire are beginning to run beneath the earth again, every cave around here will be in danger. You will have to go far away from this mountain to be safe.'

Valdis's lips move beneath her veil. 'If the water begins to boil, then we will die in this cave, Fannar, for we cannot free ourselves of this chain. Don't leave us here.'

Fannar nods gravely. 'You need have no fear of that. I will find a way to get you loose from this chain. It may take time to break the iron bands, so as soon as Ari and I return with food, we will make a start.'

'No!' I cry. 'No, you must not break the iron band. You must not. There is danger in it, danger you cannot begin to understand.'

He stares at me in astonishment. 'But I have to. If we are forced to leave the cave in a hurry, there may not be time to set you free. And as your sister says, we can't leave you both here to be scalded to death.'

'You must leave us here, Fannar. If I can find a way to remove the danger first, then I will gladly let you break the iron. I will beg you to do so. But I will not allow you to do it unless I know it is safe. If Valdis asks you to break the band, you must stop your ears and not listen to her. Whatever she says, whatever promises or threats she makes, you must ignore her.'

Fannar rubs his forehead. He is struggling to make sense of what I am saying, but he is exhausted.

'But, Eydis, we have always listened to you both and you have never misled us. You have always spoken the same word. Why should you and your sister quarrel now, and over something so important? I don't understand. What is this danger you are talking about?'

I cannot explain it to him without terrifying him and his wife and daughters. They have been through enough. For the moment they are comforted that they are in a place of safety. They need to rest, to sleep. It is hard enough for Fannar to learn about the pool. How can I tell him that his wife and children are trapped in this cave with something far worse than the Danes? And how could he live with the knowledge that it was he himself who brought that creature of death here?

'Valdis has changed. Something has entered her and she no longer speaks the truth, you must believe me. She is not to be trusted any more.'

'It is Eydis who does not speak the truth. She's gone mad. Why else would she want to die in agony in this cave? Don't listen to her, Fannar. Listen to me. Free us and we will guide you to a place of safety where the Danes will never find you.'

'Swear to me, Fannar,' I beg him, 'on the lives of your precious daughters. Swear that you will not try to break the iron bands, unless I ask you to.'

But Fannar is staring from one to the other of us, a look of complete bewilderment on his haggard face. He does not know which of us to believe, but which of us will he listen to in the end? If he chooses to trust Valdis, none of us will live to escape this cave.

Chapter Twelve

The shamans of the North say that before the world was made, there was nothing but chaos and darkness, a vast ocean which raged and foamed and would not be still. From the dark, tormented seas a tiny island emerged. Two beings appeared on the island. They were each male and female in one body, but neither being could be complete without the other.

One of these beings found a stick and broke it in two and placed it upright on the shore which was neither earth nor water, but both sea and land. The beings watched and waited. Then out of the darkness flew a white falcon and the moment it alighted on the stick, light began to creep over the island and the seas shrank back from it. The island grew bigger and bigger until it became the world.

And the falcon flew over the face of the world until he found a woman, who was fairer and more lovely than any woman who has ever lived since, and from their union, the very first shamans were born, with the power to send their spirits up into the stars.

Isabela

Cast of hawks – *two falcons working together to hunt the same quarry.*

I am lost in the forest again. I feel very small. An old woman hurries along beside me. She is holding tightly to my little hand, almost dragging me. She is my grandmother. Somehow I know that. It's dark and we are weaving between the thick tree trunks. I can see the dark smudges of others walking ahead of us. A man I know is my father carries my little brother on his back. I wish he would carry me instead. I'm tired. My legs ache. I don't want to walk any more. I want to go home to my soft bed.

Grandmother is holding my fingers much too tightly. The ring on her finger digs into the back of my hand. It hurts. I'm too hot. I am dressed in too many layers of clothes. I want to tear them off. I feel squashed and stiff. It's hard to bend my arms. There's a sharp stone in my shoe. It hurts every time I put my foot down. I keep tugging on Grandmother's hand, trying to make her stop so that I can take it out, but she yanks me forward crossly, making me run. I hate her. I want to hold my mother's hand instead, but she is carrying the baby.

My father stops. Men are stepping out of the trees in front of us. My father whips round, staring at something behind me. I turn. More men are stepping out from the shadows behind us and walking towards us. They're carrying cudgels and swords. One man ambles towards my grandmother, swinging his cudgel in his hand.

'Running away, are you, Huguenot traitors?'

'Let the children go,' my father says. 'Please . . . they are innocent.'

The man snorts. 'What man would be so foolish as to go to the trouble of hunting down a viper, and not destroy its young? You think we want more Huguenot spawn infecting France with poison?'

The man with the cudgel bounces the end of the stick against the palm of his other hand. I can hear the slap, slap of it as he walks slowly towards us through the fallen leaves. Grandmother pushes me behind her, one hand on my arm to hold me there. The man smiles at her. I can feel Grandma shaking and I want to tell her not to be scared. The man won't hurt us. He is smiling at us.

The cudgel whistles through the air. It strikes my grandmother on the side of her head and she falls. The man raises the stick again and hits her hard on her back. He is beating her over and over again. She is crying. Grandmother never cries.

I call out to my father to tell him to make the man stop, but he is kneeling on the ground, cradling my little brother against his chest. Two men are hacking at him with their swords. I turn and run, but someone grabs me, lifts me off my feet. Thick, hairy arms are crushing me. I fight and fight, but I can't get free. My lungs are bursting with the effort of trying to scream, but no sound comes out.

I woke with a violent jerk and lay sweating and trembling. The heads of both twin sisters were turned in my direction and I knew they were watching me beneath their veils. I felt the intensity of their gaze even though I couldn't see their eyes. It was almost as if they were able to see inside my nightmare.

When I first entered the cave I thought I was dreaming then. My head was thick and heavy from hunger and exhaustion, and the heat which enveloped me was the last thing

I expected, though at first I was glad of it. My father had taken me into caves before when we were away catching the passage falcons as they migrated. Some were shallow and dry, others deep and resonant, with water dripping from dark green ferns which overhung the entrance. But always the caverns were cool, even cold. I had never imagined that a cave could be warm and steamy, or that rocks on which I walked in the darkness so far below the earth could be as hot as stones that had lain all day in the summer's sun.

But then I saw Eydis, and for a moment, I believed she was some demon chained there to guard the entrance to hell. I had to stop myself from crying out. When I looked again though, I saw she was no demon, but a woman like me. She was tall and thin, clad in a brown woollen skirt, but naked from the waist up. Her breasts were bound with a simple band of cloth knotted at the front. Her head and face were covered by a black veil.

But it wasn't her clothes that made me shudder. There was a second woman, dressed exactly like Eydis, growing out of her side. Valdis, her twin sister, was joined to her at the hip. Each woman possessed their own head, arms and torso, but shared a single pair of legs. This second woman lolled out sideways from Eydis's upright body. Her arms dangled limply beneath her and the nails on her twig-like fingers were black. Her head rolled backwards from its own weight, so that when Eydis moved she was compelled to put an arm around her sister's shoulder and clasp her in a strange embrace to keep her upright, so that they could walk.

And this was not the worst of it. For while the skin on Eydis's body and arms was firm and healthy, though very pale from having lived all her life without the sun or wind, the skin of her twin was a yellowish-brown, loose and wrinkled. Her body and arms resembled the mummified hands and feet of saints preserved in the reliquaries of the great churches and cathedrals of Portugal. I would have sworn she was dead and yet I knew she couldn't be, for she turned to stare at us through her veil, and when she spoke I could see her lips moving beneath it.

Two thick iron hoops encircled the waists of both women. They were fastened to two long, heavy chains and these in turn were attached to a single iron ring embedded in the rock of the cave wall. You could see the calluses on the women's skin where for years they had chafed and rubbed. Their chains were long enough for the twins to move freely around the cave, though not to get close enough to the entrance to peer up through the slit in the rocks high above and glimpse the sun or the stars.

I'd seen the mad chained up like that. People who rave and babble nonsense, who try to savage any who approach them and tear at their own hair and flesh till they're raw and bleeding. But Eydis was not mad. I could hear the calmness in her voice, watch the sure and methodical way she tended the wounds of the poor injured man who lay unconscious in one corner of the cave. A madwoman couldn't heal. It took great skill and reason to do that.

I felt an overwhelming surge of pity for Eydis, as I would if I had seen an eagle in a tiny cage, never allowed to stretch its wings or fly. Weren't Eydis and Valdis already bound to each other for life, never able to have a moment's solitude to walk alone, to fall in love? Why did others have to add to their misery by chaining them up below the earth?

Those first two days in the cave passed in a strange kind of limbo. I felt as if I'd died and was waiting in a chamber that was neither in heaven nor hell, nor on the earth, waiting for someone to tell us where to go. Ari couldn't bear to be contained. He was constantly slipping down the passage to stand below the entrance, to see where the sun was in the sky, or if the moon had risen. Each time he went, I felt panic rising in me. The hours and days were sliding away. My father too was trapped away from the light, chained like the sisters.

I couldn't leave him there. I couldn't leave him to die. I had to escape and search for the falcons. But each time I moved towards the passage Fannar barred the way.

'Danir! Danes!' he said, gesturing upwards.

Marcos and Vítor were restless too. Perhaps the confinement was making them also feel trapped and nervous, but there was a strange enmity between them. They'd certainly never been friends, none of the three men had, yet now Marcos seemed to go out of his way to sit as far away from Vítor as he could. Once I even saw him try to strike up a conversation with Unnur, just to avoid Vítor, though she looked completely mystified, not understanding one word of what he was saying.

I thought often about Hinrik. I prayed that they hadn't hurt him, that they had let him go. He had been so terrified of being caught by the Danes, but surely they would quickly realize he was innocent of any crime? What had he done that they could possibly accuse him of?

I thought too about poor Fausto. Had poor little Hinrik been right after all when he said Fausto loved me? Was that why he'd made that brave, foolish attempt to return to the house? I'd been so certain he'd tried to kill me when he kicked my horse. Now that he was dead, I knew it must have been an accident, like Marcos had said.

What was wrong with me? How could I think that any one of these men who had risked their lives to defend me from the Danes would want to harm me? Perhaps it was the shock of knowing that everything I had been brought up to believe was a lie, that my parents, the people I had trusted the most in the world, had lied to me. It had made me suspicious of everyone. I'd even imagined that Vítor wished me harm, when in fact he'd done nothing but try to protect me. Like poor Fausto, Vítor and Marcos were both kind men and I was angry with myself for ever being suspicious of them.

But by the second night I could bear the waiting no longer.

Whatever the danger from the Danes, I had to leave the refuge of the cave and hunt for the falcons. I felt so guilty, because Fannar and his family had lost everything they had to protect us. It was a betrayal of them to put myself in danger again, but I couldn't just sit here and let my father, my mother and who knew how many more, burn.

I forced myself to stay awake and watch until the others fell asleep, though in the soporific heat of the cave it wasn't easy to keep my eyes open. But finally, when I was sure they were all lost in their dreams, I rose quietly, tiptoed out of the cave and slipped around the rocky outcrop. I groped my way along the passage, trying to place my feet as carefully as I could so as not to dislodge any of the loose stones that littered the floor. At the far end was a heap of rocks and boulders that I knew formed a rough staircase up which you could climb to reach three or four rocky ledges one above the other, like the rungs of a ladder, leading up to the long narrow slit far above my head.

As I stood at the bottom, I could just make out a single silver star shivering in the blackness overhead, but its tiny light did nothing to illuminate the rocks. When I had first entered the cave Fannar had helped me down, holding my ankles and guiding my feet on to the next ledge and the next rock, but now I couldn't see so much as a hand in front of me to find my way back up.

I cursed myself for not having the sense to bring a lamp, and wondered whether to return for one, but I remembered that even down here, the faint glow might be seen shining up through the crack at night and betray the hiding place of the others. I would have to feel my way up one boulder at a time. But as I was reaching up, trying to find a handhold, someone grabbed my shoulder. I whipped round, stifling a cry. Vítor was standing directly behind me.

'I woke and saw you were missing,' he whispered. 'I was concerned for you. Where are you going?'

'I . . . I just wanted to look out of the entrance,' I said, keeping my voice as low as possible. 'I feel so closed in and it's so hot. I need some cold fresh air.'

'I too would like the chance to breathe fresh air, but it is an extremely irresponsible thing to attempt. If you are seen and give away our hiding place, we will all suffer. You have a habit of wandering off, Isabela, first in France and then that first night in Iceland, and on both occasions you would have died, if we hadn't –'

'Don't touch her!'

We both looked up, startled, to see Marcos stumbling towards us, tripping over the stones in his haste to reach us.

'I assure you I have no intention of touching the young lady,' Vítor said. 'I was merely advising Isabela that it wasn't safe to go out. She has an unfortunate history of accidents whenever she ventures off on her own. Fortunately none has yet proved fatal, but . . .'

'You bastard,' Marcos growled. 'Don't you –'

Fannar peered around the rock outcrop. He gestured impatiently for us to return to the cave, putting his finger to his lips and gesturing upwards. 'Danir!'

We had no choice but to follow him back inside. Fannar was evidently grumbling to Ari and glowering in our direction. He lay down again but this time across the entrance to the passage, so that anyone trying to go down there would first have to step over him. We all lay down in our separate spaces. I was trembling with frustration. If it hadn't been for Vítor detaining me and Marcos waking Fannar, I could have been out there now. Why did Vítor and Marcos have to follow me around as if I was a wayward child? What did it matter to them if I left or not? The tension between them was so palpable that I was sure if Fannar hadn't woken up, they would have started wrestling each other to the ground like small boys. This confinement was getting to all of us. But I had to find a way out.

I found myself staring at the narrow ledge that ran along-side the pool. It went far back, disappearing through a tunnel beyond the pool, where the water rushed out. Was there a second cave beyond this one? Vítor, Marcos and Ari had all emerged from that tunnel the day Fannar brought us here. Perhaps if I followed the water, I would find another hole leading to the outside.

I wanted to leap up at once and try it out, but I knew I had to restrain myself until the others were sleeping. I didn't want Vítor following me again. I sat upright, pressing my back against a sharp point on the cave wall to keep myself from drifting back into sleep in the warmth. I told myself I had to stay awake so that I could try once more to escape the cave, but deep down I knew that wasn't the only reason. I was too scared to sleep in case my nightmares dragged me back into that forest where the men with swords and cudgels lay wait-ing for me in the darkness among the trees.

But in spite of all my efforts to stay awake, in that heat sleep was impossible to fight and I found myself beginning to surrender to it. My head cracked against the rock, as it lolled sideways, and I sat up sharply, rubbing the bruise. As I looked up, I suddenly saw Hinrik standing in the shadows on the opposite side of the cave. I scrambled up, overjoyed and immensely relieved to see that he was safe.

'Hinrik, you got away! How . . .'

He took a step forward, holding something out in his hand. His face, his chest and arms were bruised and bloody, but only as he moved did I see the heavy rope noose dan-gling from his neck.

He opened his palm. A small white pebble lay in his hand. 'The stone,' he said. 'I thought it was for the witch, but it was for you.'

'Hinrik, you're hurt. What have they done to you?'

'Did you say *Hinrik*?' Marcos whispered behind me. 'Is

the lad here?' He moved closer, staring about him. 'Where is he?'

I know that at twilight your eyes can be tricked into thinking dead trees are old men, or someone is seated in an empty chair. And I was sure that if I looked again I would see now that what I had taken to be Hinrik was just a rock, and what I heard was just the echo of a voice from a dream. But when I turned to look, Hinrik was still standing watching me, and my eyes couldn't turn him into shadow again. Despite the heat of the cave, a cold wave of fear drenched me. I suddenly knew he had not escaped and now he never would.

I swallowed hard, trying to keep the fear from my voice. 'I . . . I woke up and thought I saw the boy, but . . .'

Marcos yawned. 'It's this place, the damnable heat. It's enough to drive anyone crazy. But I don't think there's much chance of seeing that poor lad again. I was going to try to cut him loose back there at the farmstead, but there wasn't a hope of rescuing him, not when the fire started. Once those flames got going, if I'd tried to get anywhere near him I'd have been seen as clearly as if I was strolling around in summer sunshine.'

He half-lifted his hand and I thought he was going to pat my shoulder, but something must have stopped him for he let his hand drop. 'Don't worry. The boy comes from here. He'll know how to handle the Danes. They're bound to let him go in the end, but when they do I don't think he'll be in much of a hurry to find us again. He'll already be back with his own family by now, telling them all about his adventures and convincing his sisters they made him captain before he left.'

Marcos smiled at me as if he thought he'd reassured me. 'I should lie down, Isabela, and try to sleep again. God knows, there nothing else to do here.'

So saying, he wandered back to his sleeping place and

377

curled up again on the ground, obviously intending to take his own advice.

I turned back, praying I would see nothing except the wall of the cave, but Hinrik was still there, the noose hanging from him. I ached to tear it away, to free him from it, but I knew I couldn't. No one could take it from him now.

I sensed a movement on the other side of the cave. Eydis was awake, and her veiled head was turned as if she was gazing straight at the spot where Hinrik stood. I was certain she could see him too. She held her hand towards him, palm up, as if she was welcoming a guest. In a way that gave me courage. At least I knew I wasn't melting into madness. Hinrik turned towards her and it almost appeared as if they were speaking to each other, whispering, yet I couldn't hear their voices. It was like when I had heard the gyrfalcons calling, hearing them, yet knowing that there was no cry to hear.

Hinrik's bloodied face turned back to me and his dark, hollow eyes met mine. I was so afraid, yet how could I be scared of someone I felt so much pity for?

'Why . . . why have you come?' I whispered.

'You call the dead.'

I stared at him, unable to believe what I heard, but before I could even try to make sense of the words I was thrown off my feet, and fell sprawling on to the rocks. The floor of the cave was trembling violently. Lilja and Margrét were shrieking in fear. It was as if some beast was roaring deep beneath us in the earth. The shaking only lasted moments, but stones and rocks continued to crash down in the passage even after it had stopped. We all fled towards the pool in terror that we were going to be crushed, but at that moment there was a great hiss and a jet of stinking gas erupted from the centre of the pool. Unnur dragged her daughters into the furthest corner of the cave away from the bubbling water. Only the unconscious man remained unmoved. Not even the shaking of the rocks had been able to rouse him. The rest of us gazed fearfully at the ledge on which Marcos and Vítor had stood, just two days before. Now it was invisible behind a dense cloud of hot white steam.

When finally there was silence, Vítor and Ari ran to the passage. We all gazed about us. A deep crack had appeared, running across part of the wall of the cave, which I was sure had not been there before. Small fragments of rock still trembled on the floor where they had fallen from the roof. It was a miracle none of us had been hit. We were all holding our breath, terrified of what Vítor and Ari might discover in the passage. But they returned a few minutes later, breathing hard but looking immensely relieved.

'Some rocks have been dislodged,' Vítor said, 'but the entrance is still open and we can still climb up to it, though it will be more difficult now.'

Eydis pulled her twin upright, gripping her around her bare shoulders as she moved towards the pool. She held her hand over it for a moment as if she was commanding the waters. Then she backed away. She murmured something to Fannar and his family, pointing to the steam over the pool. Fannar looked troubled and his wife clutched her two children to her as if she was trying to defend them from Eydis's words.

Fannar marched over and seized the chains that tethered Eydis and her sister to the wall of the cave. He tugged on the ring embedded in the wall, as if he was trying to prise it loose. But Eydis stepped swiftly towards him and pushed him away from the ring. It sounded as if they were arguing, and Valdis had joined in too, her head swivelling round as Eydis supported the weight of her body in the crook of her arm.

Eventually Fannar gave up and, with a shake of his head, he stomped away, still muttering angrily. Pausing only to growl at Ari, gesturing back at the sisters and then at us, he marched into the passage and minutes later we heard him scrambling up the rocks towards the entrance. Unnur bit her lip, staring anxiously in the direction of the sound. She looked despairingly at Ari, then, much like my mother, like all mothers probably, when there's nothing else they can do, she sighed and started to rummage among the stores looking for food to prepare.

'Help me,' a voice said at my side. 'You must help us.'

I felt a sudden chill beside my arm. I did not turn to look. I knew Hinrik was standing behind me.

'I can't help you . . .' I whispered. 'I can't undo what's been done to you. Please . . . leave me alone.'

Ricardo

Crab – *a fight between hawks. If a falcon is irritable or*
trying to attack another falcon it is said to be crabby.

I was sodden with sweat in the steamy heat and I was sure I
looked as flushed as if I'd swallowed half a bottle of brandy,
though I hadn't, more's the pity, but Vítor's face thrust arro-
gantly into mine was paler than ever. He'd finally managed to
trap me in a corner. I'd been trying to avoid the little turd
ever since we arrived, and believe me, that takes some ingenuity when you're trapped in a cave, but this insufferable heat
was making me careless. I'd dropped my guard and he'd
blocked my way so that I'd no choice but to listen to him. I
knew what was coming. He'd been watching Isabela like a . . .
no, *not* like a cat watches a mouse, because at least a cat does
its own killing, if there's murder to be done. Vítor put me in
mind of a loathsome vulture hovering over the condemned
until some other predator does what it doesn't have the guts
to do.

'You do realize that we must leave this place soon,' Vítor
whispered. 'The cave will grow too hot to remain in much
longer.'

I didn't need a Jesuit to tell me that. We were all dripping
with sweat. I thought nothing could be hotter than Belém in
midsummer, but it was the steam that got to me here. My
clothes, everything, were wringing wet, and it made you so
exhausted, you didn't want to move, just lie there gasping like
a stranded fish. And as if that wasn't bad enough, the foul
vapours stank of rotten eggs.

'This is your chance,' Vítor continued. 'Ensure that Isabela remains in the cave after we leave and the steam will do the rest.'

'Leave her to be scalded alive, you mean. That's one way to ensure a bloodless death. You'll be able to swear before your confessor that your hands are as white as the snow on the mountains, not dripping with her gore. I suppose Jesuits do make confessions, or are they so pure and holy they don't need to?'

Vítor looked at me as if I was an insolent schoolboy he was itching to birch. 'I simply cannot understand why you thought nothing of strangling your lover with your bare hands and dumping her body, like a drowned puppy, for the crabs to pick at, yet now you throw up your hands like some delicate noblewoman and declare you couldn't possibly kill vermin. But if you have suddenly discovered a conscience, then surely you must recognize that I am offering you a way out? You don't need to kill the girl yourself. With everyone scrabbling to leave, you can easily ensure that you and she are the last two in the cave. Rocks have fallen before. They can easily be dislodged again to ensure that she cannot climb out.'

'You want me to leave her to die in agony, slowly broiling to death?'

Vítor gripped my arm so hard I thought he was going to break it, but he knew I could do nothing to stop him without drawing attention.

'If you had left her to be swallowed up in the bog instead of dashing to her rescue, it would all be over by now. It is entirely your fault it has come to this. But if you really are so squeamish about her dying in pain, then hit her over the head, knock her out so that she will know nothing about it. I don't know why you have to make difficulties, Cruz. It is really all quite simple.'

For a moment I wondered if he intended to trap us both

in the cave and leave us to die. That too would be quite simple, except that even he might believe that was murder, and he didn't want the sin of one death, never mind two, on his soul.

'Look,' I said, trying to resist the overwhelming urge to knee him in the balls and doing my best to adopt a friendly, reasonable, we're-both-men-of-the-world tone. 'I quite understand that if we were back in Portugal, surrounded by the king's men, the members of the Inquisition and their *familiaries*, you and I would have to kill this girl. We'd have no choice. A hundred people would know at once if we hadn't. But who is there here to report us? She's never going to catch this white falcon. We haven't even seen so much as a feather of this wretched bird, much less captured it. I'm beginning to doubt they even exist here. And with half the Danes on the island out looking for us, how is she going to set traps or whatever it is they do? And if by some miracle she does get her hands on one, I can see to it that she loses any money she has to buy a passage on a ship. She'll never get off the island.'

I adopted an ingratiating smile, not easy when your face feels as if it's melting and dripping off your bones. 'Come on now, Vítor, we've enough problems of our own trying to get out of this mess alive to bother about this girl. Between this cave and the Danes we'll need all our wits to survive ourselves without worrying about her. Why don't we just let her go? You and I can return home and tell them she'll not be coming back to Portugal, which is the truth. Neither one of us will have her blood on our hands. Then both our consciences will be clear.'

Vítor lifted his chin and glared at me as though I had just suggested that he should bugger his bishop. 'Are you suggesting that I, a Jesuit, a consecrated priest, should deliberately lie to my superiors, to the Holy Catholic Church and to my king?' His tone was cold enough to freeze steam.

'It wouldn't be a lie to say –'

'Kill her, Cruz. Kill her or I promise you that you will be returning to Portugal in chains and I will see to it that before you die you personally enjoy every single exquisite torment the Inquisition has in its mercy ever devised. Every heretic that lives is another nail in the hands of Christ. For every heretic we fail to bring into repentance or send straight to eternal hell, we his servants will be severely punished. And I do not intend to fail my Lord or my Church, Cruz. I want her dead, do you understand me? Not escaped . . . not free to live out her foul life in another land . . . but dead!'

Eydis

Cope – to trim the beak and talons of a hawk.

We no longer have the time to wait. I have told Fannar he must take his family and the foreigners from the cave tonight. He has gone to try to find a safe place for them, and a safe route to take them there. He knows, as I do, that the shaking was only a warning. There will be others, and the next could cause the passage to collapse, trapping us all in here, sealing us in our tomb.

Isabela has called Hinrik to this cave, but it is not enough. He is only a boy, as timid in death as he was in life, and who can blame him? If he stands against the draugr and the draugr overcomes him, as he surely will, then he will have the power to torment the boy for all eternity. What can an old woman and a boy do against a draugr? Though they are dead, they will not pass judgment against him. He will frighten them into silence. I need the girl to call the others, but she will not listen. I cannot make her hear me. I need her to understand what she must do. She speaks to the dead boy, but she is afraid of him, afraid of the dead.

I must speak with her directly, make her trust me, make her strong. I have to find a place to talk to her where the spirit that infects my sister cannot hear us. He must not know what we are planning. But will Isabela go there? It is a place of terror to her. Does she have the courage to enter it of her own will?

The rocks tremble again, not as violently this time, but far below I hear a rumble like thunder, deep in the earth. I dare not wait. If I cannot speak with her now it will too late for all of us. Hinrik is afraid to do what I ask, but he will do it. He knows that if the draugr cannot be destroyed, neither the living nor the dead will be safe from his terror.

I cross to my stores and rummage among the jars until I find the draught I am searching for. I measure out the contents carefully – too little and it will not work as swiftly as I need it to do, too much and it will kill her.

'Hinrik, you must make her come to me. There is no other way left now, no time, no time.'

Isabela

Jouk – *when a hawk or falcon sleeps.*

The clinging cold on my arm was lifted, and for a moment I thought Hinrik was gone, but then I saw him, standing over the body of the injured man.

It was as if all the other people in the cave were there, still talking, still moving, but their voices were distant. Yet Hinrik's voice was loud in my ear as if he was talking inside my own head.

'You must send the spirit back into this corpse.'

This wasn't happening. It couldn't be. I was imagining it. Hinrik was not here. I was dreaming, still dreaming, and yet I couldn't wake myself. But I found myself speaking as you do speak in a dream both to the dead and the living who come to you in your sleep.

'He's not a corpse. The man is sick, but he lives. Look at him, he is breathing.'

'No.' The word fell like lead upon stone. 'He drowned many months ago. But there are some men who have the power to raise a corpse and make it walk again to destroy the living.'

It couldn't be true. That man wasn't dead. Anyone could see that. He looked even healthier than Valdis and I knew she lived. And Eydis was tending him as if he was a sick, old man. If he was a corpse raised to hurt people, why would she do that?

Unless . . . unless I had mistaken Eydis's nature and there was a very good reason people had chained her up in here.

Was she the sorceress who raised the corpse? Was that why she was trying to heal him?

As if I had spoken these words aloud, Hinrik answered, 'Eydis could not go to his grave and raise him. She cannot go to any grave. You must help her. You must help us all. You must meet her, so that she can tell you what to do.'

I turned to stare at Eydis. Her head was turned towards me beneath the veil, her body was tense.

'But I have met her,' I answered stupidly.

'You must meet in the place of your nightmares. Her spirit cannot leave the cave, but she can enter your dreams. She will not enter unless you invite her. But you must do it now.'

Eydis was holding a small wooden beaker out to me. Was she offering me something to make me sleep or worse, a sleep from which I'd never wake? I stared at the injured man lying in the corner. Had she poisoned him? Had she given him one of her potions?

'You must sleep. You must help us,' Hinrik repeated. 'Trust her.'

Trust a woman whom I knew nothing of, no, not one woman, but two women grotesquely bound in one body? A monster that her countrymen had been so terrified of they had chained up in a cave? For all I knew Eydis had killed a dozen men or worse.

'The white falcons. Eydis knows about the white falcons. She knows you need them. She knows where to find them. Help us and she will give them to you. But you must sleep or you will never find them.'

How could she know about the birds? Had Hinrik told her? Eydis was leaning forward, her face turned towards me. She touched her heart and bowed her head. I knew she was making me a promise. Did she really have the power and knowledge to help me catch the falcons? Time was running out. On my own I could search for days, weeks, months, and even then not catch one. But could I trust her? I had been so suspicious of Vítor, Marcos and Fausto, and they had only ever tried to help me. I had to begin trusting people again, and Eydis might be my only chance. All she wanted me to do was dream.

No, no, I couldn't. The thought of being sent into a sleep from which I couldn't rouse myself was terrifying. Suppose the ground started to shake again and I couldn't wake up. Suppose I became one of those people again . . . that child, that woman being buried alive. I wouldn't be able to wake and escape from it. I'd be trapped with them.

'I can't. I don't want to dream . . . I don't want to go back to that forest ever.'

'Help us,' Hinrik repeated. His voice was heavy with despair.

I glanced over at the others. They were all occupied. Vítor had finally cornered Marcos and they were engrossed in a whispered conversation which, judging by their grim faces, neither was enjoying. Ari was sharpening his knife against a stone, his head jerking up every now and then, listening out for anyone approaching the entrance to the cave.

Unnur and her daughters were preparing a dish of dark grey lichen. In the farm they had soaked it in milk, but they had no milk now, just water, and even they were wrinkling up their noses as they sampled it. I didn't know whether to laugh or cry. I was about to drink a potion to send me into a sleep from which I might never wake and they were simply cooking as if they were back at their own hearth.

'Help us,' Hinrik whispered.

Shakily I walked across to Eydis. It was only a few paces, yet somehow I couldn't think how to move. Sweat was running down my face and my back was soaked with it. I crumpled down on to the rock. Eydis placed the beaker between us. Through her thick veil I could see a glint of her eyes watching me, but I knew she would not force me to drink. She would wait for me to choose.

I was shaking so much I had to grasp the beaker in both hands. I was afraid I would spill it all. I sniffed at it and caught the tang of stale sweat – valerian! I almost smiled; that was the herb Marcos had picked when poor Fausto had accused him of trying to poison us. But there was something else in this dark liquid too, something I did not recognize.

Hinrik was standing behind Eydis. This time his whisper was so faint, I only saw his lips moving, but I knew what he was begging me to do. Eydis touched her hand again to her heart, swearing. The falcons. She would give me the falcons! I raised the beaker, and without giving myself time to think, I gulped the bitter liquid.

For a moment or two I had to fight to stop myself vomiting, but I managed to master it. The flames in Unnur's cooking fire were spinning around the dark walls, the floor of the cave tipped sideways, and for a moment I thought the cave must be shaking again, but no one else seemed to notice. I was so dizzy I had to lie down. My eyes closed.

I am standing in the forest. Not a single star pierces the thick blackness. It's as if all the light in the world and in the heavens above has been snuffed out. The branches of the trees creak in the wind. The dry leaves whirl around me, stinging my skin. But I am alone. No family hurries beside me. I cling to the rough trunk. My eyes ache as I strain into the darkness. My stomach clenches as I wait in terror for the men who will emerge from behind the rough trunks, but they don't come. I don't know what to do, where to go. I'm more afraid, now that I am alone, than I had been when I was running from the men. It's as if I have been severed from life.

'You have courage. I sensed that the moment I felt you step on to this land. You have courage, but you must find more.'

I spin round, but can see no one.

'Eydis?' I ask. 'Where are you?'

'Where you are. But you must listen – there is little time. We need to tell you what you must do.'

'But I can't do anything to help you. Hinrik is dead. I can't bring him back to life. I have to leave the cave and find the white falcons. Hinrik said you would give them to me. I need two white falcons to save my father's life and the lives of others too. Please, if you know where the falcons are, you have to tell me.'

I gaze around desperately trying to see her, but I can see nothing except the trees. Yet her strong voice weaves in and out through the moaning wind and the shivering branches.

'We know what you seek, but unless you help us, you will not live to help your father. Listen to us, Isabela. The spirit of the dead man who lies in the cave has entered the body of my sister, Valdis. As long as the iron circle remains unbroken around Valdis's body, the draugr's spirit cannot leave the cave. But if we are freed from the iron, then the draugr's spirit will be freed to leave the cave.

'The mountain of fire is stirring and the water in the pool is answering. You felt the cave shake. The water is heating fast, soon the cave will be filled with scalding steam and every living thing in it will perish. That is why Fannar wants to break the iron hoops, so that Valdis and I can escape before we die.

'But once outside the cave I will be unable to control the spirit in my sister. If we are released, then we will be dragged by him into malice and evil for generations to come. We will not be able to die. We will be forced to commit acts of terrible vengeance and destruction as he grows ever stronger. The draugr devours men. Birds that fly over him fall dead from the sky. Wherever he passes, humans and animals are driven mad, so that men attack their own wives, swearing they are hideous demons, and mothers drink the blood of their own babes. As the strength of the draugr grows, so he will have the power to turn summer into eternal winter, to turn day into night, a night of terror and destruction that will not end even for those he kills, for they in turn will rise again as draugr themselves. That is why Fannar and Ari must not release us.'

'But you will die, Eydis . . . scalded to death,' I tell her. 'You can't mean to do it . . . it is . . . a terrible death. And if you do die, what will happen to the spirit of the d . . . that thing then? What will happen to you?'

The branches of the trees in the dark forest bend lower. The wind rises higher, as if a great storm is running towards us.

'If we die still bound in iron, neither his spirit nor ours can ever leave the cave. We will be trapped with him for ever.' Her voice has a terrible icy resolve as if she is a judge pronouncing her own death sentence. 'He will tear us to pieces. He will devour us. He will pour all his vengeance into our destruction, and each time he does we will become whole again, so that he can torment us anew. But even that I will accept rather than become that monster of hell and hatred.'

My fists clench against the rough bark of the tree. My own terror is forgotten in the horror of what she faces.

'No, no! You can't. There must be some other way. There has to be.'

'You are the only way. You call the dead and you must summon a door-doom of the dead to the cave before it is too late. Only they have the power now to order him to return to his own flesh.'

Hinrik had said the same words. *You call the dead.*

'But I don't understand . . . I can't call up the dead. Do you mean Hinrik? Did I call Hinrik? But I didn't call him . . . I don't know how.'

'You brought Hinrik with the stone. But there are others, those you see here in this forest. They follow you. What do you use to call them?'

'I don't call them,' I protest. 'I just dream about them, but I don't know why. I don't even know who they are.'

'And you have nothing that belongs to them?' she presses

relentlessly, as if she knows she can force a truth out of me that I don't even know myself.

I desperately try to think. 'It was dark in the forest, but I saw something pale and glinting amongst the leaf mould on a grave. I picked it up only to see what it was. I didn't mean to take it but just as I touched it there was a shriek. It was terrifying. I thought there was some wild beast behind me, so I just ran, without thinking what I was doing. I fell into a gulley and it was only later that I realized I was still clutching it.'

'Tell me what you took from that grave.'

'It was a bone, a human finger bone with a ring still on it.'

I feel her sigh like a breath of wind on my cheek. 'That is the cord that binds them to you. And that is what you must use to summon them to the door-doom. If I can be released from the iron without the draugr knowing, then together you and I can use that bone to summon the dead. But it must be done only when the moment is right. Too late and the pool will erupt before we can be freed from the iron. But if we act too soon and send the spirit back into the corpse, then the draugr will rise up and all of you will be trapped in a cave with a man who possesses the strength of ten and a thirst for vengeance that can never be slaked. He will crush you all as easily as a child smashes an egg shell before you can escape the cave.'

'But how can we free you without –'

Something catches my eye in the darkness. I turn. A little way off among the trees a pale light is seeping up from the ground, like rising mist. But it isn't mist. It glows with a pearly light as bright and white as a full moon, though there is no moon to shine on it. It hangs quite still among the distant trees. The wind which is rattling the leaves and lashing the branches doesn't even stir it. But by its light, I suddenly see that the forest floor beneath it is rising in a great mound as if something is tunnelling up from below.

A huge horned head and neck burst from the ground with

a bellow of rage. The rest of the beast erupts and a massive bull stands in the clearing, pawing at the ground. Its hide has been flayed from its body and hangs in tatters from the raw, bleeding flesh. Its eyes are great black holes and its mouth drips with blood. Before I can move, it lowers its great black horns and charges straight towards me.

I am running as fast as I can through the trees, but I know I can't outrun it. The hooves thunder behind me, shaking the earth beneath me. Its roar explodes in my head. It's getting closer and closer. I trip and plunge headlong. The beast is so close now, I can feel its foul dank breath, but I can't move.

Krery-krery-krery!

Something white soars over the top of me. The bull bellows with rage. Sick with fear, I half-turn my head. A great white falcon is hovering above the bull. It flies at its eyes, its talons outstretched, striking with hooked beak, slashing with its claws. The bull is tossing its massive head, trying to impale the bird on its horns, but the falcon is too agile for it. It swoops on the bull again and again, driving it back. With a final bellow of fury, the bull sinks back into the earth that closes over it like a wave on the sea and it is gone. For a moment the falcon hovers above me in the darkness, its wings stretched out over my head. I reach out my hand, but the white falcon vanishes like smoke in the wind.

I woke, breathing hard and soaked with sweat. Eydis's face was sunk into her hands and her chest heaved as she struggled to regain her breath. Valdis's head was jerking as if she was in a state of great agitation. She was speaking, but I couldn't understand what she was saying. First her voice was wheedling, and then sing-song like a child teasing a playmate, then came a harsh, mocking tone. Unnur and her daughters were standing transfixed, staring at her in alarm. Little Lilja ran to her mother, burying her face in Unnur's skirts.

Valdis's head swivelled towards me. Through the veil I

could just make out two large eyes that seemed to be entirely black. They had no white part at all. It was like staring into a great bottomless pit. I had seen those eyes before as the creature charged towards me in the forest. It was staring out at me from behind her face. If it had the power to follow me into my dream, what was to stop it possessing me, as it had possessed Valdis?

Ricardo

'Just ensure that she does not leave this cave alive!' Vítor turned away without even bothering to wait for a response from me.

That odious piece of dung made my skin crawl. I know now why women want to scrub themselves clean after a man has forced himself on them. Why do priests think they only have to utter that word *heretic* for every man to go running for his pitchfork? I don't care what any man or maid believes, so long as they don't try to peddle me their cant. As a child I endured years of heaven and hell being rammed down my throat by my sainted mother and the priests, until I felt like a piglet being fattened for the butcher's knife. I tell you, if you feed a man too much of anything, thereafter the merest whiff of it makes him vomit.

I sank back against the wall of the cave. Isabela was lying on the ground near the twins; she seemed to be asleep, her face buried in her arm, her curly dark hair falling in damp tangles across her slender neck. She looked so young and vulnerable. She reminded me of my poor Silvia sprawled across my bed in the heat of a summer's afternoon sleeping like a child.

What on earth was I going to do? The only reason I was here was to kill the girl, and God knows I had good enough reasons. It was simple enough; dispatch her and return home to a civilized country where I could live in comfort in my own house, with the priest's gold jangling in my pockets, or *not* kill her and face permanent exile or even be tortured to death myself, if that little weasel Vítor had his way. It wasn't exactly a difficult choice to make now, was it, so why couldn't I do it? I only knew as I watched her lying there that for some incomprehensible reason I'd never be able to harm her – other women perhaps, but not Isabela.

But if I didn't, would Vítor kill her anyway? He'd talked about bringing down the rocks to trap her in here. Would Vítor's hatred of Marranos overcome his distaste of dirtying his own hands? I had to warn her, but the problem was how to tell her who Vítor was, without also revealing that he'd been sent here to watch me commit a murder, her murder. It's not the kind of thing you can casually walk up and whisper to a girl, is it?

I glanced up at the sound of raised voices. The twin sisters seemed to be having some kind of argument. Whatever it was about, Unnur and her daughters were looking thoroughly alarmed. It couldn't have been easy for the sisters. I mean, if you quarrelled you couldn't exactly storm off and leave the other.

I have to admit the twins were a bit of a shock at first. Two women on a single pair of legs, that's not a sight you see every day. I wondered if any man had ever made love to them, now that would be an interesting threesome. Not that I harboured any ambition in that direction, in case you were wondering. I grant you, one of the pair had a nice firm body, but the other was so withered she looked more like her great-grandmother than her sister. But it did occur to me that if only they could be persuaded to come back to Portugal with me, I could make a fortune exhibiting them. I'd see that they were well rewarded, and surely a few hours each day showing themselves off to the crowd had to be better than a lifetime chained up in a cave, didn't it? It was a wonder no one here had done it already, but then no man on this island would recognize a business opportunity, even if it was dangling from his own cock.

The twins crossed over to the man lying in the corner and one of them began rubbing more ointment on him. He looked as if someone had given him a thorough beating, but even in the time we'd been here the ointment seemed to be working miracles, and no wonder, given what Isabela had told me was in it. But the poor fellow still wasn't moving. It was going to be the Devil's own job getting an unconscious man out of the cave, especially if we had to do it in a hurry.

Isabela had woken and now she clambered unsteadily to her feet. She came towards me, stumbling like a sailor after a night in the tavern. I had to catch her in my arms to stop her tripping over. I lowered her to the floor against the wall of the cave, and crouched down beside her.

'Anyone'd think you'd been drinking some of the brew the farmer's wife served us that first night. You haven't, have you?' I said hopefully. 'I could do with a few swigs of it myself – that water doesn't just smell like bad eggs, it tastes of it too.'

She shook her head, then put her hand to it as if she wished she hadn't. She sat for a long time leaning against the wall, lost in thought. I half-thought she'd drifted back to sleep, but suddenly she seemed to make up her mind about something, and she gripped my arm.

'Marcos, would you do something for me?'

'Ask away,' I said. 'What is it? Do you want me to fetch you water?'

'I . . . would you try to cut through the iron hoops around the waists of the two sisters? That pool is heating up and we'll have to leave soon. We can't leave Eydis here chained up to die. But it's going to take some time to saw through that iron. I don't think the sisters have any tools we can use. You'll have to use something like this, it's all we have.' She picked a sharp piece of stone from dozens of fragments littering the floor of the cave. 'I saw Ari sharpen his knife on one of these earlier, so if you rasp at the metal, you should be able to break the bands in time.'

'With bits of stone?' I said. 'Look, Isabela, I'd be the first to admit I'm no expert at these things. The only sawing I'm in the habit of doing is with my knife on the old horse flesh at my local inn, which the villain of an innkeeper swears is tender veal. But even I can see it's going to take a lifetime to hack through those iron bands. Much easier to chip away at the rock where the iron ring is embedded. A bit of wriggling and I could probably work it loose and free both of them at once. I'll make a start now.'

'No, no, you mustn't, please don't do that . . . promise you won't do that.'

I was taken aback by the panic in her tone and the look, bordering on fear, that passed across her face. Anyone would think I'd suggested chopping the twins in half to get them out.

'Look,' I said, 'I know it's going to be awkward for the sisters clambering about with those chains still attached, but don't worry, we can help carry them. The main thing is to get them out. Then we can find a proper file or cutters and have them free quicker than a thief can cut a purse.'

Isabela gripped my sleeve again. 'Please, you mustn't, Eydis doesn't want you to. She knows the clanging of the chains would carry for miles in these mountains, and the Danes are still searching for us. No, we have to get the hoops off. They must have rusted a little in the damp of the cave over the years, so I'm sure you can do it. Ari is already trying to free Eydis; please could you work on Valdis?'

I looked over. Ari had taken up his position behind Eydis and, judging by the way he was frowning, was already hard at work. I shrugged and lumbered towards the sisters, but Isabela seized the hem of my shirt.

'One thing more . . . this is hard to explain . . . Don't cut all the way through Valdis's hoop, nearly through, so it can be broken quickly, but don't break it, not yet. It's important . . . really important.'

'I thought getting the hoops off them was the whole idea,' I said irritably.

'Valdis doesn't want the hoop removed until the very last minute, because . . . because . . . it's the custom,' Isabela said. 'Swear you won't until I tell you to?'

'How do you know what Valdis wants?'

'I told you, I can't explain . . . but I know. Please trust me, Marcos.'

If I live as long as old Methuselah himself, I will never understand women. They are all as crazy as Icelandic horses. I resolved there and then that if I did ever manage to escape this country of lunatics with their slimy food and rabbit-burrow houses, boiling rivers and icy sun, I would never in my life again set foot in any foreign land.

I gathered up a few of the sharpest stones I could find and took up my position next to Ari, behind the two women. Eydis pulled her sister upright, clasping her tightly so that I could tackle the band around her waist. Have you ever tried to grate away at an iron hoop with a bit of stone, especially when someone is wearing it? I tried to do it without touching Valdis's skin. I told myself it was out of respect for a woman, but the truth was, her skin looked so wrinkled and brown that I couldn't bring myself to touch it. But the stone slipped off Valdis's iron band and grazed her sister's arm, a few drops of blood ran down the stone and on to my fingers, but she barely flinched.

Isabela had followed me over and now was sitting close by, watching me intently.

'Don't be afraid to touch Valdis. You'll have to grasp the hoop firmly, like Ari's doing.'

Though I was, of course, flattered that she wanted to

watch me work, I was somewhat affronted by the suggestion that Ari was more competent than I was.

'Ari has probably been sawing through iron hoops all his life,' I said. 'I imagine it's all they can think of to amuse themselves on a winter evening round here. They find themselves a nice stout hoop and saw through it. They probably even lay wagers on it. My hands were never created for manual work.'

'I know . . . but please try your best,' Isabela said.

Gritting my teeth, I grasped the hoop and started pulling it away from her loose skin. Despite the heat of the cave I was shocked to find her body was as cold as the grave. I shuddered and pulled the band as far away from her back as I could. I knew I must be making it cut into her belly, but didn't want to feel that flesh against my hand. The sooner I got this band off her the better. I sawed vigorously at the rim of it with the sharp edge of the stone.

Beneath her band I could see a thickened strip of skin, hard and rough as the sole of my foot. How long had she worn this thing? I knew only too intimately how iron bruises the flesh, how it cuts in deeper and deeper with each little movement. I remembered the raw burning of sores around my own wrists and ankles from those few weeks in the tower of Belém. The long sleeves on my doublet had hidden the scars on the ship until they healed, but they were still there.

I rasped more furiously, swearing, but not stopping, even when the stone slipped from the iron and skinned the knuckles of my other hand. The stone was still stained with Eydis's blood and now it was supping mine too.

Without warning, Silvia's face floated into my head, and my hands were not grasping stone and metal, but something soft and warm. Silva was laughing at me, taunting me, daring me. Then the laughter changed to another sound, one I'd never heard her make before, not even when she was shrieking in passion. Her eyes were wide open, but they were not mocking me any more. For a moment, only a moment, I saw something that might have been shock in those liquid dark eyes, shock and then nothing. There was nothing at all in those eyes, not even life.

'Why have you stopped?' Isabela asked anxiously. 'What's wrong? You look frightened.'

I shook my head and, breathing hard, picked up the stone which had slipped out of my wet fingers and attacked the iron again. I don't know how long we were working. Fannar returned to eat, then went out again. Several times Ari and I were forced to rest. The sweat was pouring down our bodies. There was no relief to be had even in drinking, for though water was drawn from the pool and put aside to cool, it barely seemed to get any colder and the taste was worse than the smell.

I glanced over to see how Ari was doing, just in time to see the last little fragment break on Eydis's hoop. It sprang open by no more than a baby's-finger breadth. Eydis must have felt it give, but if she did, she gave not the smallest sign of it. It would take a couple of us, one pulling on either side, to bend it wide enough for her to slip out, but that could be done quickly now that the hoop was broken. Ari went to fetch himself some more water and wipe the sweat from his streaming face. Only a few more moments and I would be joining him. Valdis's hoop was almost at the point where a few more rasps would break through it, but before I could finish, Isabela frantically beckoned me away and led me over to the far side of the cave on the pretext of finding me a cloth to wipe the stinging sweat from my eyes.

'You've almost cut through the band, Marcos. You must leave it now.'

'It won't take much more,' I said, massaging my bruised and cut hands. 'The iron has rusted on the edges. Just as well, or I think I'd never have made a dent in it. Ari has broken through Eydis's band. I'll do the same for Valdis, then it will just be a matter of pulling the hoops wide enough apart for them to slip out.'

'No, no, you must leave Valdis now, please. We can easily break the band when the time comes, but not yet. Promise you'll leave it.'

Valdis's head swivelled in my direction. She was calling out, and it didn't sound to me as if she was thanking me. In fact, she sounded more than a little angry.

'Are you sure that's what she wants? She doesn't sound too happy.'

Isabela bit her lip. 'Eydis wants it this way. She knows what she's doing. You have to trust her . . . you should rest now. You must be exhausted.'

These Icelanders were crazier than a rabid dog at the full moon, but I wasn't going to argue. My fingers were swelling up like sausages and, to be honest, I wasn't at all sure I could have managed to saw any more, even if she'd begged me to. Stretching my back, I made my way across the steamy cave towards the pail of hot water.

I staggered backwards as a sudden rumbling filled the cave and jets of stinking steam burst out of the pool, filling the cave with a dense white fog. Someone was screaming, but I couldn't see whom. The dripping cave walls seemed to cool the steam a little as it rolled towards me, but it was almost impossible to breathe in it. Ari was shouting. I could scarcely see anything in the hot steam, except the smudged shapes of people moving as they loomed in and out of the fog.

'Marcos, help me get the hoops off them!' Isabela yelled.

I stumbled blindly across the cave, slipping on the wet stones, but I couldn't see where Isabela was, never mind the sisters. Everyone was shouting. Shapes were forming and disappearing again in the steam.

I was terrified I was blundering in the wrong direction and might end up falling into the boiling pool. All I actually wanted to do was to get the hell out of that inferno as quickly as I could. If it had just been a matter of saving those two mad sisters, frankly I would have made straight for the passage and the way out, but Vítor was somewhere in this maelstrom, and I was damned if I was going to leave Isabela to his tender mercies.

I dropped to my knees, crawling over the rock. I discovered it was just a fraction easier to breathe closer to the ground. Then I saw them. Ari was crouching behind Valdis who was writhing and twisting. Isabela was frantically trying to pull open the iron hoop about Eydis's waist.

'Help me, Marcos!' Isabela looked terrified, as well she might.

'Can't you get the sisters to sit still?' I yelled in exasperation as the iron band slipped for the third time out of my sweating hands. 'We'll never get anywhere if they keep wriggling about. What the hell is Eydis trying to do, anyway?'

I was suffocating in the steam. My fingers were so wet I couldn't grip the metal. Isabela crawled away, and for a moment I thought she had given up, then she returned with a blanket pulled from the sisters' sleeping pallet.

'Use this to hold it,' she said, pushing the sodden cloth into my hands.

I wrapped my fingers in the edge of the blanket and seized the hoop in both hands, and as I pulled I felt the iron band begin to bend.

'Here,' I said to Isabela, 'take the other side, now brace your feet against my legs and pull backwards.'

We strained against each other as the hoop slowly widened, and then it shattered. The force of its breaking was so unexpected we tumbled over. There was a bellow of rage which cut over all the other screams and shouts in the cave. Beside me, Isabela had struggled to her feet, and she was staring out into the cave, her eyes wide and frozen with terror.

Eydis

*Ramage or **rammish** – a hawk or falcon which is wild and hard to catch, or an escaped bird that has fully returned to the wild and is extremely difficult to reclaim.*

The draugr is fighting to break the iron band around Valdis's waist. But he only has her hands to use. Bound by the iron, his strength is only her strength and her hands are weak, atrophied. But if Ari or the foreigner helps to break that iron before I can drive him out of Valdis, his strength will surge and I will not be able to prevent it. I must pull Isabela out of this time and take her to the place of the dead, before her iron circle is broken.

I catch Isabela's arm. 'Isabela, listen to me now as you listened in the forest.'

But I can see from her eyes she is too afraid to let me in. I will have to do this without her consent, and hope that she will understand and not fight me. I drag my lucet upwards and the long cord follows. Swiftly, before Isabela can move away, I wrap the cord around the three of us – Valdis, Isabela and me.

The black thread of death to call the spirits from their graves. The green thread of spring to give them hope. The red thread of blood to lend them our strength.

Instantly the white mist hangs still and cool. The shouts and screams are severed and there is silence. The three of us are alone. Isabela's eyes are wide with alarm. She turns her head, trying to see something beyond the white curtain of mist, but there is nothing to see.

'Where are we? Are we still in the cave? Am I dreaming again?'

I cannot afford to explain. We must act quickly.

'Isabela, the bone you took from the grave, hold it and use it to summon the door-doom.'

'I don't know how . . . what to do. I can't.'

I try to calm her. 'You can. They are all bound to you now. Hinrik through the stone he gave you, the old woman whose mummy heals your burn, those shadows who followed you from the forest. I called you to me, and now you must bring them to us. It is time.'

'You don't have the power to call up the dead, little Isabela, Isabela,' the dark voice snarls from my sister's lips. 'You know you don't. You don't even know how to begin.'

I try to make Isabela listen to me. I can see she is terrified of the creature which speaks through my sister, and fear makes us listen to fear.

'You called Hinrik to you,' I tell her gently. 'He told you that you had called him. Take out the bone, then turn and look at them. They are already here. They are the shadows you are afraid to face. Face them now and let them come to you.'

'This is just a trick to keep you here,' the dark voice snaps. 'She wants you to die in the cave with her, so that she'll always have you with her. She is dangerous. She is wicked. Why do you think they chained her up in a cave? They don't chain up good people, only evil ones. Only the wicked are punished. Only the mad are chained up. You know that, don't you, little Isabela, Isabela?'

Isabela stiffens, her expression hardens. She rubs her wrist as if remembering something she has felt. He has made a mistake, something he has said to her has made her angry, and anger drives out fear. Her fingers move towards the leather pouch about her neck, and she pulls out a small yellowing bone, encircled by an iron ring.

'Don't do it, Isabela, Isabela,' the draugr shrieks. 'Don't bring the dead here. They followed you because they are angry. You stole from them. You robbed their graves and disturbed their rest. Now they want to punish you for what you did. If you bring the dead here, they will drag you back into the grave with them. You will be buried alive. They will never let you escape.'

'Silence!' I command. 'Turn, Isabela, turn and look at them. The dead are nothing to fear. You know them, you know what they have suffered. Welcome them and let them speak.'

She is trembling. Her eyes are closed. I know she is terrified, but I know too that she is willing herself to turn.

All around us the white mist hangs in the air, still and soft as if we were encased in snow. I cannot see them, but I sense they are there in the mist, waiting, just waiting for her to call them forth. Slowly she turns and lifts her head. She holds out the bone, gripping it so hard in her fingers that the knuckles blanch to the colour of the bone she holds.

'Come,' she whispers, her voice shaking.

'Do not turn away,' I tell her. 'See them, know them.'

The mist stirs and Hinrik steps through it. His face is bloody and the noose hangs heavy from his neck. He stands, his hollow eyes fixed on her face. Isabela gives the smallest nod of greeting to him

The old woman, her cheeks hollow with hunger, shuffles out of the mist.

Valdis's lips part beneath her veil. 'Go back, Mother, Mother. I told you. I warned you. I will take you down into the grave with me. I will make you suffer without end. You too, boy, go back while you can or I promise you will die a thousand deaths and still live to die again.'

Both Hinrik and the old woman shrink back in dread. They will not stand against him, but just as I fear they are slipping back into the mist, another figure emerges from the mist. She too is old. Her head streams with blood, but she raises her chin defiantly.

'I stood against men of evil while I lived, I will stand against them in death.'

Hinrik and the old woman edge back out from the mist. I know now that they will stay.

Others are stepping into the space. A man carrying a little boy, both covered with savage slashes. A little girl follows, with blue-black marks about her neck, then a woman holding a baby that has been almost hacked in two. The woman's mouth is gaping, stuffed with earth, as are her eyes. She has been rendered blind and dumb. Two more men and a woman join them. They too are slashed and mutilated. Their clothes are faded and ragged, smeared with soil. Their eyes are dark, hollow pits. They say nothing, but silently join the circle of the dead around us.

Then, when I think there are no more to come, one last figure emerges from the mist. He is an old man. His clothes are burned almost away. His face and limbs are charred and blistered, the blackened skin cracked, the flesh gaping red-raw to the white bone beneath. His mouth is sealed with a leather gag. Isabela gasps in horror. Throwing her arms up as a shield, she backs away from the ghastly phantasm that is hobbling towards her. But he holds out his hand, palm upwards. And there are hundreds of words written upon it, in blue and scarlet, green and gold. Words that scurry across his hand and tumble from the tips of his burnt fingers to lie in heaps around his blistered feet.

'Jorge!' Isabela breathes.

He nods solemnly and takes his place in the circle.

Valdis's head swivels round to look at each of the dead in turn. I feel the draugr's agitation, but I feel something else too. Someone is trying to cut through Valdis's band. The draugr knows it. We must make haste.

'I bid you welcome,' I say. 'You have been summoned as the door-doom, the court which must pass judgment upon one of your own. Your word is law. Your decision is binding. This is the complaint I bring against him. That he has entered the body of my sister without her consent. I have healed his own corpse, but he refuses to leave and return to it. I ask the door-doom to order him to leave my sister's body and return to his own.'

The grandmother from the forest lifts her battered arm and points at Valdis.

'Speak, draugr, what have you to say in your defence?'

'Valdis is dead. She has no need of her corpse, but I have great need of it. I have every right to it, since I was called out of my grave by one who is living. If I return to my corpse, Eydis will destroy it. She will destroy me. She will send me back into the grave. You know how we suffer in the grave, our bodies rotting in the darkness, our loneliness, our despair. I was called out, and now I have tasted life again I will not return. You cannot order me to my own destruction. You are my brothers and sisters in death, you will not suffer the living to destroy us.'

The grandmother nods. 'We have listened to you. And you, Eydis, you who are of the living, what do you say?'

'If he remains in Valdis, he will make a draugr of us both, for if he is freed from the iron, he will gather such strength to him that I will not be able to fight against it. Valdis and I are joined, as we have been since we were in our mother's womb. What he does in her body, he does also in mine. He will rampage throughout the land, bringing terror and destruction, he will make draugar of those he kills and he will torment those already in their graves. All this he will do, in a body that he does not own.'

'Yes, yes,' the dark voice hisses. 'But you are the dead. You know the suffering that the living have inflicted on you. Look at your wounds, and the wounds of your children. Don't you want revenge for what they did to you? Come with me and you shall have it. You shall make them plead for mercy and you will give them none as they gave none to you. You will tear their children apart before their eyes and tear out their wives' hearts while they still beat. Jorge, Jorge, you will hear their screams like the sweetest music in your ears and drink their blood like the strongest wine to fire your belly. Hinrik, my poor Hinrik, wouldn't you like to see the Danes running in terror from you? Make them know how fear tastes?'

'Enough!' the grandmother says. 'We have listened and we have heard. Now each must judge for themselves.

'You.' She points to the old woman. 'Your mummy has healed his corpse, what do you say?'

The old woman lifts a quavering hand, glancing fearfully at Valdis, whose head turns towards her.

'Speak,' the grandmother urges. 'We all stand with you. Say only what you think to be right.'

'He must return to his own corpse,' the old woman whispers.

A howl of fury bursts from Valdis's lips.

But the grandmother ignores him, relentlessly pointing to each of the dead in turn, adults and children alike. 'My son, speak. Must he return to his own corpse?'

Their hollow eyes all stare at Valdis, as each of them pronounces their verdict.

'He must return.'

'He must return.'

The woman whose mouth is stuffed with earth can only nod, but her gesture is emphatic.

Finally, only Jorge is left to speak, but the grandmother points instead to Isabela.

'He cannot speak. You must deliver the verdict for him. You must utter what is in his heart, not yours.'

Valdis rolls her head. The words that emerge from her lips are soft, coaxing. 'He wants revenge, little Isabela, Isabela. You know he does. Jorge suffered the cruellest death of all of us. He was innocent. He has a right to justice. You can give him justice. You know what is in his heart. You know he does not want me to be destroyed. You know what he wants you to say for him. Just say it and that gag that chokes him will vanish. Say it and his wounds will be healed. Your own mother betrayed him, but you can help him, Isabela, Isabela. You can put right the wrong that was done to him. You can free him for all eternity.'

Jorge gives no sign. He stands, gazing at Isabela from out of his charred, blistered face, but nothing betrays his thoughts.

Isabela turns to me, anguish on her face. 'Is it true, can I help him? Can I release him from that?'

The grandmother speaks again, 'Say what is truly in his heart. Speak the truth, only the truth.'

'But I don't know what he is thinking, I don't.'

'What binds him to you, Isabela?' I ask her. 'How did you call him?'

'I don't know. I keep telling you, I don't know. He didn't give me a stone. I didn't take a bone.'

Jorge raises his hand and the green and scarlet words slide from his fingers, drifting to the ground like falling leaves.

For a long moment, Isabela simply stares at the words lying at his feet.

'Stories . . .' she murmurs wonderingly. 'He gave me stories that I still remember. That's how I called him.'

She lifts her head and turns to look at Valdis as the others have done.

'Jorge does not want revenge. He wants you to return.'

There is a shriek of fury. Valdis's body is lashing backwards and forward, her blackened nails are clawing at my face. It takes all my strength to hold us both upright.

The grandmother lifts her voice over the draugr's cries. 'You have entered a body that is not yours to inhabit. You have stolen a life that is not yours to live. It is the verdict of the door-doom that you leave the body of Valdis now.'

There is a great howl that tears through our bodies as if Valdis is being ripped from my side. A black stream oozes from between her lips and passes through her veil, forming itself into a great black shadow. The shadow grows and spreads as if the white mist itself is staining black. It is denser and darker than any smoke. It pours from Valdis's mouth like black blood gushing from a wound. It rises higher and higher until it towers over us, swelling up like a great black leech, breaking open the circle of the dead.

'I will not obey the door-doom,' the dark voice thunders.

'You have no right to sit in judgment over me. I am living. I am the life that will destroy the living and the dead. I will not be destroyed.'

Isabela is cowering terrified on the floor beside me, the bone still gripped in her hands. I reach down and tear it from her fingers. I raise my arms and feel the power of a falcon's wings. I know the courage of it in my heart as it plunges down in a stoop. I feel the grip of its talons in my soul, a grip that will not relinquish its hold even after death.

I lift my head and stare into the blackness writhing before me. 'The door-doom of the dead has spoken. You are of the dead. You will obey. You will return to the body you owned in life. By the power of the white falcons who were our birth and shall be our death, I command you to return.'

I thrust the bone with its iron band straight into the centre of the black shadow. A bitter cold, such as I have never known, envelops my hand. My skin is withering in it. My bone is being eaten away, but still I push against the shadow.

'No! No!' he roars.

The cold is so intense that I cannot bear the pain of it. I cannot hold the bone in it any longer. I must let go. But if I do, he will win. He will never go and I will not be able to prevent him entering us again. I will become the darkness.

Just as I think I can bear no more, just as my hand is sliding out of the icy shadow, I feel the bone growing warm in my grasp. They are with me. The dead are still with me. We will defeat him. I throw back my head and a scream erupts from my throat.

'*Krery-krery-krery!*'

The darkness shatters into a thousand tiny pieces. A great wind roars through the cave. The black shadow is caught up in it. For a moment or two the fragments are tossed helplessly in the maelstrom and then it is gone, leaving only a whirlpool of white steam swirling around us.

Ricardo

Check – when a falcon leaves the quarry it is supposed to be hunting to pursue some other prey.

A great roar filled the cave and then a high-pitched screech that was so painful it was like a dagger being thrust in each ear. It sounded as if two great beasts were hurling themselves at each other. Terrified, I looked up, and for a moment I thought I saw a crowd of people huddled together in the steam. Men and women I didn't recognize, children too, all staring down at the sisters, and looking pretty much the worse for wear, I can tell you. Where on earth had they come from? But before I could do anything, the roaring and the screeching stopped abruptly and the people just sort of dissolved. Not that they were ever really there, of course, but it just shows how that damn heat was affecting us.

I suddenly realized I'd lost sight of Isabela and stared around frantically. Finally, I saw her lying behind Eydis. Her eyes were closed, and she was not moving. God in heaven, had Vítor carried out his threat and hit her over the head to knock her out? I crawled across to her and touched her gently on the arm. She sat bolt upright, an expression of alarm and bewilderment on her face, like someone who's been woken suddenly from a sleep and can't remember where they are. I knew that feeling only too well, especially on the morning after a good night in the tavern, but if ever there was a time for taking a little nap, this was most definitely not it.

I was so distracted by Isabela that it took me several moments to realize that Ari was shouting at me, gesturing to

Valdis. I struggled over and knelt beside him. He had broken through the iron hoop, but his hands were shaking with exhaustion. The heat and moisture were making us as weak as newly hatched nestlings.

Valdis was perfectly still now, lolling away from her sister who was struggling to pull her upright so that Ari could wrench the band off. My fingers pressed against her skin as I tried to grasp the hoop and I felt again the dreadful coldness of her flesh. I snatched back my hand and found to my horror I'd ripped off a long strip of her yellow skin which was now stuck to my nails. But worse still, I realized the wound wasn't bleeding.

'She's dead, Isabela. Sweet Jesu, she's dead!'

'I know,' Isabela said faintly, 'but . . . we have to free her . . . Eydis will be trapped in here with her. Try!'

I gritted my teeth, wrapped the blanket around my fingers and seized one side of the broken hoop. How could she be dead? It wasn't possible. Just minutes before, I'd seen her thrashing around and heard her shouting. I could perfectly understand that her heart might have suddenly given out in the heat, mine was racing so hard, I was sure it too was about to collapse. But Valdis's body wasn't just dead, it was decaying.

'I've already taken Fannar's wife and daughters safely to the entrance of the cave,' a voice said.

I glanced up to see Vítor standing over us.

'Now it's your turn, Isabela,' Vítor said. 'Come and I'll guide you out and help you to climb the rocks.'

'Can't leave yet,' Isabela said. 'Have to help Eydis . . . We have to free them . . . we can't leave them here.'

'Ari and Marcos will bring the women as soon as they have released them. There's nothing more you can do. We can only climb out one at a time. We must get out now in order to leave the gap clear for them. If you stay you will only hinder them getting to safety. Hurry, the steam is building, we haven't got much time.'

He seized her arm and she turned towards him as if she had every intention of going with him.

'No, don't. We must all stay together,' I protested. I scrambled to my feet and tried to make a grab for Isabela.

'You may need help . . .' Isabela was gasping in the suffocating steam, 'getting the sisters out of the cave. If we're on the outside . . . we can help pull her through the gap.'

'Besides,' Vítor said, 'Fannar's wife and daughters are out there unprotected . . . some of us should join them.' He bent over coughing violently, struggling to regain his breath.

'Then I'll take Isabela out,' I said, but Ari tugged weakly on my breeches. I glanced down at him.

He gestured urgently at the hoop. I could hear the water in the pool bubbling like a witch's cauldron. Jets of boiling water were shooting up to the cave roof and crashing back down into the water with the roar of a deadly waterfall. I looked up and reached out to grab Isabela, but where she and Vítor had stood just a moment ago was nothing but swirling white steam.

'Hjálpa! Hjálpa!' Ari yelled at me, frantically clutching at my leg.

I crouched again and grabbed the iron ready for one last pull. Then, with a howl of fury, someone lunged towards us out of the steam. I just had time to glimpse the face of the man who minutes before had been lying unconscious in the corner. Ari sprang up and pushed himself between Eydis and the man, trying to fend him off.

'Hjálpa Valdis!' he yelled.

I grasped both ends of the iron hoop, trying to pull them apart, but my muscles had turned to water in the heat. The man slammed his arm across Ari's chest with such a powerful blow that the boy was lifted clean off his feet and tossed backwards. I heard the sickening crump as his body hit the cave wall.

I felt the squeeze of Eydis's hand on my leg and knew she was begging me to hurry, but before I could do anything the man had launched himself towards her. He threw his whole weight forward as he tried to seize Eydis. As his fingers reached for her throat, she jerked backwards, his hands missed her, his feet slipped on the wet rocks and he crashed face down to the cave floor and lay still.

Eydis fought to pull her sister's body up, so that I could once more grab the iron band encircling Valdis's waist. I seized it on either side of the break and pulled with a strength that could only have come from blind fear, and the iron band shattered.

'Ari, where are you?' I yelled into the swirling steam.

But I had the gut-wrenching feeling he couldn't answer.

'Isabela, are you there?' I could see no one and nothing except for Eydis standing beside me clasping the body of her dead sister in her arms.

'We're here, Marcos,' Isabela called from the other side of the cave. 'No, no, Vítor. I don't think that's the right way.'

'Let go of her, you bastard!' I screamed. 'Isabela, don't trust him. He means to kill you. Get away from him, get away.'

I blundered over in the direction from which I'd heard Isabela's voice, all thoughts of Ari forgotten. I had to get to her.

The steam cleared slightly just for a moment and I thought I could see two figures. But they were moving away from the passage towards the pool.

'Stop, Isabela, stand still,' I yelled. 'The water, he's taking you towards the water!'

She must have stopped then and tried to pull away from him, for I heard Vítor urging her to keep walking.

'I'm trying to get you out, Isabela. I helped you in the

forest, don't you remember? You trusted me then. Trust me now. I helped Fannar's wife out. I know the way. Come on now, take my hand. That's right. Only a few more steps and you'll be in the passage.'

I tried to run, but the ground was too slippery and I stumbled, falling down on my knees.

There was a roar behind me. The man who had attacked Ari came lumbering out of the steam to the side of me. Then he vanished again into the whiteness. Ahead of me I heard Vítor yell and Isabela scream.

I struggled to my feet, slipping and sliding until I finally managed to reach them. The man and Vítor were locked in a struggle. Vítor had drawn a knife, but the man had his arm pinned so that he couldn't use it. He was clearly far stronger, but he was having difficulty keeping a foothold on the wet rocky floor.

I grabbed Isabela. 'Come on, this way.'

'But we can't leave Vítor, and what about Ari and Eydis?' She turned back to peer hopelessly into the swirling clouds.

'I have them safe,' a calm voice said. A tall, stately woman stepped out of the mist behind me. She was carrying an unconscious Ari in her arms as easily as she might have carried a child. Eydis followed her. My brain was reeling so much in the heat, I wasn't sure if I'd imagined her, like the crowd of other people I thought I'd seen.

'Isabela, we must leave now,' I begged her.

'But Vítor . . . that man is killing him,' Isabela said desperately, half-choking in the steam, but still trying to move towards the place where we'd last seen them.

'No, Isabela. Leave them,' I pleaded. I tried to pull her but she resisted, pushing my slippery fingers easily from her arm.

The cave suddenly shook again

The tall woman turned. 'This way now before it is too late.'

We didn't stop to ask questions, even Isabela didn't protest.

How the woman could find her way so surely through the hot dense fog, I didn't know. But if she knew where the entrance was I certainly wasn't going to argue with her. I couldn't even tell which way we were facing any more.

I found the rocky outcrop that led to the passage by dint of colliding with it. Ignoring my bruises, I reached out blindly for Isabela. She grasped my hand and together we groped our way around the rock until we reached the passage. Steam filled the narrow tunnel but, protected by the outcrop of rock and with the entrance above to vent it, it was much less dense. More rocks had been dislodged in the last shaking, but there was still a way up. The tall woman went first. Ari slung over her shoulder, she climbed up as effortlessly as a man might climb his own staircase. She lifted Ari up as high as she could, then pushed him up through the slit at the top, before scrambling out after him.

I wanted to make Isabela climb out next, but she hung back.

'Let Eydis go first, we might have to help her.'

I hesitated, but Eydis had already started to climb, one arm around her dead sister's body, using the other arm to pull them both up over the rocks. At the final boulder she hesitated. The only way both sisters would fit through the hole together was if she clasped her sister's body to her own as tightly as she could, but Valdis's head was lolling backwards. Eydis had to use both hands, one to hold up the weight of the torso and flopping arms, the other to press her sister's dead head against her own neck. That meant she had no hands free to heave herself up over the edge.

I couldn't see how she'd manage to get out by herself. I would have to climb up and help her. The slit was so narrow, if she became stuck, we would all be trapped. I clambered up the rocks until I was just below Eydis. A pair of arms which I presumed belonged to the tall woman reached down through the gap to grasp Eydis under her armpits. I braced my back against the wall, trying not to think about the narrow ledge I was balancing on so precariously. I tried to work my shoulder under Eydis so that I could push her up. For the moment nothing happened. I squealed as I felt one of my feet sliding towards the edge of the ledge, and wildly flailed about, trying to grab hold of something. Then the weight lifted from my shoulder and I saw Eydis disappearing into the darkness above.

At once the woman's arm reached down again for me, and I grasped it thankfully. But as I stretched up with my other hand, the strap of my scrip around my waist snagged on the sharp rock. I felt the leather give way and the scrip containing all the money I possessed in the world tumbled into the billowing stream below. I could have howled, but there was nothing I could do to retrieve it. All that mattered now was getting out.

I looked down into the white mist. 'Come on, Isabela, climb up now and we'll pull you out.'

I heaved myself over the edge of the opening, gasping at the shock of the night air after the heat of the cave. I felt as if I'd been plunged into an icy river.

A distant cry rose up from the hole below. Shivering uncontrollably in the cold, I peered down into the pit. But all I could see was swirling white steam.

'Isabela, are you hurt? Have you fallen? Are you able to climb . . . ? Stay where you are, I'm coming back down for you.'

I was already scrambling back over the lip of the entrance again when I heard another anguished cry ring out from somewhere deep within the cave.

'Marcos!'

I leaned over, staring down the shaft into the steam-filled passageway far below me. For a few moments I could see nothing. Then I began to glimpse fragments of something dark moving through the white mist. Someone was heaving themselves up the ladder of rocks towards the opening.

'Isabela!' I called. 'Come on, you're nearly at the top. I can see you. Reach up to me. Take my hand and I'll pull you out!'

I stretched down through the slit as far as I could, trying to grasp her. Then I snatched my hand back as if it had been stung. For the face that was staring up at me from the dark pit was not Isabela's. It was Vítor's. He was clinging to a rocky ledge in the shaft, just an arm's length below me.

'Where's Isabela?' I yelled. 'What have you done with her?'

'Me?' Vítor was panting hard, gasping for breath. 'I've . . . done nothing. That man . . . has taken her down into the cave . . . nasty temper . . . she won't be troubling us agai . . .'

His voice broke off in a cry of fear as the ground began to shake violently. He flung his arm up in a desperate attempt to grab the rim of the slit and haul himself out, but he never got the chance. For just as he made to grasp it, his other hand slipped from the juddering rock, and with a scream, he fell backwards, crashing down into the passageway below.

I jerked my leg out from the hole just as a great billow of steam shot up from it, and I lost my balance and found myself rolling backwards down the steep hillside in a hail of small stones and dirt. I tried desperately to stop my fall, but only succeeded when my body crashed into a boulder. I lay there, winded, fighting to force the air back into my lungs. With a frantic effort, I finally managed to draw breath.

The ground had stopped shaking though stones were still trickling down. I heard my name being called over and over again, softly in the night sky. But I didn't answer. I didn't want to. It was over. Isabela was lying dead, buried some-where deep beneath me, and though I had never shed a single tear for Silvia, I suddenly found that I was crying, howling into the night, and I couldn't seem to stop.

Eydis

*At hack – when a falcon is left to fly free for a few weeks to
improve its condition, returning to the hack board twice a day
to be fed by the falconer.*

It has been so many years since I have breathed the cold
fresh air, or seen the purple clouds in the black sky, swollen
and silver-edged, where the moonlight touches them. Time
has flooded back into my life as swiftly as once it had drained
from it. Here was night and in time . . . in time there would
be dawn and day, sun and sunset, winter and spring. I stand
transfixed, gazing up into the vast arch of stars, and drinking
the sharp frosted air that tastes as if it is squeezed from the
sweetest berries.

A groan from Ari makes me glance down. He is struggling
to sit up, rubbing the lump on the back of his head.

'How did I get out here?'

I look round for Heidrun, but she has vanished. I smile to
myself. I knew she would not stay to be thanked.

'The nightstalker . . . did it get out?'

'No, thanks to the girl, he did not.'

'Isabela . . . where is she?' Ari tries to peer over my shoulder.

Unnur crouches down beside him, anxiously feeling his
limbs and head, as she would if one of her own children had
taken a tumble.

'I am afraid she is still down there, Ari,' she whispers.

Ari struggles up. 'I must go back, find her.'

Unnur tries to hold him down. 'No, Ari, you have a bad

bruise on your head, suppose you become dizzy again and fall.'

But he pushes aside her hands and clambers to his feet. Steam is no longer pouring from the entrance. The slit is dark and still. Ari leans over.

'Isabela! Isabela!'

We listen, but there is no answering cry beneath us. Ari slips one leg over the edge, feeling around with his foot for the outcrop of rock on which to stand.

This time it is me who holds him back. 'If the draugr is still alive down there . . .'

'Then I shall fight him. I will not leave her corpse down there for him to torment her spirit as he would have done yours. I have to bring her body out. That is the last thing I can do for her . . . But I can't feel the ledge. It's gone. It must have collapsed. What –'

I press my fingers to his mouth. 'Listen. I hear something.'

We all stand and hold our breath.

Ari shakes his head. 'It was just the wind blowing over the hole.'

The voice is faint, but this time we both hear it, a cry for help.

Ari hastily pulls his leg out and leans as far as he can into the crack.

'Isabela!'

Ari lifts his head from the hole. 'The rocks inside the tunnel fell and blocked off the cave. That must be why there's no more steam coming out, but some of the boulders have fallen from the entrance too. She can get up part of the way, but she can't reach the opening.'

'We'll have to find something to pull her out with,' Unnur says.

'I have something,' a deep voice says behind us. We turn to see Fannar clambering up the last few yards towards us. Unnur and his daughters race towards him and throw themselves into his arms. He hugs them fiercely, examining each face in turn, anxious to assure himself they are well.

'I saw the steam rising from the mountain, and felt the ground shake. I was so afraid . . .' His voice is gruff with tears, but he coughs, striking his chest vigorously as if it is just the cold night air that is catching at his throat.

'Did I hear you say the foreign girl is still down there?'

He shrugs a thick coil of rope off his shoulder and begins to fasten one end around his waist.

'I thought we might need help getting you out, Eydis, so I borrowed this from one of the farms. The owner doesn't know, but I will repay him the worth of it someday. Here!' He tosses the other end to Ari. 'Make a loop in it and drop it down to her. We need to make haste – if the earth shakes again, the whole passageway might collapse.'

They work as swiftly as they can, Ari and Fannar hauling together, but still it seems to be a lifetime before we glimpse the whiteness of a hand emerging from the hole. Unnur lies flat on her belly and grasps it. But just as Isabela's fingers close around Unnur's, there is another great shudder beneath our feet, a dreadful rumble of rocks crashing down below. Ari and Fannar both lose their balance and fall. The rope goes slack, but Unnur does not let go of Isabela's hand. Fannar manages to haul himself up on to his knees and with one last great heave, Isabela slips out of the crack and lies panting and sobbing with relief on the hillside, Unnur crooning over her and Ari standing beside them both, beaming.

We all crouch on the ground, trying to recover our breath, fearful to stand in case the mountain trembles again.

Unnur clutches her two daughters to her. 'The wounded man, you had to leave him?'

It is Ari who answers. 'He was not a man. I know now that he was a nightstalker. I should have left him to die again on the road when those Danes overpowered him, but I would not believe it. After you and the girls got out, he rose up and tried to attack Eydis in the cave . . . all of us.' Ari ruefully rubs the lump on the back of his head.

Fannar whistles through his teeth. 'A draugr . . . is it possible? I have heard of them, my own father told me about one who plagued one of the neighbouring farms for many years, but I have never encountered one. Who raised him?'

Ari glances at me.

'From what Ari tells me,' I say, 'I am sure it was the Lutheran pastor who buried his companions. It is my belief he was to have been sent to one of the families the pastor suspected of still holding the Mass. Ari said the man was wearing a crucifix. The Danes thought he was a Catholic. He would have taken work with one of the secret Catholic families, and they, thinking he was of the same faith, would in time have invited him to one of the secret Masses.'

'Ari found him on the road to my farm,' Fannar says gravely.

I nod. 'Doubtless he was raised to use his strength to kill all those at the Mass by bringing the place crashing down on them or else burn it with them trapped inside. A draugr often destroys with fire. But the pastor did not know the strength of the creature he was raising. His power was far beyond anything the pastor could control.'

Unnur clutches her two daughters tighter to her, shuddering. Memories of what the Danes had done to her home haunt her face.

For a moment or two Fannar is silent, but where the moonlight catches the side of his face I can see his jaw clenching in anger. 'And the two foreign men?' he says finally.

'Marcos escaped safely,' I tell him, 'but he tumbled down the hill when the mountain stirred. He may be hurt or unable to find his way back. We must search for him.'

Ari crouches down beside Isabela who is now sitting up, her legs drawn up to her chest, hugging herself against the cold. 'Vítor?'

She points down at the crack, and shivers.

Fannar leans over the hole and calls several times in his deep, booming voice, but there is no reply. 'If he was still alive, he would have called out. If he was crushed by those falling rocks, there is no hope. Let him rest there in peace. There is no sense in any of us risking our lives to bring up a corpse, only to bury it again.'

'But he will not rest in peace if the draugr lies down there,' Ari protested.

Fannar crosses himself. 'I am sorry for it, but I will not risk the draugr taking you too.' He seizes the hand of his younger daughter. 'We must get away from here. If the ground shakes again it might dislodge other boulders, and steam may blow out through other vents. I've seen it happen before.'

We pick our way down the mountainside. I balance the cold body of my sister in the crook of my arm. I am unused to walking on grass. I slip several times. Long ago, Valdis and I wrapped our arms about each other's waists and ran blithely down slopes, laughing if we tumbled, and rolling over for the sheer joy of it. Now I am tired and afraid; these legs which once easily carried us both now feel weak and leaden, as if poison is slowly creeping into them. They can no longer bear the weight of two.

I feel a warm arm about me, and Valdis's weight is lifted from my arm. Ari is walking next to her, helping me to hold up the sagging body. It takes courage to embrace a corpse, and a good measure of kindness too.

We find Marcos towards the bottom of the slope or rather he finds us, by the stones we dislodge as we scramble down. He seems unharmed, though no doubt bruised, but judging from his heavy tread, and the sagging of his shoulders, he does not rejoice that he is alive. He barely glances up as he approaches us.

'Marcos?' Isabela steps out from behind Fannar.

Marcos's head jerks up and he gapes at her open-mouthed,

as if her ghost has just risen up from the ground. He stands transfixed for a moment, then he rushes at her, his arms wide as if he is going to hug her. But at the last moment he lets them fall, and stands mumbling something, staring at his hands.

Fannar leads us through the pass into a high valley. We rest then, making a hasty meal of some dried meat he has also stolen, holding the fragments in our mouths, sucking them until they are moistened enough to chew. Above us tiny clouds are drifting away as if on a tide and the bright white stars prickle above us in the dark sky. I marvel at them once more. I had forgotten how many there are up there, like a black pool teeming with shoals of little silver fish. The stars blur into one as tears swim in my eyes. I wish Valdis had lived to see them too, just one last time.

'It's not safe to trust to the deep caves while the mountains are stirring,' Fannar says at length, 'but there is an old abandoned farmstead I know of, a day's journey from here. Most of it is in ruins, but the *badstofa* was built far back into the hillside and the floor dug deep. If we can get in through the entrance, the hall should be sound enough to shelter us, and if the place seems ruined, so much the better. As long as we are careful with the fire, we should be able to hide there for the winter at least.'

'But how will we feed the children?' Unnur wails. 'Everything we put down for winter is gone, the beasts too.'

Fannar squeezes his wife's shoulder. 'First we find shelter, then we worry about food. I am becoming an expert thief, though it is not a skill I ever thought to master, and I was good at catching birds when I was a boy, no doubt I can do it again. There'll be a place of honour at our fireside for you, Eydis, of course, and the foreigners too.'

'You are a good man, Fannar,' I tell him. 'But I will not be coming with you. We must part now. My sister is dead, and I swore I would lay her to rest at the river of blue ice. I must find it. I have been away from it for so long. I was only a child when I was brought into the cave, but the mountains don't change. I will find the way again. As for Isabela, she seeks the white falcons. She must not rest until she finds them, for the lives of many depend upon it. She has done all I have asked of her, and with courage. Without her, the draugr could not have been defeated, and no man, woman or child on this isle would be safe. I vowed that I would help her find what she seeks and I will not break my oath to her.'

Ari nods gravely, then turns to Fannar, biting his lip.

'Fannar, I'm bound to you for the season, but I beg you to release me from that, or at least give me leave to depart for a while. I'll guide Eydis to the blue river and then help the girl catch the white falcon. She can't do it alone, and Eydis . . .' He breaks off awkwardly. I know he is thinking that I will be of little use when it comes to climbing cliffs.

I smile. 'No, lad,' I say. 'Fannar needs you now more than ever. It will take both your strengths to see this family safe through winter, and if he should fall ill, Unnur cannot manage alone. If they are to build themselves a new life, you must be as a son to them. You cannot desert them now; they have been good to you. I will be led to the river of ice and I will guide Isabela too. I will always be there to guide her.'

Ari sighs, but he does not protest. I know he still blames himself for the draugr and will do anything he is commanded to do to make amends. Fannar and Unnur exchange looks of sheer relief at the news that Ari is staying with them, though I know Fannar would have willingly let the boy go if I had told him I needed him.

'But Eydis,' Unnur says, 'your sister is joined to you. How will you lay her to rest in the river? Can she be cut from you?'

I smile beneath my veil. 'When the time comes, the way will be shown to me.'

Chapter Thirteen

It was discovered that a parish priest was keeping a gyrfalcon in his barn. It was a bird of such great value that not even his own bishop could dream of owning such a prize. Everyone was certain there was only one way a poor man like him could have obtained such a bird: he must have stolen it. For a priest to be guilty of stealing was bad enough, but this was no ordinary theft. If he had stolen a horse or even a silver cup, as a man in holy orders he would have escaped with his life, but the white gyrfalcon must surely have belonged to no less a person than a prince or even a king. To steal from royalty was nothing less than treason, and not even the Church could protect a man accused of such a terrible crime.

The priest was found guilty and sentenced to be burned to death. The gyrfalcon was taken from him and securely tethered until it could be sent to the king. Then the priest was led to the stake and there he was bound in chains to the post and the pyre was lit. But just as the flames took hold and leapt upwards, the gyrfalcon managed to escape its leash and flew straight towards the burning pyre. It perched on the top of the stake, spreading its wings protectively to cover the head of the priest. When the people who were gathered in the square saw this, they cried out, 'It is a sign from God. The priest is innocent.' At once they pulled away the burning wood and doused the flames. Then they released the priest from his chains and set him free.

Isabela

Pounces – *the claws or talons of a falcon.*

Eydis heaved herself to her feet and hauled up Valdis's limp body, settling it against her shoulder. Her bare back gleamed like white marble in the moonlight. I was wearing the thick woollen dress that Unnur had given me the first night in the farmhouse and still I was shivering in the cold night air. Eydis must have been freezing. She had lived most of her life in the warmth of the cave, and now she was suddenly outside in the bitter wind, with nothing more than a cloth bound about her breasts to keep her from the cold. Unnur took off her own shawl and tried to wrap her in it, but Eydis gently pushed it away, shaking her head.

With her free hand, she beckoned to me and to Marcos, pointing down the valley.

'Komdu.'

She began to walk off in the direction she had indicated. I assumed that Fannar and the others would follow, but though they rose to their feet, they made no move to go after her.

'Where's she off to?' Marcos said, looking bemused. 'Do we go with her or stick with them?'

I didn't answer, but instead lifted my skirts and ran after Eydis.

'Falcons! You promised you would help me find the falcons. Please, I must find them!'

I pointed up at the dark sky and tried to imitate their call. I could barely see her in the darkness, and certainly nothing of her expression beneath the veil.

She lifted her hand and touched my cheek. It was a simple, motherly gesture, not that my mother had ever done that, but somehow I knew by it that she understood what I was asking. I trusted her. I knew she would keep her promise. I fell into step behind her and it was only after we had walked on a few paces that I realized in my haste I hadn't said good-bye to Fannar and Marcos.

I turned of to see Marcos hurrying up towards me, cursing as his feet nearly slipped from under him on the loose stones.

I looked back at Ari, Fannar and his family. They were still standing, huddled together, watching us. They didn't wave or call out, but after a moment or two little Lilja shyly raised her hand in a goodbye. My throat tightened with tears. I knew I would never see them again and they had risked so much for us. I wished I had something to give them, but even if I'd had a purse stuffed with gold, I don't think they would have taken it.

'Where are we going?' Marcos said behind me.

'I am going with Eydis,' I told him firmly, but I certainly wasn't going to tell him why, not even now. 'Why didn't you stay with Fannar?'

'Can't understand a bloody word any of them are saying. At least with you I'll have someone to talk to. Besides, you need someone to look after you.'

'I do not,' I snapped. 'I'm quite capable of taking care of myself.'

He snorted with derision. 'Is that so? Where shall I start? First there was –'

But before I could hit him with the nearest rock, Eydis turned and motioned us to be silent.

'Danir!' she whispered, gesturing round at the dark slopes of the valley.

After all the terrors of the cave I had almost forgotten that we were still in danger out here. We trudged along in silence, glancing apprehensively around us every time we thought we glimpsed movement. I'd been so thankful to escape the cave, it had driven everything else from my mind, but now it all gushed back into my head – the mutilated children from the forest, the monstrous creature that had poured out of Valdis, and almost worst of all, the horrific figure of Jorge with his charred face and the gag, that cruel gag. Did he feel pain, even now? Surely, it all must just have been a bad dream, a nightmare.

But Vítor – he had been real. He had tried to kill me. He'd pushed me into the arms of that creature. If the rocks hadn't fallen and struck it, if I hadn't got to the passage before the mouth of the cave collapsed, I would be trapped in there with it. And then Vítor falling from the ledge when the ground shook, and his body lying crumpled at the bottom. I squeezed my eyes shut, trying to block it out, but all those horrors were inside me now and there was no escaping the sight of them.

We walked and rested and walked on. None of us wanted to stop for long. We walked through the dawn, watching a pink light seep up over the mountains, staining the snow on the peaks blood-red, then fading to pink and finally sparkling white as the pale yellow sun inched over the rocks. The valleys were deserted. Once or twice in the far distance we watched a thin plume of smoke rising from a farmhouse or camp fire, but we saw no one.

As we walked I kept scanning the mountain tops and the sky for any sign of the white falcons, but there was none. I looked for anything that might be a ptarmigan, the falcons' prey, but the only birds I could see were crows and ravens. I prayed desperately that I had not been mistaken and Eydis was leading us to the white falcons. She was my last hope. If she couldn't find them, then I had signed my own father's death warrant.

Dusk came quickly again and with it the first flakes of snow began to drift down, swirling round us in the wind. Marcos was trailing further and further behind, and I could see from the way Valdis's corpse was flopping against Eydis's shoulder that Eydis was as exhausted as I was. She stopped and pointed ahead a little way up the hill to where there was a hollow. At least that would provide a little shelter from the wind while we slept.

But we had taken only a few paces towards it when I glimpsed something rising from the rocky hillside a few yards away. Even through the falling snow, it was glowing in the twilight, a white pearly light, hovering over the ground. It was like the mist I'd seen in the forest when Eydis had entered my nightmare, but I knew I wasn't dreaming now.

'Eydis, look.'

She wheeled round, flinging her arm out, pushing me back. Two great hands appeared out of the solid rock, moving as if the owner was swimming up through it. The hulk of a body followed, and two legs as thick as tree trunks, but where a man's head should have been was a mass of thick, wet seaweed, rippling and twisting as if it was still in the ocean and was caught in the swell of the waves.

With a roar the creature turned its shaggy head towards us, two burning red eyes peering out at us through the mass of weed. It lumbered down the hillside towards us. Eydis had let her sister's body drop, so that it was swinging from her waist. She lifted something high in her right hand and I saw that it was the finger bone I had taken from the grave.

With her other hand she wrenched the cord from the lucet which hung from her waist and threw it on the ground between her and the creature. She pointed the bone at it. The cord slithered towards the creature, coiling itself into a perfect circle about its feet. I thought it would simply trample over the cord, but Eydis pointed at the cord again and it burst into scarlet and blue flames. The creature reeled backwards, lumbering around, desperately looking for a way out of the circle of fire. The flames climbed higher into the darkening sky. The creature began to howl, not in rage but in terror. The flames caught at the weeds of its face, shrivelling them up as it screamed in pain. Again and again, Eydis pointed the bone, forcing the fire to burn higher, more fiercely.

The creature was trying to beat out the flames on its head with its own hands. But as the weeds turned black and dropped away I saw a face emerge. It was the corpse in the cave, the draugr, only it wasn't the face of a monster, but of a man now, terrified and in agony. It was the face of the boy burning on the pyre. It was Jorge's face. It was my father's face!

I grabbed at Eydis's arm, trying to wrench the bone from her hand.

'Stop! Stop it! You're killing him. He is a man, just a man. Let him alone!'

But she pushed me away and I fell to the ground. The man was engulfed in flames, every part of him was burning, but he was no longer moving. He stood there for a moment, rigid like a great tree, then he came crashing down. The circle of flames died down and were extinguished. The body of the man was just a heap of ash, which the wind caught and sent swirling up with the snowflakes. He was gone.

Eydis crumpled to her knees and crouched there, her head bowed, rocking the body of her dead sister like an infant in her arms. I knew that beneath the veil she was weeping.

Marcos came running up. 'What the hell happened? You're shaking. Are you hurt? I stopped to make water and when I turned round suddenly there was a fire.'

'It was . . . it's out now,' I said weakly.

'I can see that. Pity, we could have done with a fire. Couldn't you have kept just a little blaze going?' He wrapped his arms about him against the cold. 'Boiling lakes, the ground bursting into flames, that is when it's not freezing your bol . . .' He gave an embarrassed grin. 'Even hell itself can't be as diabolical as this place. I suppose at least we should be grateful it's stopped snowing, but what next – floods and whirlwinds?'

Eydis heaved herself upright. She turned her veiled head

towards me, but I walked away. I knew it was stupid to have felt sorry for that creature even for a moment. It was not alive, not really. Eydis had saved me. The creature would have ripped us to pieces. I knew that it had to be destroyed, but for the first time I understood why they had chained Eydis up in that cave and why they feared her so.

Eydis

***Creance** — a long light line attached to the leash to give the falcon the illusion of freedom. It is mainly used when a falcon is being trained.*

How can I explain to Isabela that I had to destroy him? Does she think I did not feel pity for the man? I watched him as he died at my hands. I saw the humanity return to his eyes. I heard him pleading for mercy. He had not asked to be called from his grave, nor transformed into the monster he became. It was another who did that to him, another who must bear the guilt of what they made him. But if I had relented, if I had weakened, given way to pity, he would have become that demon again.

Isabela will forgive me in time. She will come to understand one day that sometimes mercy is not kindness and pity is not love. But I saw the momentary fear in her face when she looked at me, the same fear that I had seen in others when Valdis and I were children, and it hurt me.

No matter how far the wind may blow them off course, every wild creature feels the unseen paths and lines that draw it home. Even the dead can sense the road they must travel through the stars. I thought I would not remember the way back to the river of ice, but when I close my eyes and trust to my dreams, I feel the pull like a current of water over my skin. All I have to do is follow it.

I long for a hundred eyes to look everywhere at once. To see the black rocks and golden sedges, the white clouds and blue skies reflected so sharply in the still pools that it seems as if the pools contain the real clouds and what drifts above us in the blue lake of the sky is merely a reflection. I listen to the wind rustling the dried leaf stalks, and the cry of the sandpiper. I breathe in the clean, sweet fragrance of grass, and the rich, pungent scent of the bogs. I feel the breeze pulling my hair, and the soft cushions of moss beneath my bare feet. And I wish for only one thing – that Valdis could see and smell and hear and feel the light, that glorious light that bathes the whole world.

Isabela and Marcos trail after me. Isabela is constantly gazing around, her eyes searching the rock faces and the skies for any sign of the falcons. She is not pulled towards a place, but driven to move on until she finds what she seeks. The force of it will no more let her rest than it will me.

As for Marcos, he makes me smile. Whereas Isabela delights in the vast open spaces, the colours gliding softly into one another, russet, bronze and copper, gold, gentian and green, Marcos can see nothing but mud and water, rocks to trip him and bogs to fall in. He stomps along, his shoulders hunched miserably against the cold, giving fearful glances at the emptiness as if he is constantly searching for some little corner to hide away from it all.

When night returns we seek the shelter of some rocks and nibble on the remains of the dried mutton strips that Fannar insisted on sharing with us and quench our thirst in an icy stream. We huddle against the rocks and try to sleep a little, but I am too restless to settle. I can tell from their tossing and turning that Isabela and Marcos cannot sleep either. So as soon as the moon rises high enough to gild the rocks and pools, I shake them and we move on.

It is cold. I had forgotten what cold feels like during all those years in the cave, the way it sets your teeth aching, your muscles tightening against it till they moan. My skirts are thick enough, but I have only the thin wrap around my breasts. If I was alone I would take Valdis's wrap to help cover me, but even though she is dead, I cannot expose her naked to strangers.

We make slower progress at night. The moon casts long shadows of us as we walk, but we can see the glint of its reflection to warn us of marsh pools and streams, and as long as I trust to the sense that is calling me I know we will not be led astray.

Suddenly the sharp wind carries the smell of the ice to us and, as we round the curve of the hillside, I stop as a thrill of excitement and joy shudders through me. There, between two jagged rocks, which rise like pillars on either side, is the vast, glittering expanse of blue ice, frozen in waves and peaks as it tumbles down the mountainside. It sparkles in the moonlight and, at its feet, a lake is turned to liquid silver beneath the stars. Isabela claps her hands over her mouth and gasps. We do not need words to tell each other how beautiful it looks. It is more wondrous than I ever remembered.

We start towards the edge of the river where the ice stops abruptly and little rivulets run from it towards the lake. Although I cannot see it, I know that at the far end of the valley the lake drains into the river, and the river meanders through the valleys until it pours into the great crashing waves of the sea.

I clamber up on to the first ledge of ice, feeling the frosted air rise up around me. I stand there, holding my arms up like a child to its mother. We are home. Valdis and I have come home at last.

All through those long years in the cave we would talk about all the things we remembered, the way the wind would blow over the grass in summer making it roll like waves in a green sea and the river of blue ice singing to the stars on a frosty night. We remembered how we used to gather the spring flowers and lay them in cracks in the ice and mark their place on one of the rocks close by, and every day we would run back to the river to see how far they had travelled. They would stay as fresh as the day we picked them, and before the snows of winter came and covered them we would see they had crept the breadth of our little hands closer to the sea. One day we knew they would reach it, and tumble out into the waves and float across the world.

I turn to the side of the frozen river and begin to scramble up the rocks. It is hard to climb, holding Valdis up in my arm. But I cannot rest until I know. It has been more than forty years since I have seen my father, more than forty years since my mother took us to the cave. I need to tell her that we never blamed her, not once in all those years. Perhaps she has given birth to other children since we've been gone. I hope so, for her sake. She needed a child she could cradle in her arms. Her children would be grown by now, have children of their own. Our nieces and nephews, our own family sleeping in our little bed, listening to the crackling of the frozen river, and running down in spring to place their own flowers in the ice.

There is a clatter of stones behind me and I turn, clinging to the rocks. Isabela and Marcos are climbing up behind me. I had forgotten them. Let them come, then. Our family will welcome them.

The boulders give way to a steep slope with patches of shale between the moss and grass. Valdis and I used to run down it, on our single pair of legs, heedless of falling, but now our legs ache and burn as I force them up and up.

I am almost at the top of the rise. I stop. The icy air rolls up from the river below and the moon shines down on the peaks of ice, a luminescent ribbon winding between the dark rocks. Just a few more strides will take us over the rise and I will see the house where we were born. I have become a child again.

But suddenly I am afraid. What will I read on my father's face when he opens the door, what will I see in my mother's eyes? I am suddenly conscious of the cold, decaying body of my sister, cradled in my arm. I am ashamed of our bodies now, as I was on that day she took us to the cave to shut us away out of sight where we could do no harm. But they must be told that their daughter is dead. They should be allowed to say goodbye to her. We are their flesh. They made us.

I hear Marcos and Isabela panting up the slope, behind me. Marcos curses as he trips over a stone in the darkness. I take a deep breath and stumble up over the rise.

The house squats between two long fingers of rock, still and dark. It is late. They are all sleeping. I walk towards the door. But I see something in front of it, something that had not been there when we were children. I edge closer. It is a long mound of stones silvered by the moonlight. And with a terrible understanding that makes me almost cry out with the pain of it, I recognize what it is. There is no cross, no name. It lies before the threshold, a mute curse upon the house and land. But who lies beneath it?

Something is glinting on the top of the stones, a knife, a rusty hunting knife. It is my father's blade. Only a sorcerer or a man who commits self-murder is buried beneath such a cairn, and my poor father was never a sorcerer.

I skirt the cairn and push against the door. There is no use in knocking. I know even before I enter that my call will only be answered by my own empty echo. I have no need of light. I know every inch of this long, narrow room. The cooking pot still hangs over the cold fire pit. The cords still dangle from the beams above, where once herbs and fish and meat dried in the smoke of a warming fire. I touch one of the covers that still lies upon the bed. The corner tears in my hand. It is rotting away. If my mother has left, she has taken little or nothing with her. How long has she been gone? Did she bury my father or did he harm himself after she left? I will never know. Wherever she is now I hope she has found peace.

I turn to make my way out, and in the small, cramped

space knock my arm against the long, narrow bed that runs along one wall. Something makes me look down. A river of moonlight from the open door eddies along the bed. Someone is lying beneath the rotting covers. But they will not wake. I am too late. A skull rests upon the mouldering pillow, the dark empty sockets stare upwards into the moonlight. Her long dark hair lies tangled around the bone and in her hair – two white falcon feathers.

Isabela and Marcos are waiting for me outside. They stare at me curiously, wondering, no doubt, why I have come here. I bend to pick up a stone, and groan as a spasm of pain grips my back. I have carried Valdis for so long. I place the stone carefully on the cairn. Isabela hesitates, then she and Marcos solemnly add stones too. I am grateful for their kindness.

We return the way we have come, as in life we always do, but now I am weary, so very weary. As we scramble down the last boulder, I see a tall figure standing at the foot of the ice-river. I might have guessed Heidrun would come, just as she had come that night Valdis and I were awakened.

'It is time now,' she says.

'But it is too soon. Not yet, not yet. I cannot do it yet.' I have not even grieved for those who lie in that cold, dark house. I cannot let them take Valdis from me now.

Heidrun holds out her hand.

'Wait,' I tell her.

I walk over to Isabela. I gaze deep into her bright eyes. If I had ever had a child like her, I would have been proud to call her daughter. I touch her cheek, and she does not flinch from me. I know I am forgiven. I pull the horn lucet from around my waist and loop the thong around Isabela's neck. She smiles, clutching at it, rubbing the smooth surface with her fingers as Valdis and I used to do when we were children.

I turn back to Heidrun, but before I can speak Isabela cries out. She is staring in fear up at the dark sky. A long ribbon of bright green light is ripping across it, obliterating the stars. Another, fainter, one undulates behind it. Great bands of opalescent green light begin to fill the sky, writhing and dancing. The air vibrates with singing. I spin around watching the waves of green and yellow and purple leap like flames across the dark sky, as if the whole night is afire.

Isabela and Marcos are standing motionless, gazing upwards. I do not know if she even realizes Marcos is holding her hand, for she is lost in utter awe, no longer afraid now, but consumed with the sheer wonder of it.

I gaze up the length of the blue river. The spirals of light flickering in the sky above are captured in the ice, making a thousand tiny gold-green lights tumble and spin in the heart of the frozen water. I hold out my hand to Heidrun. She takes it and helps me to clamber up on to the ice.

Isabela, still hardly able to draw her gaze away from the flames in the sky, tries to climb up and follow us. But Heidrun turns and shakes her head. She points to some rocks close to the base of the hill. She is telling them to wait there for us. What I have to do now for Valdis cannot be witnessed by them.

I watch the pair of them wandering off, still hand in hand, their heads craned up, transfixed by the rippling curtains of light in the sky. Then I turn and, clasping Valdis's body tightly in my arms, I slowly follow Heidrun up the river of blue ice, stepping carefully around the crevasses and over the rough peaks of frozen water. And as we three walk silently together, the cold green flames dance above us in the dark sky and blue ice answers them with its ancient song.

Chapter Fourteen

At the very dawn of creation there appeared in northern lands a snow-white egg, the like of which had never been seen before or since. The shell of this egg cracked open and two birds were hatched from it, the gyrfalcon and the ptarmigan, twin sisters born from a single egg, and like the egg from which they sprang, the feathers of both birds were as white as the hills in winter.

The gyrfalcon flew up high into the mountains and found a home among the rocky crags, while the ptarmigan sought shelter in the long grasses of the plateau. They lived apart for so long that the two birds forgot that they were sisters. They each built their nests and laid their eggs, but when the chicks hatched they cried for food.

The gyrfalcon saw her chicks were hungry and she went hunting. She spread her white wings and glided down across the valley and over the plateau. For a long time she hunted, but she could find no prey. Then her sharp eyes spotted something running. She stooped down upon it and, seizing her kill in her sharp talons, she carried it off to her nest. She tore at its breast until the flesh was bare and bleeding and fed it to her chicks. Only then did she look upon its face. Only then did she recognize the face of her sister, the ptarmigan. When she realized who it was she had torn apart with her cruel beak, her grief knew no bounds. And her cry of sorrow, *krery-krery-krery*, will ring out to the end of time, for she repeats her murder daily and daily repents too late.

Isabela

***Hot gorge** – when a falcon is allowed to feed on prey it has
just killed. A bird may be permitted a full gorge – to eat until
its crop is full – or a half gorge or quarter gorge.*

I woke with such a start that I must have lashed out, for my
arm hit something soft and I heard a grunt of pain beside
me. For a moment I didn't know where I was. The light was
startlingly bright as if a thousand candle flames were being
shone in my face. I was numb with cold. Then I realized that
the light was coming from a low, bright sun dazzling over the
top of a hill, and I was lying not in the warm cave, but on
damp mosses tucked under an overhang of rocks. Marcos
was lying in front of me, curled up like a baby, and groaning
as he stirred awake.

Embarrassed at finding myself pressed into a man's back,
I could not think how to extricate myself, since I was wedged
between his body and the rock. I nudged him again, hoping
it would make him move away, but he turned over and opened
his eyes, staring with a frown up at the lightening sky as if he
had never seen it before.

He crawled out from under the overhang and staggered
painfully to his feet and gazed about him. 'Sweet Jesu,
I thought I'd just dreamt this!'

I scrambled up, trying to smooth my clothes and tousled
hair. My clothes clung damply to my goose-pimpled skin,
and the breeze only made me feel wetter and colder. But
when I glanced up to where Marcos was staring, all the discomfort and cold vanished as I too gaped at the sight.

447

We were standing on the edge of a broad flat plain of dark green mosses and golden sedges. Above us towered a great mountain of sparkling bluish-white ice, tumbled down between two jagged black peaks. The frozen river flowed out around the base of the rocks, ending abruptly about four or five feet above a shelf of black sand. Little streams of water were running from beneath the ice and trickling into a wide, dark lake in whose ruffled surface the white ice and black rocks trembled. Ribbons of soft white mist drifted across the ice-river and above it the sky was such a dazzling blue it hurt my eyes to look at it.

Marcos slowly shook his head. 'That . . . that could never have been a river, could it? How could anything that deep freeze solid?'

For a few minutes all we could do was stare transfixed. Then, as the breeze once again reminded me how cold I was, I glanced around.

'Can you see Eydis anywhere?' I asked. 'I thought the other woman said to wait for her here. She should be back by now, but I see no sign of her.'

Shielding his eyes with his hand from the glare of the sun bouncing off the ice, Marcos pivoted slowly around.

'Look there. Is that one of those hot springs or is it smoke?'

I followed where he pointed. Half-hidden behind the rocks where we had taken shelter, a thin plume of lavender smoke was swirling gently in the breeze. I caught the whiff of what smelt like fish grilling.

'It's a cooking fire.' I tried to smile and discovered my face was so numb with cold I could hardly move the muscles. The thought of being able to warm my hands over a fire seemed more precious than gold right then and I turned to hurry around the rocks, but Marcos grabbed me.

'Wait,' he whispered. 'It might not be Eydis. Remember the Danes are still looking for us.'

My heart suddenly began to thump. What had been an

awe-inspiring expanse now suddenly became menacing, with little cover in which to hide.

'Get back behind the rock,' Marcos whispered. 'I'll edge round and see if I can see anything.'

I crept back under the overhang, crouching, my body tense, ready to run, though I had no idea where to make for. Marcos crept along the rocks, but even before he reached the end where he might have been seen, a woman's voice rang out,

'Marcos, Isabela, gerðu svo vel. Come and eat, you must be hungry.'

Marcos peered around the rock. 'It's that woman who took the sisters up the frozen river last night.'

The relief I felt was like being plunged into a warm bath. I crept out of my hiding place and saw the tall woman crouching by a fire she had built on a flat slab of rock. She was twisting a stick on which several small fish were skewered, their skins charred and bubbling.

'Come, warm yourselves. I am Heidrun, a friend of Eydis and Valdis. I have known them since they quickened in their mother's womb.'

We both crouched as close to the fire as we could, rubbing our hands, our clothes steaming where the heat touched them.

'Where is Eydis?' I asked.

'She is close by. Eat first, then I will take you to her.'

We breakfasted on the fish which was so fresh that it tasted as if it had only been pulled from the lake minutes before. Heidrun ate hers slowly and delicately, smiling to herself as Marcos and I burned our fingers and mouths in our haste to eat. I hadn't realized it was possible to be so ravenously hungry. Never had anything tasted so good.

But suddenly I was back in our kitchen in Sintra eating grilled sardines, hearing the thunderous hammering on the door, tense with fear as I waited for it to open, then watching as they bound my father's hands and dragged him away. What was he eating this morning? Was he even still alive? I had wasted so much precious time.

'Eydis was going to show me where the white falcons are. Do you know how far away they are from here?'

I knew even as I asked the question that it was cruel and unfeeling. The poor woman was grieving for her sister. What right had I to ask her to show me the birds in the midst of her sorrow? Yet I had to insist. I didn't know how else I was going to find them.

'They're not far. You will see them.'

We drank from the trickles of water which ran from the end of the frozen river. The ice was as wrinkled as the skin of an old crone who has lived for a thousand years, and scored by dozens of cracks and crevices. When we had drunk our fill, Heidrun climbed gracefully up on to the ice shelf, holding out a warm hand to help me scramble up. Seeing her walk on it with such practised ease, I hadn't realized how slippery it was, and I would have come crashing down had she not continued to steady me. Marcos clambered up too and almost slid straight off again.

Holding both our hands, Heidrun led us up the frozen river. Once we were away from the edge that was wet and smooth with melting water, the surface became harder and rougher, easier to find a foothold without your shoe slipping out from under you.

The coldness rose up from the ice and enveloped us. Our breath hung about in puffs of white. Although I longed to look up to see the vast expanse of ice towering above, the moment I raised my eyes, I would trip over the frozen peaks or stumble as my foot slipped into the cracks. The further we walked, the broader the crevices became until they were wide enough for a man to fall into and so deep that he would never be able to clamber up the glass walls. Follow one line of solid ice, and you could suddenly find yourself stranded with deep ravines on three sides of you and no way across.

But Heidrun seemed to be able to pick her way round this maze of crevasses, as if following a track, though there was nothing that I could see that marked the way.

Finally, as we reached the place where the ice-river angled sharply upwards, she stopped. We found ourselves facing an oval hole in the ice like the entrance to a cave, easily big enough to enter.

'Come,' Heidrun said. 'Eydis is inside.'

I had spent enough time in a cave in the past few days never to want to enter one again. Even to look at it brought panic surging up into my throat, the terror of being trapped down in the mountain. Standing there alone in the darkness, sure that the entrance had been sealed and there was no way out for me, then finally the relief of seeing that tiny pinpoint of light, a single star showing the gap was still there. Then climbing up and up and that awful moment of despair again when I realized I could not reach the world outside. Groping over the surface of the walls, desperate to find a hole, a stone jutting out, the smallest thing I could use to stand on, terrified to reach too far in case I slipped and went crashing down, perhaps to lie there mangled but still alive at the bottom.

I saw Marcos watching me, and knew my face must be revealing the horror I felt when I looked at that ice cave.

'You don't have to go in,' he said. 'I'll find her and bring her out to you.'

But Heidrun said softly, 'You must go in to her, if you want to find the white falcons. It is the only way.'

She turned, as if she expected me to follow, and ducking her head, went inside.

'You don't have to,' Marcos whispered.

But I knew that I did. Trying to fight down the desire to turn and run, I too ducked into the ice cave. But it was not like the first cave at all. It was shallow, almost egg-shaped inside. I had thought it would be dark, but I found myself bathed in an iridescent blue light, brighter and more intense

451

than a hundred lamps burning together. It was as if all the rays of sunlight outside were being sucked through the ice and concentrated in that cave. When I moved my head even slightly, the colours of every rainbow that had ever arched through the skies rippled through those walls of ice.

'Eydis is here,' Heidrun said.

Her voice startled me. I'd almost forgotten why I was in the cave. She drew to one side, so that I could see. A long low ledge of ice ran along the back of the cave. Eydis and Valdis were lying on it, their hands clasped in one another's. Then I saw something else – a single white bone, the bone which I had taken from the forest in France. The ring had been removed and the bone was clasped between the sisters' entwined fingers, just as a lover might hold a rose in death, or a Christian grasp a crucifix.

Ice was slowly creeping up over the bodies of Eydis and Valdis, over their single pair of legs, their arms and heads. Their hair was already fully embedded in the ice. Soon the rest of them would be completely encased.

'Eydis is dead,' I breathed. 'But I thought she had come to release the spirit of her twin. I thought when she'd done that she would be free.'

'She is free,' Heidrun said. 'They both are. Look at them.'

Now that their faces were no longer veiled, I saw that they were strikingly handsome, and as alike as two matched pearls. Both women's eyes were open, and as blue as the ocean, and there was an expression of childlike wonder in them.

'But, I thought she would live,' I said. 'I didn't know she had come here to die. Did she know? Did she know where you were taking her?'

'She knew she was coming here to seek life,' Heidrun said.

'But she's not alive,' I screamed. 'She's dead. All those years chained up in the cave, and she finally managed to escape, and now . . . and now . . . It isn't fair!'

I turned and blundered out of the cave, slipping and sliding on the ice, banging my shoulder on the edge of the cave entrance, but I was too angry and shocked even to notice the pain.

Marcos had remained outside, though he must have heard all that passed between us. He caught my arm, trying to stop me charging back down the river of ice.

'Wait, we need Heidrun to guide us back, otherwise we'll end up down one of those crevasses.'

'I don't care,' I yelled, but, of course, I did.

His warning was enough to make me stop, but I couldn't look at Heidrun when she emerged from the cave.

Marcos shuffled his feet awkwardly. 'I suppose we should have realized, poor woman. You could hardly cut them apart, not without killing Eydis in the process.'

'They were born as one, Eydis knew they would die as one,' Heidrun said as calmly as ever. 'They will lie there unchanged long after we are dead. The ice-river moves slowly, but one day, in time, their bodies will reach the lake and from the lake they will drift into the river and with the river they will flow into the sea and become one with it. Just as a single drop of water that falls as rain will in time become a whole ocean always moving, always changing, but always the sea.'

Without turning to see if we followed, Heidrun set off down the ice-river again, picking her way carefully between the great ravines and cracks. We followed without speaking until we reached the lip of the ice and Marcos bounded down, reaching up to help first Heidrun and then me clamber down on to the black sand and mud below.

I stood gazing back at the ice. Somewhere in that, though I could no longer see the place, Eydis and her twin lay entombed. How could I have been so stupid as even to imagine that Eydis could free herself from her dead twin? As Marcos said, it was impossible. It was obvious she'd come here to die.

Grief welled up in me as a hard lump in my throat. Tears

sprang to my eyes and I scrubbed them away. I wasn't crying for her. Why should I? I barely knew her. I was crying for poor old Jorge burning in front of that screaming mob, for the girl who'd tried to hold on to the casket of bones, for the murdered family in the forest, for poor little Hinrik, for Fausto, for my father and, though I refused to admit it, I was crying most of all for myself.

I thought of myself as far away from home in a strange land. I had longed to return to the place I knew and loved as a child, to the old familiar smells and sights, the hot summer sunshine, the scent of the pine groves and the camellias. But in that moment I finally grasped that I had no home to return to. I was a Marrano. We did not belong anywhere. There was no land we could own as ours, no place to raise a family in peace, no tomb to bury our parents in that would not be desecrated. Even that little strip of land that we might call our grave, our resting place, was not permitted to us. There was no river of blue ice waiting for me, calling for me to return to it.

Heidrun took my hand and gently pulled me round to face the calm, dark lake.

'I am not like Fannar and Eydis. I am their friend, but not of their people. They call me a *huldukona*, a hid-woman. We live among them, but we are not of them. We too were once driven out of our homes. But we still keep our own ways. We teach our children the lore which our mothers taught us and their mothers taught them since first this land was made. We do not forget who we were and who we are, and we will remember it for ever. I see it in you. You are like us. You must remain hidden. You must appear to be as one with the people you live among. But you are not. Learn the old ways of your people as we do in secret, teach them to your children, tell them who they were and make them remember. Your home is in your lore. As long as you remember the old ways and teach them, within that knowledge you will always find the place where you belong.'

'But I don't understand why you must remain hidden,' I said. 'Are you afraid of the Danes?'

She smiled sadly. 'I am afraid of nothing, except forgetting. Come.'

She walked ahead of us, leading us back to the cooking fire which still glowed on the rock. She retrieved a withy basket which she had tucked into the shelter of the rocks. She opened it and pulled out two live birds about the size of a bantam hen, with dark strips over their eyes. The backs of the birds were grey-brown mottled with white and the belly and flanks were white. They lay quietly in her hands, their big brown eyes staring up at us.

'These are ptarmigan.'

'So that's what they look like,' I said. 'They say there are great flocks of them in these mountains, but I haven't seen a single one.'

'You've seen many,' Heidrun said. 'But you haven't known it. When the snows come they'll turn white. A hillside may be covered with them, but they will not be seen. In summer they are the colour of the rocks and grey mountain grass. In autumn they look like rocks with a little frost upon them, as they do now.'

Marcos eyed them hungrily. 'Do they make good eating?'

Heidrun laughed. 'Yes, excellent, but I am afraid they will not be filling your belly. These are needed for hungrier beaks.'

She handed the birds to me and I held them, one under each arm, their wings pressed closed so that they could not struggle. Their bodies were warm and my fingers sank into the soft feathers. Beneath the skin I could feel their tiny hearts beating fast.

She nodded towards the basket. 'You will find soft leather in there to fashion into jesses and lines. You know how to snare a falcon, Isabela?'

'If we ever find one. I don't know where to look. Eydis promised me that she would help me catch the falcons. She swore . . . and I believed her. I thought that was where she was leading us. But now . . .'

'She will keep her promise,' Heidrun said calmly. 'Trust her in death as you did in life. Remember, the ptarmigan and the white falcon are sisters. Where one goes the other will always follow. Now I must leave you. Stay here until you have what you seek. You have a fire to warm you. There are fish in the lake and water in the streams. There is nothing more you need.'

Her smile was gentle as she turned and walked away. I was sure I'd seen her before, not just in the cave, but somewhere else. I suddenly realized I had not thanked her and called after her. She raised one hand in acknowledgement that she had heard me. She did not look back. We watched the tall figure stride across the plain until our eyes lost sight of her, dazzled by the sun.

Marcos stirred up the little fire, rubbing his hands, and eyed the two birds. 'What are you going to do with them? Wring their necks and leave them out as bait?'

'Falcons need live prey. Can you bring me the line from the basket?'

Marcos reluctantly held the birds while I fastened a leg of each one to a length of line. He was not used to handling birds, anyone could see that. They flapped angrily in his hands, while he leaned his head so far back to avoid the wings that he almost toppled over.

In spite of his help, I managed to tether both birds and sent him in search of stones that were weighty and rough enough to secure the ends of each line. Then I carried the birds and stones out to a flat patch of grass and set them down. The birds immediately crouched on the ground, staying so still that, had they been among rocks, I would immediately have lost sight of them. But after I had retreated, they cautiously rose and began to search among the vegetation for food.

I returned to the fire and fashioned two nooses at the ends

of the two remaining lengths of line, and laid them ready at hand.

'So, what happens now?' Marcos asked.

I shrugged. 'We wait and hope the falcons come.'

My father had used this method of trapping when he knew falcons regularly hunted in a certain place, or when a captive bird was lost, but it was not one he used often. It depended too much on luck. It occurred to me then to wonder how Heidrun had known to bring exactly the things I would need. Doubtless Eydis had told her what I was looking for and she had fetched the things in the night. I wondered if she lived close by, though I didn't recall passing any farmsteads, but then, they were so hard to see. Like the ptarmigan, their turf roofs blended perfectly into the hillside; you might walk within feet of them and not notice unless you saw the smoke rising from the hearths.

Marcos and I sat either side of the fire, occasionally feeding it with the woody stems of plants as if it was a pet and we were giving it titbits. I continually scanned the bright blue sky, but the sun glinted off the ice so brilliantly that I was forced to keep looking away. Marcos kept looking at me, half opening his mouth as if he was on the verge of saying something, but didn't know how to begin.

If I did find a bird, would he try to take it from me? He told me he had come here to capture a bird to pay a debt, though he had no idea how to set about it. But once the bird was caught, would I be able to fend him off if he was determined to take it? He had rescued me from the bog and he had warned me about Vítor. But why had he helped me? Was it just to ensure I would stay alive long enough to capture a bird for him? And what would he do when I had?

Marcos shifted his position for the umpteenth time. 'How long have we been here? My belly is beginning to grumble again. She said there were fish in the lake. I suppose she means us to use one of the lines, though I don't know what we're going to use as a hook, never mind bait. Can you catch fish as well as –'

'Quiet,' I whispered. Shielding my eyes, I stared up into the blinding blue sky.

Krery-krery-krery.

There it was again. 'White falcons,' I breathed.

'Where?' Marcos said, struggling to his feet.

I grabbed him and pulled him down.

'Keep down and stay still. I can't see them but I can hear them.'

Krery-krery-krery.

I turned in the direction of the sound. Two white specks were soaring down over the river of ice towards the ptarmigan.

'Stay here,' I whispered.

The ptarmigan had seen them too. They ran to the lengths of the line, trying to take cover in the rocks, but they were jerked back. The falcons circled above, crying out to each other. The ptarmigan froze, pressing themselves into the ground trying to hide, but though they would have been invisible against the rocks, out there in the open against the golden sedges and green mosses, they could be clearly seen.

The falcons folded their wings and stooped down in a long dive, turning upwards at the last minute to strike the ptarmigan with such force I could hear the thumps across the silent plain. They both rose in the air, the limp bodies of their prey dangling from their claws, beating their wings fiercely as they tried to lift both bird and stone to fly off with them. I saw the lines slipping on the stones and thought they were going to slide off, but they held and the falcons dropped to the ground again. They mantled their prey with their wings, covering the bodies of the ptarmigan, protecting them from any other bird that might swoop down to steal it. They lifted their heads, their huge dark eyes watching for danger. Finally, when they were satisfied they were alone, they began to tear the feathers from the warm bodies of the birds, and stab at the flesh beneath.

I watched them gulp down strips of the steaming bloody meat. Then, gripping the nooses and tingling with anticipation, I rose and strode towards the falcons.

With a cry of alarm the birds rose up into the air, circling high into the sky. Careful not to touch the bloody carcasses of the ptarmigan, I laid a noose around each bird, pegged it with a piece of woody plant stem and retreated back behind the rock, the other end of the line in my hands. I should have used a wooden peg, but there wasn't a tree to be seen anywhere. I just prayed the tough stems would be strong enough to pull against.

'What on earth did you do that for?' Marcos spluttered. 'I thought you said you knew how to catch them. If you'd just crept up on them quietly, instead of blundering in with all the stealth of a charging bull, you might have caught them. You've driven them off now. What you need –'

'Quiet,' I snapped. 'Stay absolutely still and wait.'

I watched the birds making wide sweeps in the sky, coasting on their wings on the currents of air rising from the land, their heads down, watching, waiting until all was quiet again. I was so tense, I kept forgetting to breathe, until the pain in my chest reminded me to draw breath. Would they stay? If they had killed and fed not long ago, they wouldn't bother. They would have taken those two ptarmigan from pure instinct, driven to kill because they had seen them running, trying to hide. But if they weren't really hungry they would simply fly off again. I waited, my eyes fixed on the birds. Were the circles becoming wider, were they climbing higher, would the next turn or flip of their wings carry them out of the valley?

The larger of the two, the female, began to descend towards the carcass. She landed on the ground and sauntered over, her head turning this way and that, before she stood over her prey again. Finally, she began to feed. Part of me was screaming, *pull the noose now, if you don't you'll lose her!* But I knew that as soon as the falcon felt herself caught she

459

would scream and struggle, and her mate would fly off at once. But at least I'd have one.

The jerkin, the male falcon, was flying lower. *Land!* I kept willing it. *Land, before the other takes wing again.* How hungry was it? How full was its crop? I couldn't take the risk of losing both of them. I had to do it now. My fingers were already tightening on the line when at that moment the jerkin landed. He too looked warily around before approaching his own carcass. I held my breath. Then he put his beak down and tore a lump of flesh from his prey.

It was vital I pulled both lines together and at the same pace. I tried, but the noose closed around the foot of the female just moments before the male. She let out a scream of indignation and the male's head snapped upwards; his wings flapped, but I just managed to tug the noose tight before his feet left the ground. Both birds toppled over, screeching and flapping wildly as they struggled on the ground.

Now I had to get to them before they hurt themselves and I couldn't trust Marcos to handle them. I snatched up the withy basket.

'Quickly,' I yelled at Marcos. 'Your shirt, give me your shirt.'

I will say this for him, he pulled it off without a word of protest.

I ran to the male, who was nearest, and dropped the shirt over the head of the struggling bird to quieten him. Then I raced towards the female. Scooping her up by her legs, I struggled to close her wings between my arm and chest and hold her still while I slipped the noose from her. She did not submit willingly, and I was terrified that one of her feet would fasten on me, for once they lock into flesh, nothing but killing the bird can force them loose. But I finally managed to lay her on her back in the basket and close the lid.

I walked back and wrapped the male tightly in Marcos's shirt. I removed the line and marched back with the two birds.

Marcos was shivering, but grinning so broadly, I thought his mouth would split.

'You did it! You caught them.' He looked down and his grin faded rapidly. 'But you're hurt.'

Both my arms were bleeding profusely from long gashes where talons and beaks had slashed me. My heart had been pumping so fiercely, and I had been so terrified of losing or injuring the birds, I hadn't even felt the pain, though I felt the fierce sting of it now.

'You'll have to bandage those wounds,' Marcos said, looking vaguely sick.

It was just as well Marcos was not a physician, for he was remarkably squeamish about the sight of blood.

'That will have to wait. I need to get the leather jesses on them so that I can tether them. I've no needle to sew the eyelids shut, or hoods, so I'll have to cover their heads with strips of cloth. We must keep them calm, else they will bate and harm themselves.'

Marcos, regarding the deep gashes in my arm, flatly refused to hold the birds, but under my direction he succeeded in tying the soft strips of leather to their legs and tore the bottom of his shirt for makeshift hoods which I finally succeeded in getting on the birds, though not without a few more cuts to my hands.

I tied the lines to the jesses and fastened them round the rocks, settling the birds there to perch, where they stood quietly enough. As soon as the birds were calm, Marcos insisted on going off to wet his ragged shirt in water to wash my cuts for they were bleeding and stinging ferociously.

Now that I had the birds safe, I found my legs had suddenly lost the power to hold me up. I was trembling violently. I sank down on to the ground. I had done it. I had really done it! I'd captured the falcons. My father would be released. He would come home safe and well. I could picture him now walking towards me, holding out his arms to me, the joy and amazement on his face that the miracle had happened. It was over. It was all over!

I crouched on the damp ground, waiting for Marcos to return, unable to tear my gaze from the falcons. They were a truly magnificent pair. The plumage on the underside of the birds was white with delicate markings of dark brown, as if someone had drawn on them in ink with a quill, and the plumage on the backs was as yet dark brown. They were just what I had hoped for. Both sore birds, in the first year of their lives, not yet in the full adult livery they would attain after their first moult next summer when the dark feathers would turn white. They had many years of hunting and breeding in front of them, if I could only manage to get them back alive.

Food – that was the important thing. They must be fed regularly. The ptarmigan they had killed would serve for the next couple of days, for they would surely keep fresh in this cold, especially if I packed them in a little of that ice. As soon as Marcos returned, I would send him to retrieve them, as long as I could persuade him not to roast them for his own supper. Perhaps we might spare the guts for Marcos to use as bait for fishing. Not the hearts and livers though, they must be fed to the falcons.

'Move away from those birds, Isabela,' a man's voice growled behind me.

I sprang to my feet. Marcos was on his knees, the point of a dagger at his throat, one arm twisted up painfully behind his back. Standing behind him, holding the hilt of the knife in his clenched fist, was Vítor. His clothes were torn and there was a dark patch of dried blood on his forehead, and a livid purple bruise on his cheek, but his expression was grim and determined.

'Turn around and start walking towards the ice, Isabela. Slowly! Just keep walking steadily. Don't even think of running or I will cut Marcos's throat and then I will track you down. Do falcons eat human flesh? I imagine they would eat anything if it was bloody enough, wouldn't they?'

Ricardo

Bind – *when a hawk seizes its prey in the air*
and holds on to it.

I don't know why I hadn't heard the little weasel coming. I'd never have let a man creep up on me like that in a town. You walk though a crowded street or sit in a tavern and you're constantly alert to any movement behind you – the cutpurse moving in, the hired muscle sent by the man wanting revenge – you can't afford to relax your guard for a moment. Vítor would never have taken me in the street, but that howling purgatory of empty space had sucked out even the wits I was born with.

I was just bending down to wet a torn scrap of my shirt in the lake and the next thing I knew there was a knife pricking my ribs and his odious voice whispering in my ear. He marched me back to Isabela, my arm twisted so far up my back, I was praying neither of us would stumble for one sudden jerk would have snapped it.

When Isabela turned, her face blanched as she saw us. 'Vítor . . . but I thought you were dead!'

She wasn't the only one. Why is it that filthy little cockroaches always survive, when everything else is wiped out?

'What you mean, Isabela, is you left me for dead,' Vítor said. 'But God watches over his faithful servants. I was rendered unconscious by my fall from the rocks, and when I came round, I was alone, but at least the steam was no longer filling the passageway. The ledge at the top of the shaft had fallen away, but I was able to carry a flat shard of rock up to the top of the pile of boulders and wedge it upright. Standing on that gave me just enough height to claw my way out. I eventually found Fannar and his family making for shelter. I thought you'd be with them. They were overjoyed to see me and naturally they were only too willing to point out the direction you had taken . . . But we've wasted enough time on this touching reunion. Isabela, I believe I told you to start walking towards the ice.'

He pressed the blade deeper into my throat until I was too afraid to breathe in case it pierced the skin.

Isabela flinched. 'I'll walk anywhere you want, but please don't hurt him.'

If I hadn't been so humiliated, not to mention shit-scared, I might have been flattered by her concern, but as it was, I could only echo her words in my head – *Yes, please don't hurt me!*

Unfortunately, that plea from Isabela seemed only to encourage Vítor to do just that. He jerked my arm more viciously up my back until the agony made white lights explode in front of my eyes. I could tell you, of course, that I didn't utter so much as a whimper of pain, but I suspect you know me too well by now to believe that. Isabela's face convulsed in sympathy.

'I'm going!' she said. 'Don't . . .'

She broke off, obviously realizing that another plea for mercy would only encourage him to more torture. It's refreshing to find a man who so thoroughly enjoys his work, don't you think? Inflicting pain, yes, he loved that, but we both knew he wouldn't want murder on his conscience. Wasn't this exactly why I'd been sent here? He couldn't kill anyone himself. I was gritting my teeth against the agony of my arm, but now I tried to force my jaws apart.

'Don't listen to him, Isabela. He won't kill me. He's a priest, a Jesuit. He can't commit murder. Don't do what he says.'

I squealed as he jerked my arm so savagely, I was sure I was going to pass out.

'So you've decided to start telling the truth, have you, Marcos? Very well then, let's give Isabela a little more of it, shall we? Do you know why Marcos is here, Isabela? He is a hired villain, a murderer. His real name is Cruz and he was sent to kill you. The king's advisors have no intention of letting you return to Portugal with those birds. You will die here, and when you fail to return the young king will be persuaded to execute your father. He will hate you and all your kind so bitterly that this time he will be only too eager to light the bonfire with his own little hands. And once he's lit one fire, he will learn to enjoy the thrill of lighting more, until every heretic in Portugal is burning. This man you know as Marcos is not your protector, he is your assassin.'

Isabela stared from one to the other of us in horror. 'But I thought . . . in the cave you tried to warn me . . . When were you going to kill me, Marcos? After I'd captured the birds for you?' She lifted her head and stared at Vítor. 'As for you, you must be a complete fool. You tell me he is here to murder me and then you think I'll still care if you cut his throat. Go ahead, do it!'

She turned and started to run.

'But I think you will care when I kill the falcons.' Vítor's voice was colder than the river of ice.

Isabela stopped dead, as if she'd been pierced by an arrow. She wheeled around and came racing back towards the falcons, but Vítor was closer to them than she was.

He raised his dagger and brought the hilt of it down on the side of my head, at the same time releasing my arm. I toppled over and Vítor, in a couple of strides, placed himself between Isabela and the falcons, the point of the knife pressing into the breast of one of the birds.

'Marcos is correct when he says the taking of a human life

is forbidden to me. But it is written we have dominion over the animals and may kill them for our sport. It's no sin to kill a bird, not even one as valuable as this creature. But it would be a pity to dispatch such powerful creatures too swiftly. I wonder how long they would live without wings. Shall we see?'

'No!' Isabela shouted. 'Don't harm them. I'll go wherever you want me to, but let the birds live . . . release them, please. Let them go free! Please, please don't hurt them because of me!'

'As Marcos will tell you, I do not let anything go free.'

'Then sell them,' Isabela begged him. 'They'll fetch a huge price if they are unharmed. They are worthless to you dead.'

'Oh, I wouldn't say that. Dead, they are worth a Portugal cleansed of all her heretics, a Portugal that is purified for God.'

He seemed to consider the matter, clearly enjoying the abject fear that was written through every inch of Isabela's frame as she waited for his decision.

'Perhaps you're right. They are valuable creatures, and provided they never reach the little king's hands they may help the Holy Church . . . Very well. I will spare them if you do exactly what I say, but one hint of resistance from you and I will carry out my threat.'

Isabela swallowed hard and nodded. Vítor gestured with his dagger towards the ice. With her head held high, Isabela walked past him towards the frozen river, glancing back only once to reassure herself that he had moved away from the birds.

Vítor pointed the dagger at me. 'You, on your feet and follow her! I don't want you releasing those birds while my back is turned. Besides, your work is not yet done, Senhor Cruz.'

I clambered to my feet, my head throbbing from the blow and a lump the size of a hen's egg rapidly swelling on my temple. As I stumbled along, still dazed, I clenched and unclenched my fist, trying to restore the feeling in my wrenched arm. I couldn't work out why Vítor wanted Isabela to climb up on to the ice, but I knew that whatever plan he was hatching in that scrofulous little brain of his, it wasn't going to be good for either of us.

It took me several attempts and a couple of vicious jabs in the buttocks from Vítor's dagger to clamber up on to the slippery melting ice. In my whole life I had never wanted to beat a man's face to a pulp more than I longed to pulverize Vítor's. We picked our way gingerly until we reached the drier, rougher ice. Isabela stopped and turned.

'Which way?' she asked in a tremulous voice.

Vítor's eyes narrowed as he surveyed the frozen river ahead. 'A little to your left, then keep walking.'

Isabela did as she was told. Several times she glanced back as if she was praying that somehow we would have vanished, but we had not.

If I paused or hesitated for more than a moment, I felt the point of the dagger prick into my back and heard Vítor's growl to keep walking. While I kept trying to convince myself he wouldn't kill me, his threat to mutilate the falcons reminded me that there are worse things a man might do with a knife than commit murder. The Inquisition was, after all, well versed in the art of crippling a man for life without actually taking that life even if their victims begged their tormentors to do so. And the thought of being left out here maimed, in agony and alone was enough to make me keep walking.

The cold air rising up from the ice only increased my pounding headache, and my shoulder ached so much I was beginning to fear that one of the bones had indeed been cracked.

But finally Isabela stopped. 'I can't go any further. There's a crevasse in front of me. It's too wide to get across.'

'Is that so?' Vítor sounded almost pleased by the news. 'And is it deep?'

Isabela must have realized at the same moment I did why Vítor had brought us here. She clasped her hand to her mouth, looking terrified, but said nothing.

'You, Cruz, take this length of line, which Isabela has so helpfully provided. Tie her hands behind her.' Seeing me hesitate, he added, 'I am sure she would want you to do it. She knows what will happen to her precious birds if you don't co-operate.'

Isabela stood still as I tied her as loosely as I dared. Her hands were trembling.

'I'm so sorry,' I whispered. But she gave no sign that she had heard me.

Vítor pushed past us and peered down into the crevasse. It was deep, so deep that several men could have stood on one another's shoulders and still not reached the top. The bottom was strewn with jagged shards of ice, but the sides were as clean and smooth as polished glass.

He straightened up and gave a smile of satisfaction. 'Do you recall the first night we spent on this island when that drunken peasant of a farmer was telling us his hunting stories? Now, what was it he said? Ah yes, I believe he told us how dangerous the rivers of ice could be. How if a man fell down into one of the crevasses, he would never be able to climb out again. It is a lesson you would do well to remember, Cruz. It is always wise to remain sober whilst others are in their cups, you never know what useful information you might acquire.

'You've chosen your grave well, Isabela. God has been more merciful to you than a heretic deserves. The cold will probably kill you before you starve to death or die of any injuries you might sustain in the fall. I understand dying of cold is not an unpleasant death, just accept it. Don't fight against the sleep and it will be over quickly. But while you wait down there for death, Isabela, I urge you to think of your sins and repent of your heresy. Use the time you have left well. Spend it in prayer to our Blessed Lord and the Holy Virgin, begging for their mercy. That is all the Church wants, all she has ever asked for, the full and humble repentance of heretics.'

He turned from her, jabbing the point of his dagger at me.

'Now is the time, Cruz, to fulfil the vow you made before my brothers, the oath you swore by the Virgin Mary and all the saints. Push the girl in. Do it and I will take you back to Portugal to live a life of luxury and pleasure. I will even generously divide the price I receive from the white falcons with you.'

Isabela had shrunk back from the edge. Now she looked up at me, her mouth set bravely, but I could see, behind the defiance, the terror in her eyes. 'Look after the white falcons, Marcos . . . don't let him hurt them . . . they're so beautiful.'

I had expected her to plead for mercy. I would have been grovelling pathetically on my knees, but I should have known she would never beg for her own life.

Vítor impatiently gestured with his dagger. 'Do it, Cruz. You are making her suffer more by hesitating. Come now, quickly, put the girl out of her misery and be done with it.'

'No,' I said quietly. 'I won't kill her.'

'I am not asking you to kill her. The ice will do that. Her death will not be on your soul . . . If you refuse, you will suffer more than you can ever imagine, but not before you've watched me mutilate those birds. She doesn't want that, Cruz. She wants those birds saved. She wants to give her life for them, don't you, Isabela? You want Cruz to push you in so that your falcons will be spared. Just a little push, that's all, just one.'

He took a single step towards me, jabbing at me with his dagger. It was that tiny gesture that sealed it. Enraged, I grabbed his wrist and jerked, trying to make him drop the dagger. His feet slipped from under him, and before he could stop himself he had slid over the edge of the crevasse. His fingers locked around my hand as it grasped his, almost pulling me in with him. I fell to my knees and collapsed on to my belly, trying to cling to a rough peak of ice with my other hand to prevent myself sliding over the edge. I was holding him with my injured arm, his full weight dangling from my shoulder, which, already swollen, burned like fire. He was flailing about with his other hand, trying to grasp the edge of the crevasse, but his fingers kept slipping from the ice.

'Pull me up, pull me up!' he screamed.

My hold on the lump of ice was slipping as my fingers warmed the surface. I was almost crying from the pain in my shoulder as he thrashed about. I opened my fingers, but his grip on my wrist was too strong. He would not let go, he swung himself, and with one desperate lunge managed to grab Isabela's ankle. She crashed to the ground and though she kicked and writhed, with her hands tied, she was unable to do anything to stop herself being pulled towards the edge.

Blind terror somehow summoned up the last shred of strength I possessed. I let go of the ice and, drawing back my fist, punched him as hard as I could in the face. His nose burst into a torrent of blood. With a scream he fell backwards, as in the same instance I lunged at Isabela with my other hand, just as she slid over the edge. I caught the back of her gown and for an agonizing moment she swung there in empty space as we heard the thump of Vítor's body hitting the bottom of the crevasse.

I wriggled backwards on my belly, trying to feel for a lump of ice I could hook my foot around, and then I pulled. With her arms bound, there was no way Isabela could do anything to help herself, and after the punch I'd landed on Vítor my fingers were numb. All I could do was to keep sliding backwards on my stomach and try to haul Isabela up by the weight of my body.

I heard her cry out as her shoulders and back ground hard

against the ice as I tried to haul her over the edge. I knew being dragged up like that must be agony for her, but I couldn't afford to stop. I felt the stitches in her gown begin to give way. It was now or never. I gave one huge jerk, and she landed on her back on the ice, sobbing and shaking. I crawled towards her, wrapping my arms around her and folding her into a tight embrace. I don't know which of us was sobbing the louder, but if you ever repeat that to anyone, I shall deny every word.

We didn't attempt to return to the harbour where we had disembarked. It was, as I said to Isabela, a deliberate decision on my part. I told her that if we went back we would be recognized instantly by the officious little ink-head, who would have taken great delight in clapping us in irons for the winter. But the truth was, I actually had no idea where we were or how to get back to that port.

Isabela claims it was her suggestion to follow the river from the lake to find the sea. I'd already decided that was the best course of action, but after all she'd been through, it was kinder to let her think she'd thought of it. Women like to have these little victories, it sweetens their mood.

I'll say this for the girl, she made sure we didn't starve. She was good at setting snares. Me? I've never attempted to catch so much as a mouse. I knew, of course, that someone must catch and kill animals, I'd seen enough bloody carcasses hanging in butchers' rows, but as far as I was concerned meat had always presented itself to me swimming in rich sauces and bearing no resemblance at all to the beast which gave it its name. Iceland seemed sadly lacking in rabbits or hares or any edible mammal, but the river provided ample duck, and now that we knew what we were looking for we saw that the hillsides were swarming with ptarmigan springing up like mushrooms in autumn. We shared this meat with the falcons, though somehow they always seemed to get the choice portions, while I had to make do with anything that was considered not good enough for them.

I can't say I cared much for the falcons. I was terrified that one lunge with those dagger-sharp beaks of theirs and they'd have my eye for supper. But in time I got used to carrying one on my arm, once Isabela had made a pad for me with a twist of cloth stuffed with moss, for their claws were like dragons' talons.

The first two nights Isabella removed the cloth bindings from their eyes and kept the birds constantly awake, to *man* them, as she put it. In other words, make the vicious little brutes tame and docile, and accustomed to the sight of us. I was amazed at how quickly they grew used to us. And while we still hooded them when we walked, at night their bright eyes watched us and they learned to take the raw bloody morsels she held out to them wrapped in a few feathers to help them digest the flesh.

Once we reached the sea, the ptarmigan were replaced by seabirds and eider duck. Take it from me, gulls are not good eating. So I tried my hand at fishing and managed to hook a seal, which would have been a welcome catch had it not been dead, and not just dead, but rotting and putrid. Nevertheless, I spent many hours drying the parts of it I could salvage over a fire. Isabela begged me to throw away the stinking mess, but as I told her, it was the first thing I'd caught and I wasn't going to part with it, despite her wrinkling her pretty little nose and protesting.

Even her laughing protest was a sign that relations between us were thawing. The fact that I had, in all modesty, saved her life, did make her trust me a little, though I could tell at first she was still extremely wary of me. I suppose it was only to be expected. When a woman learns you've crossed several seas with the express intention of murdering her, it's only natural she should be a tad reserved in your presence, a little jumpy when you get too close.

But I did not attempt to explain what that bastard Vítor had told her. That's another lesson I learned early in life, never offer excuses until they are asked for, it makes you look guilty. But finally, one night as we sat shivering around a tiny fire, roasting a plump little duck, she asked me if what Vítor had said was true. Of course, I told her the whole story ... well, most of the story ... some of the story ... Look, I admitted my name was Cruz, what more do you expect? One should never distress a lady with the truth.

I stared into the flames with an affecting sigh. 'It's with a heavy heart I have to tell you that I put you in grave danger, Isabela. The truth is, there are those of us in Portugal who are seeking to overthrow the Inquisition, even perhaps the throne itself if we must. We have helped some to escape the clutches of the Inquisition; we steal records and sometimes even assassinate key members of the *familiares*, making it appear as an accident so as not to arouse suspicion. It is dangerous work.'

I stole a glance at Isabela. Her eyes were wide and she sat motionless, obviously completely enthralled

'There was one man,' I continued, 'a lawyer, who was responsible for reporting many innocent people. We couldn't allow him to continue, but we couldn't simply lie in wait to stab or strangle him. They would have turned the town upside down searching for his killers, so I volunteered to break into his house one night. I had to climb over the roofs of several houses like a monkey, leaping across the gaps between them. Several times servants heard me on the roof and I flattened myself in the shadows as they wandered round peering upwards, but at last I reached his house and mercifully the shutter was open for it was a warm night.

'I flipped over the edge of the roof and swung myself in.

I almost landed on top of him and his wife as they lay in bed. As it was, I trod on the tail of their dratted cat, which screeched as if I had tried to kill it. Its cry woke the man's wife, so I had to fling myself into a chest to hide while she got up and put the cat out. I lay in that chest until I could hear them both snoring, then I tiptoed out and poured a few drops of poison into the man's open mouth as he slept. His coughing and wheezing woke his wife, but the poison was fast acting. I managed to slip out of the window again when she went running down the stairs squealing for someone to come to help her husband who was having a fit. I tell you, I came pretty close to getting caught that night.'

'I had no idea,' Isabela breathed. 'That is such a brave thing to do.' It was obvious she was impressed.

'Alas, you will not think me so very brave,' I said, 'after I confess to you what I must. You see, I was assigned to follow Vítor on this voyage. Of course, I knew from the beginning that he was a Jesuit priest working for the Inquisition, but we didn't know what his purpose was in making the voyage. Perhaps I should have dispatched him while we were still at sea, but we needed to know what he had come here to do. It was only at Fannar's house that I discovered that his purpose was to prevent you from returning home. When Ari first took us to the cave, I tried to kill Vítor then, but I confess that I failed. You see, I'm accustomed to working with poisons. I'm not skilled with a knife. Blood, you see – it always was my weakness. But my cowardice put your life in terrible danger. Can you ever forgive me, Isabela?'

She put her hand on my arm and squeezed it. 'You twice saved my life. Deeds say more about a man's heart than his words. Although . . . I did enjoy the story.' She turned her face away, and I could have almost sworn she was struggling not to laugh.

It was odd though, of all the many stories I have told about myself that was the only one that I had ever really wanted to be true. Maybe there was some point in my life when if I had taken a different path I could have been that man, that hero, fighting for a cause . . . All right, I know, just who am I kidding? You'd no more believe that of me than if I said I could have been a saint if only my parents hadn't named me Cruz!

It took us many days to work our way along the coast until we found a little harbour, surrounded by a cluster of tiny houses. Thank God, if you believe in divine providence, it was mercifully free of the accursed Danes.

A small, lateen-rigged caravel was riding at anchor, a piss-poor ship, whose captain had suffered a run of ill luck and was trying desperately to do a spot of illegal trading before the winter set in. The ship was bound for Antwerp, but from there it would be possible to work south to Portugal by sea or land. The ship was due to sail on the following day's tide. The captain needed little persuasion to take passengers – frankly, he would have taken a flock of mangy goats, he was that desperate – but the problem was money and I didn't have any left. I would get it though. I'd sooner spend a hundred years in purgatory than a single winter on that desolate island. Even if I had to stand on the street corner and sell myself as a whore to any hairy-arsed sailor or farmer who passed by, one way or another, I was determined to be on the ship when she sailed on the morrow.

But in the end I was not required to pimp myself. I had already devised another plan for getting money, one that had come to me some days before when we first reached the coast. And I have to thank that sweet angel, Eydis, for that. I would never have thought of it had it not been for watching her tending that man in the cave. Mummy! It cures everything, so of course everyone wants it, especially with winter coming on and people liable to fall sick. But the prices those Danish and German merchants demand were nothing short of extortion. It's an absolute disgrace. There ought to be a law against cheating poor hardworking people like that.

I can't tell you how pathetically grateful they were when I offered them genuine mummy for a fraction of the price, made, as I assured them, from the finest Egyptian embalmed corpses. I showed them the fine black powder, I even encouraged them to sample a few grains, and though none of them had been able to afford it before, they were certainly not going to admit that in front of their neighbours, so they all agreed that it smelt and tasted of the very finest quality. They bought every ounce I had to offer. And to think Isabela wanted me to throw away that dead seal!

I returned to the place where we were camping a little way out of the village. We had decided against seeking lodgings, for we couldn't afford for the white falcons to be seen, and there was no knowing who might be in the pay of the Danes.

I told Isabela that I had found us a ship and what the greedy oaf of a captain wanted for a passage.

She bit her lip. 'I haven't a half of that left and I still need to buy some live chickens to take on board to keep the falcons fed and buy food for the hens too until they are slaughtered. Will he take less, do you think, if I offer to cook on board?'

'I tried to argue him down,' I told her, 'but I couldn't budge him and I'm afraid he has a cook already, one of his hands. I saw him.'

'There may be another ship before the snows,' she said desperately.

'The locals say this is the last.'

'So all of this has been for nothing,' she whispered. 'Even if I find a way to get the white falcons back, it will be too late. Father will be dead.' Her face was a mask of utter misery.

There was nothing I could do to help her. I didn't have any more of the mummy left to sell. What could I do? I only had enough for my own passage. I mean, I'd have to buy food for the voyage and wine too. Sweet Jesu, I wasn't about to set foot on that hulk without a barrel or two of wine to take the edge off the misery. Then when I reached Antwerp, I'd have to find another ship to take me to Portugal and . . .

And . . . who was I fooling? I couldn't return to Portugal, not if Isabela did. Those two bastards in the tower of Belém would know I'd broken my oath and have men hunting me down within an hour. When Vítor didn't return they'd guess that something had happened to him and would no doubt try to blame me for his death on top of everything else. I didn't know what the penalty was for dropping a Jesuit priest down an ice ravine and leaving him there to die, but I had a feeling that the Inquisition would have reserved their most exquisite tortures for just such a crime.

No, I had to face it, if Isabela returned home, then I would have to remain an exile. But not here, Sweet Jesu, not on this island. There were surely more pleasant countries in the world where I could exercise my considerable talents. If I got as far as Antwerp I could go anywhere, maybe I could even sail to Golden Goa. Why not? Why not really go there? They said riches lay heaped in the streets, just waiting for a man to scoop them up.

I glanced up at Isabela. She was stroking the breast of one of the white falcons turned rosy pink in the firelight. Tears glittered in her eyes. I sighed. Then I pulled out the leather bag of money from around my neck and thrust it into her lap.

'Here, there's enough there for passage on the ship and a second ship to take you back to Portugal, if you're careful.'

Isabela stared at me. 'But I can't take it. What about you? How will you pay for your passage?'

I flapped my hand vaguely. 'I've another purse, twice as heavy, when I want to use it, but I've changed my mind about returning yet. I've decided to stay here over winter. I didn't want to tell you before, in case you were frightened I was abandoning you. But you remember Fausto telling us about the diamonds? Well, before he died, he confided to me the exact location of a mountain where they're to be found. He didn't want to say anything on the ship, for fear others might beat him to it. Those seamen always had their great hairy ears flapping. Anyway, I've made up my mind to go and look for the diamonds. In a way I owe it to Fausto's memory. Prove him right after all. I can mine the stones all winter. Those caves are pretty warm and well hidden from the Danes. Then I'll pop up again in the spring and find a ship. By that time I'll be as rich as King Sebastian himself.'

'But I can't let you stay here.' Isabela's face was a picture of concern. It was quite touching to see it.

'Do you think I'd pass up the chance to get rich?' I said, with a cheerfulness I certainly didn't feel.

'I know there aren't any diamonds,' she said fiercely. 'Just for once, why can't you . . .' Tears spilled down her cheeks. 'Thank you . . . thank you, Marcos, for my father's life.'

I saw Isabela off on the early morning tide. We smuggled the falcons aboard in baskets concealed between the cages of hens. The falcons would have to remain hidden until the ship was well clear of Iceland. When she turned to say goodbye, I took her hand. There was something I still had to tell her.

'Isabela, Vítor is not the only Jesuit who wants you dead. There are many who are very anxious you should not return, especially with those birds. I hope, with all my heart, you will get there in time to save your father's life, but if you do, you must promise me you will not stay in Portugal for one day longer than you have to. Get a boat, walk over the mountains, leave in any way you can and as fast as you can. They are determined that one day soon you will be lying in their dungeons too.'

I had watched Isabela come close to death more than once, and thought I had seen her afraid, but what passed across her face at that moment was a look of profound dread and foreboding that I had never seen on the face of any man or woman before. She was terrified of what she was about to do. She was forcing herself to go back, when every bone in her body must have been screaming at her not to return. I cursed myself for giving her the money and it was all I could do to stop myself dragging her back off the ship. But I knew even that wouldn't stop her.

'Don't go, Isabela, please don't go back.'

She swallowed hard and forced a smile. Then she reached up and kissed me on the cheek.

'You just can't help being a good man, Marcos, in spite of what you try to be. Promise me you'll never stop looking for diamonds.'

I watched the ship receding from the shore, saw her triangular sails unfurl and leap eagerly before the wind. You know me, I've never exactly pestered God or any of his saints, and I didn't intend to make a habit of it, but I reckon every man's entitled to ask for one favour from the Old Man just once in his life.

'Blessed Jesu,' I whispered, 'look after her. Let her live to grow old.'

I turned away and walked along the harbour. There were no more ships. I had just watched my only hope of escape from this midden sail off across the horizon and now I was stuck here at least until spring. Somehow I'd have to find a way to survive. But given what I'd been through in the past few weeks, I wasn't going to let a little thing like an empty purse defeat me.

There might not be any diamonds in those mountains, and I certainly wasn't stupid enough to go back into any of those caves to find out, but this mummy was proving to be a profitable little venture. Of course, I'd have to find more dead seals and other villages and towns to sell it in. Keep moving, that was the secret, never stay long enough for them to find out it didn't work. But then, who knows, maybe my powder would cure them as well as the real thing. If people believed in something strongly enough, miracles had been known to happen. Wasn't that what the priests called faith? And the more people paid for something, the more faith they had in it. The Icelanders were as poor as corpses in a common grave, but there had to be some wealthy Danish widows around somewhere, and stuck on this island they must be starving for the company of a charming man who knew how to woo a lady. Who knows, they might even consider taking another husband.

I stared down into the clear green water. A naked woman was floating just beneath the surface. Her brown skin was soft and smooth. Her raven hair fanned out all around her, undulating in the waves. An amulet in the form of a single blue eye lay between her firm, round breasts which shamelessly thrust up through the ripples at me. She was smiling, her full lips parted in lustful desire, her arms held wide to embrace me. She wanted me to come to her, to lie with her in the cold, lonely depths. Silvia wanted her revenge.

I kissed my fingers to her. 'Not yet, my sweet Silvia. Not yet. Patience was never one of your virtues. One day you'll take me down there with you, and you'll torment me for all eternity in death just as you did in life. I will pay the price for you eventually, but I'm not ready to surrender to you yet, my beauty. Haven't I always said, life is a tree laden with sweet, ripe peaches for those who know how to pluck them. And I have many more juicy peaches yet to steal, my darling, a great many more.'

Eydis

Sails – the wings of a falcon.

Isabela stands beside the rail staring at the coast slipping by, as the fragile ship weaves around the murderous rocks. She sees the towering rivers of ice inching towards the crashing waves of the shore. She sees the deep blue water surge around the barren cliffs and break on the black sand. She sees waterfalls thundering down in rainbow sprays and a thousand birds ebbing and flowing like the tides.

Soon the ship will break from the shore and there will be nothing to watch but the sea. She will mark the passage of each day and night, desperate for the ship to sail faster, frightened that she will not reach home in time or at all. A thousand anxieties swarm through her head. Can she keep the birds alive? Will she find a ship in Antwerp? Does her father still live? Will they keep their promise and release him, or will they simply take her too?

Her fingers stray to the lucet around her neck. She rubs the horn against her cheek, comforted by its cool smoothness. One day, she will begin to fashion a new cord with it. She will remember that she can call the dead. She will always fear death, but not the dead. They are her friends now and they will surround her. She will draw them to her with the cord and they will come to her. The dead can never be lost to her. The grandmother and the child, Hinrik and Jorge, Valdis and me, we all travel with her, and when the time comes to face the evil she will know we will all stand with her – the door-doom of the dead.

The black thread of death to call us from our graves.
The green thread of spring to give her hope.
The red thread of blood to lend her our strength.
Rowan, protect her.
Fern, defend her.
Salt, now bind us to her!

Historical Notes

Portugal

In 1492, Jews fleeing from the Inquisition in Spain were allowed to settle in Portugal on payment of eight crusados. The Jews were considered vital for trade and industry in the expanding Portuguese empire. But when, in 1497, King Manoel I of Portugal married the daughter of the Spanish king, his new bride insisted that both the Portuguese and exiled Spanish Jews be ordered to leave Portugal or be baptized as Catholics. The Jews were given ten months to decide.

However, just three months later, King Manoel commanded all Jews to gather at the ports. They believed they were going to be given passage out of the country, but instead they were told no Jew was now allowed to leave Portugal. Their children were seized and every Jew was ordered to convert to Christianity. Those who refused were either killed or forcibly baptized. The converts and their descendants became known as New Christians, or Marranos, which meant *pigs*.

King João III (1521–57) allowed the Grand Inquisition of the Catholic Church to establish itself in Portugal in 1536, but in the first three years it was only permitted to gather information on heretics and apostate Christians, not to act. Their particular targets were the communities of Marranos who, though outwardly Christian, were suspected of practising Judaism in secret. But the king would not allow the Inquisition to unleash its full power, because he needed the New Christians for their crafts and trade links. The Inquisition was growing increasingly frustrated.

Then in 1539, banners appeared on all the churches in

Lisbon proclaiming that Jesus was not the Messiah. A young Marrano, Manuel da Costa, was arrested and under torture confessed that he was responsible. He was executed, and the scandalized populace, whipped up by the priests, demanded that Portugal be cleansed of its heretics. The king finally granted permission for the Inquisition to round up Marranos, Muslims and Lutherans, the last being identified as anyone found in possession of a Bible translated into Portuguese. Any Christian convert who was suspected of having secretly returned to their former Jewish or Muslim faith was considered a heretic and liable to be arrested, tortured and executed. And so began the reign of terror under the Inquisition.

Some readers may be wondering what became of little King Sebastian, the child-king in the novel. In 1578, aged just twenty-four, he embarked on a war to aid the deposed ruler of Morocco, Abu Abdallah Mohammed II Saadi, in defeating his Turkish-backed uncle. Portugal had lost several important trading stations in Morocco which were vital for its route to India. At the Battle of Alcácer Quibir – the Battle of the Three Kings – Sebastian was last seen charging into enemy lines and was presumed killed. His great-uncle, Cardinal Henry, succeeded him as king until his own death in 1580, when Sebastian's uncle, Philip II of Spain, claimed the Portuguese throne.

Although Philip later claimed to have recovered Sebastian's body and interred it in the monastery at Belém, rumours persisted that Sebastian had survived the battle and had been taken prisoner for ransom, and that he would one day return to claim his throne. Over the years several men appeared, each purporting to be Sebastian and saying that he, not Philip, was the rightful king of Portugal. The last of these claimants was hanged in 1619. But the rumours lived on, and down the centuries the legend grew that, like King Arthur of England, Sebastian was merely sleeping and would one day return as

O Encoberto or *The Hidden One*, to aid his country when it was in grave peril, a belief held by some right up until the nineteenth century.

Iceland

From AD 874 when Iceland was first settled by the Norwegian Viking, Ingólfur Arnarson, it had to a greater or lesser extent been ruled by Norway. But in 1397 at Kalmar, under the terms of the Scandinavian union pact between Norway, Denmark and Sweden, the sovereignty of Iceland was transferred from Norway to Denmark. So when Lutheranism was established in Denmark in 1537, it also spread to Iceland.

At first, the Catholic bishops of Iceland declared it heresy, but even after they were replaced by Lutheran bishops, the Reformation had little impact and was largely ignored by the Icelandic clergy and laity. But in 1550, when a Catholic bishop was arrested and murdered, the Icelanders took revenge by slaughtering Danes. Denmark was then determined to impose Lutheranism on Iceland. The Lutherans seized all the assets of the Catholic churches in Iceland and stripped them bare of all images of saints and religious decoration. They closed abbeys and monasteries, driving out priests, monks and nuns. They confiscated Latin Bibles, relics and religious items from Icelandic families and from the churches. The Reformation also destroyed much of the traditional cultural life of Iceland, because many of the long-established arts such as circle dancing were considered pagan and outlawed.

In 1602, Denmark imposed a complete trade monopoly, which together with a division of the country into four commercial districts, preventing trade between the districts, brought the population to near starvation. One man had his entire house contents taken because he gave garments his wife had knitted to an Englishman in exchange for two fishing lines. Another was flogged for selling fish to a neighbour who lived just over the border in another trading district.

Independence for Iceland came slowly, beginning in 1830 when Icelanders were granted two seats out of seventy on the Danish board that governed the island, but it was not until 1 December 1918 that the Icelandic flag finally flew over its own land, and full independence was not achieved until 17 June 1944.

Huguenots

The Huguenots were French Protestants, a movement which evolved in the 1500s from a number of different religious and political movements. They were mainly townspeople, literate craftsmen and noblemen from the south of France, who were opposed to the rites and rituals of the Catholic Church and were heavily influenced by both Luther and Calvin. They sought to live a life of simple worship and adherence to biblical commandments, relying upon God rather than the mediation of the Church or priests for salvation.

The Huguenots faced constant attack and persecution from the beginning, but King Francis I (1515–47) tried at first to protect them. However, in October 1534, anti-Catholic documents appeared overnight pinned up all over Paris. One was even attached to the door of the royal bedchamber while King Francis was asleep. This action so alarmed the king that it turned his sympathies against the Protestants. Many suspects were rounded up and burned, giving the signal for open hostility and persecution of the Huguenots.

Over the subsequent years many Huguenots fled to the Netherlands, Switzerland, the New World and England. A charter of Edward VI of England in the mid-1500s permitted the first French Protestant church to be set up in England. Its descendant, which can still be visited, is now in london's Soho Square.

The elaborate, and highly symbolic, Huguenot cross we know today was of a much later design and so would not have been used on the graves in the period covered by this novel.

Black Cloud

In the novel, the little child Frída is brushed by a black cloud travelling at great speed. Several early travellers in Iceland wrote that they had witnessed or been told about this phenomenon. What all their stories have in common is that having being touched by the cloud, the victims appeared to suffer terrible pain, and babbled incoherently. They frequently tried to kill themselves, though whether this was in an attempt to end their agony or was due to hallucinations, no one seems sure. Most of the victims recovered spontaneously after a few days or weeks. It has been suggested that, if these stories have any basis at all in fact, the cloud may have been a ball of gases and ash ejected from a volcanic fissure, often heralding a bigger seismic event. This would account for the speed at which the cloud appears to travel.

Draugr

A nightstalker or draugr (the plural is *draugar*) is a revenant, or animated corpse. They appear in many early tales from all over northern Europe. These include the nightstalker Grendel in the eighth-century Anglo-Saxon saga of *Beowulf*; the ghosts described by Yorkshire's Canon William of Newburgh in his *Prodigiosa*, written in the twelfth century; and the fourteenth-century Glam, who appears in the Icelandic *Grettis Saga*. Encounters with these revenants continued to be recorded right up until the nineteenth century in Iceland.

Early tales of the draugar suggest terrifying, monstrous

creatures, whose eyes shot flames and who caused great destruction by tearing off the roofs and doors of the halls they attacked. In these stories, the draugr only appears during the hours of darkness, vanishing at dawn. But by the later half of the Middle Ages, the draugr takes the form of an apparently normal human, who remains visible and tangible both day and night, but is possessed of great physical strength and a voracious appetite. The draugr was also thought to be able to control the weather and was a shape-shifter who could take the form of creatures such as a flayed bull, or a savage cat who would sit on a sleeping person, growing heavier until it crushed their chest, suffocating them. Those who had been drowned at sea often appeared as a draugr whose head was a mass of seaweed.

Stories are told of both Catholic and Lutheran clergy in Iceland who were learned in magic and dabbled in the black arts, including the raising of corpses. They often studied the black arts through books, but legends recount how some clergy attended 'the Black School which lay over the water'. Some folklore experts have suggested that the 'Black School' referred to in the legends was in fact the University of Paris, otherwise known as the Sorbonne.

Once a draugr had been raised by a sorcerer he or she would have to do the sorcerer's bidding, which generally meant seeking out a particular man or a family against which the sorcerer had a grudge to wreak vengeance on them.

The family would often be fooled into taking the draugr into their household, believing him or her to be a stranger in need of hospitality or a servant seeking employment. Once there, not only would the draugr consume all their precious reserves of food, he or she would cause havoc – maddening livestock, spoiling crops, and terrorizing anyone who stayed in the house overnight. Whatever a man's personality had been in life, once dead he became cruel and malicious, bent on hurting the living in every way he could.

Since a draugr appeared to be a living person, it was useful to know the signs by which they could be detected. One clue that you were being addressed by a draugr was the repetition of a word or a phrase in a verse-like taunt. But the word or phrase could only be repeated by the draugr twice, for any repetition of a word three times in succession was said to invoke the Holy Trinity, at which point the draugr would be forced back into the grave.

Once the draugr had completed whatever task it had been raised to accomplish, the sorcerer had to be able to send it back into the grave, otherwise it would follow him and his descendants for nine generations, all the while growing stronger. Forcing the corpse to return to the grave was not something to be undertaken without considerable risk, for the draugr would not return to his lonely tomb willingly and was likely to seize the sorcerer in a vice-like grip and carry him down into the grave with him.

Mummy

The use of human corpses in medicine is recorded as far back as ancient Egypt, Rome and Greece. But even as recently as the eighteenth century, mummy was still included in European herbals. As early as the twelfth century, tombs in Egypt were being ransacked for embalmed corpses, and throughout the Middle Ages there was a lively trade in embalmed bodies, looted by Syrian merchants from Egyptian tombs, which were sold to European apothecaries to make mummy.

It was considered such an important medicine that no apothecary's shelf would have been complete without it. Mummy mixed with other ingredients could treat abscesses, skin complaints, paralysis, epilepsy, diseases of the liver, heart, lungs, spleen and stomach as well as treat wounds and serve as an antidote to poison. Little wonder that the wealthy liked to have a stock of it to hand.

Mummy was also used to treat ailments in valuable horses, hunting hounds and falcons. It was listed by the medieval writer Pero López de Ayala, chancellor of Castile, as one of the sixty essential preparations which a falconer should always have to hand. López believed that mummy was the most efficacious ingredient in the treatment of any wounds on a falcon, and according to him the best-quality mummy was obtained from the human head. Theophrastus Bombast von Hohenheim (1493–1541) invented *balsam of mummy* and *treacle of mummy* which both proved to be very popular. It could also be dispensed in the form of tinctures, elixirs, pills, ointments and powders.

When the supply of ancient Egyptian corpses began to run out, the merchants and apothecaries were forced to use modern cadavers. In *Othello* Shakespeare refers to a handkerchief that was said to be 'dy'd in mummy, which the skilful conserved of maidens' hearts'. Some herbalists, such as John Parkinson (1567–1650), were still of the opinion that the best mummy was obtained from bodies which had been embalmed in the Egyptian manner, but others, like Oswald Croll (1580–1609), recommended that mummy should be made from the corpse of a hanged criminal, preferably of ruddy complexion and around twenty-four years old.

Hid-woman

The tall woman, Heidrun, who befriends Eydis and Isabela, is a *huldukona*, a hid-woman, meaning a 'hidden woman', which the Icelandic people thought a safer term to utter aloud than *álfur* or elf. The name Heidrun comes from the old Norse *heiðr* meaning 'health' and *rún* meaning 'secret'.

Huldufólk were certainly not 'little people'. They were the same size or taller than humans and thought to inhabit caves or dwell on farms which were invisible to most human eyes. They lived in a parallel human-like society under the leadership of a king, engaging in activities such as farming, fishing and even holding religious services with their own consecrated priests.

Humans sometimes feared them as child stealers, bringers of curses and misfortune, often vengeful and malicious. Others regarded them as creatures who would help, protect and reward the good and innocent, and punish the guilty. *Huldufólk* often mingled with humans and the only way to tell them apart was by some small physical abnormality, for example the lack of a division between the nostrils or a ridge instead of a groove on the upper lip. Belief in these creatures was very strong in Iceland and many tales are told of encounters with them as late as the nineteenth century.

There are several Icelandic myths surrounding the origin of the hidden people. Some say they were the race of people who inhabited Iceland long before the Vikings and fled into the caves when the Vikings appeared. Others say they were shamans, priests and priestesses who worshipped the old gods and were driven into hiding after the fall of the old religion and the coming of Christianity.

But a Christian legend recounts that when God made an unannounced visit to Adam and Eve, Eve presented the children she had washed to him, but hid those she hadn't had time to bathe because she was ashamed. Asked if she had any more children, she said no, and God declared, 'Whoever is concealed from my sight, will be hidden also from human eyes.' These hidden children were the ancestors of the *Huldufólk*.

Another legend tells of the time when Lucifer led a rebellion against God and was cast out of heaven down into hell with the fallen angels. But there was a group of angels who refused to join the armies of either God or on the Devil, so they were thrown down on to earth to live inside the mountains. There they can perform both good and evil but to a degree far greater than any human.

Wildlife

Fausto failed to catch rabbits and mountain hares because although foreigners always assumed the hare and rabbit must live in Iceland, as such creatures abounded in the rest of Europe, in fact there is no evidence they ever did, despite a law being introduced in 1914 to protect these elusive animals. Over the centuries, several attempts were made to bring them in and establish them as game animals, but it would appear none survived the first winter.

The gyrfalcon or gerfalcon or gyrfalco, as readers will have already gathered, was the most prized and valuable of all the birds used in falconry and remains so today. Gyrfalcons from Iceland, Northern Greenland and Kamchatka can be brilliant white with brown/black barred scapulars and wing feathers which the Spanish called *letradod* because the marks look like the lines drawn by a quill pen. But the plumage of the mature birds can range from white to dark grey and have huge variation in the brown markings on the body, and darkness of beak and talons. The whiter the mature bird, the greater was, and is, its value.

In the nineteenth century, some ornithologists claimed that the birds found in different countries were in fact different species, because of the variation in colour and size. But modern taxonomists agree with the medieval falconers that all of the birds found in these different countries are in fact one species – the gyrfalcon, *Falco rusticolus*. Some modern scientists have suggested that the colour variation is too wide to be able to separate the gyrfalcons into different subspecies, but others have identified six different subspecies based on size and colour.

492

It is likely that some variants of gyrfalcons no longer exist today. Early descriptions of prize gyrfalcons suggest that in the Middle Ages there may have been wild gyrfalcons who were more pure white than any known today. Their possible loss may be due to changes in climate and food supplies or possibly interbreeding with darker-plumaged birds. Certainly some centuries-old breeding sites for falcons in Iceland are known to have been destroyed by volcanic activity.

The so-called 'white falcon' found in Iceland is slightly larger than the gyrfalcons of Greenland and Norway, and with its pure white plumage or livery, except for the elegant dark markings on the upper part of the body, would have been the most sought after for royal falconries. From the description of the markings, the Icelandic white falcon appears to be the type of gyrfalcon owned by one of the most avid exponents of falconry, Emperor Frederick II. This would appear to be confirmed by other early writers on falconry who say the gyrfalcons from Iceland are whiter and larger than those from Norway and therefore more prized by kings, though not necessarily better hunting birds than the Norwegian gyrfalcon.

Emperor Frederick II believed the term gyrfalcon or giro-falcon came from the Greek *hiero*, meaning 'sacred', or *kyrio* meaning 'lord', hence *kyrofalcon* – 'lord of the falcons'. However, others dismissed this as pure romance, and since that time there have been countless arguments about how the birds got their name, some claiming the origin to be variously Persian, Latin or Norse, among many others. This is not helped by the many modifications to the name as it has passed into the various European languages. The English falconers, for example called it *jerfalcon*, or just *jer*, with *jerkin* used as the name of the tiercel or male. But the meaning and origin of the name continue to remain as mysterious and elusive as the bird itself.

Glossary

Badstofa – This was the long common bedroom and living hall of Iceland farmhouses which even up to the nineteenth century had probably changed little since Viking times. In later years, in wealthier homes, the turf walls were usually wood panelled, and the floors of beaten earth were covered with wooden planks. But there was a great scarcity of wood in Iceland and poorer people simply couldn't afford to use it for walls or floors, so when it rained hard the earth floors turned to muddy puddles. Windows were either absent or kept to a minimum to conserve heat, and those few windows were glazed with fish skin or animal membranes which admitted a similar amount of light as you would get through a sheet of greaseproof paper.

The communal beds, stuffed with hay, seaweed and leaves, were used for seating during the day. Meals were cooked and eaten in the badstofa. Spinning, weaving and other crafts would also be carried out here, especially in the long winters, but there was no other domestic furniture in the badstofa, such as cupboards, tables or chairs. Clothes and personal belongings would be stored in chests or boxes kept in the separate store room, along with the food supplies.

Basilisk – A mythical beast also known as the cockatrice. In the time of the Ancient Greeks it was described as a giant serpent, but from the Middle Ages onwards it was a four-legged cock with a serpent's tail that ended either in a sting or another head. Its eyes could turn any living thing to stone. Wherever its gaze fell, it turned that place into a desert and its venom was deadly. It was only afraid of two things – the crowing of a cockerel, and a weasel, which was the only creature unaffected by its stare. The prudent traveller in the Middle Ages would therefore arm himself with a cage containing a cockerel or a weasel before exploring a foreign land.

Caravels – Two-or three-masted, ocean-going ships, which were used to travel long distances at sea. They carried around 50 to 60 tons of cargo and provisions. They were between 50 and 70 feet long and 19 to 25 feet broad. Such a ship would be crewed by approximately twenty to twenty-five men. They were sturdy and fast, so were often used for exploring distant lands. The early caravels were **lateen-rigged**, meaning they had three triangular sails which allowed them to change course rapidly. However, increasingly caravels were rigged with a square sail for the fore and main sail, using the triangular sail only for the rear mizzen mast. This allowed them to achieve faster speeds in a steady wind.

Castrati – Since women were forbidden to sing in church choirs, and boys' voices broke just a couple of years after they were fully trained, the Church needed to find a way of preserving the angelic voices they needed. From the fourth century onwards, boys between the ages of eight and twelve had their testicles removed to prevent their voices from breaking. This left them as adults able to achieve full sexual function, but they were, of course, sterile. Throughout Europe, castration centres were established in monasteries to create castrati for the choirs. By the fifteenth century, castrati were well established in all the best Catholic church choirs in Europe, including the Vatican. Alessandro Moreschi was the last known castrato in the Vatican choir. He is believed to have been castrated around the year 1866. His voice was captured on recordings made between 1902 and 1904, and he died in 1922.

Cookbox – Ships were built of wood, the timbers coated in tallow and tar, and the gaps caulked with crushed hemp and pitch, materials so flammable that even a small fire could quickly engulf a vessel and all lives might be lost if it was far from shore. Yet the sailors needed to cook food and heat metal for the blacksmith to make repairs. So they used a cookbox, which was enclosed on three sides and underneath by high metal sheets which minimized the risk of sparks escaping and also shielded the flames from the wind. The floor of the box was raised on wooden runners to allow the heat underneath to dissipate and not warp the planks of the decks. The fires were lit on bricks which lined the bottom of the cookbox. Cooking pots stood on iron grids above the fire, but their handles could be hooked to a metal rod which was inserted through the sides of the box. This ensured that in rough weather the huge pots could swing freely on the metal rod and thus remain upright through the roll of the ship without spilling their scalding contents on to the deck or men.

Door-doom (*dyra-dómr***)** – Part of ancient Norwegian law, which involved assembling a group of six, or even as many as twelve, neighbours who would act as a court ruling on local disputes, such as a man refusing to pay a debt or one neighbour accusing another of harming his cattle by witchcraft. According to ancient law, the door-doom had to be assembled at the front door of the accused's house but far enough away from it so that the accused could hold his own door-doom if he wanted to bring a counter-claim against his accuser. Once both door-dooms were assembled there still had to be enough space remaining for a wagon full of wood to be driven between the house and the door-dooms.

But there are records of door-dooms being conducted within the house. For example, if a ghost had taken up residence and was refusing to leave, it might be summoned to appear before a door-doom of living neighbours just as if it was still alive, and it would have to abide by the decision of the door-doom which could force it to leave. On some occasions, though, the door-doom might rule that the ghost had the right to stay on in the house provided it behaved itself and didn't annoy the people who lived there.

Familiaries – These were the lay agents of the Inquisition. They were not in holy orders, but were ordinary men and women recruited to work for the Inquisition. In addition to accompanying the penitents and condemned at the *auto-da-fé*, they acted as the spies of the Inquisition. Large networks of *familiaries* existed all over Europe. The Inquisition would send these agents highly detailed physical descriptions of people they wanted to find, even including observations such as a particular man who had nasal polyps and therefore breathed through his mouth. Since the populace didn't know the identity of the *familiaries* – they wore hoods at the *auto-da-fé* – it meant that fugitives had to be constantly on their guard.

Farthingale – Adopted from the Spanish court, this was a bell-shaped linen or canvas underskirt into which a series of horizontal hoops of wood or whalebone were sewn to give full shape to the heavy gowns. It caused women to walk with a gliding, swaying movement. They also wore a linen or leather corset stiffened with strips of whalebone, wood or horn at the front, back and sides, to create a narrow waist and upraised breasts and achieve an hourglass shape. This corset was held up with shoulder straps, which helped to raise the breasts, since there were no cups built into it.

Gromet – An apprentice seaman. Among the ordinary sailors the most experienced men were known as 'able seamen'. They could hoist and lower sails, make repairs to the rigging and read a ship's compass when on watch. The gromets did the hard labour, pumping the bilges, raising the massive anchors and climbing the rigging. Lowest of the low were the ship's boys who cleaned, served the officers and were required to sing hymns for services and shanties to keep time for the seamen or for entertainment.

Lucet – A cord-maker. This was usually a piece of deer horn with two prongs, a forked twig, or a piece of wood carved into two prongs, with a handle that sat in the palm of the hand. This ancient implement was used to knot wool or other materials to make a strong cord, known as a 'chain', to tie up anything from sacks to live chickens. Objects such as knives, spoons, purses, keys, drop-spindles, even the lucet itself, were hung from the waist or neck by cords. Cords were also used to fasten shoes and garments and as draw-strings for clothes and bags. In the days before the production of cheap commercially made string, so many different cords were needed for daily living that all but the wealthy had to make their own, and even small children could use a lucet, since the technique is rather like French knitting, but using two prongs instead of four.

Manticore – A mythical monster believed to live in Africa and one of the many beasts which travellers throughout the centuries feared to encounter in foreign lands. It was described as a gigantic red lion with a human face whose mouth bore three rows of teeth, and whose tail could, according to some accounts, sting like a scorpion, while others claimed the lashing tail fired poison darts like a hail of arrows. All the writers agreed its favourite food was human flesh.

Morcela – A type of blood-sausage made in Portugal, flavoured with cumin and cloves. Another classic sausage of the region is the *chouriço*, a sausage coloured with paprika.

Strappado – A method of torture by which the victims were hauled by a pulley up to the ceiling by means of ropes attached to the wrists, with heavy weights fastened to their feet. He or she was then suddenly dropped within a few feet of the floor. The violent jolt dislocated the joints. This could be repeated two or three times until the victim was persuaded to confess.

Tölt – The Icelandic horse was introduced with the first settlers and is believed to have remained unchanged for over a thousand years. They are known for their distinct gaits found in few other breeds. These include the normal *walk*, *trot* and *gallop*, as well as the *skeið*, otherwise known as the *pace*, and the *tölt*, which is a smooth running trot that does not jiggle the rider up and down like a normal trot. These beautiful, sturdy horses can keep up the *tölt* for hours across country.

Troll rune – Runes were an ancient form of writing used in Northern Europe from about the third century BC, though they have been found as far south as Italy. Ancient poems and sagas make reference to a troll rune, or letter, which if inscribed on a stick or stone would reverse the meaning of any runes written after it and turn them into a curse. The troll rune was *þurisaz* (pronounced *thurisaz*), a letter shaped like a thorn. *Thurisaz* has been variously interpreted as meaning *giant*, *troll*, *demon* or *thorn* – something evil which will wound you if you touch it. When *thurisaz* was used in a curse it meant *power*. The troll or curse rune was used to conjure spirits of the dead or invoke demons. Some authorities have suggested there were three curse runes, others that there was only one, *thurisaz*, which was repeated three times, followed by a group of three other runes or letters which together made up the curse.

Acknowledgements

I would like to thank Dr Jane Lomholt of the University of Lincoln and her family for so kindly translating the Danish phrases contained in the novel, especially in the scenes which were not entirely complimentary to her countrymen. I would also like to point out that any disparaging opinions the characters hold about countries or people are most certainly not shared by the author. I fell hopelessly in love with the beautiful and unique country of Iceland the very first time I went there, and I would like to express my gratitude to the Icelandic people for all their generous hospitality on each of my visits.

I would also like to thank my wonderful agent, Victoria Hobbs at A.M. Heath, who always seems to sense when I need an encouraging phone call or email, and my brilliant editor, Mari Evans, who is unfailingly patient and sensitive, and brings such enormous insight and dedication to her editing of the raw manuscript. Finally a huge thank you to all the team at Penguin who work on all the different aspects of the books from cover design to publicity and marketing. Without their creativity and enthusiasm this book would not exist.